Short Stories
volume one

Born in 1903, in Cork, Frank
his only real ambition was to b
to prepare a collected edition c
speak Gaelic while very young
legends. His literary career began with the translation of one of Du
Bellay's sonnets into Gaelic.

On release from imprisonment by the Free State Government for his
part in the Civil War, O'Connor won a prize for his study of Turgenev
and subsequently had poetry, stories and translations published in the
Irish Statesman. He caused great consternation in his native city by
producing plays by Ibsen and Chekhov: a local clergyman remarked
that the producer 'would go down in posterity at the head of the pagan
Dublin muses', and ladies in the local literary society threatened to
resign when he mentioned the name of James Joyce. By profession
O'Connor was a librarian and his other great interest was music, Mozart
and the Irish composer Carolan being his favourites. He will long be
remembered for his collections of short stories. Frank O'Connor died in
March 1966.

Also by Frank O'Connor in Pan Books:

Short Stories volume two

An Only Child and My Father's Son
an autobiography

Frank O'Connor
Short Stories

volume one

Pan Books
in association with Macmillan Ltd

Fish for Friday and other stories first published 1964 in *Collection Two*
by Macmillan and Company Ltd

A Life of Your Own and other stories first published 1969 in *Collection Three* by Macmillan and Company Ltd

This collection published 1990 by
Pan Books Ltd, Cavaye Place, London SW10 9PG
in association with Macmillan and Company Ltd

9 8 7 6 5 4 3 2 1

A Life of Your Own:
Acknowledgments are due to the following publications in which these stories first appeared;
Harper's Bazaar, *John Bull*, *Mademoiselle*, *New Yorker*, *Penguin New Writing*, *Saturday Evening Post*,
Woman's Day.

ISBN 0 330 31516 1

Printed and bound in Great Britain by
Cox & Wyman Ltd, Reading

Contents

Foreword

For Frank O'Connor the most important single element in any story was its design. It might be years between the moment of recognizing a theme and finding the one right shape for it – this was the hard, painful work – the writing he did in his head. But once he had the essential bony structure firmly in place he could begin to enjoy the story – to start 'tinkering' with it. It was this 'tinkering' which produced dozens of versions of the same story. The basic design never changed, but in each new version light would be thrown in a different way on a different place. Frank O'Connor did this kind of rewriting endlessly – as he admits in the Introduction to *Collection Two*, he frequently continued it even after a story had been published. Though this confused and sometimes annoyed editors, reviewers and bibliographers, the multiplicity of versions was never a problem to him. When there were enough stories to form a new collection he didn't start trying to choose between the many extant versions of them – he simply sat down and prepared to rewrite every story he wanted in the book.

That particular rewriting was directed towards a definite aim – which was to give a book of stories the feeling of being a unity rather than a grab bag. He believed that stories – if arranged in an 'ideal ambience' – could strengthen and illuminate each other. This unity was only partly preconceived, he continued to create it as he went along. He never wrote a story specifically to fit into a gap in a book – nor did he change names or locations to give superficial unity. Rather it was as though the stories were bits of a mosaic which could be arranged harmoniously so that the pattern they made together reflected the light which each cast separately. Ultimately this unity probably sprang from his basic conviction that the writer was not simply an observer: 'I can't write about something I don't admire – it goes back to the old concept of the celebration: you celebrate the hero, an idea.'

This means, of course, that Frank O'Connor had very definite ideas about the contents and arrangements of each new book of stories. If he had lived, this might have been a different book. As it is, I have had to choose, not only which and how many stories to include, but also which of the many versions of each story to print. There was also the problem of that 'ideal ambience' and the comfort of the knowledge that even his own 'ideal ambience would be shattered by the time the book appears'.

I do not doubt that I shall have to answer to the author for each of these decisions. But for the stories themselves no one need answer. They are pure Frank O'Connor.

Harriet O'Donovan (Mrs Frank O'Connor)

Fish for Friday

Contents

A Sense of Responsibility

1

The first time Mrs Dwyer saw anything queer about Susie's boy, Jack Cantillon, was when his brother, Mick, was killed in a motoring accident. Mrs Dwyer was the mother of a large, loud-voiced family. Her husband was a carpenter, known to his wife as 'poor Dwyer', whose huffy shyness had never permitted him to make anything of himself. In spite of the fact that she was twice his build and had ten times his brains, he lectured her as if she were an idiot, and she put up with it as if she were. She was a bossy, bosomy, handsome woman; very devout and very sarcastic. She had three boys who were spoiled and three girls who were not, because Mrs Dwyer never had the least regard for women's rights. 'Let them give me the money and they can have the rights,' she said, and she only voted to humour her husband, who naturally attached great importance to his vote.

Jack Cantillon had come to the house originally, courting Annie, but after he had been doing it for some time the three girls held a conference and decided he was too slow for Annie and would be better off with Susie, who was slow as well. In return, Susie gave Annie her best blue frock and a pair of new ear-rings. If Jack noticed anything queer about the change he didn't say much. He never said much anyway.

He lived with his mother in a terrace house up the road. She was a thin, ravaged, actressy woman who, according to herself, had come down in the world a lot. She was the widow of a manager in one of the big stores in town, and Jack now worked there as well. He was the elder and steadier of her two sons, but he and his mother had never got on. Her favourite was Mick, who married a girl called Madge Hunt, a good-natured, stupid, sentimental girl. Madge, like his mother, adored Mick, who was easy-going and light-hearted, and she was very shocked at the harshness of employers who expected him to work even when he wasn't feeling up to it and the unreasonableness of creditors who wanted him to

7

pay back what he owed them, whether he had it or not. She never objected when things got bad, and Mick had to transfer herself and the child back to his mother's. But a couple of years of marriage improved her sense of reality enormously, and by the time Mick was killed, not too gloriously, in an accident, and she had to go out to work, she was as hard as nails, cold and knowing.

Jack took Mick's death hard, considering that the pair of them had never been very friendly, and began calling regularly on Madge, who lived with her little boy on the road. To begin with, Mrs Dwyer saw nothing wrong in this: a decent grief is a respectable weakness, and she was nothing if not respectable. But it went on too long, till it bordered on insincerity – insincerity, or what was worse, lack of common sense. And it didn't stop there. Babs, the oldest of the Dwyer girls, who heard everything, heard from the woman who employed Madge that Jack had made her give up the daily work and paid the difference himself. What Madge's employer said was: 'There's a good brother-in-law for you!' What Babs in her loud, humorous way, said was: 'How well I wouldn't find an old fool to do that for me!' What her mother, a woman of remarkable judgement, said was: 'That's queer behaviour in a man that's supposed to be marrying our Susie.'

She wanted Susie to have an explanation with Jack, but Susie flew in a panic and said she'd be too frightened. In some ways Susie was a judgement on her mother; a dreamy, good-natured girl, but too fond of 'them old novels' to have any self-respect. Mrs Dwyer did not read novels and had plenty of self-respect. So far as the boys went, she would defend them with or without justification, but her daughters were the exclusive product of her own intelligence, and could be defended on every reasonable ground. They were personally trained, and if they failed in any particular, she would repair them without charge. Without going into difficult questions of moral theology, one might say that at a pinch she would replace them. She would certainly not let an occasion like this pass without an explanation from Jack.

'I hear you're very good to Madge Hunt, Jack,' she said one evening when she got him alone in the sitting room.

'Ah, Madge is a fine girl, Mrs Dwyer,' he said. 'And I don't think it's very good for a child of Michael's age to be left with strangers while she's out at work.'

"Tis hard, Jack,' she agreed, pleasantly enough. Never having thought of the world but as a vale of tears, she felt no responsibility to defend its inequalities. 'But won't it make it harder for you to settle down yourself?'

'Begor, I suppose it will – a bit,' he admitted cheerfully.

'And you don't think it's a long time to ask Susie to wait?' she asked reproachfully.

'It's longer than I like to wait myself, Mrs D,' he replied with a grin. 'I don't want to stay at home any longer than I can help. Of course, I may get a rise, and if I do, it will nearly cover the few shillings I give Madge. At the same time I can't be sure of it. I've told Susie already that I may have to wait, and if she gets a better offer I wouldn't stand in her way.'

'I hope she doesn't, Jack,' Mrs Dwyer replied with the least shade of pompousness. 'As you say, if she does, she'll have to take advantage of it. A girl has only one life.'

Mrs Dwyer was not pompous, but she had a mortifying feeling that Madge Hunt, who wasn't even intelligent, could get round Jack Cantillon when she failed.

'I'd have nothing to do with that fellow, Susie,' she said drily when she spoke to her daughter later. 'He hasn't enough manliness to make any girl a good husband. The Cantillons all take after their mother.'

She could hardly have said worse than that, but Susie was not the sort to drop a fellow merely because her mother told her to. 'Them old novels' had her ruined, and when she grew alarmed at the idea that Jack didn't appreciate her, her only notion of maintaining her self-respect was to make him jealous with another man. In the novels, that always showed them, usually too late.

Now, the only way she could do this in a way that would even be noticed by Jack was by flirting with his friend, Pat Farran, and Pat was anything but a good choice for that delicate office. He was tall and handsome, quick-witted and light-hearted. He was delicate. Having been brought up in a household of women and sent to work in an office full of women, he seemed at times to be half a woman himself. He could cook, he could sew, he had an eye for clothes, and never seemed to feel with women the embarrassments most normal men feel. With a girl he was just another girl, so understanding, sympathetic and light in the touch that it never struck her until later that this was the only feminine thing about

9

him. By that time, it was usually too late, and the girl's affections were engaged. Women were always trying to telephone him, and some of the things he said about them were shocking. Of course, he didn't mean them that way, but a man has enough to do trying to think as well of women as the conventions require without getting inside information, and as a rule, men didn't like him much.

Susie didn't really like him either: he didn't seem to fit into any novel that she'd ever read, but she did want Jack to see that others appreciated her, and for a shy girl it isn't easy to find an attractive man who'll make love to her at the drop of a hat. Any other man would have withdrawn from a situation of such delicacy, but Pat lacked all real niceness of feeling. He saw through Susie, was delighted with her profound satisfaction at her own guile, and full of curiosity to know how far she would take it. When he met her with Jack he pretended to be dying of love for her.

'You'll come home with me, Susie,' he would say, embracing her. 'I can't live another day without you.'

'I can't, sure,' Susie would cry, half pleased and half terrified.

'Ah, why can't you? It isn't that fellow you're afraid of?'

'But you don't know what he's like!'

'I don't? I know him since he was ten. The coldest fish in Ireland! Never cared for anyone only himself.'

'Go away, ye whoors of hell!' Jack would say, helpless with laughter as though it were all a scene from a play.

But it wasn't. Not quite. The Dwyers had a cottage in Crosshaven that summer, and as Pat spent a lot of his time there, the flirtation continued, and Susie even began to enjoy it. The cliffs at night, the noise of the sea and the company of an attractive young man who knew all about love-making gave her a certain sympathetic understanding of other seductions she had read about. Perhaps poor Tess wasn't as much to blame as she had thought! She had the idea that Pat was beginning to respect her, too, and her mother, who admitted that she liked a fellow who had a bit of the devil in him, was friendly. But of any effect it might be having on Jack, Susie couldn't see a sign, and she could only wonder if her mother wasn't right and if there wasn't something lacking in him.

All that summer Pat was unwell, and after he returned to Cork he had to be operated on. Susie had never seen Jack so depressed. Every evening he was out at the hospital. Susie discovered from

Pat's mother that Jack had offered to guarantee a loan so that Pat could get to Switzerland. When she told her mother Mrs Dwyer sniffed and said, 'That fellow will be supporting half Cork before you get him to the altar.' 'But they are great friends, Mummy,' said Susie, and her mother replied, 'Friends or not, he has other responsibilities.'

But it was too late for Switzerland. In the week after Christmas Pat died as he had lived, lightly, swiftly and making passes at the nurses with a sort of desperate gallantry that went to Jack's heart. After the funeral he took to visiting Pat's parents as he visited Madge Hunt, and busied himself with the typing up of Pat's small business interests. He was the sort of man whose sympathy could be best expressed over a set of books. But Susie realized that this was something very different from his behaviour after his brother's death. He kept a picture of Pat on his mantelpiece, and a couple of times when she called she caught him staring at it.

As time went on, and she saw it had become a sort of fixation with him, she became concerned. Women are more jealous of men than they are of other women, though Susie would have been horrified to be told that she was jealous of Pat. She put it all down to concern for Jack: his attitude was morbid, and she must try to change it. But whenever she belittled Pat he either looked pained and changed the subject or else told her that she didn't understand. This was really too much for Susie, because, after all, it was she whom Pat had made love to, and if she didn't understand him, who did?

'Ah, you're very foolish, Jack,' she said wearily. 'You let people influence you too much. I suppose it's the effect your mother had on you. I'd never let anybody influence me that way. Of course, I was very fond of Pat, but I could see through him. You never saw how shallow he was.'

'Now, Susie, don't let's argue,' he said pleadingly. 'Pat was not shallow. He had a very fine head.'

'He was very insincere though,' said Susie.

'Everybody has his own way of being sincere,' said Jack. 'Pat was sincere enough, only it wasn't in your way or mine.'

'Ah, for goodness' sake!' she said, laughing at him. 'You never knew where you were with Pat. He'd be ridiculing you as soon as your back was turned.'

'Of course he'd be ridiculing you,' Jack said almost angrily, 'but there wasn't any harm in it. He was the straightest man I ever knew.'

Then Susie realized that her only remaining hope of shaking Jack was to show him what Pat was really like. She knew from novels the effect that always produced.

'And I suppose you don't know what Pat was up to with me when you weren't there?' she asked quietly, trying to keep her voice steady.

'I know damn well what he was up to, whether I was there or not,' Jack replied with a positive grin.

'And you don't even mind that he was living with me?' she asked, beginning to sniff.

'He was what?' Jack shouted, delighting her with his furious air even though it scared her into sobs and tears. 'You bloody little bitch!'

It was the first time he had ever spoken rudely to her, and she was scandalized at the injustice of it. Anything she had said, she had said only for his sake, to help him to see things better.

'Oh, it's all very well for you to criticize,' she stormed at him through her tears. 'It's all your own fault, you and your blooming old responsibilities. I suppose you have no responsibility to me. You knew the sort he was, and you threw me at his head. Any other girl that was kept dragging on the way I was would do the same.'

'Not making you a saucy answer,' he said, rising and glaring down on her like the wrath of God, 'I don't give a damn what you did, but I'm not going to have you going round, telling lies about a dead man.'

'Lies?' she exclaimed aghast, clutching her hands on her bosom.

'What the hell else is it?'

'It is not lies,' she said, springing to her feet, really furious now. She didn't mind accusing herself of being an abandoned woman, which is what all the interesting women in fiction are, but to be accused of making it up was the final indignity.

'Of course it's lies,' he said contemptuously.

'Oh, the conceit and vanity of you! Well, he did, and I don't blame him. I don't blame him a bit. You're just like your mother, rotten with conceit. You're not natural. My mother said it herself. You don't even know the temptations people have.'

'And as I said before, I don't care,' Jack replied, squaring up to her, madder than she'd ever before seen him. 'But it could cause great pain to Pat's family to have stories like that going round about him, so don't do it again, like a good girl.'

Susie realized with stupefaction that, whether he believed her or not made no difference at all to Jack. He would still continue to think more of Pat's parents' feelings than of hers. It was no use at all practising scenes from novels on him because no novelist had ever met anyone as unnatural as Jack Cantillon. And there was no hope of sympathy at home, because her family never read novels anyway, and they would either think she was telling the truth and be ashamed of her or that she wasn't and think she wasn't right in the head. She went home in a state approaching hysterics and told her mother only that Jack was a most appalling man, a most unnatural man. 'Well, girl', her mother replied complacently, 'you can't say but that you were warned,' which was about the most useless thing she could have said, for the more Susie was warned, the more curious she became about Jack. She couldn't help wondering what worse there was to know about him, and that meant she was tied to him for a long time to come. When a girl ceases to be inquisitive about a man she is really through with him.

2

It was five years before he was in a position to marry her, and by that time Susie's spirit was broken. He was worse to her than cigarettes to another girl. She frequently thought how wonderful it would be to be married to a western islander, and to be made love to on the shore in sight of the waves, but the western islands were far away, and she would be shy about making advances to an islander, and besides, she would probably catch her death of cold.

Mrs Dwyer was not too pleased with the marriage. She had sized Jack up, and was not a woman to change her mind about people that easily, but she was prepared to tolerate him for Susie's sake. And, from the worldly point of view, he was rather a better match than the husbands the other girls had got. He was now chief clerk, and in time would probably be manager, like his father. He bought a fine dilapidated old house off the Wellington Road, with tall rooms and wonderful views, and a lavatory somewhere up in the roof that would put the western seacoast in the shade. There the two children were born, Pat and Molly. Of course, the boy had to be called Pat.

It seemed as if things were running smooth for them at last. Too smooth for Susie's comfort. Jack was all right in a pub with a few men, but he did not care for society, and he refused to dance. After his day's work, all he mostly wanted was to change into old clothes, and read, or play with the children. And she had never really got over the way he had made light of her great revelation. According to her mood, she had two entirely different versions of her relations with Pat, whose picture still stood on the mantelpiece as though nothing had ever happened between herself and him. The first and commoner version was that nothing had – which was perfectly true; the second was that something awful had happened, which was equally true, according to the way you looked at it. When she was in good humour – which was most of the time – there had been nothing between Pat and herself only what she called 'old cod-acting', but when things went against her, she looked at the photograph and scowled at the child, and realized that she was no better than a woman of the streets all because of Jack's monstrous selfishness; and when she felt like that she made him a thorough good, old-fashioned scene in which she wept and screamed and called him an old molly. Jack, staring gloomily out at the grand view of the city, tried to soothe her, but that only made her worse. Finally, when it got too much for him, he would dash down whatever he was reading, say 'F— you!' in a thick voice, and go out to get drunk. People who saw him in town at such times brought back reports of a Jack Susie had never seen – impudent, witty and scandalous. The first time it happened she was thrilled, but she soon discovered that his emotional vocabulary was limited to one word, and that when he had used it, he had no more to say for himself.

Then, trouble caught up with them again. His mother, having managed to exhaust her small means, had entangled herself in a labyrinth of minor debts that could somehow never be subjected to the ordinary processes of accountancy. Mrs Cantillon considered that sort of accountancy common, and she traced Jack's weakness for it to his father. All Jack could make out was that even if he paid her rent and as many debts as he felt should be paid, it would still be only a matter of months till she was in court again.

Jack had his father's mousy horror of the courts: Mrs Cantillon couldn't see what was wrong with them. She found district court judges very understanding and very ready to sympathize with her problems.

This presented Jack with a horrible alternative. He went up one evening to Madge Hunt to ask her advice. Curiously, Madge, who had begun as something of a nightmare to him, was now his only adviser.

She opened the door and instantly put on her best party airs. You could see at once that she was a parish priest's niece. Oh, my, the kitchen was in such a state! He'd have to come into the parlour. She was sure he'd never forgive her. Michael was out at the School of Commerce. He must be dead after the walk. A drop of whiskey was what her uncle said was the only tonic. Jack put up with it good-humouredly. She was a small woman, flowery in manner, and not as well-educated as you'd expect from a parish priest's niece – in fact, you could easily mistake her for the proprietress of a country shebeen; but he knew that under the silly convent-school airs there was a cold, clear intelligence and great integrity.

'Well, Jack,' she said candidly when he had told her his troubles, 'it seems to me you'll have to be a bit of a bastard for once in your life.'

'Tell me, Madge, would I have to take lessons?' he asked with a grin.

'I'll give you free lessons, and you'll find they'll save you a lot of trouble,' she said without answering the grin. 'Put your mother in a home.'

'That's what I find so hard to do,' he admitted.

'Well, there you are!' she said with a shrug and a laugh. 'If you were the sort of man that found it easy to be sensible, I wouldn't be sitting as comfortable as I am. Whatever I say will only reflect on myself, but that's the way life is, Jack. She'll make a wreck of your home. You know that yourself.'

'I fancy she'll try,' said Jack.

'Don't fool yourself at all, Jack,' Madge said sharply. 'There won't be any trying about it. She'll do it. You're not the man to handle her, and I'm not criticizing you. There's only one way to handle her and that's to put her in with someone who could. You could put her in with me. I don't like the woman, but I'd take

15

her for your sake, though 'twould mean more expense to you, because I haven't the room. But if you ask my opinion, she'd go to the poorhouse first. I'm not saying it to criticize your mother, Jack, because she's more to you than I am, but there's only one thing in the world she cares for, and that's her own way. You'll excuse me saying so?'

'I'll overlook it,' he said affectionately. 'Thanks, Madge. I'll talk to her about it, and see what she says.'

At the doorway she kissed him, and looked after him as he went back down the road, thinking to herself in her unsentimental worldly way that he was probably the only man in the world she could have been happy with. There weren't many women who felt that way about him. Perhaps that was why he went to her for advice.

She had seen through Mrs Cantillon though, for that was exactly what she felt about Jack's cruel proposal. First she looked at him with a timid, childlike smile as if she were wondering if he was in earnest.

'You mean the woman who killed your brother?' she asked reproachfully.

'I thought they said it was a truck,' Jack replied mildly.

'They were being charitable.'

'Then what will you do?' he asked.

'Don't ask me, Jack!' she begged with the air of a tragedy queen. 'I'll promise I'll be no burden to you.'

Then Jack, seeing she was false all through, became gloomier still, remembering how she had exploited Mick and himself, and realizing that Madge was right and that he could never, never deal with her.

Mrs Cantillon, for all her silliness, was a woman of infinite perception. She saw that in the matter of getting her own way, which as Madge had said, was all she cared about, Madge, a hard, sly, cynical woman, would see through her little dramatizations before they even took shape, while Susie, as well as being a much better cook, would be putty in her hands.

Mrs Dwyer, a woman of small silliness and excellent perceptions, saw that too. She warned Susie on no account to agree to Mrs Cantillon's living with them, and, seeing Susie's complete lack of gumption where anything you could read about in a novel was concerned, she had it out with Jack himself. This time there was no pleasantness about it. She was fighting for her daughter's happiness and security.

'I don't think you realize the dangers of in-laws in your home, Jack,' she said severely.

'I think I do, Mrs D,' he said wearily.

'I don't think you do, Jack,' she said, her voice growing hard. 'If you did you wouldn't offer your mother a home with Susie and yourself. I saw more of that sort of thing than you did, and I never yet saw it come to any good. People may mean no harm, but just the same they make mischief.'

'Mrs Dwyer,' he replied with mournful humour, 'even my mother's best friend wouldn't accuse her of meaning no harm.'

Mrs Dwyer smiled, but the smile didn't last.

'That's all the more reason why she shouldn't be in the one house with you and Susie,' she said. 'When you married Susie, you took on certain responsibilities, and they're not easy. Young people have to have their disagreements, and they have to have them in privacy. I never interfered between ye, good or bad, because I know only too well what it leads to. Marriage is something between two people, and when a third person comes into it, mother or father, priest or lawyer, there's an end of it.'

'If you think I'd be likely to let anyone come between me and Susie!' he said almost with a groan.

'You mightn't be able to help it, Jack,' she said drily. 'Your mother is your mother, whatever anyone might say.'

'If that day came I could always cut my throat,' Jack replied with one of his rare outbursts of violence. She had never seen him like this before, and she watched him with interest. 'I never got on with her,' he added candidly. 'I blamed her for the way she spoiled Mick. After my father's death I blamed her for the way she turned us against him. I knew then he was a fine man.'

'He was,' she said unemotionally. 'That's true. He was a fine man.'

'She told us lies about him. She doesn't know what the truth is. But she worked hard, and she was generous to those she liked. Old people have to live too, Mrs Dwyer.'

'They have, Jack,' she said without expression, 'but they haven't the same claims as young people. For everyone's sake, your mother would be better in a home. I have to think of Susie.'

'And I have to think of Susie and my mother,' he said gloomily.

17

'You may have to choose, Jack,' she said quietly.

'There are certain things you have no choice about, Mrs Dwyer,' he replied, and again she realized with irritation that this intolerably weak man, who allowed himself to be imposed on by his calculating mother, had a sort of doggedness that made him safe from being influenced by a woman of character like herself.

'Well, don't blame me if you wreck your home,' she said with finality.

'I wouldn't blame you, anyhow,' he replied.

'And don't expect me to go into it,' she added severely. 'I'm sure what you're doing is wrong, and that it will come to a bad end, and I won't make mischief, but I won't go where mischief is being made.'

With characteristic determination she kept her word. She did not visit Jack's house again, though the children came up regularly to see her, and Jack himself came every Sunday after Mass. She always received him with especial cordiality. She had too much pride to let herself be flouted, but it pleased her that he could take her rebuke in that impersonal way. 'God knows he's not natural,' she said to her daughters, 'but you can't help liking him.'

And that, from a woman of Mrs Dwyer's calibre, was a real concession.

3

It must be admitted that she had miscalculated Mrs Cantillon's style though not her content. She made hell of the home all right, but not in the straightforward way Mrs Dwyer expected and could have partly countered. She made no attempt to make Susie's life difficult and contented herself with making a hell of Jack's. The silliness of Mrs Cantillon had an aspect that was not far removed from genius. She knew his weaknesses in a way that Susie had never known them, because they had been largely created by herself, and she remembered with attachment childish humiliations he had endured. She knew that though a married man and a father, he had always remained something of a bachelor; had lived all his life in the one small suburb of Cork, knowing no more of his neighbours than was necessary for the small courtesies of life – weddings, christenings and funerals – while his mother boasted that she knew everything about everybody. After his day's work he liked to change ceremonially into old trousers, but his mother began to jolly him into taking Susie out. On the surface it was all the height of good nature, and Susie, who found long-extinguished aspirations for society reviving in her, took it all at its face value.

'Sure, it's all for my own sake, girl,' her mother-in-law said. 'What other chance have I of getting the children to myself, and what other chance have you and Jack of enjoying yourselves?'

The worst of it was that she could not keep from tinkering with money, which seemed to have a sort of fascination for her. Jack didn't mind the occasional bet, though she started Susie betting as well, but when he discovered from a solicitor that Susie's savings were being put into house property he lost his temper. Susie screamed at him that he'd sooner let his money rot in the bank than put it to some use, and he replied that if his mother had done the same she might have been able to pay her rent instead of living with them.

The queer thing was that as the home grew more wretched Susie came to depend more on her, and even had arguments with her own mother about it. Susie argued eagerly with her that Mrs Cantillon wasn't so much to blame as Jack. In all their disagreements it was Jack with his monstrous egotism who had been at fault. He had always been that way, even as a boy – self-centred and cold – unlike Mick, who was sunny and generous and warm. If Madge Hunt had decided that she had married the wrong brother, Susie was well on the way to believing the same.

But finding herself on the same side as Mrs Cantillon about anything was something Susie's mother did not propose to let pass.

'Ah, for goodness' sake, child!' she said. 'As if the whole road didn't know what Mick Cantillon was like.'

'He was terribly misjudged all the same, Mummy,' Susie said tragically.

'He was, I hear!' her mother retorted coarsely. 'Don't be fooling yourself at all now, Susie. Your husband may be foolish, but his brother was never any good, and his mother is downright bad, and let nobody persuade you otherwise.'

And, on the day that Mrs Cantillon was found unconscious and dying at the foot of the stairs, Mrs Dwyer walked in to look after the children, and the quarrel was over. In fact, as nobody but herself realized, the quarrel had been over for a long time. Mrs Dwyer had been impressed by something which also would have occurred to no one but herself. His mother had shaken Susie, but she had not shaken Jack. A man who could resist the influence of a bad woman was something Mrs Dwyer had never encountered before.

Mrs Dwyer was facing troubles of her own at the time. 'Poor Dwyer' had been dead for several years; Jim, the last of the boys, had married, and she was living on her own. Characteristically, this, instead of making her brood, gave her a new lease of life. What to anyone else would have been the end of a way of living was to her the beginning of another. She plunged straight into a life of dissipation, travelling to Blackrock and Douglas to visit old friends, playing cards, going to the pictures and refusing to mind her grandchildren. 'Wisha, aren't I right?' she said to Jack with a shrug. 'Aren't I fussing round them long enough? God knows, you have no notion, the comfort it is not to have anyone but yourself to look after.'

But she had left it a bit late before taking her fling. Soon afterwards she developed arthritis, and Susie came to nurse her. But it looked as though her independence was over. She couldn't be left alone in the house, and would have to go and live with one of the boys – a bitter humiliation for a strong-minded woman.

Tim, an easy-going fellow, would have had her readily enough, but easy-going fellows get easy-going wives, and it was most unlikely that Mrs Dwyer, who boasted that she had never seen the day when a properly cooked dinner wasn't served in her house, would put up with Nora and her perpetual round of sausages. Ned's wife had six children, and there was no room unless they took a bigger house. Jim, being only just married, hadn't enough furniture, and it would take a lot to make the house liveable-in. It wasn't that the boys didn't love their mother or wouldn't have died for her if the occasion arose, but they were all in difficulties themselves.

Susie, who had a heart for everyone's troubles, understood this perfectly, and her heart bled for each of them in turn, but her sister, Babs, told them roundly that they were a bloody pack of wasters and then went upstairs to tell her mother the same. 'How often did I say it to you?' she shouted, with her arms folded like a market woman. 'How often did I tell you you were ruining them, and you wouldn't pay a bit of attention to me? One of them wouldn't eat a slice of bread unless you buttered it for him, and none of us could get anything, and that's the thanks you get for it.' Babs was a forthright girl who could be counted on to make everything as difficult as possible for everyone else. Her mother listened with amusement.

'The Lord lighten their burdens!' she said drily. 'As if I'd be under an obligation to any of them!'

'Well, what are you going to do, woman?' asked Babs. 'You can't stop here.'

'I'm going up to the Little Sisters where I can be properly looked after,' said her mother. 'I have it fixed this two years past. Did you think, after all my years, I'd go into another woman's house to have her telling me what to do? What a fool I am!'

The whole family realized when it was put to them, that, regrettable as it was, it was only what they had always anticipated. A woman of strong character like their mother could never become an encumbrance in the house of a daughter-in-law. She would have to die as she had lived, saucy and strong and independent.

The only one who didn't take it that way was Jack.

'I suppose they know it's going to kill her?' he asked Susie.

'Oh, Jack, you don't think that?'

'I don't think it at all,' said Jack. 'I know it.'

'But, sure, she couldn't get on with any of the wives!'

'And do you think she's going to escape other women by going into a home?' he asked sarcastically.

'I suppose she isn't,' said Susie, who was sufficient of a fretter to be easily cast down. 'But what else can you do with her? You know what she's like when she has her mind made up.'

'I wonder if she has her mind made up,' he said lightly, and then talked about something else. But Susie could see he hadn't stopped brooding about it at all.

Next evening, after a long walk up Montenotte and back by Mayfield, he called at the Dwyers'. The walk was part protocol, part technique: to call without the excuse of a walk would have made the visit official. Babs was in charge, and her mother ordered her out to make tea for Jack. Marriage made no difference to the Dwyer girls. Inside the door, they instantly reverted to a position of dependence and would do so while she had a roof over her head. And Jack's bread would be buttered for him the way 'poor Dwyer's' bread had been buttered because men liked it that way.

'I hear you're going up to the Little Sisters?' Jack said with apparent amusement as they sat over the bedroom fire in the dusk.

'Sure, of course I am, boy,' she replied lightly. 'You know what I always thought of in-laws. Can you imagine me turned loose on one of them? Not, between ourselves, Jack Cantillon, that I'm not a better woman than any of them, as old as I am.'

'I'd put my money on you anyway,' he said, amused that even in her hour of defeat she had kept her vanity.

'God knows, Jack,' she said, leaning forward with her hands on her knees and staring into the fire, 'I don't know what sort of women are they rearing. They're good for nothing only drink and gossip – not but I always liked a little drop myself, in reason. That wife of Tim's – I don't care to be criticizing, but I don't know is she ever right. If I was a man and a woman offered me sausages for my dinner two nights in a row I'd crown her with the frying-pan. I declare to God I would.'

'You wouldn't come to Susie and me?' he asked, dropping his voice so as not to be heard by Babs. 'You'd be no trouble. The room is there since the mother died.'

'Was it Susie suggested that?' she asked with apparent pleasure that didn't take Jack in at all. He congratulated himself on observing protocol. Mrs Dwyer might just be prepared to discuss such an offer from a man, particularly a man who had only just dropped in casually on the way from a walk, but to have it made by a daughter would have been a derogation.

'Oh, I didn't discuss it with Susie,' he said hastily. 'It only just came into my mind. Of course, Susie would have to have the last word.' The last word, not the first. That had to come from a man.

'Wisha, Jack, boy,' she said, dropping protocol, 'I'm easy where I go. I had my day, and I must only be satisfied. At the same time, mind you, I'm glad to be asked. 'Tis a fright to feel that nobody wants you. I suppose vanity is the last thing that dies in us.'

'Oh, vanity!' he said. 'You never told me you were that way. Tell me, will you come to us?'

'I will not, Jack, thanks all the same. Ye had enough of in-laws to last ye the rest of yeer lives – not criticizing your poor mother, God rest her, whatever I might say while she was alive. 'Tis often I thought since how right you were, in spite of us all. I suppose 'tis only when your own turn comes that you see who was right and who was wrong. Besides,' she added, 'I wouldn't give it to say to the boys.'

'I thought of that,' he agreed seriously. 'I thought you might let me ask them. I feel sure they wouldn't stand in the way if they felt you were going to be more comfortable.'

She searched his face to see if he was smiling. He wasn't though she had too much respect for him to take his words at face value. As a card player she knew it was small use studying expressions.

'To tell you the God's truth, Jack,' she said, 'I'd hate to be in an institution. God forgive me, I could never like nuns. I don't think they're natural. But I warn you, you'd be a fool to take me in. I'd be no acquisition to you. I'd promise the earth and I wouldn't mean a word of it. Old people are a mass of selfishness We're like babies. You have no idea. You'd be waiting here for someone to bring you a cup of tea, and if your nearest and dearest died while you were waiting for it, you wouldn't care. And isn't it only natural?' she added, cocking an argumentative eyebrow at him. 'Sure what else have we to look forward to?'

'I'll talk to Susie about it,' he said, as though there was anything poor Susie could say that would make any difference. But once they got used to the idea, it seemed to the whole family that this was how it was bound to happen. Their mother would be impossible in an institution unless she were made matron at once. Jack was steady; he had a good job; he was the born burden-carrier, and in the matter of money would never be able to embarrass them as a real member of the family could have done.

But, as things turned out, Mrs Dwyer was anything but a liability. Maybe it was the thought that she had escaped the home that gave her a new lease of life. The first evening Jack came home from work she had his old trousers warming before the fire, and told him to change there. 'At my age, as if I couldn't look at a man with his trousers off!' she exclaimed. 'Do you want me to go out?'

'I do not,' said Jack.

'Wisha, why would you?' she replied cheerfully.

But in some ways she was a great trial to Susie. She looked after him as if he were a child, trying to anticipate what he really liked – never an easy thing with a man who never seemed to express a preference for anything. She started cooking special dishes for him; things she hadn't cooked for thirty years, and then lamented that 'her hand was out'. She was so pleased not to be treated as an imbecile, as 'poor Dwyer' had treated her, that she even started to read papers and books so as to be able to talk to him. 'Pick out

23

some books for me there, Jack,' she would say modestly. 'Not one of them old love stories. Something sensible.' And then she would read for an hour with great concentration and say drily: 'He got a queer one all right when he went about it. A wonder he wouldn't take a stick to her!'

When Susie started her first big row with Jack, her mother lowered her book and asked sharply: 'Susie, what way is that to talk to Jack?' and Susie broke down and went upstairs to weep. When Jack went to follow her in his usual way, Mrs Dwyer said firmly: 'Stop where you are, Jack. You only make her worse.' She put down her book and slowly followed Susie upstairs. She knew Jack didn't like it; she knew he remembered her warnings against permitting outsiders to interfere, but she also knew how her own daughters should be handled, which he never would.

'The trouble with you is that you don't know a good man when you meet one,' she told Susie, who was lying on the bed, weeping, and waiting for her husband to comfort her, the way any married woman would. 'I only wish to God that I'd had a husband like him – not criticizing poor Dwyer, God rest him.'

'God is good,' said Susie between her tears. 'I mightn't last long between the pair of ye.' As her mother chose to ignore this, she called defiantly at her through the closed door, 'Oh, ye'd be well-suited, the pair of ye!'

She mightn't have been too far wrong. On her death-bed Mrs Dwyer asked Jack and herself to see that she was buried with them. She did not ask it with any particular eagerness, but even then, she surprised Jack, because she was a woman who had always despised sentiment, disliked anyone who professed to ideals above money and security, and expressed complete indifference about where she was buried.

That caused real friction in the family, but Jack suddenly turned obstinate and even cold. Years later, Susie, searching through a few old papers in his desk, found the undertaker's bill. It came as a shock, and she wept bitterly for a few minutes, and then began to wonder why on earth he had kept it. There were still one or two things that puzzled her about him. There was no escape for her now; a woman who had not ceased to be inquisitive about the man she had married.

The Little Mother

1

Joan lived in a little terrace house near Cork Barrack with her parents and her younger sisters, Kitty and May. Mick Twomey was a builder, honest, hard-working, unbusinesslike and greatly esteemed. He was small, slight and quick-moving, with a clear complexion and red hair and moustache. Joan worshipped him, because whenever she got into some childish scrape she didn't want her mother to know about she went to him, her eyes popping, her voice a thrilling whisper, for the 'loan' of a shilling. 'And you won't tell Mummy, will you, Dad?' she would ask, and he would say indignantly: 'What business is it of Mummy's? This is between you and me, girl.' What was more, he said it in a way you could believe. It was wonderful to have someone you could trust the way you could trust her father.

Her mother was a beauty; slight, attractive and sentimental, who mourned over the wrongs of Ireland, romantic love and the sufferings of the poor, and seemed to get a great deal of pleasure from them. Her husband, who had been a revolutionary in his youth, had come to the age of being sarcastic about all three, but Mrs Twomey remained faithful to any cause she once took up. She said prayers for the success of the Republicans at elections, dreamed in a most undemocratic way of titled romances for her daughters, and entertained beggars in the house. Mick would arrive unexpectedly to find some old shawly beggar woman eating her dinner in the kitchen and slam into the sitting room in a wild rage, but in secret he adored his wife and told his daughters that they'd never be a patch on her. He knew how to take advantage of her sentimentality as well, for whenever he got in wrong with her he had only to drop a gruff remark about somebody from Killarney – Killarney being where they'd spent their honeymoon – and sure enough, in no time she would be going about the house, singing in a sweet cracked voice 'By Killarney's Lakes and Fells'. It was so easy it was mean, and it went to Mick's heart to do it, but he was old enough to value peace in the home.

The three girls were spoiled and from the time they reached the age of twelve you could find them round the gas-lamp in the evening, or slinking up dark laneways with boys who were wilder than themselves. Joan had a broad, humorous face, a gay and dashing manner and a great flow of gab. She was big round the bosom and rear and walked with a roll that her father said was like a drum-major's. Kitty, the second girl, was taller and had a better figure. She dressed better, too, because she had a passion for dressmaking and couldn't see an old frock without realizing its possibilities. She was an untidy, emotional girl who took after her mother and was, accordingly, her father's favourite. May, being only thirteen, couldn't really be very wild, but with her miniature features, she promised to be the best-looking of the three, and there was something about her quick wit and quick smile that indicated she would take full advantage of it.

Mrs Twomey, being nearer their age than her husband's, couldn't control them at all. She would fly into a rage and go for them with whatever came handiest, and then remember some identical occasion in her own girlhood and her own mother's indignation until, forgetting all about the cause of her rage, she went round singing 'Mother Machree' and the girls, forgetting their sore bottoms and injured dignity, would join in. Sometimes Mick, coming home from work in the evening, would hear them singing from the road outside, and, when he threw open the kitchen door, see the four of them sitting in darkness round the range and the fresh tears shining on their cheeks. 'Name of God, are ye at it again?' he would growl, striding over to light the gas. 'I suppose none of ye thought about supper?'

Sunday was Mrs Twomey's favourite day because after chapel in the evening the girls brought home their friends and their friends' friends. The gas-lamp was lit at the foot of the little square outside; the gas-jets hissed at either side of the fireplace in the front room, and the oil-lamp on the round table gave light to the piano. Kitty, the hostess of the three girls, made the tea and Joan played. Dick Gordon, Joan's fellow, usually started things off by singing 'Toreador' or 'The Bandolero' in a weak baritone. He was a tall, handsome young fellow with a long clear face, and while he sang

Mrs Twomey smiled fondly and discussed himself and his family in what she thought was a whisper.

She was very glad of him for Joan, though there was something missing somewhere which she attributed to a Protestant streak, way back. He wasn't interested in republicanism and was even less interested in religion. He didn't go to the Sacraments, or even to Mass, unless it was to meet somebody at it. He was a well-read boy, and, seeing that both his own family and the Twomeys were mad on religion, he had out of pure kindness of heart studied the Bible and several other religious works, only to find them all filled with people rising from the dead or ascending into the sky without any means of locomotion – things no practical engineer could credit.

'And you mean you don't really believe in God, Dick?' Mrs Twomey asked wonderingly.

'Afraid not, Mrs T,' he replied quite cheerfully, as though he were not afraid at all.

'You don't believe in anything?'

'On the contrary, I believe in everything – everything I can put my hand on, that is.'

'You will, Dick,' she said solemnly. 'One of these days when all the things you can put your hand on are no help to you, you'll see God as plain as you see me.'

'That'll be the day,' he said with cheerful irreverence.

2

Each winter Mrs Twomey, who had a weak chest, suffered from bronchitis. She had ceased to pay much attention to it herself and treated it almost like an old friend. Besides, it was an ordeal for her to stay in bed or even at home, because she liked her trips into town and her gossips with old cronies on the way.

The winter after Joan became seventeen she had one of her usual attacks and recovered, and on the first sunny day went into town to Mass. She came back, feeling weak, and that night her bronchitis was worse. By the following evening she could scarcely breathe and sat propped up on pillows. Old Dr Mulcahy, who had been in gaol with Mick, thought it best not to remove her. In the early morning she had an attack of breathlessness and became so violent that it took Mick and Joan to hold her down. Mulcahy came and gave her an injection which put her to sleep. Then he took Mick into the front room.

'We're very old friends, Mick,' he said. 'I think I'd better prepare you for a shock.'

Mick drew himself up.

'Is that the way it is, Peter?'

'I'm afraid so. Even if she gets through this I'm afraid she'll be an invalid for the rest of her days.'

'I don't care what she is, Peter,' Mick replied violently. 'So long as they leave her with me.'

'Oh, I know, I know,' Mulcahy said gloomily. 'There aren't many like her. Send the elder girl into me, Mick. I want to talk to her.'

That evening Dick Gordon came and sat in the front room, talking quietly to Mick and the girls. Now and then the gate creaked as some old neighbour came to inquire. Mulcahy had been again and gone, leaving a morphia syringe behind him. The attacks of breathlessness had become so violent that there was no other way of controlling them, and the breathing was so terrifying that none of them could stay in the bedroom for more than a few minutes.

Instead, Mick would open the door softly and tiptoe up the stairs for a few minutes at a time. Dick interjected some quiet remark that was only intended to ease the strain. Coming on to morning, Mick jumped up and rushed up the stairs, and it was only then that they realized the breathing had stopped.

'Joan! Joan!' they heard him scream in an unnatural voice. 'She's gone! Your poor mother is gone!'

Joan gathered herself up to scream as well but Dick grabbed her firmly by the shoulders. 'Quiet, now, Joanie!' he said in the low voice one might use to a child, and he smiled at her as one might smile at a child. She put her head in her hands and began to sob with the others. When they went upstairs Mick was kneeling by the head of the bed. Their mother's head had fallen feebly forward and the jaw was dropped in an expression of utter weariness.

'Take Daddy downstairs now, Dick,' Joan said, gaining control of herself. 'I can manage.'

'I'll stay, Joanie,' said Kitty.

'No, Kitty,' Dick said firmly. 'Let Joan handle this.'

They returned to the front room and Dick led Mick Twomey to an armchair by the window and then poured him out a drink. He nodded acknowledgement but when he tried to raise the glass he could not bring it to his mouth. Dick took his hand and held the glass for him. Then Dick drew the curtain and daylight came in through the drawn blind. He raised it and stood for a few moments looking out at the still square where the gas-lamp was still burning and at the fields and trees on the hillside above. 'Oh my!' he sighed with a curious boyish air and drew the blind again just as Joan entered. Her father rose with an erect and soldierly movement and drew the other girls up with him by the hand. Then he turned to Joan and presented them with a curious air of formality.

'You must be a mother to them now, Joan,' he said with a firm voice. 'They have no one else only you.'

3

That little scene made an extraordinary impression on Joan. She was over-wrought, and it seemed to her to have something of the quality of a religious dedication, as though it were a taking of vows.

When she stood with her father and sisters by the grave on a hillside over Cork Harbour, she promised the dead woman that she would try to be everything she had been to them. She had no illusions about herself. She knew her mother had been a creature apart, whose innocence had kept her emotions always fresh and beautiful. Joan felt sure that she had no such innocence, but she thought that maybe she might have character, and the thought filled her with a certain mournful pride. It was as though within a few days her whole nature had changed: as though she no longer had a father and sisters, only a husband and children; as though, in fact, her girlhood had suddenly stopped.

For months their little house was gloomy and dark. It had something to do with the deep vein of sentimentality in them all. Suddenly one of the girls would forget herself while washing clothes in the kitchen and start to hum some song of their mother's and as suddenly stop in the middle of a bar. Then would follow a few intolerable moments of widening comprehension that would end in tears.

But it couldn't go on like that. However Joan's thoughts might wander, meals had to be cooked, laundry had to be done, bills had to be paid. And though the house and furniture were now all that was left of her mother, they too were responsibilities, and Joan knew that they would have to be changed.

The house was old, and it was old-fashioned, and nothing in it had been altered in the twenty-odd years of her parents' marriage.

There was still only gas in the front room, and the furniture, bought second-hand at auctions in houses three times the size, was a joke. Joan was ashamed that they didn't have a bathroom. It struck her as all wrong in a family of girls that fellows would always be walking through the kitchen, seeing things they shouldn't see and coming in with big bumps on their foreheads after finding their way to the lavatory. Above all, she wanted to get rid of the range from the kitchen and make it into a comfortable living room. Mick did wire the house for electricity, but he made excuses about the bathroom and the kitchen, and she knew she must go slowly with him because every change would seem to him like a betrayal of her mother. He wanted to die among the things that had been hers. Joan wanted to make a new life for them all.

Besides, there was a change in herself. The excitement in her blood when dusk came and the last light lingered on the fields and trees opposite the house was no longer the same. It had used to be like a fever; the cows lowing in the fields behind, the children shouting from the gateways, the pool of light round the gas-lamp at the end of the square and the intimation of mysterious embraces; but now it was all touched with sentiment for poor human creatures whose voices would soon be stilled for ever.

It was part of her new gravity that Joan took to going to Mass every morning. Wet or fine, she plunged out after her father had left for work, and soon became familiar with the other women who did the same. If one were missing she would call on her way home to ask if there were any messages she could do. Usually there were; it was extraordinary how helpless people were when they were in trouble, and in the evening, when she had given her father his supper she would explode on him with: 'Daddy, I don't think anyone knows what goes on in a place like this.' At times like these she was very like her mother; more self-conscious, more melodramatic, but with the same absorption.

And it had a silvery sort of poetry of its own, thin and sweet and clear as if it were a world renewed. The neighbours, who only saw it from outside, admired the way a flighty girl of eighteen turned gradually into a mature, responsible young woman. But it couldn't be expected that her sisters should see it that way. Now, when Kitty was out with some fellow, Joan actually worried about her. She didn't expect anything unreasonable, only that Kitty shouldn't be out too late, but even this Kitty resented. One night there was almost a scene.

'What kept you out till this hour, Kitty?' Joan asked, quite politely, but Kitty started back as though she'd been struck.

'What's wrong with you?' she asked angrily. 'Who do you think you are?'

'Oh, just the new housekeeper, Kitty,' Joan replied with a nervous laugh. 'Who did you think?'

'I don't know,' Kitty replied coarsely. 'Whoever you are, you're getting too big for your boots.'

That night Joan wept as she so often did nowadays. Children never understood the responsibilities of guardians. And it wasn't only Kitty, of course. She remembered how often and unjustly she had blamed her mother for the same sort of thing.

But Kitty and Mary soon realized that they had lost a sister and caught a tartar. It was true that Joan always had a touch of Reverend Mother about her, and had attempted to make up in knowingness for the affection that had been diverted from her to her younger sisters, but that had been mainly swank. In essential things she had remained part of the juvenile conspiracy, treating parents as enemies, raiding their stores and smashing up their intelligence system. Now, she had real authority and harried them mercilessly, particularly poor Kitty, who had been disorderly from birth, and left a litter of dirty clothes and pots and pans behind her. Her mother had been content to clean up after her, knowing poor Kitty had other things on her mind, but Joan didn't see why she should do it. Of course, she was always polite, but then, it seemed to be the politeness that got on Kitty's nerves.

'Kitty!'

'Well?'

'In the hall, dear,' Joan would sing out. 'That thing on the floor.'

'What about it anyway?'

'Nothing, Kitty, only it looks like your good coat. I wonder if you'd mind hanging it up?'

'Would you mind?' Kitty would mutter to May. 'Would you please oblige by removing your noxious presence from the premises? That one!'

Joan realized that none of them had been taught orderly habits, and that even in their school work it came against them. May was brilliant but her marks were shocking, so she had to stay in for an hour each evening and do maths and French with Joan who rapped her knuckles with a ruler and scolded her in a shrill voice for neglecting her irregular verbs. As if the life of any pretty girl were affected by irregular verbs!

And, having deserted to the enemy, Joan was worse than any parent because she had their whole intelligence service broken up from within. She would be waiting for them at the door, her arms folded, looking up and down the road for them till she trained them to scout first. Kitty would put her head quickly round a corner and say in a despairing tone: 'Christ on a bicycle! That one is there again!' May thought this was cowardice, and said so, but even she knew that Joan was a problem. It was no good telling her you'd been dressmaking up the road when you'd really been out Mayfield with a boy because she'd done it too often herself and would be bound to find out the truth next morning at Mass from some old Biddy like herself. They had to tell the truth but they did it with bitterness in their hearts, not so much because they were afraid as because it derogated from their femininity; and in the intervals of wheedling and scolding they lapsed into mute and sullen conspiracy.

All the family learned from the new situation, but Joan, who was at the centre of it, learned most. She found it was far from being the romantic change of parts she had first imagined and not at all a matter of her father and herself on the one hand, and 'the children' as she liked to call them on the other.

At first, when she discussed money matters with Mick she was flattered by the grown-up tone of mournful candour in which he replied, but in time she began to suspect that the candour was fallacious – the accounts varied too much. It was hard to believe, and she hated to believe it, but her father was not always truthful.

One day, when she was worried about bills, she saw Kitty with a handful of silver.

'Where did you get all the cash, Kitty?' she asked lightly.

'Cash?' Kitty retorted with an attempt at brazening it out. 'What cash?'

'You needn't bother to tell me any lies, Kitty,' Joan said in an off-hand way. 'I can guess.'

'You can guess what you like,' said Kitty, now thoroughly alarmed as she saw her source of independence threatened. 'I got it from Aunt Molly, as you're so inquisitive.'

Joan was too disgusted to argue with her. Her father, thinking she kept them short deliberately, had been supplying them in secret. That was his gratitude! She could see it exactly as though he were some man who had been unfaithful to her and imagine the mockery of her rivals. Mick was horrified when she challenged him with it.

'For God's sake, girl!' he exclaimed. 'I gave her a couple of bob. What harm is that?'

'You gave it to her behind my back,' said Joan.

'Well, would you want her to know what I gave you?'

'Ah, 'tisn't alike,' she said with an angry shrug. 'I suppose you know what they think themselves – that I grudge it to them?'

'Ah, don't be silly, girl!' he said. 'How could they think anything of the kind?'

He argued, pleaded, even lost his temper with her, but she was remorseless. He had been unfaithful to her, and, like every other deceived wife, she knew her disillusionment was a weapon. Never again would he betray her. Even later, when she went beyond the beyonds and challenged him about his drinking – a thing her mother would never have dared to do – he endured it patiently. Now she had three quivering victims, a thing that might have gone to the head of a less emotional girl than she was.

4

But Dick Gordon got the worst of it, and he did not understand it at all. Joan had always been what he thought of as a good girl, but she had also had her share of devilment. A couple of times when they stayed in Crosshaven she had slipped into his bed, and Dick, who understood that part of her very well, knew that she was only trying it out. It merely meant that she felt perfectly safe with him, which she was.

But those days were over. Now, when she thought of it, Joan merely wondered how she would feel if Kitty were to behave like that with some young fellow of Dick's age, and at once it ceased to be attractive. Even Dick himself was not very reliable – a young fellow who didn't believe in God, or eternal punishment, or marriage or anything. Even if she married him, there would still be endless arguments about what children should and should not be taught. So far as he was concerned they would grow up like heathens.

It was a real problem to her and caused her a great deal of worry. She realized that in her own way she loved him, and often in the evenings she forgot herself and stood at the door with her arms folded bending forward to look down the road for him. It was only when she saw him, coming towards her with his self-confident air, that she remembered the Protestant grandmother, and in her perturbation picked a quarrel with him. No, she couldn't go to the pictures that evening. She couldn't go for a walk. She couldn't even ask him to stay because she had arranged to coach Kitty for her Civil Service exam. And then she went into the front room and bawled again.

One night, Mick opened the door and walked in with a puzzled air.

'What the hell is wrong with you, girl?' he asked crossly.

'Me?' she asked, sniffing back tears. 'Oh, nothing. Why?'

'Are you having a fight with Dick?'

'No, Daddy. It's not that.'

'Well, don't. Dick is a fine young fellow.' Long ago Mick had promoted Dick to the position of the son he lacked, and since his wife's death this attitude had become fixed in him. 'Look! Don't sit here in the dark, moaning. Put on your hat and coat and go out after him. Tell him you're sorry, whether you are or not. He won't mind.'

Whether it was that he knew her father was on his side or not, Dick had a curious thickness that made him incapable of recognizing when he wasn't wanted. There were times when she thought him the thickest man in the world. He wasn't easy at home with a respectable family who thought the Twomeys were frivolous and unstable. He had been coming to the house for years until it meant more to him than his own. The old gate that squeaked, the flower-beds and lilacs, the little front room were Dick's romance, and he was prepared to fight for them. This, she saw, was something she would have to have out with him, and it alarmed her because she was not very good at scenes. And when this one came, it was worse than she expected because she made no impression at all on Dick. It was a spring evening and they were lying in a field over the harbour – an old haunt of theirs. Dick had his hands linked behind his head, and when she told him that they must see less of one another, he merely turned to look at her with an air of pity and amusement.

'What makes you think that?' he asked mildly.

'Well, things have changed so much, and I have so many new responsibilities, I wouldn't like to keep you hanging round,' she said, getting nervous.

'Oh, I have a few responsibilities of my own, you know,' he said with a smile.

'But this may be a matter of years, Dick.'

'Well, since we suit one another, we may as well put up with a few delays,' he replied blandly.

'But, Dick, we don't suit one another.'

This time he raised his eyebrows. Dick was an engineer and tended to treat people as though they were complicated bits of machinery. Something went wrong; you opened it up and fixed it, and then it worked perfectly again. She could almost see him working on her now.

'Don't we?'

'I don't honestly think so, Dick. Not any longer anyhow.'

'Since how long?'

'Oh, a long time.'

'Exactly,' he said blandly. 'Since your mother's death.'

(Joan could almost see it as though it were evidence at the inquest – 'She had not been the same since her mother's death.')

'Ah, Dick, it's not only Mummy's death,' she said impatiently.

'No, of course not,' he went on in the same bland tone. 'But that is the most important thing. You've had a shock, and you must wait for the effects to wear off.'

'Listen, Dick, I wish you'd talk seriously for once,' she said angrily. 'I know I was young and giddy, and I didn't understand how much certain things meant to me. I suppose it's only when someone you care for dies that you do know.'

'And that is part of the shock,' he said positively.

'It isn't part of the shock,' she cried. 'That's what I'm trying to explain. You just think everything is caused by something else and it isn't. I'll get over the shock, as you call it, but I won't get over things I believed in all the time, only I didn't pay enough attention to them. You don't believe in any of the things I believe in – that's the real trouble. You want me to marry you, and God knows I always wanted to marry you, but you don't even believe in marriage. You don't believe in sin. You could go off with another girl tonight and there would be nothing to prevent you.'

'Or to prevent any of your pious believers,' Dick said with cold anger.

'At least they'd know that what they were doing was wrong,' she said.

'Oh, if it's only a feeling of guilt you think I'm lacking in, I'll do the best I can,' he said wearily. He got up and brushed himself, but he was a man who could not keep his anger at boiling point. He looked down at her and smiled.

'Give yourself time, Joanie,' he pleaded. 'You've lost a wonderful mother, and it seems like the end of the world to you, but don't exaggerate. People don't get on in marriage because they have the same taste and the same ideas. Your mother didn't get on with your father for that reason. You and I didn't get on for that reason. We got on because we had respect for one another's feelings. That's all.'

It wasn't all, and she knew it, but it was hopeless to argue with him. He came back to the house every evening just the same, though each evening he seemed a little more despondent. He was. From his limited, logical, liberal point of view her breach with him made no sense even if he was wrong about religion. Sometimes in his liberal way he assumed he must be, and that there was probably an essential flywheel missing that would enable him to enjoy ascensions, assumptions and apparitions just like anybody else. But he knew the wild side of Joan better than anyone else, and he could not understand how the laughing girl who had pushed her way into his bed in Crosshaven could disappear like that, leaving behind nothing but a soured, censorious old maid.

He even discussed it one evening with Kitty when he accidentally met her outside the office – it did not occur to him that she had arranged the accident – but her explanations only mystified him more.

'It's all just pride, Dick,' she said coldly. 'Just rotten pride and vanity. All she wants now is a man she can boss the way she bosses Daddy and us. You're too independent for her altogether.'

That evening he asked Kitty to come to the theatre with him, Joan having already refused. It was Shaw's *Saint Joan* and during the last half Kitty wept almost without ceasing.

'God, Dick,' she sobbed, 'I always wanted to be a saint.'

He was amused and touched, amused by her emotionalism, touched by her resemblance to her mother. 'What an astonishing family!' he thought. After the theatre she insisted on walking home, swinging from his arm and stopping before shop windows. Finally she detained him for half an hour under the gas-lamp at the end of the square. She knew she was in full view of Joan but this neither deterred nor incited her. She wanted to talk about the play.

'Do you think I'd let myself get burned the way she did?' she asked.

'I don't know,' Dick said with amusement, leaning against the lamp post, his feet wide and his hands behind his back. 'Maybe you would after changing your mind a few times as she did.'

'Twelve months ago I'd have been certain of it,' she said.

'And what made the change?' he asked without realizing what she was speaking of.

'You known damn well,' she said softly.

'I'm sorry, Kitty,' he said with real concern.

'Why would you be? You weren't rotten to her.'

'And if you'll forgive my saying it, neither were you,' he said with his gentle smile.

'I'm the best judge of that, Dick,' she said without rancour. 'And now, what do you think I'm going to do? Say I'm sorry and hope for another chance? Fat hope I have! It's all bloody cod, Dick Gordon, and you know it better than anyone.'

Suddenly she rushed away from him, and as she plunged up the hill he heard her sobbing as if her heart would break. There were tears in his own eyes. It was clear that Kitty had grown up with great rapidity.

5

For different reasons the same idea occurred to Joan. Next day it was obvious that Kitty had fallen head and ears in love with Dick, and Kitty in love gave off an atmosphere that simply could not be ignored. She was hoping to see Dick again the following evening, and when Joan detained her, she burst into tears and said that Joan was doing it for spite.

'What on earth do you mean, child?' Joan asked with an astonishment that was not quite sincere.

'Who are you calling "child"?' retorted Kitty. (It was the one word that was sure to madden her.) 'You pretend you don't want him, but you're mad jealous if he looks at anyone else.'

Joan gaped. It was only now that she was beginning to notice the change in her own character. Six months before, that skinny, pasty-faced little brat would not have dared to suggest that any man would look at her rather than at Joan, without Joan's showing her how wrong she was.

But Kitty continued to ignore her, and Dick, who seemed to have the hide of a rhinoceros, continued to call as though nothing much had happened except a slight change of object. From Kitty's rapt look when she had been out with him, Joan could see that he did to Kitty the sort of things he had done to herself. At a sign of approval Kitty would have broken down and told her, and Joan had no doubt at all that she told May. How could she bring up two children with that sort of thing going on?

It came to a head one Saturday afternoon when Kitty packed her bag for the weekend. Joan felt despairing. It was bad enough, having to stay at home and get everything ready for the Sunday while her mind was on something else; it was too much to be imagining a bed in Crosshaven and Kitty slipping into it beside Dick.

'Where are you going, Kitty?' she asked in her casual way.

'To Crosshaven for the weekend,' Kitty said, growing pale – casualness was something she still could not affect. 'Why?'

'Who are you going with?'

'The Caseys. They asked Dick and me. We're going in their car.'

'And did you ask Daddy's permission, Kitty?'

'No,' said Kitty, who always grew impertinent when she was frightened. 'Did you?'

It was really too much for Joan, who had no faith in her sister's capacity for keeping out of trouble, and she complained to her father. He was a bad man to complain to, because he was full of pity for humanity in general and young fellows of Dick's age in particular. He, too, thought she was jealous – it was really extraordinary, the number of people who got that impression – and of course, she couldn't really tell him about the sort of thing that went on – not without convicting herself.

'Ah, look here, girl,' he said irritably, 'wouldn't you make it up with Dick, whatever he did to you?'

'But honestly, Daddy, he did nothing to me.'

'Whatever ye did to one another, so.'

38

'We did nothing to one another, Daddy. I give you my word. It's just that we weren't really suited. You see, Dick has no religion.'

'Ah, religion my ass!' her father said furiously. 'Do you think I had any religion when I was his age? What the hell do you want him to do with you – say the Rosary? You make me sick!'

'It's not the same thing at all, Daddy,' Joan said obstinately. 'Your generation didn't have any religion, but there were good reasons for it. It's different with Dick. He hasn't any proper sense of responsibility, and Kitty hasn't either. Neither of them knows where to stop.'

'Ah, Christ, Joan,' he said, 'leave me alone with that sort of talk! I was the same when I was his age. He's only knocking round with Kitty to spite you. It only shows how fond of you he is. Damn it, didn't I nearly marry your Aunt Molly after one row I had with your poor mother, God rest her? And where would you be now if I did? Answer me that! You should never take things like that to the fair.'

All the same, Mick felt there should be something he could do about it. After an attempt at talking to Kitty who got up in her dramatic way and offered to leave the house next morning, he decided that that wasn't it. It was only when he ran into Dick Gordon accidentally one evening on Patrick's Bridge that he decided to confide in him. He was like Dick in this, that both found it easier to talk intimately to men. Men did not drop into blooming sentiment, and anyone listening to Mick would have thought he was only telling an amusing story. But Dick thought otherwise, and when he went away he already felt that he owed it to the man he would have liked for a father-in-law not to make any more trouble for him at home.

When he next met Kitty he suggested that they should give up meeting till she had got her exam and was independent. She agreed, reasonably enough as he thought, and, indeed, she settled down to work with a deliberation that surprised Joan. Though Kitty gave the impression of being frivolous and unstable, there was a streak of determination in her that was very close to desperation. Unfortunately for him, it was months before Dick realized that it was desperation rather than reasonableness, and by that time it was too late. He had lost the second of the Twomey girls without even knowing quite how he had.

6

For some months Joan had been seeing Chris Dwyer off and on. She had been astute enough to realize that he had fallen in love with her, all over a remark she had made about a concert, but that he would do nothing about it as long as she was seen round with Dick Gordon. Chris was not a dashing type at all, like Dick, and had never except inadvertently cut in on anyone.

He was a tall, good-looking young man with a long, pale face, clever eyes, a long, rather suspicious nose, and a weak, gentle mouth. He spoke in a Sunday's Well accent, swallowing half his words; dressed accordingly and even carried an umbrella. 'I really don't see what the objection to it is,' he said with his nervous laugh. 'I mean, it's so practical.' You could see that the umbrella meant something special to him, like a holy medal. Young May, who thought he was a queer, called him 'I mean'.

He came of a good family that had descended in the world, and devoted himself to the care of his mother, a woman of such invincible refinement that she didn't even understand what had happened to her income. The first time Chris asked Joan to come to a concert with him he told her the whole story of his life so that there could be no question of his inability to marry her, and Joan, who understood him perfectly, was very amused because she had no doubt of her ability to marry him whenever she wanted to.

After that, he took her out on the same evening each week, umbrella and all. He was an orderly young man who liked to know exactly where he stood. He was also in his own way a clever one, conscientious and kind; and out of his great responsibilities he made up funny little stories which he told with an air of intense gravity that made them funnier still. When Joan laughed he grew quite hysterical, and his face became that of an ingenuous boy.

Joan confided in him her troubles with her father and sisters, and Chris – after a period of meditation – responded with a new version of his life story that contained admissions about his elder brothers, Bob and Jim. Bob gambled, and Jim, who couldn't be kept out of a church had broken out in *very* peculiar ways. Joan could not get out of him exactly what they were, but they were obviously a great trial.

Between family confidences and music, Chris and herself seemed made for one another, the only difficulty being that each had so many responsibilities that there was no hope of their ever being more than friends, but even this formed something of a bond, and they were genuinely happy in one another's company. Joan had at last got rid of the range, and had the kitchen done up in bright simple colours so that she didn't mind asking him in, even if they hadn't a bathroom. Her father, of course, didn't like the living room, and had retreated to the sitting room where things were still unchanged, but Joan had ideas for that, too. Or she would have, when she had got him to install the bathroom. She felt she would never be able to deal with a man as an equal until she could say: 'Don't you want to go to the bathroom?'

All the same, she still had troubles with her family. By the time Kitty got her job and left home, May was seventeen and a handful, in some ways worse than Kitty. Kitty had a temper, and wept and used dirty words, but May was a girl of extraordinary sweetness, with a disposition as clear as her complexion. She was a slight girl, cool, resourceful and insinuating, with a smile that seemed intended merely to reveal her tiny front teeth, and she had some extraordinary ideas. For instance, she didn't believe in class distinctions, and only smiled tolerantly at Joan's insistence on a bathroom. It seemed she didn't think bathrooms were natural. She was a great believer in Nature, and Nature to her did not mean a summer bungalow in Crosshaven but a primitive cabin in West Cork with no bathroom at all. 'Do you want to go out to the haggard?' she would ask, with no consideration at all for the embarrassment she might be causing a visitor.

It was Chris, who seemed to know everything, who told Joan about May's friendship with Timmy McGovern and his crowd. Timmy represented several Dublin firms and was in line for the Dublin management of one. He lived on the College Road with his wife – one of the Geraghty girls from Glenareena (of course, Chris knew about them as well) and two kids. According to Chris, he was very popular, but not steady; definitely not steady. Even his best friend, Tony Dowse, said he was an imaginative man, and everybody knew what Tony Dowse was like!

Joan went straight upstairs and searched May's bedroom for letters. There were plenty of these, mostly from Timmy McGovern, and Joan and Chris read them together in the new living room with a sense of utter incredulity. Joan knew of old that all love letters were silly, but these were mad. They would go on for a paragraph in a jerky, spasmodic style like a broken-down car, and then soar suddenly into rhetoric about the long winding roads of Ireland or the world's not existing any longer for them when they were together.

'My goodness!' Chris said with a giggle that sounded like a cry. '"The winding roads of Ireland!" Do you know him?'

'No, Chris, why?'

'He must be a ton weight, and his feet are so bad he can hardly walk a hundred yards.'

'And a married man!'

'That's the worst of it, of course,' Chris said, sobering up.

'What am I going to do? If Daddy knew he'd go mad.'

'You'll have to talk to her,' said Chris.

'Talk to her!' cried Joan. 'Wait till I'm done with her!'

But even talking to May was not as easy as it sounded. She was too well-guarded.

'May,' Joan asked dramatically, 'what's all this about Mr McGovern and you?'

'How do you mean – all this?' May asked sweetly.

'May, it's no use talking like that,' Joan said sternly. 'I read his letters to you.'

'Then you know as much about it as I do,' replied May.

'You should be proud of them,' Joan said bitterly. 'A married man!'

'They suit me all right,' May said with a shrug and a splutter. 'And married men are much the same as other men from the little I see.'

That was typical of May. She couldn't even understand that a few words in front of a priest changed a man's whole nature – or should.

'Aren't you forgetting that they have wives, May?' Joan asked sternly. 'A lovely time his wife would have, getting those letters read out in court!' She paused to see if the word 'court' would scare May, but she wasn't as easily scared as that. 'May, where is this thing going to end?'

'We didn't decide yet,' May replied with a guilty smile as though she blamed herself greatly for letting such opportunities slip. 'I dare say eventually I'll have to go and live with him.'

'You'll what, May?' Joan asked, wondering if the girl were really sane.

'Oh, I don't mean in Cork, of course,' May said apologetically. By now she seemed to be blaming herself for a certain weakness of character. 'I mean when he gets to Dublin. It might even have to be London. People in this country are so blooming narrow-minded,' she added with indignation. 'They get in a rut by the time they're eighteen – any of them that weren't in a rut before.'

At any moment now Joan felt that May would start quoting Timmy's letters to her and tell her that Ireland didn't exist either.

'May,' she said despairingly, 'where do you get these terrible ideas from?'

'Now, Joan, it's no use talking like a schoolgirl to me,' May said with unusual sharpness. 'You should have got over that with the measles. Timmy made a mistake in his marriage, that's all. Lots of men do, actually,' she added in a worldly-wise tone that made Joan writhe. 'Either he has to put up with Eily Geraghty for the rest of his life or make a fresh start somewhere else.'

'Well, he's making a worse mistake if he thinks he's going to make a fresh start with you,' cried Joan. May only shrugged and pouted a little. The matter was obviously one she could only discuss on a high plane of abstraction. Apparently she thought that Joan probably didn't exist either.

But Joan showed her. First, she complained to her father, and as usual he behaved as though she were the guilty party. Then for ten minutes he thundered at May in the manner of an angry Jehovah, and she was quite genuinely upset, but it was obvious to Joan that she was upset on his account rather than her own. It saddened her to see a man of such independent character reduced to talk about what the neighbours would think.

But Joan had no intention of letting herself be flouted. One afternoon she went to the Grand Parade where Timmy McGovern had his office. She disliked him from the first moment. He was a fat, big-built man with discoloured teeth, a long lock of dark hair that tumbled over his left eye, small merry eyes, and small, unsteady feminine feet that seemed as though at any moment they might give up the ghost. She could see what Chris meant about the improbability of his travelling the long winding roads of Ireland in anything but a large car.

Obviously, he was scared to death and gave her a wistful smile as he led her into his private office. In fact, he had only just arrived there himself in a series of roundabout routes. He had heard talk about himself and May, and Timmy was sensitive that way. Whenever he heard talk about himself he went into hiding. He did really mean it when he said the rest of the world didn't exist for him when he was with May, but when he wasn't it could be quite alarming.

His office was a small room with a window opening on the vent, a stationery press, a table, and a couple of chairs. On the table was a photograph of May, sitting on a rock over a mountain pool, and the sight of it made Joan mad. She opened her pocket-book and put the photograph in.

'If you won't protect my sister's reputation, I have to do it, Mr McGovern,' she said. 'Now, if you wouldn't mind giving me her letters!'

'Her what?' Timmy asked in consternation.

'Her letters.'

'I have no letters,' he said, growing sullen.

'Well, I have,' she said grimly. 'Letters from you to her. And, what's more, Mr McGovern, I intend to use them.'

'I'm sorry you feel like this about it,' he said nervously, fumbling with the spring of his pince-nez.

'And how do you think I should feel? You should be ashamed of yourself! A married man with two children, writing like that to a child – a schoolgirl!'

Nothing would ever persuade Joan but that the few words pronounced in front of the priest must produce some sort of change, but with Timmy they didn't seem to have taken. His eyes clouded with tears.

'I can explain that,' he said brokenly. 'I don't think you'd be quite so unreasonable if you knew the sort of life I lead. Mind, I don't want you to think I'm complaining of my wife! She was always a good woman according to her lights, but there was never any understanding between us. Eily is a peasant, and she hasn't an idea beyond the house and the children. When I met May I knew she was the only girl in the world for me. I love May,' he added with manly simplicity. 'I'd die for her this minute.'

'Thank you, Mr McGovern,' Joan said curtly. 'She doesn't need anyone to die for her. She needs someone to look after her. I didn't come here to discuss your disagreements with your wife. I came here to get my sister's letters, and to warn you that next time you see her or write to her, I'm going straight to your wife and then to the priest.'

Joan was bluffing, and she knew it. Timmy, like everyone else in Cork was vulnerable, but he wasn't as vulnerable as all that. If he had told Joan to take a running jump for herself there was very little she could do that wouldn't make as much trouble for herself as for him; but Timmy, a romantic man, lived in an atmosphere of crisis, and he was scared by the hysteria in her voice. That is the worst of out-and-out idealism; it so rarely stands up to a well-played bluff.

'You wouldn't do that to us?' he said reproachfully.

She knew then she had him on the run. She rose and went to the door.

'The child has no other mother,' she said. 'I have to be a mother to her.'

That did it. Timmy grabbed her excitedly and closed the door she had just opened. His dark hair was ruffled, and he was scowling and dribbling. As Tony Dowse said, he was an imaginative man. He begged Joan to be reasonable; he would respect May if she were his own daughter. It was just that life was impossible without her.

'If I don't get those letters today I'm going straight up to your wife,' she said.

Timmy looked at her and sighed. It was a terrible sigh as though at last the wickedness of the world had been revealed to him. Then he opened a drawer and took out a bundle of letters. Without looking at them Joan pushed them into her handbag and went silently down the stairs. She was full of triumph. At last she felt she had grown up and spoken to a man twice her age as an equal. She was so pleased with herself that she went straight to Chris's office.

'I got them,' she said, patting her bag, and Chris smiled.

'Splendid!' he said, a little too enthusiastically. 'Wonderful! Now, if only you can keep her away from him for a week or two, everything will be fine.'

'Oh, that's all arranged, too,' she said bitterly. 'He won't see her again.' And then something awful happened to her and she burst into wild tears.

'Oh, darling!' Chris said, forgetting himself. 'I knew I shouldn't let you do this yourself. I should have seen him.

45

Look, wait a minute and we'll go out for a cup of tea. Or a drink? Maybe a drink would be better?'

'No, thanks, Chris,' she said, dabbing her eyes and trying to smile. 'I'll be all right. It's just the strain.'

But it wasn't the strain, and she stamped through Patrick Street, shaking her head and drying her eyes. She had suddenly found herself turned inside out, and instead of feeling triumphant, she felt like death. Instead of denouncing Timmy as a vile seducer, she wanted to go back and denounce him as a bloody old pansy. She knew if any man had been devoted to her as Timmy was supposed to be to May – even if it was sinful, and mortal sin at that, and even if he did have a wife and two children – and had written her those letters about reality not existing except when she was round, it would have broken her heart if he had taken fright as Timmy did.

So the scene she had planned with May took an entirely different turn from what she intended, as planned scenes usually do. May just sat there, cold and white and detached and Joan floundered and sobbed through her explanations. She knew it was none of her business, but she had done it for the best, and of course, she wasn't mature enough for the responsibilities she had taken on, and she hoped May would forgive her, but May was a hundred times the man Timmy was.

'That's what I'm beginning to think myself,' May said curtly as though from a great distance, and Joan would have done almost anything to make it up between them again but she knew she couldn't. Somewhere beneath May, as beneath her father, there was that slight streak of ice beyond which the most devoted interference could not live.

Timmy, according to Chris, who had it from Tony Dowse, took to his bed with an incurable disease and was nursed devotedly by Eily Geraghty. But Timmy knew that the doctor and Eily were in a conspiracy to conceal from him what was really wrong, so he applied for a life insurance policy, saw the doctor and went straight back to bed. When the policy was returned to him, completed, he got up, went into town and had a roaring evening with his group. 'An imaginative man', as Tony had always said, almost with admiration.

It seemed to take little out of May. She was different from Kitty in that. Within a month she was walking out with a handsome young journalist who drove a sports car, and pleading with him to get him interested in the winding roads of Ireland, but all he would say was that 'the surfaces were very bad'.

Fortunately for their own peace of mind, men rarely realize that the intellectual charms of a woman usually derive from the previous man.

7

It seemed to bring Joan closer to Chris. He wasn't scandalized as she had feared he would be. Instead, he told her a new and franker version of his life story, which contained some astonishing revelations about his brother, Bob. As usual, it was Chris who had been left with the job of clearing things up with the woman's husband. Joan admired his reserve in not having told her before. Apparently every family, even the best brought-up, had things to conceal; and respectability, far from being the dreary and monotonous virtue it was supposed to be, was athletic, perilous and exhausting. You don't get bathrooms for nothing. Joan at last succeeded in getting Mick to put in one for them, and the first night Chris came briskly up the hill, hitting his thigh with his folded paper, she nearly suffocated with pleasure at the thought that now she could say to him: 'Wouldn't you like to go upstairs?' Besides, she had rented a summer cottage in Crosshaven for a whole month.

Of course, there were drawbacks. The neighbours hadn't minded about the electric light or even the living room, but the bathroom was an innovation and unpleasant remarks were made about it. Now, when she went to Mass in the mornings she no longer knew who among the congregation did not mind the bathroom and who did, so she tended to give them all the same thin smile. As a result, people were inclined to say that the Twomeys were growing out of their knowledge.

At the same time her worries with the children continued. On her previous holiday Kitty had dodged going to Mass. Joan had discovered it by accident, and it worried her a lot. Then one morning, soon after Kitty had gone back, May got a letter from her that made her smile.

'I suppose we'd better tell Daddy about this,' she said questioningly. 'Did you know Kitty was going to have a baby?'

'A what, May?' cried Joan.

'A baby,' May replied almost enviously. 'It's this fellow Rahilly she's knocking round with. I thought she had more sense.'

'Show me!' said Joan, realizing that the bathroom was all in vain. Better, indeed, if there had never been a bathroom. Kitty was pregnant, and the father was a student of engineering, who though a boy of very fine character and intelligence, had no job and was entirely dependent on his parents. Deduct a bathroom from a baby and there was an awful lot of plain discredit left. Chris's mother would have the advantage of her at last. It was even doubtful if May's fellow could marry her, but it was no use saying that to May. She would only begin to argue about a woman's right to have a baby if she wanted it. And already Joan had a shrewd suspicion that May was beginning to feel left out of things.

Her father was no better. Weak as ever, he wanted to put the blame everywhere except where it belonged.

'Ah, I can't be angry with the girl, Joanie,' he said crossly. 'It was my own fault for letting her go to a strange town by herself. This would never have happened if she was in her own home. Sure, what is she only a child?'

'But what are you going to do about it, Daddy?' she asked.

'What can you do? You can't let her have a child up there, alone. Let her come home and have it.'

'Is it for the whole road to laugh at us?' she asked incredulously.

'Oh, them!' he said contemptuously. 'Do you think they didn't laugh at your mother when I was in gaol, and she hadn't enough to keep the house going? When did they ever do anything but laugh, for the good the laughing did them?'

'But, Daddy, what about May?'

'What about her?'

'You don't think or imagine the Mahoneys will let Jim marry her with a scandal like that in the house?'

'If Jim Mahoney is the sort to let his people decide whether he's going to marry or not, she's better off without him,' said her father. 'Anyway, what do you expect me to do? You'd think I was the father, the way you go on!'

'I thought you'd go to Dublin and talk to him.'

'How can I go to Dublin, with work ahead of me that I have to finish or pay a fine?' he shouted.

'Oh, all right, then,' cried Joan, who had heard about that fine too often to believe in it now. 'I suppose I'll have to go myself. Somebody will have to go.'

That evening she told Chris about it in a cinema teashop overlooking Patrick Street. She was surprised how little she did have to tell him, because he seemed to see difficulties and complications that she hadn't guessed at.

'This isn't a job for you at all, Joan,' he said with a worried air. 'This is a job for a man.'

'I know that, Chris,' she said, 'but Daddy won't go, and even if he did you know what he's like.'

'Pretty hopeless, I'd say,' Chris said with a nervous giggle, and talked tangentially for ten minutes about things in the office. 'Would you like me to go?' he asked suddenly.

She almost laughed at the idea of the refined and modest Chris trying to arrange Kitty's marriage for her, but at the same time she was touched.

'No, thanks, Chris,' she said. 'I'm sure you'd handle this fellow better than I could, but you'd never be able to handle Kitty. To tell you the God's truth, I don't know that I can handle her myself,' she added sadly.

'You'll have to see his father and mother, of course,' Chris said modestly. 'It's going to be very unpleasant. They may even try to buy you off. If they do, refuse to discuss it. If you do discuss it, you're lost. You have to keep threatening them with exposure. That's a purely legal thing, I needn't say. Your father would have to sue for the loss of his daughter's services. Kitty's services wouldn't be of any financial importance, but you have to stick with them. You won't want a law case any more than they will, but you have to pretend it's the one thing you're looking forward to. It's a game of bluff, really. You have to pretend you're in a stronger position than you are.'

Then, hearing himself talk, he went into a loud lonely laugh and cheered up at once.

'You'd think I was a real Don Juan, wouldn't you?' he asked.

'I was wondering how you knew all about it,' said Joan timidly.

'Oh, family business,' he said.

'Not Bob?'

'Unfortunately, yes, Bob,' he replied, almost in a whisper. 'We don't like talking about it. You have to take the line that you

49

don't care about proceedings. They settled for a hundred and fifty. Otherwise, Bob would have had to marry her.'

'My God!' Joan said.

She was really appalled at the things you brought on yourself merely by having a sense of duty. Here was Chris, pious, innocent, and interested mainly in classical music, and he had to try and outwit the outraged parents and avert a shot-gun wedding while she went to Dublin to compel some scoundrel to marry her flighty sister.

Next afternoon she set off for Dublin by the afternoon train, and was met at Kingsbridge by Kitty in a wide summer hat, looking swollen-faced, sullen and resentful. Joan felt pretty bitter herself. The evening light was flooding the river, and columns and towers and spires stood up in it, but she couldn't even enjoy it. While they sat in the front seat of the bus Kitty asked politely but without enthusiasm for her father, May and the neighbours. Each of them knew a struggle was on.

'How long are you going to stay, Joan?' Kitty asked innocently.

'I suppose that depends on you,' replied Joan.

'How does it depend on me?' asked Kitty.

'I thought I was coming here to arrange about your wedding,' Joan said.

'I know,' Kitty said with quiet fury. 'The way you arranged the wedding between Dick Gordon and me, and Timmy McGovern and May.'

'I suppose you think I should have let Timmy McGovern run away with May?' asked Joan.

'I don't see what the hell business it was of yours,' said Kitty.

'You wouldn't be long seeing what business it was if you had to get married with that scandal in the family,' said Joan. 'I suppose you'll tell me now that your Mr Rahilly is married already?'

He wasn't, but, as far as Joan could see, that was about the only thing that wasn't wrong with him. She shared a room with Kitty and another girl in Pembroke Road, and, in spite of the fact that she was worried out of her wits, she found herself staring in fascination at the sunlit rank of tall, red-brick houses opposite, or glancing out of the bathroom window at the mountains over Rathfarnham, and thinking how much nicer the world was than she had ever imagined.

She met Con Rahilly next evening in a teashop in Grafton Street. He came in with a heap of books under his arm – an overgrown schoolboy.

'Really, Miss Twomey,' he said with an anguished air, the lines over his eyes disappearing into his cropped hair, 'I'm terribly sorry for giving you all this trouble. I really am! I know you don't believe me, but it happens to be true.' Later, she learned that he had this self-pitying trick of imagining what you felt about him and expressing it.

'Well, it's no use worrying about what's already happened,' Joan said practically. 'It's just a question of what we're going to do about it.'

'I know,' he said despairingly. 'I never think of anything else. I keep racking my brains, but I don't seem to be able to think of anything.'

'I hope you've thought of marrying Kitty?' said Joan.

'You're hoping a hell of a lot,' Kitty said gruffly, but Joan knew she was ready to cry and that young Rahilly was the same.

'I don't see what the difficulty is,' she said brightly.

'That's because you haven't had the pleasure of meeting my mother,' he explained with the same mixture of misery and cheek. 'It's going to be a shock to her.'

'I suppose you think it hasn't been a shock to my father?' asked Joan, and he shuddered. Clearly, he didn't like people speaking roughly to him.

'Con doesn't mean that at all,' Kitty said hotly, and Joan saw that she was in a bad way about him.

'Then would you let him explain what he does mean?' asked Joan. 'My goodness, I can't see what all this hugger mugger is about.'

'I mean I have nothing to marry on,' he said with anguish. 'If I marry Kitty now,' my mother will throw me out.'

'And what about your father?'

'She'll probably throw him out as well. She's been threatening it long enough. She really is a woman of remarkable character,' he added with rueful admiration, and again Joan didn't know whether or not he was mocking her. 'It's not that I don't want to marry Kitty,' he added eagerly, 'She knows that. It's just that if I do, I'll have to do it quietly.'

'That would be a very peculiar sort of marriage,' said Joan.

'Oh, I know, I know,' he said wearily, clasping his hands and looking down the restaurant as though he had recognized an old enemy.

'I'm afraid my father wouldn't agree to that at all,' Joan said with growing decisiveness. 'After all, who's to support Kitty until you've finished college and got a job?'

Young Rahilly gave another shrug and looked piteously at Kitty, but even Kitty didn't seem to be able to help with this one. Instead, she lit another cigarette and pushed the packet towards him. It was a little gesture of love, but he only shook his head with a crucified air as if wondering how she could think a cigarette would make up to him for a broken heart. Joan began to like him even less.

'I suppose you think Father will support her while she hides away in a furnished room like a criminal?' she asked angrily. 'And all to spare your mother the shock! Really, Mr Rahilly, I think you're as bad as Kitty.'

'It's easy for you to talk,' Kitty said brassily. 'You don't know his mother.'

'Well, she can't eat him, Kitty,' Joan cried at the end of her patience.

'I wonder,' he said with perfect gravity. 'I've sometimes thought it might be a case of suppressed cannibalism.'

'Well, she isn't going to eat me,' said Joan.

'Look, Joan, you keep away from Con's mother,' said Kitty. 'This is my business, and I'll handle it my own way. I'll keep my job up to the last month or so, and after that I'll find something. I won't be a burden on you at all. You talk as if Con was the only one responsible, but I had something to say to it too.'

And Joan knew at once that Rahilly would accept it from her. Whatever his mother had done to him, she had deprived him of all initiative, and he would go on like that, petulantly waiting for some other woman to make up his mind for him. This time, Joan was going to do the making up.

'Oh, all right, Kitty,' she said. 'I thought I could settle this thing quietly but I see I can't. I'll just wire for Father and let him deal with it.'

'In that case I can give up all hope of getting a degree,' Rahilly said with resignation. Then he glanced at her with a certain sort of boyish frankness. 'To tell you the truth, I don't really mind,' he

added ruefully. 'I don't think I have the brains for an engineer.
I suppose I can be a clerk if anyone will take me on. I'm not the
type for a labourer – even a labourer,' again anticipating the slight
that Joan hadn't altogether intended. After that, she had no doubt
though. She had never seen a more spineless specimen.

Next morning, before Kitty left for the office, Rahilly called
at their lodgings. When they went into the sitting room he was
looking out the window. Kitty went up to him eagerly. Joan
realized that all Kitty wanted was to take him away somewhere
and nurse him, which was probably what he wanted too.

'What happened, Con?' she asked.

'Oh, what I expected,' he said jumpily. 'Into the night. Cut off
with a shilling. I can't help admiring the woman.'

'But what will you do now?' Joan asked, shocked in spite of
herself.

'Get married as soon as I can,' he replied with a shrug. 'No
point in getting thrown out for wanting to get married and then
not doing it, is there?'

'Oh, but this is silly,' she cried. 'No mother in her senses is
going to behave like that to her only son. There must be some
misunderstanding. I'll go and see her.'

'Do,' he said. 'You might like her. Several people do, I'm
told.'

It was only that afternoon on the bus out to Rahillys' that his
words came back to her, and she wondered precisely what he had
meant. She decided that he couldn't mean what he'd seemed to
mean. It was just that, like all weak people, he had no control of
his tongue.

The door was opened by a pale, dark-haired woman who
moved with a certain actressy dignity. She gave Joan a pale
smile that seemed to be directed at someone on the strand
behind her. The parlour was a small room with a high window
that overlooked the strand. Mrs Rahilly's chair was at one side
of the window from which she could view the passers-by. In the
first few minutes, Joan realized from the furniture that there was
money somewhere – not a lot perhaps, but sufficient. Joan rattled
on, raising her voice and speaking with affected brightness. She
was in a dilemma. To treat the behaviour of the 'children', as
she called them, too gravely would imply such a reflection on
Kitty as would justify any mother in having nothing to do with

her. To treat it too lightly would imply that she herself was no better and justify a mother even more. It was essential to create an impression of respectability – a little impulsive, but definitely stable. But Mrs Rahilly seemed to care very little for the stability of the Twomey character, and Joan's gay tone came back to her with a hollow echo.

'Well, what do you expect me to do, Miss Twomey?' Mrs Rahilly asked at last with a sad smile, and Joan felt at once that it would be most improper to expect anything from such a figure of tragedy.

'Well, they have to get married,' she said reasonably.

'That's what my son seems to think.'

'And doesn't it seem a pity if he can't take his degree when he worked so hard?'

'It is not only my son who had to work hard,' said Mrs Rahilly, making Joan feel she had again said the wrong thing.

'No, of course not,' she replied too eagerly. 'Everybody had to work. But that's what I mean – everyone's work going for nothing.'

'That is something my son should have thought of first, Miss Twomey,' Mrs Rahilly said with the same sad smile. 'Of course, if your family is in a position to support them and the child until Con qualifies, I have nothing to say to it. But if you mean that I should provide a home for them here' – she rose with an actressy gesture of dismissal – 'I've worked hard too. My health would not permit it.'

Now that she had Joan on her feet again she became quite friendly, almost motherly. As she reached for the door handle she rested on it and added: 'I'd better be frank with you, Miss Twomey. I don't wish to criticize my own son, but I'm afraid he would not make a good husband for your sister. His father was always a weak man. He drank, and, of course, like all drunkards, he did not keep his hand where it belonged. I had to pay back what he stole. But that is neither here nor there. My son is weaker still. I did not expect to rear him, Miss Twomey. It is his digestion. He has every delicacy in his own home, but he cannot keep it down. What business has a boy like that with a wife and family?' Then she raised her head with a calm and tragic air and added: 'If she were my sister, I'd send her to the poorhouse first.'

Joan left almost in tears with frustration. At the same time she observed a small man in a blue serge suit and a bowler hat get up from a bench. She noticed that he had a fresh-coloured kindly face and a small grey moustache. She had no doubt that she was looking at Con's father, the man who had not been able to keep his hand where it belonged. She felt dirty all over. Bitch! Bitch! Dirty bitch! she said again and again to herself.

8

That night she went back to Cork, without having effected much except to fix the date of the wedding. She was as sure as she could be of anything that Con Rahilly would not turn up, so she arranged for them to marry on the same day as May. Then, if he didn't turn up the scandal wouldn't be quite so bad. To Chris she admitted that she didn't feel too secure of herself even then. It seemed impossible that she should ever steer two such irresponsibles as Kitty and May to the altar without one or the other running off with a lover, giving birth to a baby, or something equally inappropriate.

No wonder she was hard on Kitty when her notice was up and she came back to Cork to prepare for the wedding. Joan warned her father not to encourage her in any way, and except for stolen confidences with May, who was as shameless as herself, Kitty was treated as an abandoned woman who had brought disgrace on them all – or would if she weren't stopped.

Meanwhile, her attitude to Chris changed in an extraordinary way. They spent August in a little seaside cottage in Crosshaven. Her father of course didn't come. He'd tried it once, and after forty-eight hours he was like a raging demon, complaining that there was nothing in that bloody place but the water. Kitty and May were staying there, with May's boy, a tall, athletic fellow given to practical jokes that irritated Joan. One night, when the other three had gone to a dance, Joan and Chris were sitting in a nook on the cliffs. Something about the beauty of the harbour in twilight made her despondent.

'I don't know how it is,' she said irritably. 'You work and work, and do your best for everybody, and meantime, your own life slips by.'

'Oh, I know, I know,' Chris said, taking her hand. 'It seems futile, of course, but if you're born with that sort of character you have to go through with it. You don't do it for other people's satisfaction, you know. You do it for your own as well.'

'And a hell of a lot of good it is for you,' she replied impatiently. 'Ah, Chris, nobody's born with that sort of character. You weren't born just to be censorious and bossy and quarrel over halfpence. You could get just as much out of life as the others, and more.'

'That's true, of course,' he said thoughtfully. 'Up to a point, I mean. It's funny, but everything in life is only up to a point. And families do force you into a certain mould, even if it doesn't suit you. Like me, for instance. I suppose I'm really only interested in music. But then Bob turns into a bit of a playboy, and as a result Jim gets religion in the wrong way, and I have to be the Old Reliable and look after the pair of them as well as Mother. It's silly really, I suppose. I sometimes think only children have an awful lot to be thankful for.'

'One of these days I'm going to be an only child,' Joan said.

They went back to the cottage, hand in hand. Chris went to bed and lay awake reading. Suddenly the bedroom door opened and Joan stormed in in her nightdress. He had never seen her like this before. She was angry, amused and very, very beautiful.

'For God's sake, push in there, Chris Dwyer!' she said shrilly. 'I have to have someone to talk to, or I'll go out of my blooming mind.'

Chris, who was always modest, blew out the candle. As a romantic lover, Chris was no great shakes, but he knew desperation when he saw it, and he put his arm about her and patted her gently as one would pat a child.

And then, to Joan's great astonishment, he stopped patting her, and said a number of things that astonished her and made her want to weep, so that she was not quite up to it when he treated her as Dick Gordon had never done. Then he yawned and asked if it wasn't wonderful and said they should go to Italy at once. He had always wanted to go to Italy and something had always stopped him, but this time he was determined about it. When they heard the voices of the others from the cliff, Joan jumped out of bed and rushed into the hall. Suddenly, at the door she stopped and shouted back at him in laughter and delight—

'Now, Chris Dwyer, you've got me into trouble, and you'd better marry me quick!'

9

In that haze, it seemed even more impossible for Joan to do what she had set out to do, but she did it. To her great surprise, Con Rahilly arrived in time for the wedding – when driven to it, those dependent mother's boys sometimes showed extraordinary manliness. His father had shaken him silently by the hand and slipped him a five-pound note borrowed specially for the occasion, and Con said he was going to get it framed. Mrs Rahilly had refused to leave her room or even to say goodbye. 'You can't beat the true Irish mother,' Con said with his abstracted air. He had already rented a furnished room in Leeson Street, and the father of a college friend had made a small job for him, selling women's underwear – of all things! Chris, with whom he stayed, could make nothing of him and thought he wasn't quite right in the head, but Joan's father, for some reason, took a fantastic liking to him, laughed at his grisly jokes, told him there would always be a room in his house for him, offered to back a loan for him, and then told Joan that Kitty had picked the best man of them all. When she asked what he meant, he said Con was the only man that he'd trust with a rifle – a typical obscure joke from an old revolutionary.

It was a lonely house when the double wedding was over and the guests had gone. Now that her task was completed and her responsibilities almost at an end, Joan felt empty inside. It was as though her mind could not settle on the present and ranged back over the years to the time when she had been a little girl. She sat over the fire in the front room with her father, talking into the early hours of the morning. Though neither of them mentioned it, it was her mother's death they were both thinking of – the sitting there at the same hour, listening to that ghastly breathing overhead. This, too, was a sort of death, and the new life that was waiting for her was something that she shrank from.

'I suppose Chris and I will be getting married too, as soon as we can,' she said lightly. 'I hope you won't mind?'

'Mind?' he asked. 'Why should I mind?'

'Because I'm afraid we'll have to go and live in Dublin.'

'Why in Dublin?' he asked.

'Oh, well,' she said, dabbing her eyes, 'Chris is mad on classical music, and you can't hear a single thing in this blooming place. There are concerts and all sorts in Dublin.'

'And what about Chris's mother?' he asked. 'Is she going with you?'

'Indeed, she is not,' said Joan. 'She can stay with Bob if she wants someone to look after her. She won't find him as easy to get on with as Chris, but that's her look-out. What about you, though? Wouldn't you like to live with May?'

'I would not,' he said flatly.

'Chris said to tell you you could always come and live with us,' she said, realizing for the first time how big it was of Chris.

'Ah, Chris has enough responsibilities without me,' her father said. 'I'll be all right, you'll see. I'll get some old woman in to cook my supper and I'll be fine.'

And she knew he would do his best to die where he had lived, among the little memorials of the woman he had loved, and for one wild minute she felt she wanted to do the same. She put her head in her hands and began to sob quietly. Her father got up and re-filled her glass. Then he stood, looking down at her.

'What's wrong, child?' he asked quizzically.

'I don't want to go to Dublin,' she sobbed. 'I don't want to leave Cork. I want to stay here and look after you.'

'If you don't want to you don't have to,' he said gently.

'I do.'

'Why?'

'I'm – I'm having a baby – oh, Jesus!'

At first she thought he was going to hit her, and then she saw he was almost on the point of laughing.

'Here!' he said, thrusting the glass on her. 'Take a pussful of this! What's wrong with having a baby?'

'I'd be disgraced if I stayed on here.'

He poured himself a drink.

'Is it Chris?'

'Yes.'

'And ye're getting married?'

'Yes.'

'What the hell disgrace is there? Isn't it your own business?'

Snivelling into her glass, she saw him back in his own chair, grinning at her as he had grinned when she had come to him for the 'loan' of a shilling.

'It isn't. I'm a liar and a hypocrite. I bullied you and the girls and ye have every reason to despise me.'

'Do you think I despise you?'

'You have good reason to. And Dick Gordon was so good, and I was rotten to him, and I was rotten to May and rotten to Kitty, and they'll never forgive me.'

'Come here to me!' he said, and she got up like a sleep-walker and crossed the room to him. 'Come on! You can sit on my knee. It's a long time since you did. Now, I want you to listen to me. You know I was fond of your mother, and what sort of life do you think I gave her? I had the best wife the Lord God ever gave a man in this world, and I treated her as I wouldn't treat a dog. I wake up in the middle of the night and think about it and cry, and a hell of a lot of good that is to her or me! But even if I was as decent a man as I wanted to be, what sort of life do you think I'd have given her? A damn poor life, but all I had.'

Then his voice took on the curious formality she had noticed once before.

'If your mother is anywhere, she's here tonight, and what she has to say, I'm saying for her. We're proud of you, and we're delighted you're getting married. There's nothing we'd hate more than to see you without kids of your own. You're a great girl, and we're glad you're getting a fine steady fellow like Chris. And thank Chris from both of us for offering me a home, but I'll stick with the one that she made for me.

'Now, it's a long time since I put you to bed, and probably it's the last time, but it's time little girls were asleep. Come along! Sleepy bye!'

More Stories (1954)

The Sorcerer's Apprentice

1

Their friends said that, whenever Jimmy Foley named the day, Una slipped a disc. For five years now they had been keeping company, and three times Una had slipped a disc, or its equivalent. Jimmy blamed Una, who was an only child, and, according to him, spoiled to death by her father. Una blamed Jimmy's mother, an old lady of great sweetness, who deferred so much to Jimmy that she couldn't even stay in the same room with him and hear him contradicted.

The third time she slipped a disc she went to Dublin to recover. Joan Sheehy was an old school friend, a tall, dark, intense girl, who was very happily married to a Dublin solicitor. They lived with their two children in an old-fashioned house on the strand. As usual, Joan and Una had no opportunity for intimate discussion till Una went to bed. Then Joan came in in her dressing gown; first she sat in the armchair, then on the bed, and finally threw off the dressing gown and slipped into the double bed beside Una. That way they could talk better.

They were interrupted by slow and heavy footsteps descending the stairs and Joan sat up with a long-suffering air.

'Bother that fellow!' she said. 'He's worse to me than a baby.'

Slowly the door opened and Mick Sheehy, a tall man with a dark moustache, stumbled in. He was clutching a pillow as if it were a baby, his pyjamas were dangling about his crotch, and his eyes were closed. Joan jumped up and made room for him.

'Lie there and keep quiet!' she said fiercely. 'I'm not done talking to Una yet.'

'What are ye talking about?' he asked, wedging his shoulder comfortably into Una's hip. 'Anything interesting?'

'Only about herself and Jimmy.'

'Oh, that!' he said with a noisy yawn and composed himself to sleep again between the pair of them, his hands crossed piously on his stomach. Una, who was a well-read girl, wondered what Joan would say if any Irish writer reported a scene like that.

'I don't mind what you say, Una,' Joan said, pushing her husband rudely against Una. 'I think it's high time you stopped making excuses and settled down. My God, girl, you must be thirty, and if you go on like this you won't get married at all.'

'But what's going to happen if I marry someone like Jimmy that I don't agree with?' Una asked indignantly.

'What has agreeing got to do with it?' Joan asked. 'Do you think for an instant I agree with this? Wouldn't you fight with him?'

'Me?' said Una, looking at him as he lay between them, making funny faces and snoring. 'God, I'd murder him!'

'I want to murder him too,' said Joan in her intense way, 'but I love him just the same. Men are like that, Una. You're too damn critical – honest to God, you are. There was Ned Buckley,' she went on, ticking the names off on her fingers. 'You said *he* had no religion. Mick Doyle had too much religion. He went to Mass every morning and never talked about anything only the lives of the saints.'

'Oh, God, Joan, Mick was awful,' Una said in horror. 'Do you know I nearly lost my religion over him.'

'Never mind your religion,' Joan went on remorselessly. 'We know about that. Then there was Paddy Healy, who had a lovely voice only he drank too much. I forget the rest. Damn it, Una, you had a fair choice. What the hell is wrong with Jimmy?'

'You have no idea, girl,' Una said despondently. 'Jimmy wouldn't let you have an opinion of your own. He thinks you shouldn't even open your mouth about anything except what's in his silly old paper. It's easy to see you never had anything to do with a journalist.'

'And journalists have nothing to do with it either,' said Joan. 'Do you think any man wants you to have an opinion of your own?'

'But this is different, Joan,' Una said positively.

'They're all different, girl,' said Joan.

'But Jimmy is different, Joan,' said Una. 'I'm sure it's his mother. She has him ruined.'

'And you're the very one who told me that I was ruining Tommy!' said Joan. 'What's the good of talking? They're all ruined! There's something wrong with every man if you look at him long enough. Not that you'd need to look at this lump,' she added, giving a friendly kick to the sleeping form between them, which grunted with pleasure and threw a hand over her stomach. It clawed at her impatiently till, with a sigh, she pulled her nightdress up, and at once it relaxed and its owner began to snore again.

'Ah, it's not like that at all, Joan,' Una said thoughtfully. 'Daddy says I attract the wrong sort of man.'

'And, in the name of the Almighty God,' Joan said piously, 'when did your father ever see the right sort of man for you? Look, I don't want to interfere between the pair of ye, but surely you're grown-up enough to realize that your father doesn't want you to marry at all? Damn it, Una, every fellow that got as much as a squeeze off you, your father got jealous of him. Do you think I didn't see it? Every boy you ever brought to the house was treated as a tolerable sort of leper. Either his mother came from Blarney Lane or his grand-uncle was in the asylum. And you know, Una, I have to be frank. Sometimes I think you and your old fellow are lick alike. If only you could get rid of your mother, you'd be settled for life. I hate saying it, but, honest to God, you are turning into a proper old maid.'

'Ah, no, I'm not, I'm not,' Una said, trying to look as though she knew things that were lost on her friend. All the same she was scared. The last thing in the world she wanted to be was an old maid, and she was beginning to realize that old maids were not wallflowers at all, but girls who had more charm than was good for them.

'You see, Joan, what's wrong with me is indecision,' she said with an air of great enlightenment. 'Somehow or other, I can't make up my mind.'

'And you know what happens to girls who can't make up their minds?' asked Joan.

'I do, I do,' Una said glumly. 'They don't marry at all.'

'Oh, no,' said Joan. 'Nothing as comfortable as that. Girls who can't make up their own minds soon get their minds made up for them. And mark my words, that's what's going to happen to you, Una . . . Sheehy,' she added with a further friendly kick. 'Back to bed, boy! Back to bed!'

2

As Una thought afterwards, Joan could have been prophetic, because the following evening, Denis O'Brien came to supper. Denis was in his middle forties, married and separated, poor and plain. He had a plump, bright, beaming face, a small, dark moustache, a high, bald forehead, a quiet voice and the most insinuating manners. The nicest thing about him was his eyes, which were very gentle, but the least bit mad. He was a lonely man who got little in the way of nourishment except what he provided for himself, which was mainly bacon and eggs, but he was always welcome at the Sheehys. He did not leave till very late, but Una noticed that while Mick drank steadily, Denis only supped at his glass of beer. She liked that little touch of asceticism in him.

'Isn't he nice?' Joan asked in her enthusiastic way when he left. 'Isn't he a real pet?'

'He's a pity anyway,' said Una, who didn't know whether he was a pet or not.

'Ah, what a pity he is!' Joan exclaimed. 'A flat of his own and every doll in the office falling over him.'

'Now, that's only hearsay, Joan,' Mick said, staring at his wife over his glasses. 'We know nothing about his private life, and we shouldn't repeat things we hear . . . I quite agree with you, Una. He is a pity.'

A couple of evenings later Una heard a knock and found him standing on the doorstep against the glowing strand, hatless, his greying hair very long behind his bald brow, and his trousers, which needed pressing, flapping about his heels. His clothes were cheap, but he wore them with an air of well-bred carelessness that made them seem better than they were.

'Oh, come in, Denis,' she said. 'I'm delighted to see you. I'm all alone and the kids are asleep.'

It wasn't only that she was bored. She was glad to see him, and afterwards she felt that she might have been a little less flirtatious, but he invited that sort of behaviour. He had the sort of insinuating manner that is a compound of father and elder brother; apparently he kissed girls on sight and without intending much harm, held their hands, patted their shoulders and invited their confidences.

In no time at all, Una was holding forth to him about her troubles with Jimmy, and Denis was advising her in the manner of an old family friend. Naturally, he was advising her to marry Jimmy. Everybody seemed to be doing that. In his excitement he got up and stood before the fireplace, the light from the strand catching his round sunburned face and kind, anxious eyes. She could see why the girls in the office would fall for him — a man who took them as seriously as that. He talked in a solemn, unctuous, almost clerical tone, with flashes of what might almost be religious mysticism. Being a very pious girl, Una could not see what mysticism had to do with marriage. What she wanted from marriage was security, the hope that in ten years time she wouldn't regret her bargain.

'But, Una,' he said, burying his right fist in his left palm, 'there's no such thing as security in marriage. You can be friends with a man for twenty years, and when you marry him, you find out things about him you never guessed at. Everybody keeps a bit of himself to himself, even if it's only something to die with. Sooner or later, you have to take a chance, and it's better to take it before you get too set in your ways. That's hell, when you have to smash yourself up again, just to adjust.'

'Haven't you ever regretted taking a chance, Denis?' she asked pertly.

'No, dear, I haven't,' he replied without taking offence. 'My wife represented what I could grasp at that age, and I couldn't predict – not infallibly that is,' he added carefully, as though infallibility were his rule on all other occasions – 'how either of us would develop. What I mean is that when we separated we weren't the same people who got married. That's where the Church goes wrong. People become different, and it's no use trying to be wise before the event.'

'It's not much use being wise after it,' she retorted.

'No, dear, it isn't,' he retorted imperturbably, as though nothing she said could interrupt the flow of his gab. 'That's true. You have to use your common sense in deducing the line of development you're both going to follow. You've got to ask yourself if a girl or a fellow who's been sleeping around before you married them is going to change just because of living with you. But you can abuse your common sense just as you can abuse your feelings, you know.' By now, he was very excited and striding to the door and back, giving her brooding glances. 'You can put too much responsibility on your common sense as you can put too much responsibility on a boy or girl with an unstable family, and all that happens is that it collapses under it, exactly as a boy or girl will collapse if you ask too much of them. Think of all the women you know who made fools of themselves in their thirties.'

'And what about all the men who make fools of themselves in their forties?' she asked, and that stopped the flow all right. She noticed that when you did stop the flow, he was so pleased that he went off into a roar of laughter that seemed almost as uncontrollable as the sermonizing. There were tears in his eyes as he turned to her and said, 'Doesn't Jimmy ever knock you about, Una? That's what I'd do if you were my girl.'

To Una's great surprise, Joan Sheehy didn't seem at all pleased that Denis agreed with her about Una's marrying. On the contrary, she became as irritable as hell.

'And do you mean to tell me you talked to *Denis* about *Jimmy*?' she asked.

'Oh, only generally, of course,' said Una.

'God help you if you go round talking like that about him when ye're married,' said Joan. 'Sheehy would take a gun to me.'

All the same, Una went to the pictures with Denis the following evening and returned to his flat for coffee. She was curious to know where he lived. It was in one of the city squares in a third-floor apartment of two draughty rooms with high windows, the kitchen cut out of the bedroom, and, in a return room upstairs a bathroom that seemed to be connected directly with a cave of the winds. Even from downstairs you could hear the gale roaring up into the lavatory basin. The sitting room wasn't too bad. It had a big print of Rembrandt's 'Golden Helmet' over the mantelpiece and bookshelves along one wall. Una could see that a lot of them were religious books, a thing she hardly expected.

All the same it was pleasant to turn off the light and sit by the window and talk about all the fellows she had. Denis was a good listener, and everything she said moved him to comment and generalization.

'It's no good telling me what you think of Jimmy now, Una,' he said at last. 'You and Jimmy are at a dead end. You've taken it as far as it will go. You'll think differently when you're married because then you'll change again.'

'As much as all that?' she asked in mock alarm.

'You'll be surprised,' he said. 'And mind,' he added menacingly, pointing at her, 'it won't be all for the better. It may even be for the worse.'

'And all after one night?' she exclaimed in the same tone.

'Not necessarily after one night,' he said, rolling over her in his usual infallible way. 'Maybe not till after a good many nights – and days. You make too much of the nights you know,' he said, laughing uproariously again as the meaning of her little joke broke in upon his monologue. 'Damn it all, you can sleep through the nights, girl. It's the blooming days that get you down.'

'Denis, do you think I'm an old maid?' she asked.

'No, dear, I don't,' he replied, refusing to be put off his new tack. 'Girls like you, with lots of energy, if you're not married by the time you're thirty, start exaggerating things. Your minds have gone off in one direction and your bodies in another. You see, Una, you talk too much about sex. You've got sex in the head instead of where it belongs. Where it belongs, it's not all that important. When you get it in the head it makes everything go cockeyed. That's why you're so afraid of committing yourself. That's why you and Jimmy fight the way you do. You see, your mind and body have to work together, in harmony, the way they did when you were a kid. But when one of the principal bodily functions gets into the head, then they can't work together.'

Una found him so entertaining that she stayed late and almost ran home. When she reached the strand, Mick had already gone to bed, but Joan was waiting up for her in her dressing gown. She seemed in an unusual state of tension, even for her.

'Will I get you a glass of hot milk, Una?' she asked nervously.

'No, love,' Una replied with a sly grin. 'Was there something you wanted to say to me?'

'As a matter of fact, there was,' Joan said tragically, collapsing into a chair. 'Una, do you think you're being fair to Denis?'

'Aren't I?' Una asked in mock surprise, though she knew what was coming.

'You know that Mick and myself are very fond of him?'

'And I know he thinks the world of you,' Una said firmly.

'And don't you think you're not being fair? Honest now, Una! Aren't you amusing yourself with him?'

'You mean, you think he's not amusing himself with me?' Una asked in a gentle parody of her friend's tone.

''Tisn't alike, Una,' Joan said nervously, clasping and unclasping her long beautiful hands. 'You're young. You have a fellow you'll probably marry eventually. Denis has nobody.' Joan shook her head as though she were imitating some bad actress on the movies, which she wasn't – Joan had been that way from childhood. 'Una, can you even understand what it means, having nobody – nobody at all in the world? When he's sick or lonely, this is the only place he can come. He's not a young man any longer; when he sees his kids it has to be in Mick's office; he has only a little job in the Corporation, and he'll never do any better because he's too proud and honest. He won't take bribes and he won't lick boots. And even then he has to pay more than half he earns to that bloody bitch! God forgive me, there are some women I'd like to strangle, and that's one. All I'm saying, Una, is if anyone is going to get hurt, it's going to be him, not you. And, God damn it, the man has been hurt enough!'

Una was suddenly deeply moved. It was clear that Joan's lecture was the result of some discussion between Mick and his wife. Mick gave a false impression of sluggishness, but it was clear that he liked Denis. Joan didn't merely like him; she loved him, and Una didn't in the least resent the fact that she was as jealous as hell.

'All right, love,' she said. 'I'll sleep on it.'

'And you don't mind my talking to you?'

'I wouldn't change an iota of you for all the women that were ever born,' said Una, giving her a kiss, and then Joan began to sniffle and Una had the job of consoling her for what she thought of, no doubt, as an exceedingly sinful attachment. God help us all! Una thought.

3

The more Una thought of it, the more she felt that Joan was right. She had been flirting with Denis, regardless of the consequences to him, though she had to admit that she was humanly flattered by the suggestion that it was she rather than Denis who had been doing the flirting.

The following evening she met him coming out from work and they went to sit in Stephen's Green. She was at her brightest and most eloquent. She admitted that she was becoming too attracted by him, thought she took more blame for this than she felt she deserved. At the same time she could not resist pointing out to him how irresponsible he was, and what little concern he showed for the kids. Up to this he had listened politely, but suddenly it was as if he had pulled down the shutters on her. 'Let the kids out of it, Una, like a good girl,' he said.

She knew that had been a bad mistake, but at least, her conscience was clear and that night she rang up Jimmy and told him she had been having a violent flirtation with the father of two children. Una never could keep a good thing to herself.

'Some people have all the luck,' Jimmy said darkly.

'Why? What's wrong with the flappers?' she asked.

'Not biting this weather,' he replied.

'Maybe I'd better come back,' she said.

'Maybe you'd better,' said Jimmy, and she laughed and said good night. If only Jimmy were always that way there was no one who suited her half as well.

But next morning, she woke in a real agony of mind, thinking not of Jimmy but of Denis. She dressed before the window, looking out at the long back gardens of the old houses, and feeling older than they. She was sure she had not been deliberately hypocritical with Denis, but the very thought of what she had said to him about the children, about whom she didn't give a damn, and the cold way he had cut her off, made her squirm. 'God!' she thought desperately. 'I *am* becoming an old maid!' At the same time she wished that she were not so damnably critical of herself: self-knowledge was all right in its own way, but if you took it too far, it made you feel like a worm. She rang up Denis and arranged to meet him again after work.

The explanation, which somehow turned into an apology, was all right, but the consequences were simply awful. At midnight, through no apparent fault of her own, she found herself in bed with him in a single bed in the back room with the kitchen attached. She was lying in a most extraordinary position that made her want to giggle. God, she felt, could never have intended anything as absurd as this. She was angry with Joan who had failed to warn her of her real danger, because what a dozen men with twice his attraction had failed to do, this round-faced, ageing man had done with no great difficulty, and now she was no longer in danger of being an old maid. In fact, the sooner she could find somebody to marry her, the better.

What made her still angrier was that Denis seemed to be deeply attached to religious emblems, and there was a crucifix over the bed and a copy of the *Imitation* on the shelf beside it. It reminded her of a friend of her father's who, having lost his religion, played 'Nearer My God to Thee' on the clarinet.

At one o'clock Denis was fast asleep and snoring, and somehow the snoring struck her as far more compromising than anything that had happened before. She rose and dressed hastily, and then stood for a long time, peering down at the round, red, innocent face with the gaping mouth and drooping dark moustache. Then she glanced at herself in the mirror on the dressing table and frowned. Her face, except for a few abrasions, seemed just the same. 'His mistress,' she whispered in a horrified tone, and the face in the mirror looked back at her and echoed: 'His mistress.' She tiptoed hastily out of the room, took off her shoes to descend the long, dark stairs, closed the great front door almost soundlessly behind her, and was startled by the echo of her own footsteps from the other side of the square. They sounded like those of a secondary personality that had taken her place and was now returning furtively from its midnight adultery.

'Adultery!' she added aloud in the same horrified tone, just to make sure that this was what her mind had suggested, and as she reached the canal bridge, she began to run as though she could outstrip the adultery that was stealing up on her. All she wanted was the quiet of her own little back room, where she could meditate on the strangeness of her behaviour, away from Denis's snores and kicks. She was alarmed and disillusioned; alarmed because a pious girl like herself had suddenly behaved in this irresponsible and irremediable way; disillusioned, because, so far as she could see, it had produced absolutely no effect on her character. If *this* was what was supposed to change people, she thought, they must be a damn sight more susceptible than she was.

But next morning, she woke appalled by her own danger. It was all very well for Joan to worry about Denis, but it wasn't Denis who had to do the worrying now. He wasn't the one who was liable to have the baby. 'Baby' for some reason sounded in her mind like 'mistress' and 'adultery'; things that didn't happen to decent girls. Merely because she had begun to behave in this queer way, she decided that the time had come to marry Jimmy, so she rang him up to tell him she was returning. Even to hear his nice Sunday's Well accent was a relief, so she hurried into town and spent a lot of money on a really beautiful pullover for him. In a wave of self-mockery, she decided that if men only knew what pullovers meant, they wouldn't wear them at all; but the sheer extravagance of it, and the crowds in the sunlight of Stephen's Green reassured her and helped to banish the memory of the night, and the stealthy echoing steps in the dark and silent square proclaiming to all who listened 'Adultery! Adultery!'

4

She cooked Denis's dinner that evening in his flat, though how anyone could cook in that cubbyhole off the bedroom was beyond her. But she was a good cook, and she wanted to show off to him. He seemed touched by the sight of her, making a muck of his kitchen, and shambled behind her, begging her not to use three pots when one would do. It looked like the kitchen of a man who used only one pot.

But she could see his attitude to her had changed. Now, he was all for her staying on in Dublin as long as possible.

'The sooner I get back to Cork and marry Jimmy, the better for all parties,' she said ruefully.

'You still want to marry Jimmy?'

'I thought that was what you were advising me to do,' she said in mock alarm.

'Things were different then,' he said.

'They were,' she agreed. 'They weren't quite so urgent.'

'You know, Una,' he said, walking restlessly about the room, 'I think I might be able to get a divorce. I don't say I could. I might.'

'But I thought your wife was a Catholic, Denis.'

'Annie is whatever it suits her to be. I never raised the matter with her because, to tell you the truth, I didn't expect I'd want to marry again.'

'Well, even if she's not, I am,' said Una. It wasn't even as if she wanted to marry Denis. Emotionally, she had been taken at a disadvantage, but her judgement was still clear. The sight of all those religious books had reminded her again of the man playing 'Nearer My God to Thee' on the clarinet. 'Even if you did get a divorce, I couldn't possibly marry you.'

'Not in this country. I understand that,' Denis said, not understanding her at all. 'But after all, I don't see why I should have to live here for the rest of my life. I could go to England. Other people have had to do it.'

'England!' Una thought despairingly. He was making it sound worse and worse. It would be bad enough to live with a man you didn't believe you were married to, but as well as that, to give up her family and friends, and never again be able to walk up the Western Road in the evening light! The very idea of it was punishment enough for any sin she had committed.

'You don't know my father, Denis,' she said. 'Mind you, he's broad-minded enough in his own way. I think if I was to tell him what happened between us, he'd only ask me was I able to look after myself, but if I was to marry a divorced man, out the door I'd go. Straight! And after all, you can't blame him. Damn it, that's what he believes.'

After that, she refused to repeat her performance of the previous evening. The rational side of her was in control again, and, as she said, it was one thing to make a fool of yourself when you felt free, but a different thing entirely to do it in cold blood when you realized how dependent you were on another man.

All the same, when she embraced Denis for the last time at Kingsbridge Station, Joan's face suddenly went black with rage and even Mick looked a bit embarrassed. It was only too plain that whatever there was between them was no mere holiday flirtation. Una managed to keep from weeping until the train pulled out and then began to sob uncontrollably. In a nice rational mood you could make love-making seem unimportant enough, but it changed your character all right. Suddenly, seeing the look of consternation on the face of a young officer who was sitting opposite her, she began to giggle through her sobs.

'It's all right,' she said. 'It isn't a death. Only a fellow.'

'Oh, is that all?' he said in relief. 'In that case you'd better have tea with me.'

'I'd love to,' she sniffled. 'Just give me time for one more bawl. God, I am an idiot!'

It was pleasant and restful to slip back into the routine of home and Jimmy, though even the pullover did not entirely wipe out her feeling of guilt towards him. It was only then that she really began to notice the change in herself. She felt big and motherly and mature. For the first time she realized how many of their quarrels had originated in her own unsettled state, and how much better a man he was than she had imagined. At the same time she realized that he was not an easy man to understand because he had so little understanding of himself. He was resentful about any criticism of orthodoxy because he wasn't really happy with it. There was an objective, critical side to Jimmy that he rarely exposed, and didn't expose at all except to a passive listener.

Jimmy himself noticed the change and said that the holiday seemed to have done her good.

'Joan always has that effect on me,' she replied eagerly.

'Was it Joan or that fellow with the five children – what's his name?'

'Ah, that's something I'll have to confess to you one of these days,' she said with a laugh. 'There's more to that than you think, boy.'

It was half joke and wholly earnest, because in fact Denis was never far from her mind. Their queer little love affair was like a dark background of woods that threw every figure that moved against it into startling relief. It was the secrecy that gave it such power. There was no one she could tell, and because of this it lent to everything a quality of dramatic irony. Jimmy's mother would be knitting and describing some wonderful sermon, or Una would be walking down a hill with her father, and bang! there it would all be again, and again she would be alone with the echoing footsteps in the silent square, now romantic and faraway. Sometimes she wondered if Jimmy had any such dark secret from her, and, deciding he hadn't, wished for his own sake that he had.

But one night they had a thundering row after Jimmy's mother had gone to bed. Like all their rows it was about nothing – a current political scandal about a distillery – and Una said that political scandals always seemed to be about a distillery or a bacon factory, thus reviving an earlier row, and Jimmy said pompously that she used the word 'scandal' with a rare lack of discrimination. Una, who had forgotten how violent their quarrels could be, was appalled as she heard herself shouting at him. She even refused to let him see her home, and said that anyone who accosted her would probably be a pleasant relief.

By the time she reached home she saw that the old pattern had re-asserted itself exactly as before, and this time it wasn't her fault. Whatever she might have done, at least she had straightened herself out about certain things, but Jimmy was as big a mess as ever. He took the wrong side in an argument and stuck by it because in life he had taken the wrong side and couldn't break free.

Immediately, this made her again feel prudent and mature. She looked at her own angry face in the mirror over the fireplace and said authoritatively: 'Una, girl, someone in this blooming group has to act grown-up.' So she rang Jimmy up and apologized and proposed that they should go to Glengarriffe for the weekend. He was still hurt, and still sounded like a small boy of twelve, but though he accepted her apology ungraciously, he agreed to go with her.

Glengarriffe had always been a great haunt of theirs, and by the time they began to drive between lake and mountain Jimmy was already in high spirits. Whenever he let himself go, he was the best of company; considerate, sly and full of crude schoolboy jokes. After supper at the hotel, they walked down the sea front and watched the moon rise over Cab Dhu. They knew all the boatmen and chatted with them about the latest visitors, and leaned on the sea-wall, watching the moon's reflection in the bay like a great silver tree of quivering leaves.

When Jimmy said goodnight to her in her bedroom she grabbed him tight.

'Jimmy,' she asked, 'aren't you going to stay?'

'Are you sure you want me to?' he asked with a sombre smile, and she knew the same idea had been in his own mind.

'That's right,' she said reproachfully. 'Put all the responsibility on the girl! The least you might have done is to let me swoon respectably.'

She turned her back and pulled her frock over her head. When she saw him standing there still, tall, embarrassed and silent, she gave him a playful push on to the bed. She felt in command of the situation again. Denis had been right about that at least. She and Jimmy had come to a dead end, and, by hook or crook, they must break out of it. And with Jimmy it was all so much easier. He wasn't only someone who attracted her, but someone she loved; someone she had known since her girlhood, whom she trusted and understood.

He fell asleep in her arms, but Una remained awake till morning in a daze of happiness and fulfilment. She had seen her duty and done it, and to hell with everybody! Before the maids began their work she waked him and sat cross-legged on the bed, watching him pull on his trousers and socks. It was only when he raised the blind that she noticed his unusual gravity. It was as though the sky must look very dark over the mountains.

'What's it like outside, Jimmy?' she asked.

'I wasn't looking,' he said without glancing at her. 'It seems all right. I was just thinking we'd probably better get married at once.'

'Oh, do you think so?' she asked. She felt rather let down. This was not how a lover should sound after a first night with a girl he'd been courting for years. But maybe all Irishmen were like that. To do anything at all with them, you had to seduce them, and then they could hardly wait to make respectable men of themselves again. And yet Jimmy had never looked more attractive. He leaned against the window-frame in his white shirt sleeves, and the morning light caught his big-boned obstinate face and brought out the deep vertical lines between his eyes.

'We don't want to have to rush it,' he said. 'Your father wouldn't like that at all. Neither would my mother, I dare say.'

'I dare say they wouldn't,' Una said coolly. 'To tell you the truth, I wasn't thinking of them.'

'Unfortunately, I have to think of them.'

'Jimmy,' she cried in consternation, 'you're not upset about it, are you?'

'Aren't you?' he asked in his Sunday's Well accent, giving her a dark look.

'Me?' she said with a laugh. 'I'm enchanted, of course. I thought I'd never see the day.'

'Maybe upset is the wrong word,' he said pompously, and then nodded towards the bed. 'But we don't want any more of *this*.' The contempt in his tone as he said 'this' angered her. It reduced it all to a child's messy game.

'We haven't had such a lot of it,' she said sharply. 'Do you mean it's too furtive?'

'Oh, yes,' he said almost with a shudder. 'And *wrong*!'

'Wrong?' she repeated angrily. 'I thought we were supposed to be engaged.'

'I don't see what that has to do with it.'

'If you want to know, I don't think it's half as wrong as quarrelling over old distilleries,' she snapped. 'At any rate, it's human.'

'That only makes it worse,' he said coldly. 'We stuck it so long, we could have stuck it a little longer. After all, we're not just out together for a good time.'

He sounded as though he were explaining the policy of his paper, and at any other time it would have made her really furious. Now, she felt despairingly that he was probably right. Their squabbles and misunderstandings had been part of the normal behaviour of two responsible grown-ups who took marriage seriously.

'Honestly, Jimmy,' she said, 'there are times when I think I'm not right in the head. This is all my fault.'

'Oh, no, it isn't,' he said, showing what she called his 'Sunday's Well' character. 'I'm entirely to blame.' She knew he didn't mean a word of it, but she liked it just the same.

'You are not, Jimmy,' she said flatly. 'I made you come here deliberately, with that intention. I only wish you'd told me to go to Hell.'

'Oh, intentions!' he said wearily. 'Do you think I don't have intentions, too? No, it's not that. It's just that things have changed between us, and I don't seem to be able to talk to you as I used to do.'

'But that's exactly what I felt about you, Jimmy,' she said. 'That's why I felt we had to do something desperate.'

'Yes,' he added bitterly, 'and it's all the fault of the damn fellow in Dublin. He's the one who made you change.'

The suddenness and bitterness of the attack took her by surprise. Then she got out of bed and put her arms on his shoulders.

'You really think that?' she asked.

'I know it, girl,' he said with tears of rage in his eyes.

'Well, you're wrong,' she said earnestly. 'I swear you're wrong. I'm just the same as I always was, and Denis did nothing to me. You do believe that, don't you? You have to believe that. If you don't, we'd better chuck it.' Then, as the falsehood touched the chord of hysteria in her, she began to sob and pull her hair. 'Oh, I'm just a bloody fool. I do my best – honest to God I do my best – but everything I do goes wrong, God, it's beastly!'

'It isn't beastly, Una,' he said. 'I know you acted for the best. So did I. It's just that it's not right for us. We're not the sort.'

And again she saw it through his eyes, something beautiful that had been irretrievably spoiled by a few hours of boredom and dissatisfaction and could never be the same again because innocence had gone out of it.

When Jimmy left her she threw herself on the bed and really bawled. Now, she didn't know where to turn to or what to do. She had tried everything, and everything had been wrong. And yet she knew she wasn't worse than other girls. She had sense enough to realize that, as girls went, she was rather better than most. She had acted with the best of intentions out of what she had thought a sense of responsibility. In fact, when it came to good intentions, she was almost tripping over them. And yet she had done worse than any flighty irresponsible girl would have done. She had let herself be seduced by Denis, and seduced Jimmy in her turn. And what was worse, she had lied to Jimmy, lied to him in the most flagrant way.

She wasn't really apologizing for that. Now that Jimmy was out of the room she was very cross with him, but she was crosser still with Denis. She could almost imagine him laughing at her folly. So now she thought she could get along on her own, did she? She thought there was nothing left for her to learn? Like the sorcerer's apprentice she had learned how to produce magic but not how to control it!

It made her so angry that she actually began talking to him as though he were there.

'All right, you old bastard,' she muttered vindictively. 'You started it, with all your old talk. "Everything would be fine once we made the breakthrough." Well, I made the breakthrough, and where the hell am I? I'm worse off than I was before. What did I do wrong? As you think you're so smart, maybe you'll tell me that?'

And suddenly, almost as though he had opened his mouth and replied to her, she knew what she had done wrong, and the very idea of it made her feel sick. She dressed and went downstairs to the telephone. It was on the wall beside the back door, near the kitchen. The back door was open and there were hens strutting by in the early morning light. She had minutes to wait for her call, and she stamped nervously up and down the yard, afraid that at any moment Jimmy would appear, as good-looking as ever, and ask her to go for a swim. In that state she felt she couldn't even talk to him. Even the memory of the night they had spent together made her feel dirty all over. 'Prostitution,' said that queer voice in her head, and she shuddered and wished the phone bell would ring.

Suddenly it sounded and she grabbed at it. A meek, sleepy voice answered her. As it expanded into awareness she could almost see that awful bedroom with the kitchen attached and her heart overflowed. In her excitement she began to stutter.

'Denis,' she said, 'about that divorce business you were mentioning—'

'Yes, dear,' he replied snugly.

'You didn't do anything about it, I suppose?'

'As a matter of fact, I did, dear,' he said, coming gradually awake. 'Why?'

'Oh, nothing,' she said lightly. 'Only, I've been thinking about it myself. That it might be the best way, I mean.'

'It's the only way, dear,' he said in his most infallible tone, and Una almost chuckled at how little he knew. 'And I'm pretty sure now it's going to be possible. Gum, it *is* early, isn't it? You haven't been lying awake thinking of it, have you?'

'Not altogether,' she said drily.

'Where are you speaking from, Una?' he asked with concern. 'Not from home, surely?'

At this she chuckled. It wouldn't do at all to tell him that she was speaking from a hotel where she'd been spending the night with another man. He mightn't understand.

'I'll see you soon and tell you all about it,' she said, and when she had hung up, she went briskly down the sea-road in the morning sunlight, singing and not caring much where she went. She would get a cup of tea and a slice of home-made bread in a country cottage, and thank God, that was about all she wanted. All the same she knew perfectly well that she would tell Denis where she had rung from, and why, and knew that though he might be furious for a couple of hours, it would really make no difference. So far as he was concerned, innocence had not gone out of it.

Being a pious girl she thanked God for having discovered in time what was wrong with her. In her simple way she had thought she was learning the business of love, and she was, but in a way that no one had told her of. Now she realized that even Denis didn't know the half of it. Every man and woman is a trade in himself, and however bad a bargain she might have in Denis, Denis was the only trade she knew.

More Stories (1954)

The Old Faith

The Pattern at Kilmulpeter turned into a great day. Mass was said in the ruins of the cathedral and the old bishop, Dr Gallogly, preached. Father Devine, who was a bit of an antiquarian, had looked up the details of St Mulpeter's life for him. There were a lot of them, mostly contradictory, and all very, very queer. It seemed that like most of the saints of that remote period, St Mulpeter had put to sea on a flagstone and floated ashore in Cornwall. There, the seven harpers of the King had been put to death through the curses of the Druids and the machinations of the King's unfaithful wife. St Mulpeter miraculously restored them to life and, through the great mercy of God, they were permitted to sing a song about the Queen's misbehaviour, which resulted in St Mulpeter turning her into a pillar-stone and converting the King to the one true faith.

The Bishop had been Professor of Dogmatic Theology in the seminary; a job that had suited him excellently for he was a man who dogmatized about everything. He was a tall, powerfully built, handsome old man with a face that was both broad and long, and high cheek-bones that gave the lower half of his face an air of unnatural immobility but drew attention to the fine blue, anxious eyes. He had a quiet manner and a low voice, but with a touch of the piledriver about him.

For a dogmatic theologian he showed great restraint on reading Devine's summary of the saint's life. He raised his brows a few times, and then read it through again with an air of resignation.

'I suppose that's what you'd call allegorical, father,' he said anxiously.

'So long as you don't call it historical,' said Devine, who had a tongue he couldn't control.

The Bishop rarely showed signs of emotion, and he seemed quite unaffected by the scene in the ruined cathedral, though it impressed Devine – the crowds of country people kneeling in the wet grass among the tottering crosses and headstones, the wild countryside framed in the mullioned windows, and the big deeply moulded clouds sailing overhead. The Bishop disposed neatly of St Mulpeter by saying that we couldn't all go to sea on flagstones, which required great faith in anyone who attempted it, but the family Rosary was just as good.

After Mass, Father Devine showed the Bishop and some of the other clergy round the ruins. Suddenly, a couple of men who had been hiding in the remains of a twelfth-century chapel took to their heels. One of them stood on a low wall, looking down on the little group of clergymen with the expression of a terrified rabbit. The Bishop raised his umbrella and pointed it accusingly at him.

'Father Devine,' he said in a commanding tone, 'see what that fellow has.'

'I have nothing, Your Eminence,' wailed the man on the wall.

'You have a bottle behind your back,' said the Bishop sternly. 'What have you in that?'

'Nothing, Your Eminence, only a drop of water from the Holy Well.'

'Give it here to me till I see,' said the Bishop, and when Father Devine passed him the bottle he removed the cork and sniffed.

'I'd like to see the Holy Well that came out of,' he said ironically. 'Is it any use my preaching to ye about poteen?'

'Ah, 'tis a wild, windy quarter, Your Eminence,' said the man, beginning to scratch himself, 'and I have the rheumatics something terrible.'

'I'd sooner the rheumatics than the cirrhosis,' grunted the Bishop. 'Bring it with you, father,' he added to Devine, and strode on with his umbrella against his back.

The same night a few of them had dinner with him at the Palace – Father Whelan, an old parish priest, who was a cross between a saint and a half-wit; Father Fogarty, who was a bit of a firebrand, Devine and Canon Lanigan. The Bishop and the Canon never got on because the Canon's supporters were giving it out that the Bishop was doddering and needed a coadjutor. Besides, the Canon gave himself too many airs. He was tall and thin, with a long nose and a punchinello chin, and he let on to be an authority on Church history as well as on food and wine. The last item was enough to damn him in the Bishop's eyes, because he maintained almost *ex cathedra* that the best food and wine in the world were to be found on the restaurant car from Holyhead to Euston.

When Lanigan made a fool of himself by recommending Châteauneuf-du-Pape, the Bishop turned to Father Devine.

'Talking about drink, father,' he said with his anxious glare, 'what happened to the bottle of poteen you took off that fellow?'

'I suppose it's in the hall,' Father Devine said vaguely. 'I can assure you I wasn't indulging in it.'

'You could indulge in worse,' said the Bishop with a dirty look at the Canon. 'Many a good man was raised on it. Nellie,' he called, turning his head a few inches, 'bring in that bottle of poteen, if you can find it . . . You can have it in your tea,' he added to the Canon. 'Or is it coffee you want?'

'Oh, tea, tea,' sighed the Canon, offering it up. He knew only too well what the Bishop's coffee was like. According to the Bishop, it was the best bottled coffee in the world.

When the housekeeper brought in the poteen, the Bishop took out the cork and sniffed at the bottle again with an anxious air.

'I should have found out who made it,' he said. 'When they can't get the rye, they make it out of anything.'

'You seem to be quite an expert, my Lord,' said Devine with his waspish air.

'Why wouldn't I?' asked the Bishop. 'Didn't I make it myself? My poor father – God rest him! – had a still of his own. In milk he used to give it to me, for colds. Or like a liniment, rubbed on the chest. Not that I tasted it now in sixty, sixty-five years.'

He poured a stiff glass for each of them, and drank his own in a gulp without any change of expression. Then he looked anxiously at the others to see what they thought of it. Lanigan put on an air of consternation, but the Bishop knew that was only showing off. Father Fogarty drank it reverently, as though it were altar wine, but he was a nationalist and felt that anything that came from the people had to be treated accordingly. Father Devine disgraced himself; spluttered, choked, and then went petulantly off to the bathroom.

Meanwhile, the Bishop had decided that it was good poteen and treated them to another round, which they seemed to feel it might be disrespectful to refuse. Father Devine did refuse, and with a crucified air that the Bishop did not like at all. The Bishop, who knew everything and had one of the most venomously gossipy tongues in the diocese, was convinced that he was a model of

Christian charity and had spoken seriously to Father Devine about his own sharpness.

'Was it on an island you made this stuff?' the Canon asked blandly.

'No,' replied the Bishop, who didn't know what irony was. 'A mountain.'

'A rather desolate one, I fancy,' Lanigan said dreamily.

'It had to be if you didn't want the police on top of you,' said the Bishop. 'They'd have fifty men out at a time, scouring the mountains.'

'And bagpipes!' said the Canon, bursting into an old woman's cackle at the memory of the hilly road from Beaune to Dijon with the vineyards at each side. 'It seems to go with bagpipes.'

'There were no bagpipes,' the Bishop said shortly. 'As a matter of fact,' he added nostalgically, 'it was very nice up there on a summer's night. They'd hide the still in a hollow, and then sit round and tell stories. Very queer stories, some of them, like that life of St Mulpeter Father Devine wrote out for me.'

'Ah, the people were half-savage in those days,' the Canon said.

'They were not,' the Bishop replied mildly, but from his tone Father Devine knew he was very vexed. 'They were more refined altogether.'

'Would you say so, my Lord?' asked Father Fogarty, who, as a good nationalist was convinced the people were rushing to perdition and that the only hope for them was to send them all back to live in whitewashed cabins.

'Ah, a nicer class of people in every way,' Father Whelan said mournfully. 'You wouldn't find the same nature at all in them nowadays.'

'They had a lot of queer customs all the same, father,' said the Bishop, who always spoke with peculiar affection to Whelan. 'I remember they used to put the first mug of poteen in hiding under a rock. Would that be something to do with the fairies?' he asked Devine.

'Well, at any rate, you can't deny that the people today are more enlightened,' the Canon said warmly.

'I deny it *in toto*,' retorted the Bishop. 'There's no comparison. The people were more intelligent altogether, better balanced and better spoken. What would you say, Father Whelan?'

'Oh, in every way, my Lord,' moaned Father Whelan, taking out his pipe.

'And the superstitions, my Lord?' the Canon hissed superciliously. 'The ghosts and fairies and spells?'

'They might have good reason,' said the Bishop with a flash of his blue eyes.

'By Gor, you're right, my Lord,' said Fogarty, in a loud voice, and then, realizing the attention he had attracted, he blushed and stopped short.

'"There are more things in heaven and earth, Horatio, than are dreamt of in our philosophy,"' added the Bishop complacently.

'Omar Khayyam,' whispered Father Whelan to Father Fogarty. 'He's a fellow you'd want to read. He said some very good things.'

'That's a useful quotation,' said the Canon, seeing he was getting the worst of it. 'I must remember that the next time I'm preaching against fortune tellers.'

'I wouldn't bother,' the Bishop said curtly. 'There's no analogy. There was a parish priest in our place one time, a man called Muldoon. Father Whelan might remember him.'

'Con?' defined Father Whelan. 'I do, well. His nephew, Peter, was on the Chinese Mission.'

'A well-meaning man but a bit coarse, I thought,' said the Bishop.

'That was his mother's side of the family,' explained Whelan. 'His mother was one of the Clasheen Dempseys and they were always a rough lot.'

'Was she so?' the Bishop asked with a great air of enlightenment. 'I never knew that. It would explain a lot. He was always preaching against superstition, you might remember, and he had his knife in one poor old fellow up the Glen called Johnnie Ryan.'

'Johnnie the Fairies,' said Father Whelan. 'I knew him too.'

'I knew him well,' said the Bishop. 'A gentle poor man but a bit soft in the head. He was their Living Man.'

'Their what?' cried Father Devine in astonishment.

'Their Living Man,' said the Bishop.

'Whose Living Man?' asked Divine with a baffled air.

'The fairies,' explained the Bishop. 'They had to have a Living Man to go with them, or else they had no power. That was the way I heard it anyway. I remember him well playing the Fairy Music on his whistle. They taught it to him.'

'You wouldn't remember how it went?' Father Fogarty asked eagerly. Devine could see the scheme forming in his head, for the convent school orchestra to play it. He could even imagine it on the programme – 'The Fairy Music, by kind permission of his Lordship the Bishop of Moyle.'

'I was never much good at remembering music,' said the Bishop. 'Anyway, I was only a child. Of course, there might be something in it. You'd often see queer lights on the mountain over our house. They said it was a fairy funeral. They had some story about a man from our place who interrupted a funeral like that one night. The fairies left down the coffin and ran away. The man opened the coffin and there was a girl inside. A fine-looking girl, too, I believe. When he breathed on her she woke up. They said she was from the Tuam direction – a changeling or something. I never checked the truth of it.'

'From Galway, I believe, my Lord,' Father Whelan said respectfully.

'Was it Galway?' asked the Bishop.

'I dare say with enough poteen in, a man could even believe that,' said the Canon indignantly.

'Still, Canon, strange things do happen,' said Father Fogarty.

'Why, then, indeed, they do,' agreed Father Whelan with a sigh.

'Was this something that happened to yourself, father?' the Bishop asked kindly, seeing the young man straining at the leash.

'It was, my Lord,' said Fogarty. ''Twas when I was a kid, going to school. I got fever very bad and the doctor gave me up. The mother – God rest her – was in a terrible state. Then my aunt came to stay with us. She was a real old countrywoman. I remember them to this day arguing in the kitchen, about what they ought to do. "Don't be a fool, woman!" said my aunt. "You know there's ways."'

'Well, well, well,' Father Whelan said, shaking his head.

'Then my aunt came up with a scissors,' Father Fogarty continued excitedly. 'First, she cut off a bit of the end of my shirt, and then a bit of hair from behind my ear, and then a bit of fingernail, and she threw them in the fire. All the time she was muttering to herself like an old witch.'

'My! My! My!' exclaimed Father Whelan.

'And you got better?' said the Bishop with a quelling glance at the Canon.

'I got better, all right, but that wasn't the strangest part of it.' Fogarty leaned across the table, scowling, and dropped his eager, boyish voice to a whisper. 'Inside a year, her two sons, two of the finest young fellows you ever laid eyes on, died.' Then he sat back, took out a cigar and scowled again. 'Now, wasn't that extraordinary?' he asked. 'I say, wasn't it extraordinary?'

'Ah, whatever was waiting to get you,' Father Whelan said philosophically, emptying his pipe on to his plate. 'I suppose it had to get something. A similar thing happened to an old aunt of my own. The cock used to sleep in the house, on a perch over the door – you know, the old-fashioned way. One night, the old woman had occasion, and when she went to the door, the cock crowed three times and dropped dead at her feet. Whatever was waiting for her, of course,' he added with a sigh. 'The cock gave them away, and they took their revenge on him.'

'Well! Well! Well!' the Canon exploded. 'I'm astonished at you, Father Whelan, absolutely astonished! How can you even repeat such old wives' tales?'

'I don't see what you have to be astonished about, Canon,' said the Bishop. 'It was no worse than what happened to Father Muldoon.'

'That was a bad business,' muttered Father Whelan, shaking his head.

'What happened him?' asked Devine.

'I told you he was always denouncing old Johnnie,' said the Bishop. 'One day they had words and he struck the old man. It wasn't fair. The old man was too feeble. Within a month Muldoon got a breaking out on his knee.'

'Poor fellow, he lost the leg after,' Father Whelan said, stuffing his pipe again.

'I suppose next you'll say that was the fairies' revenge?' said the Canon, throwing discretion to the winds. It was too much for him, a man who knew Church history, had lived in France and was a connoisseur of wine.

'That was what Father Muldoon thought,' said the Bishop smugly.

'More fool he!' retorted the Canon.

'That's as may be, Canon,' said the Bishop. 'Anyway, the doctors couldn't do much for him. He went back up the Glen again to ask Johnnie's advice. "I had nothing to do with it, father," said Johnnie, "but you can tell the doctor from me that he might as well take the leg off you while he's at it." "Why so?" says Muldoon. "Because it was the Queen of the Fairies that fired the shot at you, father, and the Queen's wound never heals." No more it did,' added the Bishop. 'As you say, father, he ended his days on a peg leg.'

'He did, God rest him, he did,' muttered Father Whelan mournfully, and there was a long pause. It was clear that the Canon was routed, and soon after they all got up to go. Father Fogarty had left his car outside the Seminary, and the Bishop, in a benevolent mood, offered to guide them across the field by the footpath.

'No, I'll do that,' Devine said irritably. In his cranky way he was fond of the Bishop and he didn't want him perambulating through the fields at that hour.

'Ah, I need the little walk,' said the Bishop.

He, the Canon and Father Fogarty went first down the palace steps. Father Devine followed with Father Whelan, who went down sideways with the skirts of his coat held up.

'That was a very good drop of poteen,' the Bishop was saying. 'For some reason, bad poteen strikes at the extremities. I used to see the people at home, talking as clearly as yourself or myself, and then dropping off the chairs, paralysed. You'd have to take them home on a door. The head might be quite clear, but the legs would be like gateposts.'

'Father Devine,' Father Whelan whispered girlishly, stopping in his tracks.

'Yes, father, what is it?' Devine asked gently.

'What his Lordship said,' whispered Father Whelan guiltily. 'That's the way I feel. Like gateposts.'

And before the young priest could catch him, he put out one of the gateposts which failed to alight properly on its base: the other leaned slowly towards it, and he collapsed in an ungraceful parody of a ballet dancer's curtsey.

'Oh, my, my, my!' he exclaimed guiltily. Even in his liquor he was melancholy and gentle.

The other three turned round slowly, very slowly, to study him. To Devine they looked like sleep-walkers.

'Hah!' the Bishop said with quiet satisfaction. 'It wasn't as good as I thought. We'd want to mind ourselves.'

And off the three of them went, arm-in-arm, as though they recognized no responsibility to their fallen colleague. Paddy, the Bishop's 'boy', who had been anticipating trouble, immediately appeared, and he and Devine carried the old man back to the hallway. 'Father Whelan isn't feeling well,' he explained unnecessarily to the housekeeper. Then, the two of them took the hall bench and set out after the others. They were in time to see the collapse of the Canon, but in spite of it, the other two went on. Devine shouted a warning, but they ignored him. Father Fogarty had begun to chuckle hysterically. It occurred to Devine that he was already beginning to rehearse his story of 'the night I got drunk with the Bishop'.

Devine and Paddy left the Canon and pursued the other two. They had gone wildly astray, turning in a semi-circle round the field, till they were at the foot of the hill and before a high fence round the plantation. The Bishop never hesitated but began to climb the wall.

'I must be gone wrong, father,' he said anxiously. 'This never happened to me before. We'll go over the wall and up the wood.'

'I can't,' shouted Fogarty in a paroxysm of chuckles.

'Nonsense, father!' the Bishop said sternly, holding on to a bush and looking down at him from the top of the wall. 'Why can't you?'

'The fairies have me,' roared Fogarty.

'Pull yourself together, father,' the Bishop said sternly. 'You don't want to be making an exhibition of yourself.'

Next moment Fogarty was lying flat at the foot of the wall, laughing his head off. Devine shouted again to the Bishop, but the Bishop only turned his back contemptuously and slid down at the other side of the wall. They found him there under a tree in the starlight, quite powerless but full of wisdom, resignation and peace. When they lifted him on to the bench he reclined there, his hands crossed meekly on his breast, like an effigy on a tomb-chest.

'The most remarkable example of historical regression I've ever seen,' Devine told young Fogarty when he woke up later with a terrible head. 'I must write a paper on it for the Archaeological Society. I didn't mind your retreat into the Early Bronze Age so much, but I was afraid you'd forget yourselves and go neolithic on me all of a sudden.'

'Ah, how bad the neolithic fellows were!' groaned Fogarty. 'I'm damn full sure they never felt as bad as I do.'

'The neolithic fellows?' Devine said in mock surprise. 'And have the Bishop proposing to build Lanigan into the wall of the new cathedral? My dear fellow, believe me, you can take this historical regression business too far.'

More Stories (1954)

Vanity

There are a lot of things bishops have to put up with beside old age, loneliness and domestic discomfort, and the worst of these is coadjutors. To be God Almighty – the just and moral Governor of your own private universe – for years, and then have an assistant God Almighty tagged on to you is enough to break the spirit in most men. The Bishop of Moyle, the Most Reverend Dr Gallogly, called his coadjutor the Stump, the Spy or the Boy, according to the way he felt about him. Mostly it was the Boy. The Boy had nasty supercilious ways that the Bishop detested. He let on to know a lot about French history, gave himself out as an authority on food and wine, jeered at Dr Gallogly's coffee – the best bottled coffee on the market – and mocked at his statement that the best food and wine in the world were served on the train from Holyhead to Euston. As a one time Professor of Dogmatic Theology, the Bishop was vulnerable to that sort of criticism.

Worst of all, the coadjutor had the illusion that at eighty-six the Bishop was past his prime while the Bishop himself knew that he had never been younger or livelier. Just to prove it, he would suddenly order round his car, drive a couple of hundred miles to Dublin and interview three Ministers. The Bishop was such a nice, friendly, inquisitive old man that the Ministers fell over themselves, telling him things he wanted to know, and then, of course, everybody in Moyle learned about them except Lanigan. Lanigan let on to be amused at this because it showed up the Bishop's senile fatuity, but, being an inquisitive man himself, the Bishop knew Lanigan was furious, and only pretended indifference out of vanity. Vanity – the besetting sin of people in religion, according to the Bishop – was Lanigan's weak spot, and the Bishop continued to play on it.

Whenever the notion of going to Dublin struck the Bishop he always made inquiries about people from Moyle whom he might call on there. He knew they liked that. Everyone is impressed by a Bishop, and it gave people like that an advantage over their city friends, and later they came home and said what a wonderful old man he was – so modest! – so considerate! – another thorn in the coadjutor's side.

One morning before setting out he made inquiries and discovered that one of his curates was in a nursing home for an operation.

'Father O'Brien?' he exclaimed, hitting his brow. 'What's he being operated on for? Surely, he's only – what is he, father?'

'Forty-five, my Lord.'

'Forty-five? And having an operation like that? Sure, there's no sense to it. Remind me to go and see Father O'Brien, Paddy,' he added to his chauffeur.

Even the Bishop's best friend would not have pretended that this was all kindness, though the Bishop had plenty of that. It was mainly delight and wonder at himself for having reached the age of eighty-six without a pain or an ache while a whole generation of priests was growing up who couldn't get to forty-five without an operation. 'Motor cars!' he said to himself. 'It's all the blooming motor cars!'

And every step he climbed up to the first floor of the nursing home the Bishop vacillated between good nature and complacency: good nature because he was genuinely glad to be able to do a good turn for a lonesome young priest, far from his family and friends, and a furious complacency because it wasn't the young fellow of forty-five who was coming to visit the sick old man of eighty-six. The two emotions mingled in the triumphant smile with which he opened the curate's door and trumpeted joyously: 'Father O'Brien, what does this mean? Do you want me to suspend you?' That would get back, too.

The Bishop was no fool, but he was so pleased with himself that he talked with more freedom than usual about the Moyle clergy and their families, particularly the families. 'If you want to know about a man, father, find out about his family,' he pronounced oracularly. 'Now, there's Dr Lanigan. To understand Dr Lanigan, you would have to know his brother, Mick, the way I did. Now, Mick was a clever sort of man, and a conscientious one in his own way, but he died when he was only sixty of some sort of children's disease that was never known to kill anyone else, and for years before he died he was suffering from religious scruples. Scruples! You see, father, that whole family was a bit neurotic.'

The Bishop returned to his hotel, saying to Paddy, his 'man', 'That'll show them, Paddy,' and Paddy grinned with perfect comprehension. Nobody resents a coadjutor more than a bishop's man. The lounge of the hotel was crowded and several people were waiting for the lift. By this time the Bishop's complacency had assumed monstrous proportions. 'Ah, I can't be bothered waiting for that old machine,' he said testily, loud enough to be overheard, and went up the stairs 'like a hare' according to Paddy, though this was a slight exaggeration.

He negotiated the main flight of stairs successfully, but when he came to one of six steps leading from one level to another, he tripped. He had only six steps to fall, but he knew they might as well be twenty. He was dished. He didn't move; he knew it wasn't safe. 'Pride goeth before a fall,' he thought ruefully. 'I should have waited for that blooming old lift.'

But when an old waiter appeared he did not lose his composure.

'I think I'm hurt,' he said placidly. 'Don't tell anyone. Get something to lift me in on and call Dr Jameson.'

It was agony being transferred to the stretcher and laid on the bed, but pain was the least of the Bishop's troubles, and the tears in his eyes were as much humiliation as anything else. He was only beginning to realize the full extent of the disaster that had overtaken him. After an irreproachable life of eighty-six years he was suddenly, because of what he thought of now as 'a mad vagary', no longer his own master, and as much the property of stretcher-bearers, doctors and nurses as any poor curate. Lanigan had his chance at last. No longer would they think of him in his own diocese as a marvellous old man. The shock of it was almost enough to make him lose his reason. But his voice remained steady and unemotional, the voice of a theologian.

'Am I bad?' he asked the doctor, who was a brisk, moon-faced young man.

'It looks as if you've broken your shoulder and your leg,' said the doctor. 'We'll have to get you to hospital to see if there's anything else.'

'Am I going to die?' the Bishop asked almost hopefully. If he were going to die there would be no further problem.

'I doubt it,' said the doctor, who was privately convinced that the Bishop wouldn't leave hospital outside a box. 'You must be pretty tough.'

'Ah, I'm tough enough,' the Bishop replied complacently. 'Couldn't you do whatever you have to do here?'

'I couldn't, my Lord.'

'Why couldn't you?' the Bishop asked angrily. He hated to be contradicted in that positive way – it is one of the drawbacks of having been Almighty God.

'Because I've got to have an X-ray taken at once.'

'Then why can't you get it taken here? They must have portable ones. I don't like hospitals.'

'Why? What's wrong with hospitals?'

'They're too public,' the Bishop said flatly. 'When a man has a bit of authority, the way I have, he can't be making a spectacle of himself. He has too many people round him, trying to make out he's not fit to look after himself. They treat you as if you were a child.'

'But an accident can happen to anybody,' said the doctor.

'An accident can happen to a young man,' the Bishop said. 'If the same thing happens to an elderly person, people go on as though you did it out of spite. Boland, the manager here, is an old friend. He'll keep quiet about it. If I went into a hospital 'twould be all round Moyle tomorrow.'

'It'll be all round Moyle anyhow.'

'Not if I can help it,' the Bishop said, clamping his long thin lips.

'But people will have to know.'

'Why will they have to know?' the Bishop asked with sudden fierceness. It was bad enough to endure helplessness and agonizing pain without being contradicted into the bargain. 'What business is it of theirs? Or I could go into hospital under a false name.'

'You couldn't do anything of the sort,' said the doctor. 'You'd have to tell the nuns.'

'I would *not* tell the nuns,' said the Bishop with renewed irascibility. 'You don't know nuns the way I know them. I wouldn't tell a nun anything.'

'They'd have to know you were a clergyman.'

'Ah, a clergyman in this country can have no privacy,' the Bishop said, becoming weaker and more fretful. 'The first thing they'd want to know is what diocese I was from, and then they'd have a nun or a nurse checking up on me. I'm in a most unfortunate position. What sort is the Reverend Mother in that place?'

'Ah, she's a nice homely sort.'

'Never mind how homely she is. Where is she from?'

'I never asked her.'

The Bishop was so upset by this that it took him a full minute to collect his thoughts. He was astonished that a professional man wouldn't inquire about a thing like that, and wondered if the young doctor was quite as good as he was supposed to be.

'Send her over here to talk to me,' he said. 'I see I'll have to make my own arrangements.'

'Do you know, my Lord, you're a very obstinate old man,' said the doctor with a grin.

'That's what has me where I am,' the Bishop replied ambiguously. He never minded being told he was obstinate or even pigheaded because it showed he was making the right impression.

Ten minutes later the doctor returned with Reverend Mother and left her alone with the Bishop. She was an elderly, softmannered, gigglesome woman who almost smothered the Bishop with solicitude. Knowing it was only her stock-in-trade, he let her moan on, and then rested his good hand lightly on hers. From the gentleness of his face, you might have thought he had become reconciled to his fate, but that was only the Bishop's stock-in-trade as well – his manner for hysterical females.

'The doctor is a bright young man, Mother,' he said earnestly, 'but I don't find him easy to talk to. Laymen can never understand the difficulties of people in religion. The reason is that every calling has its own graces and its own temptations. Now, the great temptation of religious people is vanity.'

'I wonder, my Lord,' she said coyly.

'You needn't,' the Bishop said firmly. 'That's what makes it so hard for people in religion to be growing old. You're a young woman yet,' he continued with brazen flattery, 'so you mightn't know. Tell me, where are you from?'

'Mayo, my Lord,' she said. 'Mayo, God help us!'

'Are you from Mayo?' the Bishop asked with a sinking heart. He did not trust nuns, and he did not trust Mayo people. 'But as I was saying, your turn will come. You'll see the young people pushing you out to make way for themselves, watching and criticizing, waiting for you to make a slip.'

'Ah, you needn't tell me, my Lord,' she said in a wail. 'I saw it already.'

'Ah, you're an observant young woman,' the Bishop said ingenuously. 'Now, Mother, this is something I wouldn't like to admit to a lay person, but I know you'll understand. I have a coadjutor and we don't get on – I know this won't go any further. He thinks I'm not able to look after myself. If it got round that I had an accident, he'd be saying I wasn't fit to make decisions on my own. Now, you must have had cases like that before.'

'My Lord,' she said in mock-girlish alarm, 'I don't think you know what you're asking.'

'In fact, if I'm not mistaken, 'tisn't so long since you had a certain member of the Government in your place.'

'Well, of course, we always have special patients.'

'They called it pneumonia, I believe,' the Bishop said gravely. 'However, it was greatly appreciated in government circles.'

'Ah, 'tisn't alike, my Lord,' she said anxiously. 'A Minister is one thing but a Bishop – how could I?'

'There is nothing an intelligent woman can't do if she puts her mind to it, Mother,' he said.

'No, nor anything an inquisitive woman can't find out if she puts her mind to it, my Lord,' she replied wryly.

That evening, the Bishop was comfortably settled in a room corridors away from the rest of the building with two old nuns to guard him. The old nuns had long ceased to be active: Sister Dympna was crippled with the rheumatics and Sister Martha was slightly gone in the head, but they rejoiced in their new responsibility, exulted in the fact that at last somebody reliable was needed, and revenged themselves on those who had slighted them by silence and cunning.

The Bishop was in great pain, but even this did not take from his feeling of triumph. The curate was upstairs, probably lying awake and marvelling at the Bishop's sturdy health while unknown to him, the Bishop was lying awake, helpless as himself but knowing something he didn't know. The essence of authority consists in keeping your secrets.

But after a few days even the Bishop became aware of the fury of curiosity his secret roused. Reverend Mother was the only nun permitted to visit him and nurses were not allowed in his room at all. But the trouble with the Bishop's gallant old watch-dogs was that they had lost their teeth. They were easy game for the younger nuns and nurses, because Sister Dympna's bad legs and Sister Martha's bad head meant that once they left the room there was no guarantee that they would ever get back. On the third day the door opened suddenly and a middle-aged scraggy nurse came in and looked at him in apparent astonishment.

'I'm sorry,' she said. 'I must be in the wrong room. Are you Mr Murphy?'

Now, if there was one thing the Bishop could not stand it was inquisitiveness. He was an inquisitive man himself, so he understood the vice in all its manifestations.

'No, I'm Mr Dempsey,' he said. 'Who are you?'

'My name is Fitzpatrick,' she said smoothly, and he knew as if God had revealed it to him that it wasn't. 'You wouldn't be one of the Dempseys from Limerick?'

'No. My family came from Kanturk,' he said curtly.

'We had a nurse one time from Kanturk,' she said, screwing up her eyes. 'Lucey, her name was. You wouldn't know her?'

'She must be from another part of Kanturk,' said the Bishop.

'I dare say,' she said, realizing she had met her match. 'What happened to you anyway?'

For a moment the Bishop was so mad that he nearly asked her if she knew who she was talking to. Then he recollected that she probably didn't.

'A fall I got off my bicycle,' he said, glaring at her.

'At your age!' she said with a sweet smile. 'I'm astonished at you.'

She left him in a state of blind rage. Never, never, since the time he was a boy had anybody spoken to him in that coarse familiar way. Then he broke into a chuckle. As a young priest he had noticed how conversation changed when he entered a room, and wondered how people really behaved when there wasn't a priest around. Now, in his old age, he had discovered. 'The religious life is too sheltered,' he thought. 'Too much play-acting about it. "Father, what do you think of this?" and "Father, what would you say to that?" No wonder the Jesuits were supposed to have spies to report on what people said. No wonder at all they had the reputation of being so clever. He waited impatiently for the nurse to come back.

Instead, there came a young and good-looking nurse who didn't even pretend to have strayed in by accident. She gave him a guilty look and then shrugged and smiled, but all the time her small, keen, beautiful eyes wandered about the room, searching for a clue.

'They say you were in America,' she burst out without preliminaries.

'What makes them think that, girl?' the Bishop asked good-humouredly.

'How would I know?' she replied with another shrug. 'I suppose because you don't seem to have a family.'

'Well, I'll tell you the truth,' said the Bishop slyly. 'I haven't. I was never what you'd call a marrying man.'

'Why would you?' she asked. 'I suppose you can get them without.'

The Bishop was so stunned that he almost gave himself away again. He stared at the nurse, but her charming little face still remained vague and sweet and innocent.

'Isn't that a shocking thing for a girl like you to say?' he asked.

'What's shocking about it?' she asked lightly. 'I suppose you didn't do without them. I'd know a queer a mile off.'

This left the Bishop very thoughtful indeed. Even in a long life there were apparently many things that had escaped his eye. He shook his head over it. 'Too sheltered,' he muttered again to himself. 'Too blooming sheltered. We don't know the half that's going on. We might as well have blinkers.'

What really surprised him was that he was becoming quite attached to his own anonymity, and grew quite hopeful when he heard a woman's step outside his door. He felt a match for any of them now. When the first nurse came back and told him a dirty story, he guessed at once that it was to test some new theory of his identity and let on to be very amused by it, though he had never realized that women knew dirty stories. 'We live and learn,' he thought. 'I don't know do even the Jesuits know the whole thing.'

It took the Bishop the whole of ten days to recover from his fractures, but it was a great day for him when he left the hospital by the back door. The two old nuns knelt for his blessing, and wept because they would again be regarded as old and useless. The curate was still upstairs.

'I suppose you'll go straight to the hotel?' said the doctor.

'I'll do nothing of the sort,' said the Bishop, whose only plan was to put a couple of hundred miles between himself and the hospital before they found anything else wrong with him.

'You're a very lucky man,' said the doctor. 'I can tell you now I was sure you were for the long road. I have a patient of twenty-two that the same thing happened to, and he'll never walk again. I can't even keep you quiet.'

'Ah, poor fellow! poor fellow!' the Bishop said perfunctorily. 'I suppose he hadn't the stamina.'

The Bishop was like a boy. He had always been a great student, and never before had he noticed how beautiful was the road back to Moyle. Illness, he thought, was a great thing, because it made you see more of life. For the future he must meet more laymen, and not laymen like the old crawthumpers who were always round the palace, but broadminded people he could describe his adventures to.

It was something of a disappointment to him when he got home to find a large crowd waiting for him outside the gate of the palace. When the car stopped they began to cheer, and Jerry Cronin, on behalf of the County Council, stepped forward shyly to congratulate him on his recovery. Then they all dropped on their knees and the Bishop gave them his blessing.

'Tell me what's all this about, Jerry,' he said, propelling Cronin to the car. It didn't occur to the Bishop that in a small town the presence of two bishops is nearly as good as a boxing match.

'Ah, well, you know, people were very upset when they heard of the accident, my Lord,' said Jerry.

'And I suppose they knew all about it inside twenty-four hours?' the Bishop asked with a glare.

'Oh, sooner than that, my Lord, sooner than that,' said Jerry.

'Nuns, nuns, nuns!' said the Bishop petulantly. 'Take a fool's advice, Jerry, and never trust a nun. And whatever else you do, never trust anybody from Mayo.'

More Stories (1954)

A Brief for Oedipus

To watch a law case between husband and wife is like watching a performance of Oedipus. You know that, whatever happens, the man has no chance, because every judge has a mother fixation and any lawyer would as soon take a brief for Oedipus.

It has been said that the nearest a man ever got to averting the Furies was the day Micky Joe Spillane defended a countryman called Lynam whose wife was suing for legal separation on the usual grounds of cruelty and adultery. Separation was all she could get, and, indeed, all she wanted; and even this she could not get without proving cruelty, which, in the present-day decline of manliness, is not as easy as it sounds.

Mrs Lynam at least had no trouble about that. The adultery was admitted, if not actually gloried in, and all that was needed to prove the cruelty was to put the Respondent in the box. He was a big, good-looking man with a stiff, morose manner – one of those Irish countrymen who are deceptively gentle, who are so generous that they will give you the shirt off their back, and will then knock you unconscious over some trifling remark about politics.

His wife was a trim, mousy little woman of about half his height and a quarter his weight, with an anxious face and a gentle, bedraggled, virginal air. She was pathetically anxious to make a good impression: she cocked her little head as she listened to her counsel's questions, as though they were in French, and replied to them in something like the same way, raising her colourless little voice and illustrating her answers with vague, half-completed gestures.

You could see that O'Meara, the judge, adored her. 'Come over here where we can hear you, ma'am,' he said, pointing to a seat beside him on the bench. Poor O'Meara was a bad case: he had blood pressure as well as a mother fixation.

Once or twice as she gave her evidence she glanced forgivingly at her husband who only stared back with a gloomy hatred that was

97

awe-inspiring. Most men are embarrassed, hearing what they are supposed to have done to their wives, but Lynam paid attention to nobody, and just watched his wife as if he were wondering why the blazes he hadn't taken a hatchet and finished the job while he was at it.

'And what did he do then?' asked her counsel, Kenefick, having gone through the demolition of the house, chair by chair and cup by cup.

'He called me – do I have to repeat it, my lord?'

'Ah, not at all, ma'am, not at all,' he said encouragingly. 'Write it down.'

The clerk gave her pencil and paper. Mrs Lynam wrote as she talked, slowly and carefully, raising her eyes to the ceiling. Then she handed the paper to the clerk, who passed it to O'Meara. O'Meara glanced at it expressionlessly and passed it down to counsel. Tom Lynam, black with rage, whispered something to his solicitor, Quill, but Quill only shook his head. He had never liked the case from the first day, and if he had had his way, would have settled it out of court. He had allowed himself to be over-persuaded by his truculent client and by his counsel, Mickie Joe, who had got into a tantrum and said it was a scandalous case and should be fought in the public interest. Public interest, indeed! Quill felt it was his own fault for briefing an unstable man like Mickie Joe.

'And did he say anything else?' Kenefick murmured sympathetically.

'Only if I didn't get out of the house in five minutes, sir, that he'd do to me what the Jews did to Jesus.'

'What the Jews did to who?' O'Meara asked incredulously.

'Jesus, my lord,' she repeated, bowing reverently for the second time. 'Our Blessed Lord, my lord. Crucify me he meant.'

'Huh!' snorted O'Meara, his blood pressure going up. Adultery and cruelty were bad enough, but when you had blasphemy thrown in Ireland was certainly going to the dogs.

'Now tell my lord what happened then,' prompted Kenefick, scaling up the sympathy to the degree of emotion the judge seemed to require.

'So then I told him I could not go out of the house at that hour and the state I was in,' Mrs Lynam continued with growing animation. 'And with that, he dragged me off the sofa and twisted my wrist behind my back.' ('Wrist' and 'back' she illustrated by another feeble gesture that she did not complete.)

'And this was at a time when you were seriously ill?'

'I was at death's door, sir,' she said candidly. 'The whole day I wasn't able to get up off the sofa even to feed the children. That was what he had against me the whole time,' she said, shaking her little head vivaciously. 'Shamming, he said I was.'

'And then what happened?' Kenefick asked, yearning over her.

'He kicked me right out the front door sir,' she replied, raising her hands as though to avert the crash. 'I fell on the path on my hands and knees. Tommy – that's our little boy – ran out and began to cry, and my husband said for him to get to bed quick or he'd do the same to him.'

'And your little boy is – how old?' Kenefick asked with a positive tremolo in his voice.

'Five, sir, the fourteenth of February.'

'And did your husband make any effort to see if you were injured by the fall?'

'Why, then, indeed, he did not, sir,' she replied with a smile that was like a rainbow – an optical illusion between two downpours. 'Only to give me another kick into the flower bed. Then he made use of a filthy expression and banged the door behind him.'

'And those were the marks that you showed next day to Dr O'Mahoney?'

'They were, sir. The very same. A week he made me stop in bed, with my back.'

After this, it was scarcely necessary to emphasize her husband's bad behaviour with Nora Magee, a woman of notorious bad character, for in fact, she had had a child by him, he had been seen minding it, and rumour in the town held that Nora had never had it so good.

'And did you have any conversation with your husband about this woman?' Kenefick asked gravely.

'A dozen times, sir,' she replied. 'I asked him a dozen times, practically on my bended knees, to give her up, for the children's sake if not for mine.'

'And what was his reply?'

'His reply, sir, was that the child was a Lynam, and he wouldn't give up one Lynam for all the Hanafeys that were ever pupped . . .

Hanafey is my maiden name,' she added. 'He meant the children took after me.'

At this Kenefick sat down, looking old and broken, and Mickie Joe got up. Now, the best day he ever was, Mickie Joe was no great shakes as a lawyer. He had begun life as a schoolmaster and given it up for the law. He really loved the art of oratory, and would sit with a childish expression of delight, listening to a good sermon or a good speech or a good summing up, but his own voice was like a train-whistle, and the only effect he had on an audience was to make it laugh. If it laughed too much, he would stop and scold it, which only brought more laughter.

He had a tendency to identify himself with his client, a thing no real lawyer will do. A client is a fact, and a true lawyer hates facts. He is an artist – a dramatist and actor – whose job it is to make little dramas out of the sordid and trivial material his clients provide. The one thing he hates is to be reminded by the characters themselves of what the real story is. Mickie Joe had very little of the artist in him, and as a result, had a tendency to get rattled when his client got the worst of a case and start barging his opponent like an old market-woman.

Kenefick had obviously told Mrs Lynam not to be afraid of him and she wasn't. She clutched the arms of her chair, raised herself in it as if in anxiety to give the best that was in her and answered patiently and quietly. Yes, sir, she had been educated in a convent. Yes, indeed, she was a very old friend of Sister Dominic. *And* of Father O'Regan, the parish priest. Yes, she had asked their advice before beginning proceedings because it was a thing she would not take on herself. Yes, she was a member of the Women's Sodality and the Children of Mary as well as the St Vincent de Paul. Kenefick looked up doubtfully at Mickie Joe, wondering where the hell he was going from that, unless it was to prove that Mrs Lynam was a saint as well as a martyr.

Kenefick saw soon enough and it startled him even more.

'And when you went to the Women's Sodality, who got your husband's supper?' Mickie Joe asked in a wailing voice.

'Ah, well, sometimes he got it for himself.'

'And the children's supper as well?'

'He might get that, too, of an odd time.'

'And when you were at Mass, I dare say he got his own breakfast?'

'Unless he waited till I got in.'

'But you always got it for him when you came in?'

'Always, except when I wasn't able.'

'And I take it, Mrs Lynam, you weren't always able?'

'Well, no, I wasn't,' she admitted candidly. 'Not always.'

She still didn't take him seriously or realize her danger, but she was the only one who didn't. Breakfast, after all, is a serious matter.

'You were able to go to Mass, but you were not able to get your husband's breakfast?' asked Mickie Joe. 'Is that what you're telling my lord?'

'I often went to Mass when I wasn't able either,' she replied with a noble pathos that would have silenced anyone else but Mickie Joe. He was still hot on the trail of the missing breakfast.

'You went to Mass when you weren't able, but you didn't get your husband's breakfast when you weren't able?' he asked in his shrill monotonous voice. 'Is that what you mean?'

'I think I should explain that,' she said, looking nervously at the judge. 'I'm rather delicate, of course. I have a pain in my back. I hurted it years ago in a fall I got on the ice. Doctor O'Mahoney treated me.'

This was a really dangerous admission which any other counsel would have been after like a greyhound, but Mickie Joe didn't even seem to realize that it had been made. By this time he was getting furious.

'And you suffer from headaches, too, I suppose?' he went on.

'I do, sir,' she replied, with one small hand sketching a gesture at her stomach. 'Bilious.'

But O'Meara was tired of Mickie Joe. He liked his breakfast as well as the next, but for a judge with a mother fixation to listen to the poor victim being badgered like that was too much.

'Really, Mr Spillane,' he asked in a distant voice, 'do we have to go into the lady's bilious headaches?'

But for once Mickie Joe did not give way. He looked reprovingly at O'Meara over his pince-nez and his voice went off into an unearthly wail.

'My lord, if the Petitioner is presented to the court as something out of a medical museum, I can hardly say much more.'

'Oh, go on, Mr Spillane, go on!' O'Meara said. All the same he blushed. It was beginning to dawn even on him that you couldn't always treat Mickie Joe as a figure of fun. He did not quite know why. It never occurred to him that the one man who can stand up to a mother fixation in fair fight is a woman hater.

And, in a curious way, Mickie Joe's passion was beginning to affect the general view. It wasn't only that you couldn't any longer afford to bully or patronize him. A picture was beginning to emerge of a woman who was not only useless but was at the same time bold, ruthless and designing.

The court had begun to fill as it usually does when a case grows interesting, and Lynam himself seemed to pluck up courage. Instead of glowering at his wife, he looked back defiantly at the court as though to see whether anyone now believed the lies that had been told. A tall, bald man at the back gave him an encouraging wave and Lynam returned the salute austerely.

'Did you and your husband go out together much, Mrs Lynam?' Mickie Joe asked, changing his tack abruptly.

'Well, you can't do much with two children, can you, sir?' she asked with soft reproach.

'That depends, ma'am,' he said with a wintry smile. 'Don't other people do it?'

'I dare say they have servants,' she said nervously.

'You don't mean that people in the humbler walks of life have no friends, do you, ma'am?' he asked.

'Or neighbours, of course,' she added, filling out her original reply.

'I'm glad you thought of the neighbours,' he said. 'I was coming to them.'

'But you can't always be asking them for favours, can you?' she said.

'When you quarrelled with your husband, ma'am, didn't *you* go to the neighbours?'

'Sure, when I was crippled with the kicks he gave me!'

'But you couldn't ask them to mind the children when he wanted to go out and enjoy himself?'

'Ah, 'tisn't alike,' she said, showing irritation for the first time.

'No, ma'am, it isn't,' he agreed. 'How old did you say the little girl was?'

'Ten.'

'And you mean to say a girl of ten couldn't look after her brother for a couple of hours?'

'Well, I can explain that,' she said hastily. 'You see, they don't get on – you know the way it is between girls and boys – and you wouldn't like to leave her alone with him.'

'Do you mean she'd beat him?'

'Well, she mightn't *beat* him exactly,' Mrs Lynam replied nervously, 'but she might be tormenting him.'

'Mrs Lynam,' he asked severely, 'isn't it true that those children of yours are utterly ruined?'

'Ruined?' she cried indignantly, starting up with an outraged glance. 'Certainly not. I never heard such a thing!'

'On your oath, ma'am, wasn't that what your husband meant when he said they weren't Lynams at all?'

'How could he?' she asked. 'There isn't a word of truth in it.'

But Lynam looked at Mickie Joe with such an expression of astonishment that everyone knew there was. Mickie Joe knew it too, and for the first time a prim, watery smile of satisfaction played on his thin, old-maidish mouth.

'Did many of your husband's friends visit you?'

'Some of them, yes,' Mrs Lynam replied anxiously, trying to grasp the drift of the question. She was afraid of him now, all right.

'He had a lot of friends when he married you?'

Kenefick rose with an air of deep distress to say his learned friend was straying from the point, but even O'Meara realized that straying was the one thing Mickie Joe was not doing.

'Answer the question, ma'am.'

'He had – of a kind.'

'Of the wrong kind, you mean?'

'Well, not my kind.' It was not exactly a tactful answer.

'He was what you'd call a popular man?'

'Well, he was an athletic sort of man. I don't know you would call him popular exactly.'

'And at the time of this unfortunate break-up, how many of them were still coming to the house?'

Mrs Lynam's eye sought out the tall bald man at the back of the court and confirmed an impression that he might have a story to tell.

'Well, I'm sure I couldn't say,' she replied doubtfully. 'Mr Malone was at the house two or three nights a week.' You could almost hear the note of grievance in her voice.

'And what happened the rest?'

'I'm sure *I* couldn't say, sir.'

'They just stopped coming, and you never once asked your husband "What's wrong with Joe or Pat or Willie?"'

'No. What business was it of mine?'

'I'm asking the questions, Mrs Lynam. You never gave them reason?'

'Never,' she replied earnestly.

'Never let them see that they weren't your – kind, as you call it?'

'Certainly not,' she replied self-righteously. 'I hope I always behaved like a lady.'

'And I dare say,' Mickie Joe drawled with the first really pleasant smile he had shown that day, 'when this last remaining friend – this Last Rose of Summer left blooming alone – came to bring your husband out, it sometimes happened that they couldn't go?'

'Well, I explained about my back,' she said, sketching another gesture behind her.

'You did, ma'am, fully,' Mickie Joe agreed with a wicked chuckle. 'We're better acquainted with your back now than we are with any other part of you.'

The bald man at the back was having the time of his life. It was his day as much as Mickie Joe's. He smiled and nodded amiably at the judge, the clerk and even the pressman. The Last Rose of Summer – a shy, neighbourly man – was clearly delighted that at last someone was getting down to business. Lynam, who had been staring in surprise at Mickie Joe, whispered something to his solicitor, but Quill only shook his head and frowned. As producer of the show, Quill was beginning to be impressed by the performance of his great new star, and, like any other theatre man, had no time to spare for the author's views.

'Tell me, ma'am,' Mickie Joe asked keenly, 'when did you last have relations with your husband?'

'When did I what, sir?' she asked in a baby voice, putting her finger to her mouth.

'When did you last go to bed with him with a view to matrimony?' Mickie Joe translated boisterously.

'Oh, I forgot to mention that,' she said hastily. 'He has a room of his own, of course.'

'Oh, has he?' Mickie Joe asked with a new light in his eye. 'But that wasn't the question I asked you. I asked how long it was since you had relations with him.'

'Well, with my back . . .' she began pathetically, and suddenly Mickie Joe interrupted her with a positive squeal of rage.

'Ah, give your back a rest, ma'am!' he cried, growing purple. 'Give your back a rest! It isn't your back we're discussing now. How long is it, I say.'

'Oh, I suppose a couple of years,' she replied doubtfully, and he pounced on her.

'Two years?'

'Two or three.'

'Or four?'

'I don't think 'twas as long as that,' she said wonderingly. 'What difference does it make?'

'Only the difference between a human being and a monster, ma'am,' he said. 'So in those impassioned scenes in which you begged your husband, "almost on your bended knees", to come back to you, you didn't want him to come back? And when he was at Mrs Magee's, looking after his child, he was in the only decent home he ever had?'

Mickie Joe, of course, had made his usual mistake and lost all restraint. At once, Kenefick was on his feet, protesting, and O'Meara rebuked Mickie Joe, who stood there humbly with his head down, thanked O'Meara for the rebuke, and went on just the same.

'Would it be true to say that you don't think much of marriage, ma'am?'

'Oh, I wouldn't say that,' she replied almost patronizingly. 'The Church of course takes a rather high view of it.'

'I was asking about you, ma'am, not the Church,' Mickie Joe said icily. 'The Church is quite capable of speaking for itself. But weren't you always grousing to Sister Dominic about married life?'

'I went to her for advice,' Mrs Lynam said anxiously, clearly wondering whether Mickie Joe was guessing or Sister Dominic gossiping.

'And to Father O'Regan when you were trying to turn him against your unfortunate decent husband?'

'I never tried to turn Father O'Regan against him,' she cried.

105

'Never! All I asked Father O'Regan to do was to talk to him and tell him to be more natural.'

'Natural?' repeated Mickie Joe bitterly. 'Four years sleeping in a room by himself? Is that what you call natural?'

'Natural, reasonable – call it what you like. Ah, now, Mr Spillane,' she went on angrily, ''tis all very well for you to be talking. That sort of thing may do all right for young people that don't know better, but for people of our age, 'tis disgusting. Positively disgusting!'

She had said too much. Even she knew that, though she didn't know how much damage she had done herself. A judge with a mother fixation may overlook the prospect of having to get his own breakfast but not that of four years in the spare room. There is a limit to human endurance. Even the policemen at the back of the court who had wives of cast iron were looking disapprovingly at the gentle, insinuating little woman who had revealed herself as a grey, grim, discontented monster with notions above her station.

When the court adjourned Mickie Joe had not done with her though he could well have left his case there. She was probably the only one who didn't yet know that she had lost, but even she was badly shaken. She grabbed her handbag and waddled quickly out. To everyone's astonishment, Tom Lynam hurried after her. Kenefick made an alarmed face at Mickie Joe who went after Lynam as fast as he could. Neither he nor Quill wanted to see their client finish off the job in the hall.

But when they got out Lynam was talking to her in a low voice. She was half turned away from him as though interrupted in flight. At last he came over to Mickie Joe and Quill.

'She wants to settle this,' he muttered apologetically, blushing and stammering.

'I'm damn full sure she does,' said Quill. 'Tell her there's nothing to settle.'

'I know that, Mr Quill,' said Lynam gloomily. 'I know you and Mr Spillane did your best for me. But I wouldn't like her to have to answer any more questions. She thinks I made them up. Sure, I never told Mr Spillane half the things he said.'

'You mean you're going to go back and live with that woman?' Mickie Joe asked with cold anger.

'That's what she wants, sir,' said Lynam.

'And do you know that in forty-eight hours she'll be making

your life a hell again?'

'She says she'll try to do better the next time,' Lynam said, staring at him.

'Is it a woman that five minutes ago was perjuring herself black in the face only to destroy you?' Mickie Joe asked savagely. 'How could you believe daylight from a woman like that? And next time she gets you here you won't be so lucky.'

'She says she won't go to court again,' Lynam said, scowling.

'And when she does, she needn't be afraid of me,' Mickie Joe said shrilly. 'You can find someone else to represent you. A man is only wasting his time trying to save people like you. It is like trying to keep a lunatic from suicide.'

'Nor I wouldn't have you again,' Lynam shouted, flaring up. 'Nor I wouldn't have had you today if I knew what you were going to do. I don't know who your spies were but they were no friends of mine, and for the future I'll see you keep your tongue off my wife.'

He was flushed and incoherent, and Quill realized again that he was an ugly customer to cross. But Mickie Joe was good enough for him.

'Fitter for you to make her keep her tongue off yourself,' he hissed. 'You would if you were man enough.'

'Mickie! Mickie!' said Quill, pulling his arm.

'What's that you said? I'll show you whether I'm man enough or not.'

'Come on, man, come on!' Quill said in alarm.

But all that evening Mickie Joe was in a terrible humour. He knew now that he would never see justice done to a husband in a court of law. You might as well hold a brief for Oedipus against the Fates.

More Stories (1954)

Father and Son

There were times when Dan felt Mildred's English superficiality as a sort of judgement. Flurry (short for Florence, a great name among men of the MacCarthy family) was their child. Bawn and Tim were Dan's children by his first wife. Mildred had made an excellent stepmother. Girls, even small ones, soon get to know whether they have the right accent and the right frock, and, as Mildred knew everything about accents and frocks, Bawn and she got on fine. Boys are different. Boys don't care about frocks. Tim was older than Bawn: he stole, he told lies, and, to show his contempt for Mildred, hacked his way through the house in his heaviest boots, speaking in a common Cockney accent. Mildred had been very patient with him, explaining everything, affecting nothing and boxing his ears when he cheeked her. But it hadn't worked. One day he kicked her savagely. Mildred, a woman of great spirit and resource, had kicked him back, but Dan, mad with rage, had decided he must go to boarding school. Mildred, who had been to a boarding school herself, thought that this was really taking things too far.

'Oh, Danny, you do make an awful fuss about things,' she sighed in her weary, well-bred way. 'Anyway, it's nothing to the kick I gave him. He'll be sore for weeks, the poor little bugger.'

In spite of her words Dan knew she was as conventional as they came; it went with the accent and the frocks, and it suited him fine, but, he knew that though they got on better than most husbands and wives, she still had the guilty feeling that he was Min's husband, not hers, Tim's father, not Flurry's.

During the holidays, Min wrote to say that she would like to see the kids again before they grew out of her knowledge and asked Dan to find her a room for the weekend in some pub nearby. As he read the letter he was full of foreboding. It was as though he were being haunted by the ghost of his first marriage.

'Something wrong?' Mildred asked when the children had left the dining room.

'Only Min wanting to come for the weekend,' he said expressionlessly.

'Well, there's nothing wrong with that, is there?'

'Only that it may prove a little awkward. She wants us to get her a room.'

'Why on earth doesn't she stay here? There's heaps of room . . . Or do you think she might be embarrassed?' she asked, seeing his face.

'I wasn't thinking of her,' he replied coldly.

'Then why don't I take Flurry to Helen's for the weekend and let you have the house to yourselves?' she asked reasonably.

'Can you ever think sensibly for five minutes?' he asked angrily.

'Really, ducky,' she sighed in that maddening, superficial way of hers, 'you do make a crisis out of everything.'

'Let's put it the other way round,' he said sternly. 'Suppose you'd been married instead of me, and your first attempt came here to see the kids, would you have liked my going off with Flurry and leaving you here with him?'

This reversal of parts was a favourite device of Dan's, guaranteed, according to him, to produce a really objective estimate of any situation, though it never seemed to work with Mildred. Her long, bony, aristocratic face took on its usual smooth smile.

'Really, Dan, one of these days you'll end up like a fly, walking upside down on the ceiling.'

'Never mind about me,' he said curtly. 'Isn't it true?'

'Then in that case I can go to Helen's with an easy mind,' she said blandly. 'What have I said wrong now, ducky?' she asked when she saw his scowl.

'Never mind,' he said. 'You wouldn't understand.'

And she wouldn't. It was no use telling Mildred that nothing in the world was so over as a marriage that was over. It was not until she was leaving with Flurry for Helen's that she really realized how depressed he was.

'Maybe I shouldn't go,' she said.

'It's a bit late to change your mind now,' he said, rubbing it in.

'Danny, don't let Min upset you!' she begged. 'I'm a silly bitch, but you knew that when you married me. And I'm not going to get more sensible with age.'

He made a suitable gloomy reply, and later set off down the road to meet Min's train. He knew it was all going to be desperately unpleasant.

In fact, it proved the opposite. Min came out of the little suburban train, holding out her arms to him as though she had only been away for a holiday. She was older and fatter, and he thought she had a shade too much make-up on, but she was as lively and natural as ever. Within five minutes they were sitting in the bar opposite the station, chattering away like the old cronies they were. They had so much to talk about; there were so many of the old neighbours who had died or married or had families. When they got out of the bus and Min saw the big house, with Bawn peering anxiously out the front door for them, she pretended to change her mind.

'Is this Mildred's house?' she asked. 'My God, I feel like the new maid!'

Bawn came running up the path and Min gave her a great hug.

'Child of grace!' she cried. 'Where did you get the looks from? Not from your father?'

Tim appeared, a bit red and a fraction of a second off the beat, and Dan could have murdered him. He had a heavy, sullen, angry face, though he did warm up a little when he saw Min.

'Oh, Tim,' she cried, 'you've grown such a great big man!'

Dan and she got the supper together. She was all lit up, and it wasn't only the effect of the children and himself. It was plain inquisitiveness as well. She poked her nose shamelessly into cupboards and rooms, commenting loudly on the taste and utility of everything. Dan suddenly felt curiously guilty at having put her to sleep in the spare room. He could hardly have put her anywhere else, because there wasn't room for another bed in Bawn's little den, but with all of them together, it seemed uncouth, as if he were emphasizing a gap that was already only too plain.

It wasn't that she attracted him any more but that he could not erect artificial barriers between himself and someone who at any moment could let drop a remark that brought back all their past life together. Her remarks about the neighbours had already reminded him of Tim's infant crush on the tall girl next door who used to advise him about the garden. Those two nice sisters and their kindly old mother – how could he have forgotten them so completely?

The telephone rang and Dan answered it. It was a long-distance call, and he was sure it must be Mildred, reassuring herself about him. Instead, it turned out to be a man, who apparently wanted to reassure himself about Min, and he found himself raging against Mildred – and the man. Then he grinned, amused at his own touchiness.

Min returned from the hall, red and laughing, obviously delighted at having been rung up and embarrassed at having to explain it.

'Just a friend giving me a tip for the big race tomorrow,' she said modestly.

'Oh, still keen on the horses!' said Dan. The horses had been one of the things they disagreed on. He was a prudent and censorious man, and Min had far too much wildness in her for his taste.

He felt a bit of a fool when he went to her room to show her how the electric fire worked. She did one of her sly schoolgirl acts, joining her hands behind her back and raising herself on her toes. She felt none of his awkwardness and was getting great fun out of his embarrassment. At last, she made him laugh too and he threw a cushion at her.

'Ah, don't stop, Dan,' she said. 'Mildred's made a proper toff out of you.'

She went to the kitchen and made another pot of tea, and they sat over the electric fire till late into the night, discussing the children.

'Of course, Bawn is lovely,' she said thoughtfully. 'Anybody would get on with Bawn.'

'Ah, Tim is all right too,' Dan said defensively. 'It's just that he's so moody. That's why I sent him to school. Not that it seems to have done him much good.'

'I fancy there are times when Tim hates the whole damn lot of us,' Min said. 'He's more sensitive than Bawn, really.'

'Don't let me disillusion you,' he said and kissed her goodnight.

'Goodnight, love,' she said, and gave him a warm embrace in which there was no mockery. After it he found himself very wakeful. He was all churned up inside, going over his own conduct and Min's and getting so heated over it that he felt like going downstairs and having it all out with her again. Then he wondered if she wasn't feeling the same. For a few moments he even fancied he heard her crying.

Crying in a sleeping house had always been a peculiar horror to him. He imagined he heard it even when there was nothing to hear but the wind. It was like no one you knew crying about anything you could understand. It was more like the whole world crying in its sleep. A couple of times this weakness had got him into extraordinary situations, even to holding the hand of a drunken old woman in a boarding house while she complained of her daughter-in-law. Faces you saw in the street or about the house rarely told you anything; it was only faces that you scarcely saw at all that told the truth.

Now, in his cautious way he got up and stood on the landing for several minutes listening. Either the crying had ceased or he had been imagining it. All the same, he tiptoed down the stairs and listened at Min's door till he heard her breathing evenly.

Next morning, when he returned from a brief visit to the office, Bawn beckoned him into the kitchen.

'Daddy, I wish you'd talk to Tim about the way he's carrying on,' she said.

'Why? What's Tim up to now?' he asked with no great interest. As a small child Bawn had made quite an art of getting Tim into trouble and she hadn't altogether got over it yet.

'He won't even make an effort to be nice to Mummy,' she said angrily. 'I'll fling something at him if he goes on. He just sits there with his book and his disapproving air as if Mummy were the Penitent Thief or the Prodigal Son or something.'

'It's probably only strangeness, you know,' Dan said defensively.

'You can call it that,' snapped Bawn. 'I call it plain snobbery. Mum isn't good enough for him now. And the trouble is, she cares more about that fellow's big toe than about my whole body.'

Dan reflected for a moment on the remarkable understanding that girls showed of their mothers, and wondered whether this wasn't the reason that their mothers usually appreciated them so little.

'If I catch him at it, I'll knock the snobbery out of him,' said Dan. 'Where is Mummy?'

'In your room, dolling herself up,' Bawn replied guiltily. 'You can't even see your face in that old bathroom mirror.'

Dan gave a snort of amusement. It was plain that whatever grief Tim had caused them, Min and Bawn had been having a heavenly time, trying on Mildred's dresses. However differently they might feel about her personality, they were at one when it came to her frocks.

'By the way, did Mummy tell you her friend had bought a new house?' Bawn asked, trying hastily to divert him.

'Which friend?' asked Dan cautiously.

'The lady who rang her up last night.'

'Oh, the *elderly* lady,' said Dan, amused at Min's access of modesty and relieved that there were limits even to Bawn's understanding of her. 'Yes, I believe she goes in for house property.'

But he also realized that Bawn had not been making it up about Tim. At lunch he was sulky, silent, superior, scowling at them all from under heavy brows.

When Min asked him when they got up at school he corrected her bluntly.

'We rise at seven,' he said. 'We retire at nine thirty,' he added.

'And when do you go to bed?' asked Dan.

'At nine thirty,' he said. 'I told you.'

Bawn handled it magnificently in a way that, Dan knew, would have really endeared her to Mildred. A high-spirited, working-class, Irish girl in a snobbish English school, she had a hard time of it, but she made it sound so funny that Dan and Min both laughed outright. The attention they paid her seemed to irritate Tim.

'It's entirely your own fault if they treat you like that,' he said in his deep authoritative voice.

'How is it Bawn's fault, Tim?' Dan asked, trying to keep the rancour out of his tone.

'She behaves exactly like the Stuarts,' said Tim. 'She treats other girls as the Stuarts treated their parliaments.'

113

'I'd sooner be Charles II than your old Cromwell anyway,' Bawn said.

'I was not defending Cromwell,' said Tim.

'And how do you manage, Tim?' asked Dan.

'I model my conduct on Queen Elizabeth,' Tim said solemnly.

'And if Queen Elizabeth had the girls in our school to handle, she mightn't be such a model either,' spluttered Bawn.

That evening they all went to the pictures and had tea in the kitchen when they got home. Having had one restless night Dan went straight to bed. This was a bad mistake, as he discovered when he tried to sleep. He put the light on again and began to read. Then he thought he heard a noise downstairs and opened the bedroom door. This time there could be no mistake about it. He could distinctly hear the weeping. He went straight downstairs to Min's room. He would have done the same if Mildred had been there. All he wanted was to take that stupid, pig-headed woman in his arms and comfort her for the wrong she had done to himself and the children.

'Asleep, Min?' he asked, opening her door.

Her breathing was enough to tell him he had guessed wrongly. Then real panic swept over him. He closed Min's door quietly and rushed back to Tim's room. He switched on the light.

'What's going on in this house?' he asked in a jovial voice.

Tim started up with a brave show of astonishment, but his red eyes betrayed him.

'Hullo, Dad,' he said. 'What time is it?'

'Too early for me,' Dan said, sitting on the side of his bed. 'I suppose you didn't hear any noise?'

'No, Dad,' said Tim. 'Did you?'

'My imagination, I suppose,' said Dan.

'It might be the pictures,' said Tim. 'Pictures keep me awake too.'

'No, I don't think it's the pictures,' said Dan. 'I think it's having Mother in the house, don't you?'

'What's that, Dad?' Tim asked, sitting up and feeling for his hand.

'Don't you find it upsetting, after all these years?'

'I suppose I do,' said Tim, and Dan saw the flash of fresh tears.

And suddenly Dan realized that he must tell the child everything, good and bad. Dan was a cautious, secretive man. He knew perfectly well that more harm was done by well-intentioned people who tried to explain themselves than was ever done by those who kept their mouths shut. But he knew as well that Tim and he were in the same trouble and that Tim could not handle it alone. This was something that even Mildred wouldn't understand. It was something that could happen only between father and son. He hadn't even told Mildred the full story of his married life, and now he went through it to the end, not seeking words, nor evading them when they came – trying to be fair to Min but not trying too hard. After all, it wasn't fairness the boy wanted but some understanding of the human reality behind, even if it hurt.

Tim was in a state of enchantment. He sat up in bed, his hands about his knees, his eyes fixed on Dan's as though he might miss some shade of meaning. It reminded Dan of the way he had sat years before, listening to *Treasure Island*. Then he had tried to project himself into a world where boys were strong and brave. Now he was trying to project himself into a world in which grown-ups were hurt and powerless, striking out wildly at people they loved.

'So that's how it is,' Dan concluded gently. 'I was fond of your mother once, and I'm still fond of her, but we've been apart too long. She has new friends, like the man who rang her up the first night she came. I have new friends. The real reason I wasn't sleeping was that I'd behaved like a pig. I didn't go to her room to say goodnight as I should have done.'

'Why didn't you, Dad?' asked Tim, and Dan knew he wasn't being merely critical. He was trying to get Dan to explain to him his own behaviour.

'I suppose I was modelling my conduct on Queen Elizabeth,' said Dan with a grin and Tim smiled sadly. Probably that bit of rudeness had been on his conscience too.

'For all I knew,' said Dan, 'she was lying awake, brooding on it. I knew it might be years before I could make up for it. I knew one of us might die even before I got the chance. That's how the damn thing happens, Tim. You pass a room, and wonder if it's worth your while dropping in, and day after day for the rest of your life, you pass it again and feel you'd give anything on God's earth for the chance of one word with somebody who isn't there to hear it. Nobody knows how cruel he is until it's too late. So I just went down to see if Mother was asleep.'

'And was she?' asked Tim.

'Don't worry,' said Dan. 'I'll make up for it tomorrow. Goodnight, old man.'

'Goodnight, Dad,' said Tim. And then, in a sniffle, 'Don't worry about Mummy. She knows you like her all right.'

Dan noticed the slight emphasis on the 'you'. Half an hour later he heard Tim's door open and shut. This was something he hadn't calculated on, but he decided it was better to leave it that way. If it was Min's turn for a sleepless night she might as well resign herself to it.

The weekend was a great success, and the children were to spend part of the Christmas holidays with Min. They all saw her off and the children's eyes were red. When they sat together in the front room it was as though the bottom of the world had dropped out for them. Then Tim suddenly started up and charged into the hall.

'There's Mildred,' he said, as though he had been waiting for her and from the hallway Dan heard his voice. 'Hullo, Mildred, welcome home! Hullo, Flurry, old scout! You sit down and I'll get the tea, Mildred.'

'Don't attempt it,' Bawn cried, storming out after him. 'You'll only make a mess of the kitchen again.'

'Please, Bawn, put Flurry to bed for me,' said Mildred. 'Poor Flurry is exhausted.'

'I am not,' screamed Flurry. 'I want to play.'

Dan saw that Mildred only wanted to get him alone. She was all lit up about something, and though he was glad to see her, he suspected her of making fun of him.

'What is it?' he asked.

'Don't you know?' she whispered. 'Didn't you hear? What on earth have you done to Tim? Do you know he kissed me?'

More Stories (1954)

Private Property

My mother was never really happy about my being in the secret revolutionary army, and Father hated it. Father was a natural conservative who hated change on principle, and he had a shrewd idea of the sort of family whose lack of balance would cause them to be mixed up in it. Having relatives in the lunatic asylum would naturally be a predisposing factor. Another would be having come from some backward place like Carlow. Father disliked my great friend, Mick Ryan, for no other reason than that.

Now, I was a well-balanced young fellow. I will say that for myself. I didn't drink; I smoked very little; I was regular at work and contributed my fair share to the housekeeping. So I didn't fly off the handle as another might have done, and I did my best to explain to Father that this was all only passion and prejudice on his part, that nothing would ever improve if it depended on people like him, and that it didn't really matter who a man was or where he came from. It had no effect on Father. He didn't want things improved. He wanted them to last out his lifetime the way they were.

He tried to keep me in check by making me be home at ten, but I felt that as a revolutionist as well as a wage earner, I had to stick out for half past. It was the old story. He wouldn't give me a key and go to bed like a sensible man. One lock wasn't enough for him. The world was too uncertain with thieves and murderers forever on the prowl. He had three separate bolts on the front door and had to bolt them himself before he could sleep. There was no use arguing with a man like that.

We of the secret army met in a Gaelic League hall in a back street and discussed dispatches from Dublin telling us to be armed and ready for the great day. I didn't see how we were to arm ourselves at all, the way things were going. Our Quartermaster – a stocky little stone-mason called Johnny Forrestal – was a bitter old pill who had been a revolutionary from the age of fifteen and had been

117

in five gaols and on three hunger strikes. He was above suspicion, and almost above criticism by kids like ourselves, but he had no luck. As soon as ever we scraped together a few pounds from the men's subscriptions and bought a couple of rifles the police nosed them out. It was making us all depressed, and the Adjutant, Tom Harrison, was really savage. He said Johnny was too old, but I knew it wasn't Johnny's age that came against him; it was his vanity.

Johnny simply couldn't walk down a street in that stocky portentous way of his without advertising that he was a man who had fought in two wars and was only waiting his chance to fight in a third. He had toadies who gave him all the admiration he needed, and I suspected that he spilled everything to them.

But if Johnny was tough, Harrison was tougher. He was a grocer's curate from down the country and looked like a seminarist in mufti. He was a man who never hesitated to speak his mind, and as this was a privilege Johnny liked to reserve for himself, there was always bad blood between them.

'I tell you again there's a spy in the camp,' Harrison shouted one night we were discussing the latest catastrophe.

'Maybe you'd tell us who he is,' Johnny said with a face on him like one of his own tombstones.

'If I knew he wouldn't be there long,' said Harrison.

'You'd shoot him, I suppose?' Johnny asked with a sneer.

'I would shoot him.'

'He got no information out of me anyway,' Johnny said in a surly tone. 'I could keep my mouth shut before some people here were born.'

This was Johnny at his old game of turning the discussion into a vote of confidence, and he'd done it too often for my liking.

'I'm afraid I agree with Tom, Johnny,' I said.

'Then why don't you do the job yourself?' asked Johnny, leaving it to be understood what would happen if I did.

'I don't want to make a personal matter of it, Johnny,' I said, keeping my temper.

'And I *do* want to make a personal matter of it,' said Harrison, losing his. 'Damn it, we're only wasting our own time till we learn to keep our equipment safe. I say Larry is the man for the job.'

So that was how, at the age of seventeen, I came to be Brigade Quartermaster, and, though it may sound like self-praise, they never had a better. Mick Ryan was a tower of strength to me. He was a tall, handsome, reckless devil who worked on the railway, and the pair of us made a grand team because he made me do things that ordinarily I'd have been too shy to do, while I stopped him doing things he would have done when his imagination ran away with him. In the evenings we went into pubs on the quays, talking to sailors and giving assumed names. When we began, we had only one Smith and Wesson pistol belonging to Mick's brother who was in the British Army, and even for this we had only Thompson gun ammunition, but within six months we were getting in guns from Hamburg and Lisbon and packing them away in a dump we had built on the hill behind the church. Mick and I had dug it out ourselves and propped it with railway sleepers. We even put an old bed in it so that we could sleep there. Not that I ever stayed out all night, but Mick was a bit of a rambler.

By this time the police were beginning to realize that it wasn't old Johnny Forrestal they had to deal with and they panicked. Dwyer, the superintendent, called the detectives together and warned them that there would be sackings if something wasn't done. They did their best but it wasn't very good. You could see that someone had tipped them off about me and Mick because our houses were watched by detectives with bikes, and we made a new game out of giving them the slip.

To tell the truth, I was a bit flattered by all this attention. It was the first time that anyone had taken me seriously. At first, Father couldn't believe it, and after that he was stunned. He stood for hours behind the curtains in the front room, watching the detectives, and sometimes getting mad with the detective and sometimes with me. He discovered that the detective's wife kept hens, so he dropped poisoned bread in her garden. At the same time he tried to make me stay in at night, but no Brigade Quartermaster with an ounce of self-respect could let himself be locked in at ten. Father locked me out, but behind his back Mother left the window open. Then he fastened the window catch himself but I got over the back wall. After that he contented himself with muttering prophecies to himself about what was in store for me.

'Aha, they think they're cleverer than their fathers, but they'll be taught. Mark my words! The rope will teach them. *Then* they'll see how clever they were.'

I made a point of it that no one should know the whereabouts of the dump except Mick, myself and Harrison. Mick was opposed even to Harrison's knowing, but, seeing that both of us were liable to be picked up any day, I thought this was carrying secrecy too far.

Besides, I knew that Mick was prejudiced against Harrison for reasons that had nothing to do with the organization. In his own way Mick was as bad as Father. It was one of the main drawbacks of the movement – private quarrels – and I was forever begging Mick to keep out of them and think only of the principle. But Mick hadn't a principle in his head; he liked or hated people, and that was all there was to it.

Now the reason he hated Harrison was this. Harrison was married to the sister of Mick's friend, Joe Ward, another member of the organization and as decent a poor devil as ever drew breath, only for his misfortune. He had married a flighty woman who bore him four kids but omitted to make a proper home for them because the horses took up all her spare time and money. Between illness and debt poor Joe was half-distracted. Mick, being a single man and very open-handed, was always helping him, but Harrison – at least according to Mick – would do nothing for him. This cut poor Joe to the heart because he was an emotional man, always laughing or crying; he dearly loved his sister, and, when she married Harrison, he had given them a magnificent clock as a wedding present – something he could badly afford.

Now, I didn't doubt that for a moment, but I could see Harrison's point of view as well. That was always my trouble; being a reasonable man I could see everyone's point of view. After all, Harrison was a married man, too, with a kid of his own, and he wasn't earning so much in the grocery and bar that he could afford to be generous on Mick's scale. Besides, I had the feeling that helping Joe was really an acute case of casting your bread upon the waters. Personally, I would have been damn full sure it wouldn't come back.

But for the sake of the organization I tried to keep the peace between Mick and Harrison. I praised them both to one another, and any little admission I could wring out of one I passed on to the other. It was all for the cause. I was a conscientious officer, even if I was only seventeen, and in those days I was innocent enough to believe that this was all that was needed to keep Ireland united.

That was where the ferry-boat left me. It began innocently enough the day Joe Ward discovered that his wife had been to a money-lender and borrowed seven pounds. To poor Joe, weighed down with troubles, this seemed like the end of the world. He was never what you'd call a well-balanced man, and for a while he was probably a bit off his head. Instead of going to his sister, who might have raised a few shillings for him unknown to Harrison, or to Mick, who would have borrowed the money himself to help him, he went to the pub where Harrison worked. He stood at the door with his hands out and the tears streaming down his long clown's face and said dramatically: 'Look at me, Tom Harrison! Look at me! Happier men floated out Lough Mahon.'

Now, in spite of what happened afterwards, I want to be quite fair about this. Though Mick called Harrison a mean bastard, my own impression of him was that he wasn't a bad chap at all, really, and that, given time to get used to the idea, he might have done something substantial for Joe. I understood his position. I might have taken the cautious line myself, for after all, where was this thing going to end?

'Begor, Joe,' he said, 'if I had it you'd be welcome, but the way it is with me, I haven't.'

'I'm sorry for your troubles, poor man,' said Joe with withering scorn and stalked out on him. Of course, Harrison was leaping. After all, he had only been playing for time, and while it's bad enough to be asked for money, it's a hard thing to be insulted when you don't fall over yourself giving it. I sympathized with Harrison. As I say, the only excuse I could see for Joe was that he wasn't in his right mind at the time. I saw his point of view, too, of course. That's the worst of being a fair-minded man; you can't buy any friends with half-hearted sympathy.

Well, next evening, when I was pushing my bicycle back up Summerhill from work, who did I see but Harrison, coming towards me, looking very serious. He barely saluted me.

'Nothing wrong, is there, Tom?' I asked.

'Plenty, I'm afraid,' he said stiffly, and made to go on.

'Nothing to do with the organization, Tom?' I asked, turning the bike and walking back down the hill with him. Of course, it was the organization that was on my mind.

121

'Oh, nothing,' he said in the same tone. 'A purely private matter.' You could take it to mean I should mind my own business, but I didn't think he intended it that way. I could see he was very upset. 'Larceny!' he said then. 'Burglary! My house broken into and looted while I was at work. Oh, nothing to do with the organization!'

'For God's sake!' I said. 'Was much taken?'

'Oh, only a clock!' he snapped, and then, in case I might think he hadn't enough cause to be in a state about it: 'A valuable clock.'

The word struck a familiar chord, but for a while I couldn't place it. Then I remembered where I'd heard of that clock before.

'That wouldn't be the clock Joe Ward gave you, Tom?' I asked.

'It would,' he said, stopping to give me a suspicious glance. 'It is. How do you know about it?'

'Oh, only that Mick Ryan mentioned it to me once,' I said in confusion.

'Whoever gave it, the clock is my property now,' said Harrison, moving on.

'And what are you going to do about it?' I asked.

'I'm going to put the police on him,' Harrison said defiantly, and I knew by his truculent tone that he was a bit ashamed of himself. To us, of course, the police were never anything but enemy spies. It gave me a nasty turn. Besides, I was tired and beginning to feel that to keep our fellows together would take more than compliments.

'On who, Tom?' I asked.

'Who do you think? On Ward, of course. It's about time that fellow was taught a lesson.'

I had not been thinking of anyone in particular, and the name gave me a start. Then I could feel myself getting red with embarrassment.

'Oh, was it Joe took it?' I said.

'Walked into the house and took it from under my wife's eyes,' Harrison said indignantly.

'And you're going to put the enemy police on him?' I asked.

'Who else is there, man?' he retorted hotly.

'Well, I was thinking that maybe the organization might do something,' I said.

'And while I was waiting for the organization to do it my clock would be sold.'

'Oh, I'm not criticizing you,' I said. 'I was only thinking of the effect it would have on young fellows in the organization – an officer going to the enemy about another member.'

'But damn it, man, if someone broke into your house tonight and stole valuable property wouldn't you do the same?' he asked.

'If I had any property, and the man was a common thief, I dare say I would,' I admitted.

'There's nothing uncommon about Joe Ward only his impudence,' said Harrison. 'Now it's all very well to talk, Larry,' he went on in a more reasonable tone, 'and you and I agree about most things, but whatever government you have, you must protect private property. Even an army of occupation has to do that.'

'Oh, I'm not denying it, Tom,' I said, making the best I could of an argument that was a bit abstract for me. 'Only I don't think you're being fair to poor Joe. I don't really, Tom. My own impression is that the man can't have been right in the head.'

'He was sufficiently right in his head to come to my house while I was out at work,' said Harrison.

So we went on together, past the church at the foot of the hill and over the New Bridge, with me still arguing for the sake of appearances. It was the organization I was thinking of, and the scandal and disagreements that were bound to follow, with some of the lads backing Harrison and others backing Joe Ward, but nothing was farther from Harrison's mind. He hadn't a principle in his head any more than Father or Mick. All he could think of was his blooming old clock. I knew if he didn't do something about it he wouldn't sleep, only lie awake, noticing the silence in the house, and mourning for his clock as if it was someone that had died on him. I felt gloomy and desperate. It was a spring evening, coming on to dusk, and the metal bridges and the back streets full of old warehouses gave me the creeps. There seemed to be no hope for idealism, the way things were.

I remained outside on the quay while Harrison went into the barracks. It was a big, red-brick building with a few lights burning. I wondered if I should be there at all and what I'd say about it to the lads at our next meeting. I decided that there was nothing wrong in waiting since the man was so upset. It was the same thing as with Mick. He'd get in a bake, and do something he shouldn't, and then regret it after. It all came of a want of principle.

Nothing happened for a long time, and I began to wonder whether Dwyer, the superintendent, hadn't taken the chance of locking Harrison up. There was a light in his office, which I recognized because I had plans of the whole building in the dump. I saw a figure come to the window and look up and down the river and decided that I'd better get a move on quick. I jumped on the bicycle and started to ride away. Then I glanced back and saw two detectives get into a car and follow me. I got cold all over because I knew I had no way of escape. But then the car passed me out and I realized that they had not been following me at all. I decided to follow them instead. I had a good notion of where they were going, and I knew Harrison would be inside till they came back.

They stopped outside a tenement house on another quay. There were no curtains in the windows and no lights but candles. A couple of women were leaning out of the windows and they began to pretend the police had come to call on them. The detectives paid no attention and walked straight in the hallway as though they knew where they were going.

When they came out three minutes later, each of them was carrying a clock. Joe Ward followed them out in his shirt sleeves, a thin, consumptive man with glasses and a mad air. He stood on the steps of the house and addressed the detectives and the crowd that had gathered. Like all emotional men, he laughed as if he was crying, and cried as if he was laughing, and only that I knew him so well I'd have laughed at him myself.

'There's the great Irish patriot for you!' he bawled, waving one arm wildly. 'There's the great Republican chief, General Tom Harrison, putting the Free State police on his own poor misfortune brother-in-law, and all over an old clock! A clock I gave him for his wedding when 'tis a dose of poison I should have given him! There's the great patriot, a fellow that wouldn't lend you a bob if the children died of hunger at his feet. God help Ireland and God help the poor! Give me back my own clock anyway, ye robbers of hell! Give me back the clock I bought with my own couple of ha'pence!'

They ignored him and drove off. This time they got well away from me and I only arrived back at the barracks in time to see Harrison coming out. He had his own clock under his arm, wrapped up, and you could see the comfort it gave him. He wasn't the same man at all. That is the only way I can describe him. He was bubbling with good nature towards myself and the whole world, and nothing would do him only to unwrap the clock for me to admire it. It was a good clock all right.

'Ah, it may teach that fellow some sense,' he said, but there wasn't a hint of indignation left in him, nothing but his own basic good humour. 'He should know better than to think he can get away with things like that.'

With the picture of Joe fresh in my mind, I didn't feel like discussing it. I had the impression that poor Joe would get away with damn little in this world or the next. In a curious way I began to understand Mick Ryan's attitude to Harrison. It was against my principles but I couldn't help it.

'Who did you see inside?' I asked.

'You'd never believe,' said Harrison with a chuckle.

'Not Dwyer, surely?' I asked. I could hardly believe that Dwyer would concern himself about a thing like a stolen clock.

'Oh, one of the detectives recognized me, of course,' said Harrison. 'Dwyer came down himself and brought me up to his office to wait. He took it more seriously than I did, as a matter of fact, but I suppose he has to; it's his job. He told them to bring in every clock in the place. They brought two.'

'I saw them at it,' I said.

'Did you follow them?' he asked eagerly. 'What happened?'

'Joe came out and made a bit of a scene. There was a crowd.'

'Tell me, Larry, was he mad?'

It was all too palsy-walsy for me.

'He was upset. You'd hardly blame him.'

'I do not blame him, Larry,' Harrison said gravely. 'I'm genuinely sorry for that unfortunate wretch. We all told him what that woman was like, but he wouldn't believe us. God knows, if there was anything I could do for him, I'd do it.'

The benevolence that clock produced in Harrison was simply astonishing. He was so full of good nature that he never even noticed that I didn't share it with him.

'Tell us about Dwyer,' I said to get away from it.

'Oh, he stood me a drink, man,' said Harrison, beginning to chuckle again. 'You should have come in with me. You'd have enjoyed it.'

'I saw him in the window.'

'Oh, he saw you as well. There are no flies on Dwyer.'

'Did he ask any questions?'

'Questions? He never stopped.'

'About what?'

'About you and Ryan and the dump. Oh, naturally pretending to have a great admiration for us all, particularly you. He said he was like that himself when he was younger. Like hell he was . . . Stand in here for a minute.'

He whispered the last words, glancing hastily over his shoulder to see if we were being followed, and then pulled me into a dark archway. He was very excited.

'Do you know that he offered me money to tell him where the dump was?' he whispered angrily. 'Big money! He said the organization was riddled with spies; that every gun Johnny Forrestal bought was reported to him twice over inside twenty-four hours. They meet him after midnight at some hideout of his in town.'

I believed him, unfortunately, and my feeling of gloom deepened. Of course, I had always suspected that there was a spy, but it was a different thing to be sure of it. For the future I knew that I should trust nobody. All the same I wasn't feeling so kindly towards Harrison as to look for sympathy from him.

'I was afraid of that,' I said. 'I guessed Johnny talked too much. Dwyer isn't getting the information now though.'

'That's what I told him,' said Harrison. 'He said he was getting plenty, but that's only bluff. Otherwise, why would he offer to bribe me? . . . But imagine it! Fellows you'd be drinking with one minute stealing down there the next to swear your life away. What sort of conscience can they have?'

'If they have a conscience,' I said despondently. In the badly lit street, supperless, cold and tired, I was beginning to wonder if there was any opportunity for idealism, and if Father wasn't right after all.

'Dwyer laughed at me when I said that,' said Harrison ruefully as he walked on. '"Nonsense, man,' he said. 'I could put a call through on that telephone this minute and bring in two men you know well that are giving information about you, and you'd damn soon see they're not so different from yourself. Poor devils! Maybe they got into a spot of trouble over a woman and they wanted the money.'"

'They couldn't do without women, I suppose,' I said. Naturally, at seventeen they were about the last thing I wanted.

And then, three weeks later, the dump was raided and everything in it seized, including Mick Ryan with all the Brigade papers on him. It was a pure fluke that I wasn't there myself. Mick, who was a resourceful chap, got rid of the papers by distributing cigarettes wholesale to the detectives and lighting them with letters he pulled from his pockets. Only for that, I'd have been in gaol with him. From the barracks he slipped me out a note that just read: 'Shoot Harrison'. Mick was a dramatic sort of fellow on occasions.

Of course, I didn't shoot Harrison. To begin with, I hadn't any absolute proof, though I didn't need it. I was sick at the loss of my priceless dump, all the lovely rifles and automatics smuggled in from all over Europe, and all sold over an old clock. If I were to have Harrison shot it would mean that I would have to start again from the beginning, and I didn't have the heart. I just dropped out of the organization altogether.

Father was very cocked-up about Mick's arrest because it confirmed his old prejudice against Carlow people, and the first night the detective failed to show up near the house he positively purred. He gave me five shillings for myself and told me that in future I could stay out until eleven. 'Or so,' he added. He didn't want to seem severe, and he had been a bit wild himself at my age.

It was the first time he had been civil to me for a year and a half, and I got so sentimental that I broke down and told him the whole story. To my astonishment he flew into a wild rage and wanted to know why I didn't chuck a bomb into Harrison's house. That very night he took a pot of white paint and a brush and painted the front wall of Harrison's house with the words 'Spies and Informers Beware'. God, you can never tell with Conservatives!

I took the five bob, but I was home by half past ten. I had decided to go to the School of Commerce in the evenings. I was beginning to see that there was no future in revolutions – not in Ireland, anyway. It may be different elsewhere.

Domestic Relations (1957)

Fish For Friday

Ned McCarthy, the teacher in a village called Abbeyduff, was wakened one morning by his sister-in-law. She was standing over him with a cynical smile and saying in a harsh voice:

'Wake up! 'Tis started.'

'What's started, Sue?' Ned asked wildly, jumping up in bed with an anguished air.

'Why?' she asked dryly. 'Are you after forgetting already? There's no immediate hurry, but you'd better get the doctor.'

'Oh, the doctor!' sighed Ned, remembering all at once why he was sleeping alone in the little back room and why that unpleasant female was in the house. She only came when Kitty was having a baby, and she went round like a Redemptorist missioner on an annual retreat.

He dressed in a hurry, said a few words of encouragement to Kitty, talked to the kids while swallowing a cup of tea, and got out the car. He was a well-built man in his early forties with fair hair and pale grey eyes, nervous and excitable under his placid manner. He had plenty to be excited about. The house, for instance. It was a fine house, an old shooting lodge, set back at a distance of two fields from the main road, with a lawn leading to the river and steep gardens climbing the wooded hill behind. It was an ideal house, in fact, the sort he had always dreamed of, where Kitty could keep a few hens and he could garden and get in a bit of shooting. But scarcely had he settled in than he realized it was a mistake. The loneliness of the long evenings when dusk settled on the valley was something he had never even imagined.

He had lamented it to Kitty, and it was she who had suggested the car, but even this had drawbacks because it needed as much attention as a baby. When Ned was alone in it he chatted to it encouragingly; when it stopped he kicked it viciously, and the villagers swore he had actually been seen stoning it. This and the fact that he sometimes talked to himself when he hadn't the car to talk to had given rise to the legend that he had a slate loose.

He drove down the lane and across the footbridge to the main road. Then he stopped before the public house at the corner which his friend, Tom Hurley, owned.

'Anything you want in town, Tom?' he shouted.

'What's that, Ned?' said a voice from within, and Tom himself, a small, round, russet-faced man, came out with his wrinkled grin.

'I have to go to town. Is there anything you want?'

'No, no, Ned, I think not, thanks,' Tom said in his hasty way, all the words trying to come out together. 'All we wanted was fish for the dinner, and the Jordans are bringing that.'

'I'd sooner them than me,' Ned said, making a face.

'Och, isn't it the devil, Ned?' Tom said with a look of real anguish. 'The damn smell hangs round the shop the whole day. But what the hell else can you do on a Friday? Is it a spin you're going for?'

'No, for the doctor,' said Ned.

'Och, I see,' said Tom, beginning to beam. His expression exaggerated almost to caricature whatever emotion his interlocutor might be expected to feel. 'Ah, please God, it'll go off all right. There's no hurry, is there? Come in and have a drop.'

'No, thanks, Tom,' Ned said with resignation. 'I'd better not start so early.'

'Ah, hell to your soul, you will,' fussed Tom. 'It won't take you two minutes. Hard enough it was for me to keep you sober the time the first fellow arrived.'

Ned got out of the car and followed Tom inside.

'That's right, Tom,' he said in surprise. 'I'd forgotten about that. Who was it was here?'

'Och, God, you had half the countryside in,' Tom said, shaking his head. 'It was a terrible night, a terrible night. You had Jack Martin, the teacher, and Owen Hennessey, and that publican friend of yours from town – what's that his name is? – Cronin. That's right, Larry Cronin. Ye must have dropped just where ye stood, glasses and all. The milkman found ye next morning littering the floor, and ye never even locked the doors after ye. Ye could have had my licence taken from me.'

'Do you know, I'd forgotten about that completely,' said Ned with a pleased smile. 'My memory isn't what it was. I suppose we're getting old.'

'Och, well, 'tis never the same after the first,' said Tom, and he poured a large drink for Ned and a few spoonfuls for himself. 'God, isn't it astonishing what the first one does for you, Ned?' he added in his eager way, bending across the counter. 'You feel you're getting a new lease of life. And by the time the second comes you're beginning to wonder will the damn thing ever stop. God forgive me for talking,' he said, lowering his voice. 'Herself would have my life if she heard me.'

'Still, there's a lot of truth in it, Tom,' said Ned, relieved to feel that the gloom in his mind was nothing unusual. 'It's not the same thing at all. And I suppose that even that is only an illusion. Like when you fall in love and think you're getting first prize in the lottery, while all the time it's only Nature's little way of putting you on the spot.'

'Ah, well, they say it all comes back when you're a grandfather,' said Tom with a chuckle.

'But who wants to be a grandfather?' asked Ned, already feeling sorry for himself with his home upset, that unpleasant woman bossing the house and more money to be found somewhere.

He drove off but his mood had darkened. It was a grand bit of road between his house and the town, with the river below him on the left, and the hills at either side with the first faint wash of green on them like an unfinished water-colour. Walking or driving, it was a real pleasure to him because of the prospect of civilization at the other end. The town was only a little run-down port, but it had shops and pubs and villas with electric light, and a water supply that did not give out in May, and there were all sorts of interesting people to be met there. But the prospect didn't cheer him now. He realized that the rapture of being a father doesn't go on repeating itself and it gave him no pleasure at all to look forward to being a grandfather. He felt decrepit enough the way he was.

At the same time he was haunted by some memory of days when he was not decrepit but careless and gay. He had been a Volunteer and roamed the hills for months with a column, wondering where he would spend the night. Then it had all seemed uncomfortable and dangerous enough, but at least he had felt free. Maybe, like an illusion of re-birth at finding himself a father, it was only an illusion of freedom, but it was terrible to think he wouldn't be able to feel it any more. It was associated in his mind with high hills and wide views, but now his life had descended into a valley like the one he was driving along. He had descended into it by the quiet path of duty – a steady man, a sucker for responsibilities, treasurer of the Hurling Club, treasurer of the Republican Party, secretary of three other organizations. He talked to the car as he did whenever something was too much on his mind.

'It's all Nature, old girl,' he said despondently. 'It gives you a set of illusions, but all the time it's only bending you to its own purposes as if you were a cow or a tree. You'd be better off with no illusions at all. No illusions about anything! That way, Nature wouldn't get you quite so soon.'

Being nervous, he did not like to drive through the town. He did it when he had to, but it made him flustered and fidgety so that he missed seeing who was on the streets, and a town was nothing without people. He usually parked his car outside Cronin's pub on the way in and walked the rest of the way. Larry Cronin was an old comrade of revolutionary days who had married into the pub.

He went in to tell Larry. This was quite unnecessary as Larry knew every car for miles around and was well aware of Ned's little weakness, but it was a habit and Ned was a man of more habits than he realized himself.

'I'm leaving the old bus for half an hour, Larry,' he called through the door in a plaintive tone that expressed regret for the inconvenience he was causing Larry and grief for the burden that was being put on himself.

'Ah, come in, man, come in!' cried Larry, a tall, engaging man with a handsome face and a sunny smile that was quite sincere if Larry liked you and damnably hypocritical if he didn't. His mouth was like a showcase with the array of false teeth in it. 'What has you out at this hour of the morning?'

'Oh, Nature, Nature,' Ned said with a laugh, digging his hands into his trouser pockets.

'How do you mean, Nature?' asked Larry, who did not understand the allusive ways of intellectuals but admired them none the less.

'Kitty, I mean. I'm going for the doctor.'

'Ah, the blessings of God on you!' Larry said jovially. 'Is this the third or the fourth? You lose count after a while, don't you? You

131

might as well have a resiner as you're in. Ah, you will, you will,
God blast you! 'Tis hard on the nerves. That was a great night we
had the time the boy was born.'

'Wasn't it?' said Ned, beaming at the way people remembered
it. 'I was only talking to Tom Hurley about it.'

'Ah, what the hell does Hurley know about it?' Larry asked
contemptuously, pouring out a half tumbler of whiskey with the
air of a lord. 'The bloody man went to bed at two. That fellow is
too cautious to be good. But Jack Martin gave a great account of
himself. Do you remember? The whole first act of *Tosca*, orchestra
and all. "The southern sunlight" he called it. You didn't see Jack
since he came back?'

'Was Jack away?' Ned asked in surprise. He felt easier now,
being on the doctor's doorstep, and anyhow he knew the doctor
would only be waiting.

'Ah, God he was,' said Larry, throwing his whole weight on the
counter. 'In Paris, would you believe it? He's on the batter again,
of course. Wait till you hear him on Paris! 'Tis only the mercy of
God if Father Clery doesn't get to hear of it.'

'That's where you're wrong, Larry,' Ned said with a smile.
'Martin doesn't have to mind himself at all. Father Clery will do
all that for him. If an inspector comes round while Martin is on
it, Father Clery will take him out to look at the antiquities.'

'Begod, you might be right, Ned,' said Larry. 'But you or I
couldn't do it. God Almighty, man, we'd be slaughtered alive.
'Tisn't worried you are about Kitty,' he asked gently.

'Ah, no, Larry,' said Ned. 'It's only that at times like this a man
feels himself of no importance. A messenger boy would do as well.
We're all dragged down to the same level.'

'And damn queer we'd be if we weren't,' said Larry with his
lazy, sunny smile, the smile Ned remembered from the day Larry
threw a Mills bomb into a lorry of soldiers. 'Unless you'd want to
have the bloody baby yourself.'

'Ah, it's not only that, Larry,' Ned said gloomily. 'It's not that
at all. But you can't help wondering what it's all about.'

'Why, then indeed, that's true for you,' said Larry, who, as a
result of his own experience in the pub had developed a gloomy
and philosophic view of human existence. After all, a man can't be
looking at schizophrenia for ten hours a day without wondering if
it's all strictly necessary. 'And 'tis at times like this you notice it

– men coming and going like the leaves on the trees. Ah, God, 'tis a great mystery.'

But that wasn't what Ned was thinking about either. He was thinking of his own lost youth and what had happened to him.

'That's not what I mean, Larry,' he said, drawing neat figures on the counter with the bottom of his glass. 'What I mean is you can't help wondering what happened yourself. We knew one another when we were young, and look at us now, forty odd and our lives are over and we have nothing to show for them. It's as if when you married some good went out of you.'

'Small loss as the fool said when he lost Mass,' retorted Larry, who had found himself a comfortable berth in the pub and lost his thirst for adventure.

'That's the bait, of course,' Ned said with a grim smile. 'That's where Nature gets us every time. A small contribution, you'll never miss it, and before you know where you are, you're bankrupt.'

'Ah, how bad Nature is!' exclaimed Larry, not relaxing his grin. 'When your first was born you were walking mad round the town, looking for people to celebrate it with, and there you are now, looking for sympathy! God, man, isn't it a great thing to have someone to share your troubles with and give a slap on the ass to, even if she does let the crockery fly once in a while? What the hell about an old bit of china?'

'That's all very well, Larry, *if* that's all it costs,' said Ned darkly.

'And what the hell else does it cost?' asked Larry. 'Twenty-one meals a week and a couple of pounds of tea. Sure, 'tis for nothing!'

'And what about your freedom?' Ned asked. 'What about the old days on the column?'

'Ah, that was different, Ned,' Larry said with a sigh, and at once his smile went out and his eyes took on a dreamy, faraway look. 'But sure, everything was different then. I don't know what the hell is after coming over the country at all.'

'The same thing that's come over you and me,' Ned said with finality. 'Nature kidded us, the way it kidded us when we got married, and the way it kidded us when the first child was born. There's nothing worse than illusions for getting you into the rut. We had our freedom and we didn't value it. Now our lives are run for us by women the way they were when we were kids. This is Friday and what do I find? Hurley waiting for someone to bring home the fish. You waiting for the fish. I'll go home to a nice plate of fish, and I'll guarantee to you, Larry, not one man in that flying column is having meat for his dinner today. One few words in front of the altar and it's fish for Friday the rest of your life. And they call this a man's country!'

'Still, Ned, there's nothing nicer than a good bit of fish,' Larry said wistfully. 'If 'tis well done, mind you. *If* 'tis well done. And I grant you 'tisn't often you get it well done. God, I had some fried plaice in Kilkenny last week that had me turned inside out. I declare to God if I stopped that car once I stopped it six times, and by the time I got home I was after caving in like a sandpit.'

'And yet I can remember you in Tramore, letting on to be a Protestant to get bacon and eggs on Friday,' Ned said accusingly.

'Oh, that's the God's truth,' Larry said joyously. 'I was a divil for meat, God forgive me. I used to go mad seeing the Protestants lowering it, and me there with nothing only a boiled egg. And the waitress, Ned – do you remember the waitress that wouldn't believe I was a Protestant till I said the 'Our Father' the wrong way for her? She said I had too open a face for a Protestant. How well she'd know a thing like that about the 'Our Father', Ned!'

'A woman would know anything she had to know to make you eat fish,' Ned said, finishing his drink and turning away. 'And you may be reconciled to it, Larry,' he added with a mournful smile, 'but I'm not. I'll eat it because I'm damned with a sense of duty, and I don't want to get Kitty into trouble with the neighbours, but please God, I'll see one more revolution before I die, even if I have to swing for it.'

'Ah, well,' sighed Larry, 'youth is a great thing, sure enough . . . Coming, Hanna, coming!' he boomed as a woman's voice yelled from the room upstairs. He gave Ned a nod and a wink to suggest that he enjoyed it, but Ned knew that that scared little rabbit of a wife of his would be wanting to know about the Protestant prayers, and would then go to Confession and ask the priest was it a reserved sin and should Larry be sent to the Bishop. And then he remembered Larry during the Dunkeen ambush when they had to run for it, pleading with that broad smile of his, 'Ah, Christ, Ned, let me have one more crack at them!' 'No life, no life,' Ned said aloud to himself as he sauntered down the hill past the church. And it was a great mistake taking a drink whenever he felt badly about the country because it always made the country seem worse.

Someone clapped him suddenly on the shoulder. It was Jack Martin, the vocational-school teacher, a small, plump, nervous man with a baby complexion, a neat greying moustache and big, blue, innocent eyes. Ned's face lit up. Of all his friends Martin was the one he warmed to most. He was a talented man and a good baritone. His wife had died a few years before and left him with the two children, but he had not married again and had been a devoted if over-anxious father. Yet two or three times a year, and always coming on to his wife's anniversary, he went on a tearing drunk that left some legend behind. There was the time he tried to teach Verdi to the tramp who played the penny whistle and the time his housekeeper hid his trousers and he got out of the window in his pyjamas and had to be brought home by the parish priest.

'MacCarthy, you scoundrel, you were hoping to give me the slip,' he said delightedly in his shrill nasal voice. 'Come in here one minute till I tell you something. God, you'll die!'

'If you wait there ten minutes, Jack, I'll be back to you,' said Ned. 'There's only one little job I have to do, and then I'll be able to give you my full attention.'

'All right, all right, but have one little drink before you go,' Martin said irritably. 'One drink and I'll release you on your own recognizances. You'll never guess where I was, Ned. I woke up there, as true as God!'

Martin was like that. Ned decided good-humouredly that five minutes' explanation in the bar was easier than ten minutes' argument in the street. It was quite clear that Martin was 'on it'. He was full of clock-work vitality, rushing to the counter for fresh drinks, fumbling over money, trying to carry glasses without spilling them, and talking thirteen to the dozen. Ned beamed at him. Drunk or sober, he liked the man.

'Ned, I'll give you three guesses where I was.'

'Let me see,' said Ned in mock meditation. 'I suppose 'twould never be Paris?' and then laughed boyishly at Martin's hurt air.

'You can't do anything in this town,' said Martin. 'Next, I suppose you'll be telling me what I did there.'

'No,' said Ned gravely. 'It's Father Clery who'll be telling about that – from the pulpit.'

'Ah, to hell with Father Clery!' said Martin. 'No, Ned, this is se-e-e-rious. This is vital. It only came to me in the last week. We're only wasting our time in this misfortunate country.'

'You're probably right,' Ned said urbanely. 'The question is, what else can you do with Time?'

'Ah, this isn't philosophy, man,' Martin said testily. 'This is se-e-e-rious, I tell you.'

'I know how serious it is all right,' Ned said complacently. 'Only five minutes ago I was asking Larry Cronin where our youth was gone.'

'Youth?' said Martin. 'But you can't call that youth, what we have in this country. Drinking bad porter in public houses after closing time and listening to someone singing 'The Rose of Tralee'. Sure, that's not life, man.'

'But isn't that the question?' asked Ned. 'What is Life?' Ned couldn't help promoting words like 'time' and 'life' to the dignity of capital letters.

'How the hell would I know?' asked Martin. 'I suppose you have to go out and look for the bloody thing. You're not going to find it round here. You have to go south, where they have sunlight and wine and good cooking and women with a bit of go.'

'And you don't think it would be the same thing there?' Ned asked quietly.

'Oh, God, dust and ashes! Dust and ashes!' wailed Martin. 'Don't go on with that! Don't we get enough of it every Sunday in the chapel?'

Now, Ned was very fond of Martin, and admired the vitality with which in his forties he still pursued a fancy, but he could not let him get away with the notion that Life was merely a matter of geography.

'But that's a way Life has,' he said oracularly. 'You think you're seeing it, and it turns out it was somewhere else all the time. Like women; the girl you lose is the one that could have made you happy. Or revolutions; you always fought the wrong battle. I dare say there are people in the south wishing they could be in some wild place like this. I admit it's rather difficult to imagine, but I suppose it could happen. No, Jack, we might as well resign ourselves to the fact that wherever Life was, it wasn't where we were looking for it.'

'For God's sake!' cried Martin. 'You're talking like an old man of ninety-five.'

'I'm forty-two,' Ned said with quiet emphasis, 'and I have no illusions left. You still have a few. Mind, I admire you for it. You were never a fighting man like Cronin or myself. You kept your youthfulness longer. You escaped the big disillusionments. But Nature has her eye on you as well. You're light and airy now, but what way will you be next week? We pay for our illusions, Jack. They're only sent to drag us deeper into the mud.'

'Ah, 'tisn't that with me at all, Ned,' said Martin. 'It's my stomach. I can't keep it up.'

'No, Jack, it's not your stomach. It's the illusion. I saw other men with the same illusion and I know the way you'll end up. You'll be in and out of the chapel ten times a day for fear once wasn't enough, with your head down for fear you'd catch a friendly eye and be led astray, beating your breast, lighting candles and counting indulgences. And that, Jack, may be the last illusion of all.'

'I don't know what the hell is after coming over you,' Martin said in bewilderment. 'You're – you're being positively personal. And Father Clery knows perfectly well the sort of man I am. I have all Shaw's plays on my shelf, and I never tried to hide them from anybody.'

'I know that, Jack, I know that,' Ned said sadly, overcome by the force of his own oratory. 'And I'm not being personal, because it isn't a personal matter. It's only Nature working through you. It works through me as well only it gets me in a different way. My illusion was a different sort, and look at me now. I turn every damn thing into a duty, and in the end I'm good for nothing. I know the way I'll die too. I'll disintegrate into a husband, a father, a schoolteacher, a local librarian, and fifteen different sorts of committee men, and none of them with enough energy to survive. Unless, with God's help, I die on a barricade.'

'What barricade?' asked Martin, who found all this hard to follow.

'Any barricade,' Ned said with a wild sweep of his arms. 'I don't care what it's for so long as it means a fight. I don't want to die of disseminated conscientiousness. I don't want to be one of Nature's errand boys. I'm not even a good one. Here I am arguing with you in a pub instead of doing what I was sent to do.' He paused for a moment to think and then broke into his boyish laugh, because he realized that for the moment he had forgotten what it was. 'Whatever the hell it was,' he added. 'Well, that beats everything! That's what duty does for you!'

'Ah, that's only because it wasn't important,' said Martin.

'That's where you're wrong again, Jack,' said Ned, beginning to enjoy the situation thoroughly. 'Maybe it was of no importance to us but it was probably of great importance to Nature. What *was* the damn thing? My memory's gone to hell.'

He closed his eyes and lay back limply in his chair, though even through his self-induced trance he smiled at the absurdity of it.

'No good,' he said briskly, starting up. 'It's an extraordinary thing, the way it disappears as if the ground opened and swallowed it. And there's nothing you can do about it. It'll come back of its own accord, and there won't be any reason for that either. I was reading an article about a German doctor who says you forget because it's too unpleasant to think about.'

'It's not a haircut?' Martin asked helpfully, and Ned, a tidy man, shook his head.

'Or clothes?' Martin went on. 'Women are great on clothes.'

'No,' said Ned, frowning. 'I'm sure it wasn't anything for myself.'

'Or for the kids? Shoes or the like?'

'It could be, I suppose,' said Ned. 'Something flashed across my mind just then.'

'If it's not that it must be groceries.'

'I don't see how it could be. Williams deliver them every week, and they're nearly always the same.'

'In that case it's bound to be something to eat,' said Martin. 'They're always forgetting things – bread or butter or milk.'

'I suppose so, but I'm damned if I know what,' said Ned. 'Jim,' he said to the barman, 'I'm after forgetting the message I was sent on. What do you think of that?'

'Ah, I suppose 'twas fish, Mr Mac,' said the barman.

'Fish!' said Martin. 'The very thing.' 'Fish?' repeated Ned, stroking his forehead. 'I suppose it could be, now you mention it. I know I offered to bring it for Tom Hurley and I had a bit of an argument with Larry Cronin about it. He seems to like it.'

'I can't stand the damn stuff,' said Martin, 'only the house-keeper has to have it for the kids.'

'Ah, 'tis fish all right, Mr Mac,' the barman said. 'In an hour's time you wouldn't forget it, not with the stink of it all round the town. I never could stand it myself since the last war and all the poor unfortunates getting drowned. You'd feel you were making a cannibal out of yourself.'

'Well, obviously, it has something to do with fish,' said Ned with a laugh. 'It may not exactly be fish, but it's something very like it. Anyway, if that's the case, there's no particular hurry. We'll have another of these, Jim.'

'Whether it is or not, she'll take it as kindly meant,' said Martin. 'The same as flowers. Women in this country don't seem to be able to distinguish between them.'

Two hours later, the two friends, more talkative than ever, drove up to Ned's house for lunch.

'Mustn't forget the fish,' Ned said with a knowing smile as he reached back for it. 'The spirit of the revolution, Jack – that's what it's come to.'

At that moment they both heard the wail of a new-born infant from the front bedroom. Ned grew very white.

'What's that, Ned?' asked Martin, and Ned gave a deep sigh.

'That's the fish, Jack, I'm afraid,' said Ned.

'Oh, God, I'm not going in so,' Martin said hastily, getting out of the car. 'Tom Hurley will give me a bit of bread and cheese.'

'Nonsense, man!' Ned said boldly, knowing perfectly well what his welcome would be if he went in alone. 'I'll get you something. That's not what's worrying me at all. What's worrying me is why I thought it could be fish. That's what I can't understand.'

Domestic Relations (1957)

Androcles
and the Army

'Politics and religion!' Healy said when Cloone, the lion-tamer, announced that he was joining the army for the duration of the war. 'Even a lion-tamer you can't trust not to get patriotic on you. The next thing will be the Clown getting religion and wanting to join the Trappists.'

He argued, he pleaded, he threatened proceedings for breach of contract, but Cloone only retorted with arguments about the danger of the country. Threatened by the Germans, threatened by the English, threatened even by the Americans, she needed all her children. She did like hell, thought Healy, and his long red mournful nose shuddered and began to ascend like a helicopter.

'Look, Cloone, there's nothing wrong with the bloody country,' he said patiently. 'It's the show I'm thinking of. 'Twill only be the mercy of God if we can keep going at all. You know yourself there isn't another man in Ireland within a hundred miles of you, and if there was anyone outside it half as good, I couldn't get him in. Not with a war on.'

'Ah, damn it, I know, I know,' Cloone said in anguish. 'I like the show as well as you do, and I like my lions better than I like the show, but if I have to choose between my lions and my country, I have to choose my country. It's as hard on me as it is on you, but war is always like that. Look at the sugar rationing!'

Healy pleaded up to the very last minute. He knew that not only could he not get another lion-tamer, but that even if he could, the man would be nothing like as good as Cloone. He hated to admit it, because he was a professional, and Cloone was nothing but an amateur, a Dublin stone-mason who wasn't happy at home. But because he was a professional, Healy knew an artist when he saw one. What others could do by fear, Cloone could do by a simple dropping of his voice. Healy could not see what magic there was in that sudden change of pitch, but he could see the result all right, because an angry lion would suddenly uncoil his tightened springs of muscle and roll over to be stroked like a cat. And Cloone would play with it like a cat, his blue eyes soft with emotion, and mutter as though to himself, 'God, Ned, isn't he beautiful?' 'Beautiful my ass!' Healy would think, as his helicopter nose began to ascend, but he wouldn't say it. It was plain enough that the lion knew what Cloone meant, and there was no saying but that he might understand what Healy meant as well.

Anyone seeing Cloone with animals would be bound to think of St Francis of Assisi, but Healy knew that that was the only thing saintly about him. He had a wicked temper, and brooded for months on imaginary insults and injuries. He would begin to mutter about a half-crown that he said had been unjustly stopped from his pay six months before and go on nagging till Healy asked God for patience with him. 'Listen, Cloone,' he would say, 'I told you fifty times that there was nothing stopped. If you don't believe me, I'll give you the bloody half-crown to take your puss off me.' Then spasms of outraged pride would run through Cloone like electric shocks, and he would cry, 'It isn't the money, Ned. It's not the money. It's the principle.'

But Healy, who had been in show business from the time he was five, knew that artists had no principle; and it took a man like himself who hated animals but loved human beings to put up with it at all. Cloone knew that, too. He knew that Healy had some sort of hold over him and he didn't like it. 'I tame lions, but Healy tames me,' he said one night in a public house with a sort of exasperated giggle that showed he was half ashamed of it.

But even Healy could not persuade him to stay on during the war. And it wasn't just because the show was only a ghost of itself, stripped by restrictions and regulations; it was pure unqualified, blood-thirsty patriotism – a thing Healy could not understand in a mature man. 'If you can ever say an artist is mature,' he added darkly.

It was a wrench for Cloone, because he really loved the few animals that had been left him, he liked Healy and the others, and he enjoyed the wandering life and the crowds of the small towns and fair greens. He had taken to the life as though he had never known any other. He left with a breaking heart to be shut up in a Nissen hut, dressed in uniform, stood to attention, stood at ease, presenting arms and forming twos and fours, as if he himself was only a mangy old circus lion. Besides, he was an

141

awkward, excitable man who could never remember his right from his left, and he shouldered arms when he should have presented them and had to listen to the tongue-lashings of a sergeant without even replying. It often reduced him to mutinous tears, and he lay on his cot at night, exhausted, thinking of himself as a caged old animal with his spirit broken. Then he shed more tears because he felt he had never understood wild animals before.

All the same, his desperate sincerity stood to him. They had to make a corporal of him in the end, and in the way of other great artists, he was prouder of his two miserable stripes than of all his other attainments. Drinking in a pub with another man, he could not help glancing at his sleeve with a girlish smirk.

Then one day he opened a local paper and saw that Doyle's World-Famous Circus was visiting Asragh for one evening the following week. Filled with excitement, he went off to ask for a pass. Everyone in the battalion knew his trade, and there was no difficulty about the pass. The trouble was that the whole battalion felt it had a personal interest in the circus and wanted passes as well. On the afternoon of the show two lorry-loads of troops left for town, and the Commandant, looking darkly at them, said, 'Well, boys, if the Germans come tonight, the country is lost.'

In the main street the soldiers scattered to the public houses to wait for the circus, but Cloone hurried off joyously to the fair green. In his temperamental way he threw his arms round Healy and sobbed with pleasure till Healy grabbed him by the shoulders and inspected his uniform, the green gloves tucked in the shoulder strap and the natty little cane.

'God Almighty, John, you look a sight!' he said with affectionate malice.

'Ah, how bad I am!' Cloone said, giving him a punch. 'I'm all right, only for the hair,' he added self-consciously. 'I feel lost without the old wig.'

''Twould take more than a haircut to make a soldier of you,' said Healy.

'How well they had to give me the stripes!' said Cloone, looking admiringly at his sleeve.

'You're like a baby in a new sailor suit,' said Healy. 'Come in and have a drink.' They went into the caravan, and Healy poured half tumblers of neat whiskey for the pair of them. 'Ah, John, I thought you had more sense, boy,' he added as he handed one to Cloone.

'Oh, God, Ned, I know, I know,' said Cloone, wriggling miserably on the edge of the bed. 'I'm not suited to the life at all. But when you have it in the family! The father was in the Rising, and the two uncles were in the Volunteers, and I'm the same. Even now, when I'm in the Army I can never hear the Anthem without the heart rising in me.'

'I know. Like a pony when the band strikes up,' Healy said cruelly.

'Ah, 'tisn't alike, Ned,' Cloone said sadly. 'But believe me, the day I get my discharge, I'll be back. Tell me, who have you on the lions?'

'Who do you think?' Healy asked gloomily. 'Darcy – the Strong Man.' The description was added not by way of information, but as a sneer, for Healy, who had a wretched stomach and suffered agonies from it had seen the Strong Man screaming his head off with an ordinary toothache. It had left an indelible impression on his mind.

'Ah, God, Ned, sure Darcy could never handle a lion!' Cloone said in consternation. 'Darcy is too rough.'

'Darcy is too frightened,' Healy said candidly. 'Here, let me fill that for you.'

'Is he any good at all with them?' Cloone asked tensely.

'He's good all right,' Healy replied with a frown, for, though he didn't like Darcy much, he was a fair man. 'He's very conscientious. They don't like him; that's the only thing.'

'But how could they, Ned?' Cloone asked feverishly. 'Lions could never get on with a Strong Man. Lions are sensitive, like women. What possessed you to give them to Darcy?'

'I was damn grateful to Darcy for helping me out of the hole you left me in,' Healy said candidly. 'And I'll never criticize any man that does his best.'

It was like old times for Cloone, sitting in the twilight with his friend, sniffing the thick circus smells all round him and talking to the old hands who came in to ask how he was doing. He told them all about the importance of the army and the danger to the country, and they listened politely but with utter incredulity. It was at times like this that you could see Cloone wasn't really one of them, Healy thought sadly.

When he went off to take the gate, Cloone with a foolish smile nodded in the direction of the big cage and said, 'I'll slip round and have a look at Jumbo and Bess.' They might have been two old sweethearts, the way he talked of them.

'Plenty of time, John,' Healy said. 'They won't be on for half an hour yet.'

From Healy's point of view the main satisfaction of the evening was the number of soldiers who came, officers and all. Healy couldn't help liking a bit of style, and style was something that was disappearing from the Irish countryside. He was only sorry for the miserable show he had for them, and the two lions that were all he had left when the rationing was done. And then their turn came and Darcy stood ready, a huge and handsome man with a self-conscious air.

'Ladies and gentlemen,' the Cockney ringmaster explained, 'owing to Emergency restrictions, Doyle's collection of wild animals – the greatest in the world – has been considerably depleted. But the two lions you are about to see are not just ordinary animals. No, ladies and gentlemen, these two terrible lions are the most savage ever to be captured alive. In the capture of these lions – especially for Doyle's Circus – no less than eight famous big-game hunters lost their lives, as well as an untold number of simple natives.'

Then the band – what was left of it – played; the big cage was rolled on; Darcy whipped the curtain back, and then – after a moment of incredulous silence – came a laugh that chilled Healy's blood. For, inside the cage, with his tunic open and his cap off, was Cloone, sprawled on the ground against the bars, embracing Jumbo with one arm and Bess with the other. The two lions had a smug, meditative air, as though they were posing for a family photograph. At the uproar from the audience, they raised their heads sharply and fresh screams broke out, because Jumbo was seen to be holding Cloone's green gloves in his jaws while Bess sedately held his cane. There was an atmosphere of intense domesticity about the scene that made Healy feel that instead of a cage there should be a comfortable living room with a good fire burning. As a turn, it was superior to anything that had yet been seen, but the circus hands felt it was disaster.

'Oh, my God!' muttered the ringmaster. 'This is awful. This is the end. How could a thing like this happen, Darcy?'

'That's Cloone,' said Darcy with a puzzled frown.

'I know damned well it's Cloone,' the ringmaster said severely. 'I hadn't imagined it was a casual visitor. But how the hell did he get in, and how are we to get him out? Come along now, John,' he called pathetically. 'You don't want to hold up the show.'

But Cloone was too far gone to notice anything except that he had the whole audience to himself.

'Bess wants me to desert,' he announced. 'She says the old war is after going on long enough.'

This delighted the soldiers because, for some reason Bess looked exactly as though she had been saying something of the kind.

'Leave the man go home to his mother,' said a voice.

'Oh, Christ!' said the ringmaster. 'We'll be the laughing stock of the whole country. Darcy, you go in and get him out, there's a good man!'

'Is it me?' Darcy asked angrily. 'How the hell can I go in with him there? They'd ate you, man.' All the same he was a conscientious man, if a bit slow-witted, and after a moment he muttered despairingly, 'Where's me hot bar?'

Two policemen who had been sitting near the front approached with their uniform caps in their hands to indicate that this was merely friendly curiosity and that nothing had yet occurred to require their official attention.

'Now, lads, what's the disturbance about?' the sergeant asked amiably. 'Wouldn't you come out of that cage like a good man and not be obstructing the traffic?'

Cloone began to giggle as the humour of it struck him.

'The door is open,' he said. 'Can't you come in and join the party.'

'What's that?' asked the sergeant.

'Come in and meet the family,' said Cloone.

'You're only making trouble for yourself,' the sergeant said sternly.

'Cowardy, cowardy custard!' Cloone said archly.

The sergeant glared at him for a moment and then put on his official cap. It had something of the effect of the judge's donning of the black cap in a murder trial. The younger policeman with a shy air put on his own.

'Someone will have to get him out,' the sergeant announced in an entirely different tone, the one that went with the cap.

'All right, all right,' Darcy said irritably, fetching his hot bar. He opened the door of the cage cautiously and the two lions rose and growled at him. Cloone jumped to his feet.

'Put that down,' he said in an outraged voice. 'Put it down, I say.'

'Get out of my way, God blast you!' snarled Darcy. 'Haven't I trouble enough without you?'

In a moment the atmosphere of domesticity had vanished. It was clear that Darcy hated the lions and the lions hated Darcy. For a few moments they eyed the Strong Man hungrily and growled; they slunk slowly back to the separate compartment at the end of the cage. Darcy, white in the face, slammed the gate behind them, and the ringmaster and the policeman, followed by Healy, entered the other compartment.

'Come home now, John,' Healy said softly.

'That's no way to treat my animals,' Cloone said.

'John! John! Remember the uniform.' A remark that, as he said later, he'd have to answer for on the Last Day because he cared as much about the uniform as he did about the danger to the country. But he was a man-tamer as Cloone was a lion-tamer: each made his own sort of soothing nonsensical noise.

'All right, all right,' Cloone muttered. 'Just let me say goodbye to them.'

'Don't let that man open the gate again or I won't be responsible,' Darcy shouted in a frenzy.

'I'll be responsible, Darcy,' Healy said shortly. 'Go on, John. Do it quick, and for God's sake don't let them out on us. Come on outside, boys.'

And there they had to stand outside the cage powerlessly while Cloone said goodbye to his pets. He opened the gate of the inner cage and stood there for a moment, overcome with emotion. The lions seemed to be overcome as well. After a moment Jumbo tossed his big head as though suppressing a sob and padded up to Cloone. Cloone bent and kissed him on the snout. Bess growled in a way that suggested a moan and came to lick his hand He kissed her as well. 'I'll be back, Bess, I'll be back,' he said with an anguished air. Then he drew himself up and gave them both a military salute. 'Company, present arms!' yelled one of the soldiers, and as Cloone staggered out they rose to cheer him. As Healy said, 'There was never the like of it seen in show business. If you could put it on as an act, you'd be turning them away.'

But for Cloone it was anything but show business. He strode straight up to Darcy.

'You bloody big bully!' he said with tears of rage in his voice. 'You had to take a red-hot bar to frighten these poor innocent creatures. Like every other bully you're a coward.'

He gave Darcy a punch, and the Strong Man was so astonished that he went down flat on the ground. There was fresh uproar in the audience. The soldiers were getting out of hand. Darcy rose with a dazed expression as the two policemen seized Cloone from behind. To give them their due they were less afraid of what Cloone would do to Darcy than of what Darcy might do to Cloone. He was one of those powerful melancholy men whose tragedy is that they can't have a little disagreement with a man in a pub without running the risk of manslaughter.

Cloone pulled himself away, leaving his unbuttoned tunic in the policeman's hands, and then made a dash for the side of the tent. He disappeared under the canvas with the two guards close behind and a score of soldiers after the guards to see that Cloone got fair play. As they were unbuckling their belts for the task, two officers got up as well and rushed out through the main entrance to see that the guards got fair play. It was all very confusing, and the show was as good as over.

They ran Cloone to earth in the kitchen of a cottage down a lane from which there was no escape. By this time he had had the opportunity of considering his own behaviour, and all the fight had gone out of him. Once more he was only a broken-spirited old circus lion. He apologized to the woman of the house for the fright he had given her, and she moaned over him like a Greek chorus, blaming it all on the bad whiskey. He apologized to the police for the trouble he had given them and begged them not to spoil their night's pleasure but to let him surrender himself. He apologized all over again to the two young lieutenants who appeared soon after. By this time he was trembling like an aspen leaf.

'I'm sorry I disgraced ye the way I did,' he muttered. 'I'll never forgive myself. If 'twasn't for the lions I wouldn't have done it.'

At his court martial he appeared on a charge of 'conduct prejudicial to good order and discipline, in that he, Corporal John Cloone, on the 18th day of September of the current year had appeared in public with his tunic in disorder and minus certain articles of equipment: viz. one pair of gloves and one walking stick (regulations).' The charge of assault was dropped at the instance of the President who suggested to the Prosecutor that, considering the prisoner's occupation in civil life, there might have been provocation.

But armies are alike the world over, and whatever their disregard for civilian rights, they all have the same old-maidish preoccupation with their own dignity, and Cloone lost his stripes. Healy asked him what better he could expect from soldiers, people who tried to turn decent artists into megalomaniacs like themselves. As if anybody had ever succeeded in turning a soldier into anything that was the least use to God or man!

Achilles' Heel

The Catholic Church has only one weak point which is well known to all the faithful. This is the type of woman who preys on celibates, particularly priests' housekeepers. The priest's housekeeper is a subject in itself, because tests have shown that when transferred to males who are not celibate it pines away and dies. To say that it is sexless is to say both too much and too little. Like the Church it pursues chastity for higher ends, which – in the matter of priests' housekeepers – means the subjection of men in a way that mere wives cannot comprehend. Wives, of course, have a similar ambition, but their purposes are mysteriously thwarted by love-making, jealousy and children; and it is well known that many wives break down and weep with rage when they think of the power of priests' housekeepers. *Their* victims, being celibate, have no children, and are automatically sealed off from other women, so that even women who have business to transact with them find they have to do it through the housekeeper.

The Bishop of Moyle was no exception. His housekeeper, Nellie, had been with him since the time he was a Canon, and even then, unknown to himself, he had always been referred to by his congregation as 'Nellie and the Canon'. 'Nellie and the Canon' disliked all-night dances, for instance, so all-night dances simply stopped. There was even a story that Nellie had once appeared on the altar and announced that there would be no eight o'clock Mass because she was keeping the Canon in bed. Even in those days she could not have been very old, and by the time I speak of her, she was a well-preserved woman with a fussy, humble, sugary air that concealed a cold intelligence. In private, her great rival, Canon Lanigan, used to call her 'La Maintenon', but when he visited the Bishop's he was as unctuous as herself, and affected to admire her cooking and even her detestable bottled coffee.

For all Nellie's airs and graces, she wasn't in the least taken in by the Canon; she knew he preferred old French mish-mash to her own simple, straightforward cooking, and she even warned the Bishop against him.

'God forgive me, my Lord,' she said meekly, 'I can't warm to Canon Lanigan. There's something about him that's insincere. Or am I just being silly? I know I'm a foolish old woman, but you knew that yourself the day you engaged me.'

Anyway, Nellie's cooking was not aimed at the Canon but at her own dear simple man – a giant with the heart of a child, as she often said herself in her poetic way. His only real fear was that he might fade away for want of proper nourishment. It wasn't that he was greedy, but that he didn't have much else to worry about. He knew what the appetites of old-fashioned clerics were like, and comparing his own accomplishments and theirs, he couldn't see for the life of him how he was ever going to reach the age of ninety. After eating a whole chicken for his dinner, he would sit in his study for hours with his hands folded on his lap, brooding on it, till Nellie stuck her head through the door.

'You're all right, my Lord?' she would cry.

'Ah, I'm not, Nellie,' he would say despondently over his shoulder. 'I'm feeling a bit low tonight.'

''Tis that chicken,' she would cry, making a dramatic entrance. 'I knew it. I said it to Tim Murphy. There wasn't a pick on it.'

'I was wondering about that,' he would say sadly, fixing her with his anxious blue eyes. 'I thought myself 'twas on the slight side.'

'What you want is a nice grilled chop.'

'I wonder, Nellie, I wonder,' he would mutter, shaking his head. 'There's a lot of eating in a chop.'

'Or cutlets, if you prefer them.'

'Well, cutlets make a nice late night snack,' he would say, beginning to relax.

'They do, but they're too dry. What you want is a good plate of nice curly rashers, with lots of fat. Sure, 'twas my own fault. I knew there was nothing in that chicken. I knew there should be rashers along with it, but the way I am, the head is going on me. I'm getting too old. One of these days I won't be able to remember my own name. . . And a couple of chips – sure, 'twould be the making of you.'

The Bishop was anything but a stupid man, but he did tend to take Nellie at her own valuation. He could easily have imagined her in various sorts of trouble. He could have imagined her lending her little savings to the breadman on foot of a proposal of marriage, or getting into debt with a bookmaker. When at last she came to him with her troubles, he couldn't conceive of her having any difficulty with the Revenue Commissioners, and she, it appeared, couldn't either.

'Ah, you said it yourself, my Lord,'she said ingenuously. 'This diocese was ever notorious for slander. But why would they try to fix it on me? I suppose they want to get their own candidate in – someone that would do their whispering for them. It is something I never would do, and I won't do it now, my Lord, even if they do say you are too old.'

'Who says I'm too old?' the Bishop asked with a flash of his blue eyes.

'Oh, don't ask me to tell you things like that,' she said with disgust. 'I'm fifteen years with you, and I never carried stories yet, let Canon Lanigan say what he likes.'

'Never mind about Canon Lanigan,' said the Bishop, feeling he was never going to get to the bottom of it. 'What did this fellow from the Revenue say?'

'Is it Tim Leary?' she asked. 'Sure, what could he say? Ah, 'tisn't that at all, my Lord, but the questions he asked me, the sly rogue! And the things he said! "The biggest smuggler in the whole country" – wasn't that a nice thing for him to say?'

'He called you "the biggest smuggler in the whole country"?' repeated the Bishop, between amusement and rage.

'Ah, how could he call me that?' she replied. 'Sure, the tongue would rot in his mouth. Is it a poor defenceless old woman like me? But that's what he meant all right, my Lord. Sure, I knew well what he had in his mind the whole time. Whiskey, petrol, tea, and things, my Lord, that I declare to you, as if I was going before my Maker this minute, I never heard the names of.'

'Ah, that fellow must be a bit soft in the head,' the Bishop said with a worried air. 'Which Learys does he belong to? Is it the Learys of Clooneavullen?'

In spite of the fact that he had been a Professor of Dogmatic Theology, the Bishop was convinced that you could explain everything about a man just by knowing who his parents were. The grace of God was all very well, but it wasn't the same thing at all as belonging to a good family.

'Aha!' she said, wagging a finger at him. 'Didn't I say exactly

151

the same thing myself? That his own father couldn't read or write, and he accusing me!'

'Never mind about his father,' the Bishop said earnestly. 'Sure, hadn't he an uncle up in the lunatic asylum? I knew him myself. What business has a fellow like that interfering with the likes of me? You tell him to come up here tomorrow, and I'll talk to him myself.'

'You will to be sure, my Lord,' she said complacently. Then at the door she stopped. 'But sure, why would you talk to a little whipper-snapper like that – a man like you that have the ear of the government? You would only have to tell them to send him somewhere else. How well he didn't mind going over your head. Ah, well, I suppose they told him you were too old.'

The Bishop meditated for a moment on that. When she mentioned his getting old she touched on his sore spot because he knew a lot of people thought he was getting old. And he saw her point about people's going over his head, which might, or might not, be the work of clerical opponents like Lanigan. He knew the secrets of power as well as Nellie did, and the most important of these is never to deal directly with your inferiors. Of course, in the eyes of God, they might be anything but inferiors, but nobody knew exactly how they *did* look in the eyes of God, so the best thing was to put them down before they became a menace.

'Very well,' he said in a detached voice that made Nellie's heart flutter. 'Where's my pen?'

It was a voice he used only when some parish priest had been seen drunk in a public place or a gang of young curates had started a card school. 'Give me my pen till I suspend Father Tom,' he would say in a dry voice to his secretary, or else, 'Give me my pen till I scatter them.' It was the voice of ultimate authority, of the Church Militant personified in her own dear man.

In spite of good detective work Nellie never did get to see the Bishop's letter to the Minister, Jim Butcher, but, on the other hand, the Bishop did not see the Minister's reply either: Nellie thought it might worry him too much. It ran:

'Dear Doctor Gallogly, how pleasant to hear from you again. Mrs Butcher was saying only yesterday that it was a long time since we saw you. I have had careful inquiries made about the matter you mention, and I am sorry to inform you that the statements of the local Revenue Officer appear to be fully substantiated. Your housekeeper, Miss Ellen Coneely, is the owner of licensed premises on the other side of the Border which have long been known as the headquarters of a considerable smuggling organization, and their base on this side is believed to be the Episcopal Palace. You will realize that the Revenue Commissioners hesitate to take any steps that might embarrass your good self, but you will also realize that this traffic involves a considerable loss of revenue. I should be deeply grateful for your Lordship's assistance in putting an early end to it. *Mise le Meas. Seumas O Buitséir, Aire.*'

Nellie turned cold when she read it. Things were worse than she imagined. It wasn't only Tim Leary she had to deal with but shadowy Commissioners and Ministers in Dublin who might be up to any sort of blackguarding. Nor could she rely on the Bishop himself to deal with them. He was a good, kind man, but the fire had gone out of him. She took up her own pen and wrote:

'Dear Sir, His Lordship, the Most Reverend Doctor Gallogly, Bishop of Moyle, has passed on to me your letter of May 3rd and asked me to reply to it for him. He says it is all lies and intrigues and not to bother him any more about it. He says is it likely he would not know what was going on in his own home, or is it a daylight robber you think he is. This campaign was started entirely by Timothy Leary, and as the Bishop points out, what better could you expect of a man whose uncle died in the Moyle Asylum, a wet and dirty case. The public house you talk of is only another matter of the lies. It does not belong to me at all, but to my unfortunate brother, a Commandant in the Army of Freedom (how are you?), and now a helpless invalid with varicose veins and six children. How would the likes of him be a smuggler? Timothy Leary will not be allowed to enter this Palace again. What do we pay taxes for? We were better off when we had the English. Your obedient servant, Ellen Coneely.'

There was something about this letter that gave Nellie great satisfaction. Though she did not recognize it, it illustrated to perfection the Achilles Heel of Catholicism, for though Dr Gallogly was entirely innocent of its contents, they left the Minister and his staff with a strong impression that the Bishop of Moyle was now the ringleader of a powerful smuggling gang. No doubt the poor old man was not responsible; old age took people in all sorts of different ways, but it was embarrassing because you couldn't possibly go raiding the Bishop's Palace for contraband. The very thought of what the newspapers would say about that made the Minister wince: the *Irish Times* would report it smugly, with the implication that whatever could be said against Protestant bishops, they drew the line at certain things; the *Irish Independent* would assert that instructions for the raid must have come from Moscow, while the *Irish Press* would compare it to the Casement forgeries.

'For God's sake, leave it as it is, Peter,' the Minister told his secretary. 'This thing is dynamite.'

Nellie, scared by the Minister's letter, worked feverishly and openly to get rid of the contraband in her possession, and Tim Leary knew it and was mortified.

Then one day a man was caught crossing the Border with a keg of whiskey strapped under his car, and Tim was able to trace the keg to Paddy Clancy's liquor store. Paddy had no alternative but to admit that he had sold the keg to the Bishop.

'Give us a look at the Bishop's account, Paddy,' Tim said irritably, and poor Paddy felt it would be safer to produce the ledger. It was an ugly moment. He was never a man to interfere in other people's business, but he knew of old that the Bishop's account was peculiar. Tim Leary looked at it in stupefaction.

'Merciful God, are you trying to tell me the Bishop drinks all that?' he asked.

'I wouldn't know, Tim,' said Paddy. 'I dare say bishops have a lot of entertaining to do – parish priests and that.'

'A gallon a man a night!' Tim cried. He was a rather hysterical young fellow, Paddy thought, and anyway took his job too seriously.

'Now, that's all very well, Tim,' Paddy said severely. 'I'm not in a position to ask my customers questions.'

'Well, I'm going to ask a few,' Tim said, headstrong as ever. 'And unless that man is an out-and-out criminal, he'll answer them, what's more. Give us that ledger.'

Paddy watched him from the door striding off up the street and decided that he wouldn't last long in his job – a young fellow who took things to the fair like that.

At the Palace, Nellie tried hard to head him off. She said first that the Bishop was out. Then she said he was sick, and finally that he had given orders not to admit Tim. Unfortunately for her, she could not get Tim to keep his voice down, and she knew to her cost that with the appetite of a child, the Bishop also had a child's curiosity, and a beggar could hardly come to the door without his peering out and listening. Suddenly, there was a step in the hall and the Bishop came out.

'That will do, Nellie,' he said mildly and came up to Tim with a threatening air, a handsome old man with a baby complexion and fierce blue eyes.

'Now, what do you want, young man?' he asked sternly.

'I'm investigating the smuggling that's going on in this locality and I'd like a few words with you, my Lord.'

'I already wrote to the Minister, young man, and told him I didn't know what I had to do with it.'

'If you'll listen to me for a few minutes I'll soon show you what you have to do with it,' said Tim.

'Aren't you a very saucy young fellow?' the Bishop said in a tone of reproach. 'What part of the world do you hail from?'

'I'm from Manister,' replied Tim, who couldn't be aware of the significance the Bishop attached to heredity.

'I thought you were John Leary's son from Clooneavullen,' the Bishop said in surprise.

'I'm nothing of the sort,' Tim said shortly. 'My father was a schoolmaster.'

'You're not Jim Leary's boy?' the Bishop said softly, resting his old hand on Tim's.

'I am, then,' said Tim, pleased to be identified at last.

'Come in, come in,' the Bishop said, giving his hand a squeeze. 'Your father was Headmaster there when I was a curate. No son of Jim Leary's is going to leave my house without something.'

'I'm on duty, my Lord,' said Tim, following him into his sitting room.

'Ah, sha, aren't we all?' asked the Bishop, going to the sideboard. With shaky hands he produced two glasses and a bottle of whiskey. He put a few spoonfuls in one glass and almost filled the other, which he gave to Tim.

'Now, you can tell me,' he said comfortably. Tim was beginning to realize that he liked the old man, a weakness of his that made him a bad investigator.

'Well, a fellow was caught trying to cross the Border three days ago with a keg of your whiskey slung under his car,' said Tim.

'A keg of my whiskey?' repeated the Bishop with amusement. 'But what would I be doing with a keg of whiskey?'

'That's what *I* was wondering,' replied Tim.

'I never bought a keg of whiskey in my whole life, man,' the Bishop said candidly. 'I wouldn't know what to do with it. A drop like this just to keep someone company is all I ever see of it. I haven't the constitution for whiskey.'

'If you'll take one look at your account in Paddy Clancy's ledger you'll soon see the sort of constitution you're supposed to have,' said Tim . . . 'Or maybe this is the one with the constitution,' he added fiercely as Nellie walked in with a bundle of bills in her hand.

'That's enough of the whispering and intriguing,' she said. 'I admit what I have to admit. 'Twas only to keep my unfortunate angashore of a brother out of the workhouse, a fellow that never did a hand's turn only fighting for Ireland. 'Twas people like me that had to do the real fighting. I will go if I'm made but I will not leave this house without my reference.'

'You could keep a houseful of of brothers out of what you made on the petrol alone,' Tim said angrily. 'And I suppose you forget the tea and the butter.'

'That will do,' the Bishop said firmly. 'Go away, Nellie,' he added over his shoulder in his dry voice, his episcopal voice.

Nellie looked at him in stupefaction and then burst into a howl of grief and went out, sobbing to herself about 'the fifteen good years of my life that I gave him, and this is all the gratitude I get'. The Bishop waited till her sobs had subsided in the kitchen, and then leaned forward with his hands joined between his knees.

'Do me a favour, Tim,' he said. 'You don't mind if I call you Tim?'

'I'm honoured, my Lord,' said Tim.

'But don't call me Paddy,' added the Bishop, an old joke that did not ring true. 'Tell me, how many people know about this?'

'You might say that, by this time, 'twas common property,' said Tim.

'And what do they think about me?' asked the Bishop.

'You must know yourself they have a great regard for you,' said Tim.

'They have,' the Bishop said drily. 'They have so much regard for me that they don't mind if I turn my house into a smugglers' den. They didn't suggest what I might be doing with the Cathedral?'

Tim saw then that the Bishop was more affected than he let on to be.

'What will they do to Nellie?' the Bishop added.

'Send her to gaol, I hope,' said Tim. 'Not to mention the fine, that will be worse for her.'

'What sort of fine?'

'It'll have to be calculated,' said Tim. 'But it'll probably run into a couple of thousand pounds.'

'A couple of thousand?' exclaimed the Bishop. 'Sure, I haven't that much money myself, Tim.'

'You may be damn full sure she has it,' said Tim.

'Nellie?' said the Bishop.

'And more along with it.'

'For the love of God!' the Bishop said softly and sat back, crossing his legs. 'And here was I, thinking she was only an old fool! Oh, after this, they'll say I'm not even fit to look after myself. They could put in a coadjutor on me over a thing like this.'

'They wouldn't do that,' Tim said in alarm.

'Oh, indeed they would,' the Bishop said gaily. 'And they'd be fully entitled. And that's not the worst of it. Do you know what's the worst thing about being old, Tim?' he added, leaning forward again. 'I'll tell you. By the time you finish your lunch you start worrying about your dinner. I suppose a man must have something to look forward to. When I was a young priest I didn't care if I never saw a dinner. And if they put Nellie in gaol, 'twill kill me. At my age I'm not going to be able to get another housekeeper like that.'

Tim was a generous young man, and, after all, the Bishop had been a friend of his father.

'Do you think you'd be able to control her for the future?' he asked.

'I do not,' replied the Bishop with his outrageous candour. 'A priest never controlled a woman yet. We haven't the experience, I suppose.'

'Begod, I'd soon control her if I had a free hand,' said Tim.

'Oh, I'll give you all the hand you want,' said the Bishop with an episcopal wave of his hand. ''Tis more in my interest than yours, before they have me married to her.' Then he got up and gave Tim a pat on the shoulder. 'You're a good boy,' he said, 'and I won't forget it for you. Butcher is a good enough fellow, only he's ruined with that wife of his.'

That afternoon the Bishop stood by the window with his hands behind his back and watched while Tim Leary loaded the lorries with commodities the Bishop had thought had gone from the world – chests of tea, bags of sugar, and boxes of butter. Nellie herself did not put in an appearance, but that night when she opened the door and said, 'Dinner is served, my Lord,' the Bishop sat down to a dinner in a thousand – juicy roast beef and roast potatoes with the tenderest of young peas drowned in butter. The Bishop ate his way through it, but he never addressed a word to her. He was thinking of the way he had had to coax and beg for it, an old man with nothing else to look forward to.

After that, he went to his study and took down the history of the diocese that had often comforted him before when he had dreamed of what his own name would look like in future editions, but that night it only made him feel worse. Looking back on the men who had held the see before him he couldn't think of one against whom there had been a breath of scandal, except for one eighteenth-century Bishop who had turned Protestant. He was beginning to think that turning Protestant wasn't the worst thing that could happen to a Bishop.

Then the door opened and Nellie looked in coyly.

'What way are you feeling now?' she whispered.

'Let me alone,' he said in a dry voice without even looking up. 'My heart is broken.'

'Ah, 'tisn't your heart at all,' she said. ''Tis that beef. 'Twasn't hung long enough. There isn't a butcher in this town will take the trouble to hang beef. Would I get you a couple of scrambled eggs?'

'Go away, I said!' he retorted, but she heard the tears in his voice.

'You're right,' she said. 'There's nothing in eggs only coloured water. O God, would I fry you a couple of rashers?'

'I tell you I don't want rashers, woman,' he said in a cry of pain.

'The dear knows, they're not worth it,' she admitted sadly. 'What are they only old bones with the hair still growing on them? What you want is a nice little juicy bit of Limerick ham with a couple of mashed potatoes and milk sauce with parsley. 'Twould make a new man of you.'

'All right, all right,' he cried angrily. 'Do what you like but leave me alone.'

Even the prospect of the ham could not lift his sorrow. He knew that whenever a woman says something will make a new man of you, all she means is that it will help to make an old one of you before your time.

The Wreath

When Father Fogarty read of the death of his friend, Father Devine, in a Dublin nursing home, he was stunned. He was a man who did not understand the irremediable. He took out an old seminary group, put it on the mantelpiece and spent the evening looking at it. Devine's clever, pale, shrunken face stood out from the rest, not very different from what it had been in his later years except for the absence of pince-nez. He and Fogarty had been boys together in a provincial town where Devine's father had been a schoolmaster and Fogarty's mother had kept a shop. Even then, everybody had known that Devine was marked out by nature for the priesthood. He was clever, docile and beautifully mannered. Fogarty's vocation had come later and proved a surprise, to himself as well as to others.

They had been friends over the years, affectionate when together, critical and sarcastic when apart. They had not seen one another for close on a year. Devine had been unlucky. As long as the old Bishop, Gallogly, lived, he had been fairly well sheltered, but Lanigan, the new one, disliked him. It was partly Devine's own fault. He could not keep his mouth shut. He was witty and waspish and said whatever came into his head about colleagues who had nothing like his gifts. Fogarty remembered the things Devine had said about himself. Devine had affected to believe that Fogarty was a man of many personalities, and asked with mock humility which he was now dealing with – Nero, Napoleon, or St Francis of Assisi.

It all came back: the occasional jaunts together, the plans for holidays abroad that never took place, and now the warm and genuine love for Devine which was so natural to Fogarty welled up in him, and, realizing that never again in this world would he be able to express it, he began to weep. He was as simple as a child in his emotions. When he was in high spirits he devised practical jokes of the utmost crudity; when he was depressed he brooded for days

159

on imaginary injuries: he forgot lightly, remembered suddenly and with exaggerated intensity, and blamed himself cruelly and unjustly for his own shortcomings. He would have been astonished to learn that, for all the intrusions of Nero and Napoleon, his understanding had continued to develop when that of cleverer men had dried up, and that he was a better and wiser man at forty than he had been twenty years before.

But he did not understand the irremediable. He had to have someone to talk to, and for want of a better, rang up Jackson, a curate who had been Devine's other friend. He did not really like Jackson, who was worldly, cynical, and something of a careerist, and he usually called him by the worst name in his vocabulary – a Jesuit. Several times he had asked Devine what he saw in Jackson but Devine's replies had not enlightened him much. 'I wouldn't trust myself too far with the young Loyola if I were you,' Fogarty had told Devine with his worldly swagger. Now, he had no swagger left.

'That's terrible news about Devine, Jim, isn't it?' he said.

'Yes,' Jackson drawled in his usual cautious, cagey way, as though he were afraid to commit himself even about that. 'I suppose it's a happy release for the poor devil.'

That was the sort of tone that maddened Fogarty. It sounded as though Jackson were talking of an old family pet who had been sent to the vet's.

'I hope he appreciates it,' he said gruffly. 'I was thinking of going to town and coming back with the funeral. You wouldn't come, I suppose?'

'I don't very well see how I could, Jerry,' Jackson replied in a tone of mild alarm. 'It's only a week since I was up last.'

'Ah, well, I'll go myself,' said Fogarty. 'You don't know what happened to him, do you?'

'Ah, well, he was always anaemic,' Jackson said lightly. 'He should have looked after himself, but he didn't get much chance with old O'Leary.'

'He wasn't intended to,' Fogarty said darkly, indiscreet as usual.

'What?' Jackson asked in surprise. 'Oh no,' he added, resuming his worldly tone. 'It wasn't a sinecure, of course. He was fainting all over the shop. Last time was in the middle of Mass. By then, of course, it was too late. When I saw him last week I knew he was dying.'

'You saw him last week?' Fogarty repeated.

'Oh, just for a few minutes. He couldn't talk much.'

And again, the feeling of his own inadequacy descended on Fogarty. He realized that Jackson, who seemed to have as much feeling as a mowing machine, had kept in touch with Devine, and gone out of his way to see him at the end, while he, the devoted, warm-hearted friend, had let him slip from sight into eternity and was now wallowing in the sense of his own loss.

'I'll never forgive myself, Jim,' he said humbly. 'I never even knew he was sick.'

'I'd like to go to the funeral myself if I could,' said Jackson. 'I'll ring you up later if I can manage it.'

He did manage it, and that evening they set off in Fogarty's car for the city. They stayed in an old hotel in a side-street where porters and waiters all knew them. Jackson brought Fogarty to a very pleasant restaurant for dinner. The very sight of Jackson had been enough to renew Fogarty's doubts. He was a tall, thin man with a prim, watchful, clerical air, and he knew his way around. He spent at least ten minutes over the menu and the wine list, and the head waiter danced attendance on him as head waiters do only when they are either hopeful or intimidated.

'You needn't bother about me,' Fogarty said to cut short the rigmarole. 'I'm having steak.'

'Father Fogarty is having steak, Paddy,' Jackson said suavely, looking at the head waiter over his spectacles with what Fogarty called his 'Jesuit' air. 'Make it rare. And stout, I fancy. It's a favourite beverage of the natives.'

'I'll spare you the stout,' Fogarty said, enjoying the banter. 'Red wine will do me fine.'

'Mind, Paddy,' Jackson said in the same tone, 'Father Fogarty said *red* wine. You're in Ireland now, remember.'

Next morning they went to the parish church where the coffin was resting on trestles before the altar. Beside it, to Fogarty's surprise, was a large wreath of roses. When they got up from their knees, Devine's uncle, Ned, had arrived with his son. Ned was a broad-faced, dark-haired, nervous man, with the anaemic complexion of the family.

'I'm sorry for your trouble, Ned,' said Fogarty.

'I know that, father,' said Ned.

'I don't know if you know Father Jackson. He was a great friend of Father Willie's.'

'I heard him speak of him,' said Ned. 'He talked a lot about the pair of ye. Ye were his great friends. Poor Father Willie!' he added with a sigh. 'He had few enough.'

Just then the parish priest came in and spoke to Ned Devine. His name was Martin. He was a tall man with a stern, unlined, wooden face and candid blue eyes like a baby's. He stood for a few minutes by the coffin, then studied the breastplate and wreath, looking closely at the tag. It was only then that he beckoned the two younger priests towards the door.

'Tell me, what are we going to do about that thing?' he asked with a professional air.

'What thing?' Fogarty asked in surprise.

'That wreath,' Martin replied with a nod over his shoulder.

'What's wrong with it?'

''Tis against the rubrics,' replied the parish priest in the complacent tone of a policeman who has looked up the law on the subject.

'For heaven's sake, what have the rubrics to do with it?' Fogarty asked impatiently.

'The rubrics have a whole lot to do with it,' Martin replied with a stern glance. 'And, apart from that, 'tis a bad custom.'

'You mean Masses bring in more money?' Fogarty asked with amused insolence.

'I do not mean Masses bring in more money,' replied Martin who tended to answer every remark verbatim, like a solicitor's letter. It added to the impression of woodenness he gave. 'I mean that flowers are a Pagan survival.' He looked at the two young priests with the same anxious, innocent, wooden air. 'And here am I, week in, week out, preaching against flowers, and a blooming big wreath of them in my own church. And on a priest's coffin, what's more! What am I to say about that?'

'Who asked you to say anything?' Fogarty asked angrily. 'The man wasn't from your diocese.'

'Now, that's all very well,' said Martin. 'That's bad enough by itself, but it isn't the whole story.'

'You mean because it's from a woman?' Jackson broke in lightly in a tone that would have punctured any pose less substantial than Martin's.

'I mean, because it's from a woman, exactly.'

162

'A woman!' said Fogarty in astonishment. 'Does it say so?'

'It does not say so.'

'Then how do you know?'

'Because it's red roses.'

'And does that mean it's from a woman?'

'What else could it mean?'

'I suppose it could mean it's from somebody who didn't study the language of flowers the way you seem to have done,' Fogarty snapped.

He could feel Jackson's disapproval of him weighing on the air, but when Jackson spoke it was at the parish priest that his coldness and nonchalance were directed.

'Oh, well,' he said with a shrug. 'I'm afraid we know nothing about it, father. You'll have to make up your own mind.'

'I don't like doing anything when I wasn't acquainted with the man,' Martin grumbled, but he made no further attempt to interfere, and one of the undertaker's men took the wreath and put it on the hearse. Fogarty controlled himself with difficulty. As he banged open the door of his car and started the engine his face was flushed. He drove with his head bowed and his brows jutting down like rocks over his eyes. It was what Devine had called his Nero look. As they cleared the main streets he burst out.

'That's the sort of thing that makes me ashamed of myself, Jim. Flowers are a pagan survival! And they take it from him, what's worse. They take it from him. They listen to that sort of stuff instead of telling him to shut his big ignorant gob.'

'Oh, well,' Jackson said tolerantly, taking out his pipe, 'we're hardly being fair to him. After all, he didn't know Devine.'

'But that only makes it worse,' Fogarty said hotly. 'Only for our being there he'd have thrown out that wreath. And for what? His own dirty, mean, suspicious mind!'

'Ah, I wouldn't go as far as that,' Jackson said, frowning. 'I think in his position I'd have asked somebody to take it away.'

'You would?'

'Wouldn't you?'

'But why, in God's name?'

'Oh, I suppose I'd be afraid of the scandal – I'm not a very courageous type.'

'Scandal?'

'Whatever you like to call it. After all, some woman sent it.'

'Yes. One of Devine's old maids.'

'Have you ever heard of an old maid sending a wreath of red roses to a funeral?' Jackson asked, raising his brows, his head cocked.

'To tell you the God's truth, I might have done it myself,' Fogarty confessed with boyish candour. 'It would never have struck me that there was anything wrong with it.'

'It would have struck the old maid all right, though.'

Fogarty turned his eyes for a moment to stare at Jackson. Jackson was staring back. Then he missed a turning and reversed with a muttered curse. To the left of them the Wicklow mountains stretched away southwards, and between the grey walls the fields were a ragged brilliant green under the tattered sky.

'You're not serious, Jim?' he said after a few minutes.

'Oh, I'm not suggesting that there was anything wrong,' Jackson said, gesturing widely with his pipe. 'Women get ideas. We all know that.'

'These things can happen in very innocent ways,' Fogarty said with ingenuous solemnity. Then he scowled again and a blush spread over his handsome craggy face. Like all those who live mainly in their imaginations, he was always astonished and shocked at the suggestions that reached him from the outside world: he could live with his fantasies only by assuming that they were nothing more. Jackson, whose own imagination was curbed and even timid, who never went at things like a thoroughbred at a gate, watched him with amusement and a certain envy. Just occasionally he felt that he himself would have liked to welcome a new idea with that boyish wonder and panic.

'I can't believe it,' Fogarty said angrily, tossing his head.

'You don't have to,' Jackson replied, nursing his pipe and swinging round in the seat with his arm close to Fogarty's shoulder. 'As I say, women get these queer ideas. There's usually nothing in them. At the same time, I must say I wouldn't be very scandalized if I found out that there was something in it. If ever a man needed someone to care for him, Devine did in the last year or two.'

'But not Devine, Jim,' Fogarty said, raising his voice. 'Not Devine! You could believe a thing like that about me. I suppose I could believe it about you. But I knew Devine since we were kids, and he wouldn't be capable of it.'

'I never knew him in that way,' Jackson admitted. 'In fact, I scarcely knew him at all, really. But I'd have said he was as capable of it as the rest of us. He was lonelier than the rest of us.'

'God, don't I know it?' Fogarty said in sudden self-reproach. 'I could understand if it was drink.'

'Oh, not drink!' Jackson said with distaste. 'He was too fastidious. Can you imagine him in the DTs like some old parish priest, trying to strangle the nurses?'

'But that's what I say, Jim. He wasn't the type.'

'Oh, you must make distinctions,' said Jackson. 'I could imagine him attracted by some intelligent woman. You know yourself how he'd appeal to her, the same way he appealed to us, a cultured man in a country town. I don't have to tell you the sort of life an intelligent woman leads, married to some lout of a shopkeeper or a gentleman farmer. Poor devils, it's a mercy that most of them aren't educated.'

'He didn't give you any hint who she was?' Fogarty asked incredulously. Jackson had spoken with such conviction that it impressed him as true.

'Oh, I don't even know if there was such a woman,' Jackson said hastily, and then he blushed too. Fogarty remained silent. He knew now that Jackson had been talking about himself, not Devine.

As the country grew wilder and furze bushes and ruined keeps took the place of pastures and old abbeys, Fogarty found his eyes attracted more and more to the wreath that swayed lightly with the hearse, the only spot of pure colour in the whole landscape with its watery greens and blues and greys. It seemed an image of the essential mystery of a priest's life. What, after all, did he really know of Devine? Only what his own temperament suggested, and mostly – when he wasn't being St Francis of Assisi – he had seen himself as the worldly one of the pair, the practical, coarse-grained man who cut corners, and Devine as the saint, racked by the fastidiousness and asceticism that exploded in his bitter little jests. Now his mind boggled at the idea of the agony that alone could have driven Devine into an entanglement with a woman; yet the measure of his incredulity was that of the conviction he would presently begin to feel. When once an unusual idea broke through his imagination, he hugged it, brooded on it, promoted it to the dignity of a revelation.

'God, don't we lead terrible lives?' he burst out at last. 'Here we are, probably the two people in the world who knew Devine best, and even we have no notion what that thing in front of us means.'

'Which might be as well for our peace of mind,' said Jackson.

'I'll engage it did damn little for Devine's,' Fogarty said grimly. It was peculiar; he did not believe yet in the reality of the woman behind the wreath, but already he hated her.

'Oh, I don't know,' Jackson said in some surprise. 'Isn't that what we all really want from life?'

'Is it?' Fogarty asked in wonder. He had always thought of Jackson as a cold fish, and suddenly found himself wondering about that as well. After all, there must have been something in him that attracted Devine. He had the feeling that Jackson, who was, as he recognized, by far the subtler man, was probing him, and for the same reason. Each was looking in the other for the quality that had attracted Devine, and which, having made him their friend might make them friends also. Each was trying to see how far he could go with the other. Fogarty, as usual, was the first with a confession.

'I couldn't do it, Jim,' he said earnestly. 'I was never even tempted, except once, and then it was the wife of one of the men who was in the seminary with me. I was crazy about her. But when I saw what her marriage to the other fellow was like, I changed my mind. She hated him like poison, Jim. I soon saw she might have hated me in the same way. It's only when you see what marriage is really like, as we do, that you realize how lucky we are.'

'Lucky?' Jackson repeated mockingly.

'Aren't we?'

'Did you ever know a seminary that wasn't full of men who thought they were lucky? They might be drinking themselves to death, but they never doubted their luck? Nonsense, man! Anyway, why do you think she'd have hated you?'

'I don't,' Fogarty replied with a boyish laugh. 'Naturally, I think I'd have been the perfect husband for her. That's the way Nature kids you.'

'Well, why shouldn't you have made her a perfect husband?' Jackson asked quizzically. 'There's nothing much wrong with you that I can see. Though I admit I can see you better as a devoted father.'

'God knows you might be right,' Fogarty said, his face clouding again. It was as changeable as an Irish sky, Jackson thought with amusement. 'You could get on well enough without the woman, but the kids are hell. She had two. "Father Fogey" they used to call me. And my mother was as bad,' he burst out. 'She was wrapped up in the pair of us. She always wanted us to be better than everybody else, and when we weren't she used to cry. She said it was the Fogarty blood breaking out in us – the Fogartys were all horse dealers.' His handsome, happy face was black with all the remorse and guilt. 'I'm afraid she died under the impression that I was a Fogarty after all.'

'If the Fogartys are any relation to the Martins, I'd say it was most unlikely,' Jackson said, half amused, half touched.

'I never knew till she was dead how much she meant to me,' Fogarty said broodingly. 'Hennessey warned me not to take the Burial Service myself, but I thought it was the last thing I could do for her. He knew what he was talking about, of course. I disgraced myself, bawling like a blooming kid, and he pushed me aside and finished it for me. My God, the way we gallop through that till it comes to our own turn! Every time I've read it since, I've read it as if it were for my mother.'

Jackson shook his head uncomprehendingly.

'You feel these things more than I do,' he said. 'I'm a cold fish.'

It struck Fogarty with some force that this was precisely what he had always believed himself and that now he could believe it no longer.

'Until then, I used to be a bit flighty,' he confessed. 'After that I knew it wasn't in me to care for another woman.'

'That's only more of your nonsense,' said Jackson impatiently. 'Love is just one thing, not half a dozen. If I were a young fellow looking for a wife I'd go after some girl who felt like that about her father. You probably have too much of it. I haven't enough. When I was in Manister there was a shopkeeper's wife I used to see. I talked to her and lent her books. She was half crazy with loneliness. Then one morning I got home and found her standing outside my door in the pouring rain. She'd been there half the night. She wanted me to take her away, to "save" her, as she said. You can imagine what happened to her after.'

'Went off with someone else, I suppose?'

'No such luck. She took to drinking and sleeping with racing men. Sometimes I blame myself for it. I feel I should have kidded her along. But I haven't enough love to go round. You have too much. With your enthusiastic nature you'd probably have run off with her.'

'I often wondered what I would do,' Fogarty said shyly.

He felt very close to tears. It was partly the wreath, brilliant in the sunlight, that had drawn him out of his habitual reserve and made him talk in that way with a man of even greater reserve. Partly it was the emotion of returning to the little town where he had grown up. He hated and avoided it; it seemed to him to represent all the narrowness and meanness that he tried to banish from his thoughts, but at the same time it contained all the nostalgia and violence he had felt there; and when he drew near it again a tumult of emotions rose in him that half-strangled him. He was watching for it already like a lover.

'There it is!' he said triumphantly, pointing to a valley where a tapering Franciscan tower rose on the edge of a clutter of low Georgian houses and thatched cabins. 'They'll be waiting for us at the bridge. That's how they'll be waiting for me when my turn comes, Jim.'

A considerable crowd had gathered at the farther side of the bridge to escort the hearse to the cemetery. Four men shouldered the shiny coffin over the bridge past the ruined castle and up the hilly Main Street. Shutters were up on the shop fronts, blinds were drawn, everything was at a standstill except where a curtain was lifted and an old woman peered out.

'Counting the mourners,' Fogarty said with a bitter laugh. 'They'll say I had nothing like as many as Devine. That place,' he added, lowering his voice, 'the second shop from the corner, that was ours.'

Jackson took it in at a glance. He was puzzled and touched by Fogarty's emotion because there was nothing to distinguish the little market town from a hundred others. A laneway led off the hilly road and they came to the abbey, a ruined tower and a few walls, with tombstones sown thickly in quire and nave. The hearse was already drawn up outside and people had gathered in a semicircle about it. Ned Devine came hastily up to the car where the two priests were donning their vestments. Fogarty knew at once that there was trouble brewing.

'Whisper, Father Jerry,' Ned muttered in a strained excited voice. 'People are talking about that wreath. I wonder would you know who sent it?'

'I don't know the first thing about it, Ned,' Fogarty replied, and suddenly his heart began to beat violently.

'Come here a minute, Sheela,' Ned called, and a tall, pale girl with the stain of tears on her long bony face left the little group of mourners and joined them. Fogarty nodded to her. She was Devine's sister, a schoolteacher who had never married. 'This is Father Jackson, Father Willie's other friend. They don't know anything about it either.'

'Then I'd let them take it back,' she said doggedly.

'What would you say, father?' Ned asked, appealing to Fogarty, and suddenly Fogarty felt his courage desert him. In disputing with Martin he had felt himself an equal on neutral ground, but now the passion and prejudice of the little town seemed to rise up and oppose him, and he felt himself again a boy, rebellious and terrified. You had to know the place to realize the hysteria that could be provoked by something like a funeral.

'I can only tell you what I told Father Martin already,' he said, growing red and angry.

'Did he talk about it too?' Ned asked sharply.

'There!' Sheela said vindictively. 'What did I tell you?'

'Well, the pair of you are cleverer than I am,' Fogarty said. 'I saw nothing wrong with it.'

'It was no proper thing to send to a priest's funeral,' she hissed with prim fury. 'And whoever sent it was no friend of my brother.'

'You saw nothing wrong with it, father?' Ned prompted appealingly.

'But I tell you, Uncle Ned, if that wreath goes into the graveyard we'll be the laughing stock of the town,' she said in an old-maidish frenzy. 'I'll throw it out myself if you won't.'

'Whisht, girl, whisht, and let Father Jerry talk!' Ned said furiously.

'It's entirely a matter for yourselves, Ned,' Fogarty said excitedly. He was really scared now. He knew he was in danger of behaving imprudently in public, and sooner or later, the story would get back to the Bishop, and it would be suggested that he knew more than he pretended.

'If you'll excuse me interrupting, father,' Jackson said suavely, giving Fogarty a warning glance over his spectacles. 'I know this is none of my business.'

'Not at all, father, not at all,' Ned said passionately. 'You were the boy's friend. All we want is for you to tell us what to do.'

'Oh, well, Mr Devine, that would be too great a responsibility for me to take,' Jackson replied with a cagey smile, though Fogarty saw that his face was very flushed. 'Only someone who really knows the town could advise you about that. I only know what things are like in my own place. Of course, I entirely agree with Miss Devine,' he said, giving her a smile that suggested that this, like crucifixion, was something he preferred to avoid. 'Naturally, Father Fogarty and I have discussed it already. I think personally that it was entirely improper to send a wreath.' Then his mild, clerical voice suddenly grew menacing and he shrugged his shoulders with an air of contempt. 'But, speaking as an outsider, I'd say if you were to send that wreath back from the graveyard, you'd make yourself something far worse than a laughing stock. You'd throw mud on a dead man's name that would never be forgotten for you the longest day you lived . . . Of course, that's only an outsider's opinion,' he added urbanely, drawing in his breath in a positive hiss.

'Of course, of course, of course,' Ned Devine said, clicking his fingers and snapping into action. 'We should have thought of it ourselves, father. 'Twould be giving tongues to the stones.'

Then he lifted the wreath himself and carried it to the graveside. Several of the men by the gate looked at him with a questioning eye and fell in behind him. Some hysteria had gone out of the air. Fogarty gently squeezed Jackson's hand.

'Good man, Jim!' he said in a whisper. 'Good man you are!'

He stood with Jackson at the head of the open grave beside the local priests. As their voices rose in the psalms for the dead and their vestments billowed about them, Fogarty's brooding eyes swept the crowd of faces he had known since his childhood and which were now caricatured by age and pain. Each time they came to rest on the wreath which stood at one side of the open grave. It would lie there now above Devine when all the living had gone, his secret. And each time it came over him in a wave of emotion that what he and Jackson had protected was something more than a sentimental token. It was the thing that had linked them to Devine, and for the future would link them to one another – love. Not half a dozen things, but one thing, between son and mother, man and sweetheart, friend and friend.

The Weeping
over Children

Joe Saunders and his wife, Brigid, had been married a year when they had their first baby – a little girl they called Nance, after Brigid's mother. Brigid was Irish, and Joe had always had a feeling that there must be some Irish blood in himself. She was a Catholic, and, though Joe was an unbeliever, he liked it in her, and encouraged her to put up holy pictures and statues all over the house. He even went to Mass with her occasionally, but she said he put her off her prayers with his air of devotion, which made him laugh. She often made him laugh, and he liked it, because he had a natural gravity that turned easily to melancholy and even tears. She had good breeding as well, and he liked that too, though she sometimes upset him by the way she unconsciously patronized his mother and sisters. They were common, and he knew they were common, but he didn't like it to be rubbed in. Brigid had kept her girlish gaiety and her delight in flirting shamelessly with any man who fancied her. It amused Joe, because for all her charm, he knew the wild, chaste, innocent streak in her, and realized that the smart operators would get absolutely nowhere with her.

After Nance's birth Joe felt that life had done him proud. There were times when he saw everything with a sort of double vision, as though he were not only doing whatever he was doing – like pushing the pram round the estate, or creeping into the back room at night to see that the baby was covered – but watching himself do it, as though he were someone in a film or a book, and the conjunction of the two visions gave the thing itself an intense stereoscopic quality. He was sure that this must be what people meant when they talked of happiness.

But he realized that it was different for Brigid. Though at times she could forget herself and play with the baby like a girl with a doll, she was often gloomy, tearful and irritable. This was not

171

like her. Joe's great friend, Jerry Cross, called it something like post-partem psychosis, and though Joe had no great faith in the long names Jerry liked to give things, he accepted his advice and took Brigid for a week to Brighton. It did her good but only for a short while. Joe – a sensitive man – sometimes thought he knew exactly how she felt – a wild girl with a vivacious temperament, who loved outings and parties, trapped by a morsel of humanity who took everything and gave nothing.

Joe was attentive to the point of officiousness, seeing that she went to the cinema and visited friends. But even to old friends she had changed, and had taken a positive dislike to Jerry Cross. Though Jerry was great at giving women little presents, he didn't seem to like them much, and now Brigid chose to interpret this as dislike of herself. With a sort of schoolgirl pertness that drove Joe to despair she mocked Cross about his over-heated bachelor flat, his expensive gramophone and collection of records, and his liqueur cabinet that always seemed to contain some new exotic drink that Jerry would press on his visitors, rubbing his hands and saying in his anxious way: 'It's not bad, is it? I mean, it really is not bad. You think that, too, Joe.' Twice, to protect Cross, Joe had to reprove her, and though he did it gently, it cut him to the heart to have to do it at all.

'Why can't you be nicer to Jerry?' he asked as they were going home one night. 'He hasn't so many friends.'

'He has no friends at all, if you ask me,' Brigid said coldly. 'He's too bloody selfish to afford them.'

'Selfish?' Joe exclaimed, stopping dead. 'A man who put a cheque for two hundred quid on my mantelpiece while I was out of the room!'

'We know all that,' Brigid said contemptuously. 'Damn well he knew you wouldn't take it.'

'He knew more than I did,' Joe said, resuming his walk. 'Anyway, it wasn't the money that mattered at the time. It was his confidence in me. It gave me confidence in myself. I tell you, Brigid, there are things between men that you'll never understand, not till the day you die.'

But argument had no effect on Brigid except perhaps to give her fresh grounds for spite. One evening at Joe's house, Cross was boasting innocently of some shady deal he had refused to be connected with, and Brigid, with mock admiration, drew him skilfully out. It was one of Cross's little weaknesses that he liked to think himself a really shrewd businessman – 'a bloody dreamer' was how an uncle had described him to Joe.

'You always play it safe, Jerry, don't you?' she asked at last.

'What's that, Brigid?' Cross asked eagerly, too pleased with himself to be aware of her malice.

'Brigid!' Joe said warningly.

'Anyone who had anything to do with you would want to watch out,' she said.

Cross got up and clutched the lapels of his coat as though he were about to make a speech. It suddenly struck Joe that he was a little man who lived in expectation of having to make speeches – unpleasant ones, in his own defence.

'I assure you, Brigid, that nobody who had anything to do with me ever had to watch out, as you put it,' he said over-loudly, speaking as it were to a faraway audience. 'I do play it safe, though. You're right there, I do. And I'll play it safer for the future by not calling here, as I have been doing.'

Then he made for the door, and Joe, holding his coat for him, realized that he was shivering violently. Joe opened the door, put his arm round Cross's shoulder and walked slowly to the gate with him. Cross walked close to him, so as not to break the embrace, and yet Joe knew he did not feel it in a homosexual way. The estate road went uphill to the bus stop on the tree-shaded suburban road, and the two men walked together like sweethearts till they reached it. Then Joe took Cross's hand in his own two.

'Try not to think of it, Jerry,' he said in a low voice. 'She doesn't even know what she's saying. The girl is sick in her mind.'

'She is, Joe, she is, she is,' Cross said with pathetic eagerness. 'I thought it from the first, but now I'm sure. I'm sorry I was so sharp with her.'

'You weren't, Jerry; not so sharp as I'd have been.'

It was only when he had waved goodbye to Cross from the pavement that Joe gave way to tears. He walked slowly up and down the road till the fit had passed. As he entered the house, Brigid was waiting for him in the sitting room, sitting exactly as when he had left.

'Come in, Joe,' she said quietly. 'We have to talk.'

'I'm sorry, Brigid, but I don't want to talk,' he said, feeling sure that if he did he would break down again.

'I want to talk,' she said in a flat tone. 'It may be the last chance we'll get. I'll have to clear out.'

'What's that?' he asked incredulously.

'I have to clear out,' she said again, and he knew that she meant it.

It was at moments like these that all the wise passivity in Joe came on top. In his time he had been humiliated, hurt so that the pain had never left him, but he knew you had to give in to it, let the pain wash over you, if you didn't want it to destroy you.

'Why do you think you have to clear out, dear?' he asked mildly, taking a chair inside the door and joining his hands before him.

'Because I don't want to destroy your life the way I destroyed my own,' she said.

'Well, I should have something to say to that,' he said. 'So should the baby, of course. Unless you're proposing to take her with you.'

'I'm not,' she said with artificial casualness. 'I dare say your mother can look after her.'

'I dare say she could,' he said calmly. 'But it's not my idea of what a child needs.'

'At least your mother won't insult your friends,' Brigid said bitterly. He knew then that she had no illusions about her behaviour to Cross and his heart softened.

'You mean more to me than any of my friends, dear,' he said. 'Even Jerry – and Heaven knows, he means quite a lot. But why do you have to do things like that? They hurt you as much as they hurt other people. What is it, Brigid? Why don't you trust me? Is it another man?'

For a moment Joe thought she really was going to strike him. Then the humour of it seemed to dawn on her, and she gave a weak grin.

'You have a very poor opinion of yourself, haven't you?' she asked pertly. 'Even that jenny-ass, Cross, wouldn't think of a silly thing like that. I never looked at the side of the road a man walked at since I married you.'

There was no mistaking the absolute truthfulness of that, and again he felt the sense of relief, and with it the old tenderness and admiration.

'Naturally, that's what I hoped, dear,' he said. 'And damn it all, nothing else matters.'

'Not even the ones I met before I met you?' she asked mockingly, and her tone struck him cold again.

'I see,' he said. 'You mean there was someone else?'

'Naturally,' she said angrily. And then, as though reading his thoughts, she reverted to her tone of exasperated amusement. 'Now, I suppose you think I'm breaking my heart over him? I am, like hell! I hope to God I never lay eyes on him again. I wish I could say the same thing about his child.'

'His child?' Joe repeated stupidly. Now he felt that the world really was collapsing about him. 'You mean you had a child already?'

'What do you think brought me over to London in the first place?' she asked reasonably.

'I don't know,' Joe said with simple dignity. 'I just thought you might have been telling me the truth when you said you came over for a job. I suppose you're right to think I'm a bit simple-minded.'

'I never thought you were simple-minded,' she retorted with the fury of a hell-cat. 'I thought you were too good to be true, if you want to know what I really thought.'

'And you have this child where? With your people?'

'No, outside Cork,' she said shortly. 'I suppose I wanted her as far away as possible. And, as I'm about it, there's another thing. I pinched some of the housekeeping money to support her. After I left the job I had nothing of my own.'

'You could scarcely have left the child to starve,' he said lightly. 'That doesn't count beside the other things.'

'What other things?'

'All the lies you've told me,' he said bitterly. 'I didn't deserve that from you. Look, Brigid, it's no use pretending I'm not hurt – not by what you've just told me. That was your business. But you might have told me before you married me.'

'So that you needn't have married me?' she asked bitterly.

'I mean nothing of the sort,' said Joe. 'I don't know what I should have done, but I don't think it would have come between you and me. You were unfair to me and unfair to the child. You might have trusted me as I trusted you.'

'As if the two things were alike?' she retorted. 'I told you I thought you were too good to be true. You weren't, but to get to know you that way I had to marry you first, and to marry you

175

I had to tell you lies. At least, that's how it seemed to me. And a hell of a lot of good it did me!'

Joe sighed.

'Anyway, we have to think what we're to do about this child, and that's something we can't decide tonight.'

'There's only one thing to do, Joe,' she said. 'I'll have to go back to London and get a job.' She said it manfully enough, but he knew she didn't mean it. She was begging him to find some way out for her.

'We don't have to break up this house,' he said with determination. 'Damn it, it's our own. We can still bring her to live with us.'

'But I don't want her to live with us,' she said angrily. 'Can't you understand? It was all a miserable bloody mistake, and I don't want you to have to live with it either. It's just that I feel such a bitch, having everything in the world I want while she has nothing.'

'I see that,' Joe said gently. 'I see it's not an easy question. We'll have to think of something, that's all.'

He thought a lot about it that night, though less of what they were to do with Brigid's child than of the disaster that had overtaken his beautiful world. Again he could see himself acting, doing whatever he felt he had to do, but beyond that he could see it all as though it were happening to someone in a book or a movie. He could almost hear his own voice as if it were in the third person. '"We'll have to think of something, that's all," he said.' And he supposed that this must be what people meant when they talked of grief.

Yet when Brigid waked him, bringing him a cup of tea in bed, it seemed to have taken nothing out of her. Unburdening herself of her secret seemed to have restored all her native liveliness, in fact.

When he got home that evening, he was astonished to see Cross waiting for him in the front room, and he knew from Cross's manner that Brigid had made her peace with him. At any other time this would have made him happy, but now it merely seemed an irrelevance. As he saw Cross off, Cross said urgently, 'You won't think me interfering, Joe, but Brigid came to the office and told me about your little trouble. I guessed there was something upsetting her. I only wanted to say how sorry I am.'

Joe was amused at Cross's delicacy, and touched that Brigid, for all her fierce pride, had humiliated herself so abjectly before him, but this didn't seem to matter either.

'I know, Jerry, I know,' he said, squeezing Cross's arm, but Cross was full of the subject.

'It's going to be terrible, however you arrange things,' he said, 'and I only want you to know that I'll be delighted to do anything. Delighted! Because I have a great admiration for Brigid, Joe. You know that.' Joe realized that by ways that could have been no great pleasure to her, Brigid had at last managed to pierce Cross's defences. Being Cross, he was doing more than interceding for her. He was hiding the cheque on the mantelpiece.

After supper Joe said to Brigid:

'I've been thinking this thing over, dear, and I see only one way out. We have to bring the child here.'

'I've been thinking it over too, and I don't see the necessity for that at all,' she said hastily. 'Cross thinks the same. To tell you the truth, I think 'twould be impossible for everybody.'

Joe could see exactly what she was thinking about. Now that the burden of secrecy had been lifted, she had fled to the opposite extreme of self-confidence. Only a wild outburst of self-confidence could have given her the courage to go to Cross at all. But with self-confidence she had regained all her old devious personality, and was plotting like mad to retrieve as much as possible from the wreck and avoid humiliating herself before the neighbours and before Joe's decent, common working-class family.

'Not impossible,' he said. 'Difficult, I grant you. We've made a good many friends on the estate, and it's not going to make our position here any better. But others have had to do the same and worse.'

'It's easier for a man than for a woman,' Brigid said ruefully.

'It's harder for a woman because she does more to make the position she finds herself in,' said Joe sternly. 'It's not easy for anybody. All the same, it doesn't count compared with a child's life.'

'And there's your mother to be considered,' she said.

'Exactly. There's Mother, and there's Barbara and Coralie, and we know what they'll think and say. They'll make you pay, Brigid, and I'll suffer for it. But that's not the worst. The worst is that we may get the kid too late for her to be able to fit in. Still, bad as that is, it will be easier now than it would be in ten or fifteen years' time.'

'I don't know, Joe,' Brigid said earnestly. 'I cracked up on you before because I was trying to handle it on my own. I won't crack up on you again, and I think there are a lot of things I can do without making ourselves miserable into the bargain.'

'Such as?'

'Well, it was really Jerry who suggested it – getting her over here to a decent home where we can keep an eye on her, taking her on holidays with Nance, and seeing that she goes to a good school when she's old enough.'

'And I suppose Jerry offered to help?'

'He did,' she admitted. 'He's damn decent.'

'He is decent,' said Joe. 'All the same, he's wrong. Dead wrong.' Like many gentle souls, Joe had a streak of iron in him, and when he made up his mind about something he could be very obstinate. 'Jerry is a bachelor. He doesn't even know what he's talking about. You can cut off a man or woman as a loss, and feel that maybe they'll keep afloat, but you can't do that to a child. A child is too helpless. And this time, it isn't only you who have to live with them but me as well, and if anything happened to that child, I'd be a murderer. I've got my faults, Brigid, but I'm not a murderer.'

A fortnight later they were flying in from the sea over Dublin, and Joe knew that Brigid was losing her nerve. Every moment seemed to leave her more panic-stricken. When they travelled into the city on the tall, bumpy, swaying bus, she kept silent, but in the hotel room she broke down.

'Look, Joe, I can't face it,' she said.

'Now, Brigid, you've done things a great deal more difficult than this,' he said comfortingly.

'I haven't, Joe,' she said. 'You don't understand, I tell you. I can't go down to Cork tomorrow and meet people I used to know, and start inventing excuses for coming back.'

'You don't have to invent excuses,' he said patiently. 'You're just here with your husband on a holiday – what's wrong with that?'

'And with a two-year-old baby in my arms?' she said bitterly. 'I tell you, Joe, I don't give a damn what happens to the child. I'm not going down.'

She frightened Joe. It was as though behind this façade of a capital with its Georgian squares and flashy hotels and expensive restaurants there was a jungle of secrecy and panic. But he did not want Brigid to see how he felt about it.

'Very well, dear,' he said patiently. 'I'll go. I dare say your family can direct me.'

'I suppose they could,' she said doubtfully. 'But if you have any consideration for them, you'll keep as far from them as you can.'

He knew it was unsafe to argue with her. She was close to hysteria or he would have said it was rather peculiar to have a foreigner searching in unfamiliar country for a child of this family who had already been neglected for two years.

'Very well, dear,' he said. 'If you say so, I shall.'

The trip on the train to Cork was pleasant, and his only regret was that Brigid wasn't there to share it with him and point out the places of interest: it seemed like the waste of a good excursion. The city itself seemed pleasant enough too, and he had a good view of the river and quays from his bedroom window. Downstairs, he talked to the hotel manager, who was big-boned, deep-voiced and amiable and threw himself into the business of getting Joe to his destination as though he had no other aim in life. 'Throw' seemed the word that suited him, for he literally heaved himself across the desk, looking at a map and studying a timetable, bellowed softly to members of the staff who might help, and even called in casual passers-by. This scared Joe who did not want his business made public too soon. It would be time enough for explanations when he returned to the hotel with a baby – a difficult moment enough, as even he realized.

But the last ten miles of his journey seemed the most difficult of all.

'It's all right, Mr Coleman,' said Joe. 'I'll hire a car.'

The hotel manager glanced at the clock in the hall and said in his deep voice:

'You won't hire any car. I'll take an hour off after dinner and drive you.'

'That's very kind of you,' whispered Joe, 'but it might be better if I did take a car. You see, it's rather a delicate matter.'

'Oh, sorry, I didn't mean to be inquisitive,' Coleman said with a touch of resentment.

'Don't be silly!' Joe said with a laugh. 'You're not being

179

inquisitive. I haven't anything to hide, and anyhow I'd have had to tell you sooner or later. Sit down for a moment and let me explain.'

The two men sat in a corner of the lounge and Joe explained. The hotel manager listened with a vague smile.

'So far as I'm concerned, I can keep my mouth shut,' he said. 'But don't be surprised if a lot of the staff know who you are already. If they don't know tonight they'll know tomorrow. They'll also know who your wife is. This may seem a big city to you, but it's not big enough for those who have to live in it. Mind,' he added with a smile, 'I wouldn't let that disturb me too much either. Will I get a cot into your room?'

'Not tonight,' said Joe. 'I've tried to sort this thing out. It isn't easy for a man, you know, but I don't think it would be fair to the kid to bring her back tonight, particularly with no woman around. Even if Brigid was here it would be a shock. No, I thought I'd go to this house first, and let the kid get to know me before I bring her back.'

'Tomorrow I have the whole morning clear,' said Coleman.

'No, I didn't mean it that way either,' said Joe. 'I can afford to hire a car. Damn it, having come all this way, I can't be stopped by the hire of a car.'

'No reason you should unless you want to,' Coleman said gruffly. 'I think you're wise not to bring her back tonight though. I'll see you in the lounge after dinner. I'd stick to the roast beef, if I were you.'

After dinner the two men set off in Coleman's old car. After a few minutes Coleman spoke.

'This isn't an aspect of life you get much advice on when you go into the hotel business,' he said in his good-humoured way. 'But, if you'll excuse my being personal, Mr Saunders, you seem to me a rather unusual sort of man.'

'Do I?' Joe asked in genuine surprise. 'I should have said in my circumstances most men would have felt the same.'

'Felt the same, I've no doubt,' said Coleman. 'I'm not so sure they'd have acted the same, though. Naturally, the first thing I did when you told me your story was to ask myself what I'd have done in your place.'

'Yes?' Joe said eagerly.

'And I decided – don't think me impertinent now! – that I'd think twice about it.'

'Don't worry, old man,' Joe said with a loud laugh. 'I did. I thought three times about it, as a matter of fact.'

But those few words seemed to have cleared the air between them. They had passed the city boundaries and were driving along a river bank with a tree-lined walk at the other side of the water. The main road led along a smaller river wooded to its bank. Finally they reached a little village with a church and public house where they went off on a by-road up the hill. They came out of it above the river and harbour, stopped to inquire their way, and drove slowly for some miles along a deserted upland road. It was darkening, and Coleman drove more carefully. There was a cottage on their right and two small children with bare feet were playing in the roadway outside. He stopped the car suddenly.

'I have a feeling this is it,' he said, and bellowed to the children: 'Is this Mrs Ryan's?'

'What's that, sir?' asked a little boy.

'Mrs Ryan's, I said.'

"Tis, sir.'

'And is this Marie?' Coleman asked, pointing to the little girl who accompanied him.

'No, sir, 'tis Martha,' said the child.

'Then where is Marie?' Coleman asked, and suddenly a tall, rough-looking woman with rosy cheeks appeared by the white gatepost. Afterwards Joe thought he would never forget that first impression of her with the white gatepost and dark fuchsia bushes, cut out against the sky.

'Is this the gentleman from England I have?' she called. 'Marie is inside, gentlemen. Won't you come in?'

Joe got out first and held out his hand.

'I'm Joe Saunders, Brigid Healy's husband,' he said. 'And this is Mr Coleman, the hotel manager from Cork. He was kind enough to give me a lift.'

'I was after giving up expecting ye,' she said, showing her big teeth in a smile. 'Come in, let ye! I'm afraid the house is in a mess, but 'tis only the children.'

'You don't have to apologize, Mrs Ryan,' Joe said. 'I come of a large family myself.'

But even Joe's large London family had not prepared him for the little cottage, even if the shadows inside gave little opportunity for deciding whether or not it was in a mess. An open door into the bedroom suggested a big bed that had not been made, and the walls of the kitchen were bare but for a grocer's calendar inside the door. Sitting round the open fire were three other children whose faces he could scarcely see, but it was clear that the bare-legged two-years-old who roasted her feet before it was Brigid's child. Suddenly he wondered what he was doing there.

'This is Miss Healy's little girl, gentlemen,' said Mrs Ryan. 'She's the spit of her mother, but ye can't see. I'll light the lamp. I suppose ye'd like a cup of tea after yeer journey?'

'No, thanks, Mrs Ryan,' said Joe. 'We've only just had dinner. Besides, we won't stay long. We thought we'd come back tomorrow morning for Marie, just to give you time to get her ready . . . Hullo, Marie,' he said, taking the child's hand. 'I bet you don't know who I am.'

'Hullo, Marie,' Coleman said with casual amiability and took her hand as well. She looked up at them without expression and Joe suddenly recognized her resemblance to Brigid. That gave him a turn too.

'Run out and play with Martha and Michael,' Mrs Ryan shouted to the other boy in the room. 'And bring Kitty along with you.' Silently the two children got up and went out, closing the half door behind them. It was not as though they were frightened but as though they saw no reason for disobeying, and for some reason this struck Joe as even worse. He felt that a natural child should be curious. Mrs Ryan lit the lamp, squinting up at it.

'Wisha, sit down, let ye,' she said, pulling up two chairs and wiping the seats vaguely with her apron. 'And how is Miss Healy? You'll have to forgive me. I forget her married name.'

'Saunders,' said Joe, sitting down and opening the little case he had brought with him. 'She's fine, Mrs Ryan. She probably told you we have a little girl of our own now. She wasn't well or she'd have been here herself. I don't want to rush you. These are a few clothes I brought, and perhaps you can tell me if they'll fit.'

He passed the frock, overcoat and hat to her and she held them to the light with a vague smile. Then she peered at the shoes.

'Wisha, aren't they lovely?' she said. 'Aren't you the lucky girl, Marie? Ye're sure ye won't have the tea? 'Twouldn't take me a minute to boil the kettle.'

'Certain, thanks,' said Joe, who only wanted to get out of the house quick. He crossed to the half-door, and again he caught an image he felt he would never forget of the lamp-light on the hedge and white-washed gatepost where four children were crowded together, talking in whispers. 'Better come in now,' he said with a laugh. 'I bet you heard every word we said. Are they all yours, Mrs Ryan?'

'Ah, no, sir,' she replied almost reproachfully. 'We had no children of our own. 'Tis on account of my husband's death I had to take them.'

The four children came in and stood fidgeting by the dresser, two little boys and two little girls, apparently well fed if not well dressed or clean, but somehow lacking all the spontaneity of other children. Joe took out a fistful of coins and distributed them. The children took the money meekly, without gratitude.

'Well, Marie,' he asked, stooping over the child on the stool, 'how do you think you're going to like me for a daddy?'

'She's strange,' Mrs Ryan said apologetically. 'Most of the time she have plenty to say for herself.'

'I'll bet she has,' said Joe. 'And in a couple of days she'll be giving me cheek as well. Won't you, old lady?'

They sat and talked for a few minutes longer. Then Joe said good night, kissed Marie and patted the other children on the head. It was already dark on the road, and he was glad of the headlights that made the green banks seem theatrical but concealed his face.

'Well, I don't know how you feel, but I'm ready for a drink,' said Coleman. 'A large one, at that.'

'What I should like is to buy a few toys for the other kids,' said Joe.

'Too late for that, I'm afraid,' said Coleman. 'The shops are shut until Monday. You might be able to pick up a few cheap toys in a sweet-shop, and a couple of bags of sweets. If you mean they won't have the money long I'm inclined to agree with you.'

As they entered the hotel the tall night porter looked up from his evening paper and said, 'Night, sir. Night, Mr Saunders,' and already Joe knew that his business was being discussed. The waiter who brought them their drinks in the lounge seemed to know as well, but Joe had the idea that he approved. He might have been a father himself. He might even have known Brigid and Marie's father. The pair of them might have sat drinking in this very lounge like any of the couples who sat there now. It was only the other side of the picture that he had been looking at that evening in a lonesome cottage on the hills. He felt very depressed.

Next morning he was more cheerful. He woke to the sound of bells. He had never heard so many bells, or else they sounded louder in the hollow of the city. A pious people all right, he thought. On their way out of town he saw the well-dressed crowds on their way to Mass. In the first village they came to there was a large group outside the church and a similar one outside the public house.

The four elder children were waiting for them in the roadway, and as they approached, two of these rushed in to give warning. They had all been washed and two of them even wore boots. When they went into the cottage Marie was sitting stiffly on a low chair by the door, as though she had been glued there to keep her from soiling her new dress, and she looked up at them blankly and pointed to her shoes. 'Look! Shoes!' she said shrilly, and Joe, stooping to admire them, saw that they were too big.

'We'll get you properly fitted tomorrow, old lady,' he said.

He distributed the few presents he had managed to buy, shook hands with Mrs Ryan, and carried Marie to the car. The other children followed, and he shook hands with each in turn, and then laid his hand gently on each one's head. Over the low wooden gate he could see the tall figure of Mrs Ryan, holding the doorpost and gazing up and down the deserted road.

As the car started he turned to wave to the little group of children. They stood in the roadway, their presents clutched in their hands, and he saw that they were all weeping quietly. It seemed to him that they were not weeping as real children weep, with abandonment and delight, but hopelessly, as old people weep whom the world has passed by. He was the world and he had passed them by. He knew now why he had not dared to kiss any of them. If he had kissed them he could not have left them there. His first thought was to prevent Marie's seeing them, but he realized that he needn't have worried. She was leaning forward, enchanted, trying to touch her beautiful new shoes. Coleman drove with his eyes fixed on the winding roadway over the hills, and his fat sulky face was expressionless.

'I wonder if you saw what I did?' Joe said at last to break the silence, and Coleman stared at him despairingly.

'I'm in dread I'll never forget it,' he said.

A Life of
Your Own

Contents

A Life of
Your Own

Jane Harty, the chemist, lived alone in a little bungalow on the outskirts of the town. She had long ago decided that it was the only way to live a life of her own. In a city you could be one of a group without adopting its standards, but girls who took lodgings in the town accepted a discipline stricter than that of home.

She could not live that way, and after her parents' death and her brother's departure for London, she gave up trying. She ran a battered old car and went off on free weekends by herself, without telling anyone except the Sullivans where she was going. They were her only friends in town. Celia had been to school with her and had married the headmaster of the Technical School. When she got a fit of the blues she merely packed her bag and went to stay with them, and they never asked any questions.

The bungalow wasn't very comfortable, and she could afford to have a cleaning woman in only once a week, but it had a garden and a bit of a view, and she could live better in the town than in Dublin, where she would only be a nonentity. The poor people feared and distrusted doctors, and they came to her with their troubles, domestic and medical. They knew she didn't mind tramping down to a dirty cottage at night with a prescription, or looking at a sick child or arguing with a drunken husband. She was one of themselves. Of course, they knew things about her as well. They had known her parents, and knew she was looked on as a bit of a freak by the swanky people, all because she wouldn't play the game and fell in love with unsuitable men. Unsuitable men seemed to be the price you had to pay for trying to live a life of your own.

One night she came back from Dublin, and when she opened the door of the bungalow she felt a sudden stab of fear. She stepped back and asked angrily, 'Is there somebody there?' There was no reply, and she muttered to herself, 'You're getting neurotic, Harty.' She went in and turned on the light in the sitting room.

One glance was enough to show that it wasn't nerves. Through the open door of the bedroom she could see clothes scattered on the floor. How anybody got in she didn't know, but the key was under the mat, and in fact anyone could have done it. She searched the two rooms and the kitchen but found nothing missing. Yet it gave her a sick and desolate feeling, like the touch of something dirty.

Next morning she went to the police station and made her complaint to the sergeant, a beefy, boozy man by the name of Lenihan.

'Ah, it's them kids again, Miss Harty,' he said gloomily.

'What kids are they, Joe?'

'That rough gang down the River Road,' he said. 'They didn't take anything?'

'Not that I could see.'

'Pity about that,' he said moodily. 'If there was anything taken we could keep an eye out for it. Young Humphreys lives up your way. I'll tell him to watch for anyone going in that direction. In the meantime, you'd better leave word with us when you're away.'

'For God's sake!' Ned Sullivan drawled when she told him and his wife about it that night. 'When one of them leaves the barrack they hear his boots at the other side of town. I'll have a word with a couple of the kids. The best way of keeping kids from being juvenile delinquents is to turn them into policemen.'

Sullivan was like that; ugly, attractive, slow-moving and cynical, and Jane squirmed when Celia talked to him, because it was clear that she didn't realize how remarkable he was.

But neither the police nor the Technical School kids were round when the intruder came again. Jane arrived home on Sunday night from Galway. The first glance was enough to show that her visitor was no child. She felt sick again, but this time anger got the upper hand. She drove back to Humphreys' house, which was on a terrace by the main road. Madge Humphreys answered the door. She was a school-teacher, who was supposed to read what she called 'the clawsicks' to her family each evening till their spirit was broken. She told Jane her husband was out, and that she had better report to the barrack, but at that very moment Humphreys appeared, a tall, big-boned young man, grinning and pulling on his jacket. 'Ah, Madge, a policeman is never off duty,' he said. 'I might as well go and see what's up.'

When Jane showed him the living room he said softly, 'Oh, Chrisht!' In the kitchen doorway he halted. 'These yours?' he asked, nodding to the tea things, and she shook her head, anger giving way to hopelessness. She had merely tried to have a life of her own, and even this was being denied her. 'Better check and see is anything missing from the bedroom,' he said, and she preceded him, looking helplessly round. 'Try your clothes first,' he said gently, and she began to fold them and put them back. Humphreys sat down and lit a cigarette.

'Well?' he asked, and she burst into a loud angry laugh.

'Nothing I can see only a pair of pants,' she said roughly, and then, catching the startled look on his face, realized the significance of what she had said.

'Better make sure of it,' he said, and she checked again.

'They're gone all right,' she said. 'Frilly ones – they were a present. I wouldn't wear the blooming things.'

'That's bad,' he said, and went back to the living room.

'You'll have a drink as you're here,' she said.

'I'd better not,' he said with a boyish grin. 'It's Madge. She starts getting nervous when I'm out.'

'I'm going to have one anyway,' said Jane, knowing well what it was Madge got nervous of – another woman who might talk to him about some things beside 'the claw-sicks'.

'Tell me, do you remember was any fellow annoying you?' he asked.

'Nobody,' she said. 'Unless that fellow on the phone.'

'Oh, was he after you too?' Humphreys asked with interest. 'That's someone I'd like to lay my hands on some time. What did you do?'

'What could I do?' she asked, taking her drink. 'The first time I was so appalled, I listened. It's funny; I suppose it's like being hypnotized. After it, you start to get sick. I never knew people could be like that. The second time I did what Ned Sullivan told me, and he's left me alone since then.'

'What was that?'

'Oh, I told him he was a very sick man and that he should get treatment at once.' She gave an engaging grin. 'You know – Dr Harty, the well-known nerve specialist, giving a free opinion and wondering all the time when she'll start screaming.'

'Was he cross?'

'Leppin' mad.'

'That was clever of Ned Sullivan,' said Humphreys. 'But I don't think it's the same man. This is probably someone you know quite well. Any idea who it could be?'

'Not a notion.'

'Someone who comes into the shop for small things you'd expect his mother or sister to get for him?' he asked shrewdly.

'I can't think of a soul,' she said offhandedly. 'Anybody that isn't normal, I mean.'

'They all look normal enough to begin with,' he said grimly. 'They won't look so normal in five years' time. If you think of anyone let me know . . . The bloody house is probably full of fingerprints,' he added gloomily. 'For all the good they'd do us.'

As he was leaving he studied the lock and said, 'I think I'd get a new lock for the door. And you might as well get a spare key and leave it at the barrack. I could drop in some evening and see if he'd come. Anyway, you'd better call at the barrack tomorrow and have a word with the superintendent. Not that he'll know more than I do, but it might make things easier for us.'

She did as he advised and understood what he meant. The superintendent was a bright and cheerful young man who was obviously much happier with papers than with people. Papers didn't answer back in the same way.

'We could all be killed in our beds, and 'twould only make an interesting statistic for that idiot,' she said to the Sullivans.

'You're in no danger like that,' Ned said thoughtfully. 'That fellow won't come near the place as long as you're there. He's still too shy. You'll find there's a loving Irish mother in the background who takes him to Confession herself every Saturday and writes out a list of his sins for him, the way he won't forget. He may get dangerous, but it won't be for a long time yet, and it won't be over you. Damn it, I feel I ought to be able to go for a walk and put my hand on him! You'll have to think of someone like that, Jan.'

'Ah, for God's sake, I'd have to think of half the town,' she said jokingly, but he didn't smile.

'You would, you would, but this is something different. Lord God, it's unknown the lives people have to lead in towns like this!' he added, growing bitter himself.

It was after that she began to crack. Two or three times she stopped the car outside the gate and blew the horn to warn the intruder. Now she had almost a horror of seeing him, for fear she might know who he was. And once more she returned from a weekend and saw that he had been there. He must have come before darkness fell for he had taken down a few of her books. In the bedroom there was the same childish disorder of clothes, but written in lipstick over her bed were the words 'I love you.'

She called the guards station and Humphreys answered.

'All right, all right,' he said quickly. 'Don't touch anything. Somebody will be along in a minute. And meantime, don't worry. You're all right.'

'Would you ask whoever is coming to tell Ned Sullivan?' she asked and was slightly shocked after she had said it. But Ned was the only one she wanted to talk to now.

It was Lenihan who came and inspected the house. Ned came after him, walking slowly. Lenihan exasperated her, examining locks and window-catches.

'This is how he got in all right,' he said sagaciously, indicating the catch on the bedroom window. 'That catch is too easy to open. Blast him anyway! He doesn't miss much.'

''Tis nice to know how he got in,' Ned said sarcastically. 'It would be more practical if we knew how to keep him out.'

'Oh, we'll get him yet, Mr Sullivan,' said Lenihan, shaking his head over it. 'He'll come too often, the way they all do. But if I was you, Miss Harty, I wouldn't bother my head about him. Sure, he's only a poor harmless ould sexual maniac. The country is full of them. So long as he wouldn't take anything valuable.'

'I haven't anything valuable for him to take,' she replied.

'No. Only your peace of mind,' Ned said shortly.

When Lenihan had gone he gave a sigh.

'It's no use relying on those fellows,' he said. 'They have no notion who that fellow is. Either that, or they know and they're not telling. It could be somebody that they don't want to make a fuss about. But they're right enough about the danger. They don't see the real danger you're in.'

'What danger?' she asked curiously.

'That fellow would drive you as mad as himself,' Ned said flatly. ''Twould be like living with a ghost. It gives me the horrors, not to mind you. I'm going to get myself a drink if you have one.'

195

'Do you really think they know?' she asked as he got the tumblers.

'They may. This is probably someone you saw being picked on or ignored some place and made a fuss of. Or you stopped and gave him a lift. It was probably the first time a woman treated him as a human being, and it went to the poor devil's head.' He glanced at her inquiringly, but her face was a blank, and he knew that this was what she did normally and that it would have made no impression on her mind. 'Oh, how the hell do I know? But you'd better start making plans to get out.'

'Out?'

'You can't stay here.'

'But where am I to go?'

'Somewhere they won't notice your seven-league boots,' he replied with mournful humour. 'You have them all frightened: Humphreys' wife is frightened, Lenihan is frightened; you probably scared the wits out of the superintendent as well. I'll hear it all in due course, in Slattery's pub. Sex is a game, girl,' he said almost angrily. 'You have to play a three to beat a two, but you play your ace every time. You simply can't afford to live naturally in a place like this.'

'That's a comforting thought,' she replied bitterly. 'In that case you'd better go home to Celia, quick. She'll be wondering what happened to you.'

'She won't. She told me I was to spend the night or bring you back with me.'

Anger was Jane's first response. It was as though Celia were condescending to him. And then she realized how unfair she was. Celia was merely showing that she knew the gossip and didn't care.

'Tell Celia I'd go back with you if I could,' she said with a sob. 'If I gave in now I'd never sleep here alone again.'

'And do you intend to go on staying here alone?' he asked.

'But where else have I to go, Ned?'

'Go to Dublin, go to London, get to hell out of this!' he cried. 'And God knows I'm not saying that for my sake.'

It was as though her tears had been waiting for the words. He took her in his arms and patted her awkwardly. 'I know, love, I know,' he said, as though he were speaking to a child, and she knew that he did know, and that it would always be this way with her, falling in love with the wrong man or the man she could not have, exactly as though each time she did it coldly and deliberately.

'Go on, Ned! Go home!' she said, and he understood that too. It was better for him to go now, for otherwise it would only mean the same old remorse and guilt for her. She tried to smile at him from the door, and then went back quickly and poured herself another drink. Then she opened the living-room window and stood, looking out at the country road, the bogs and the fields, now vague shapes in the darkness. At the end of the garden she seemed to see the poor simpleton, staring at her, crushing a pair of her pants in his hands and muttering, 'I love you.' She rested her hands on the window-sill and leaned out as though she could see him.

'Are you there?' she called.

There was no reply, only the whisper that always ran over the dark uplands at night, and she raised her voice.

'Come in, whoever you are!' she said. 'There's nobody here at all. The guards are gone. You're perfectly safe.'

For some reason she was convinced that he was there, listening to her but paralysed, trapped in the snare of his own crazy character even more than she was in hers. And yet all she wanted was to come to terms with him, to lure him out of himself and make him realize that there was a world of warmth and friendship in which he could exist. Then she slammed the window and gave way to an agony of hopelessness. When people had mocked and criticized her she had been afraid, but she had not given in, but now she was really afraid because what she had to deal with was a loneliness deeper than her own.

She knew now that Ned was right and that she no longer had a place of refuge from the outside world. She would never be able to live alone again; never again would she have a life of her own.

(1965)

The Impossible Marriage

It wasn't till he was nearly thirty that Jim Grahame realized the trick that life had played on him. Up to that time he had lived very much like any other young man, with no great notion that he was being imposed upon. His father had died ten years before. Jim, an accountant in a provision store, had continued to accept his father's responsibilities, and his mother, a lively, sweet-natured little woman, had kept house for him in the way that only mothers can. They lived on in the house into which she had married; a big, roomy, awkward house on the edge of the country where the rent they paid was barely enough to keep the building in repair. Jim had never been very shy with girls, but none of them he had met seemed to him to be half the woman his mother was, and, unknown to himself, he was turning into a typical comfortable old bachelor who might or might not at the age of forty-five decide to establish a family of his own. His mother spoiled him, of course, and, in the way of only children, he had a troubled conscience because of the way he took advantage of it. But spoiling is a burden that the majority of men can carry a great deal of without undue hardship.

Then, by the seaside in Crosshaven, one Sunday, he went for a walk with a girl called Eileen Clery, who lived in the same quarter of Cork as himself, though he had never noticed her before. She wasn't the sort of girl who thrusts herself on people's attention, though she was good-looking enough, with a thin face that lit up beautifully when she smiled, and pale hair with gold lights in it. He tried to flirt with her, and was surprised and a little offended by her quick, almost violent, withdrawal. He had not mistaken her for a flighty type, but neither had he expected to meet an untouchable.

The curious thing was that she seemed to like him, and even arranged to meet him again. This time they sat in a nook on the cliffs, and Jim became more pressing. To his astonishment, she began to cry. He was exasperated, but he pretended a solicitude he did not altogether feel, and when she saw him apparently distressed, she sat up and smiled, though her tears still continued to flow freely. 'It's not that I wouldn't like it, Jim,' she said, drying her eyes and blowing her nose into a ridiculous little scrap of a handkerchief, 'only I don't like thinking about it.'

'Why on earth not, Eileen?' he asked with some amusement.

'Well, you see, I'm an only child, and I have my mother to look after,' she said, still sniffing.

'And I'm an only child, and I have a mother to look after,' Jim replied triumphantly, and then laughed outright at the absurdity of the coincidence. 'We're a pair,' he added with a rueful chuckle.

'Yes, aren't we?' Eileen said, laughing and sobbing at once, and then she rested her head on his chest, and made no further difficulties about his love-making.

Now, all books on the subject describe attraction in similar terms: tanned chests and voluptuous contours which really have very little to do with the matter. But what they rarely mention, the most powerful of all, is human loneliness. This is something that women face earlier than men, and Eileen had already faced it. Jim, though he had not faced it in the same way, was perceptive enough to see it reaching out before him, and up there on the cliffs overlooking Cork Harbour, watching a score of little sailing boats headed for Currabinny, they realized that they were in love, and all the more in love because their position was so obviously hopeless.

After that, they met regularly every week in Cork, to walk, or go to the pictures when it rained. They did it in the way of only children, taking precautions that became something of a joke to those who knew them. One evening, a girl crossing the New Bridge saw Jim Grahame standing there, and when she came to the second bridge was amused to see Eileen. 'Excuse my interfering, Miss Clery,' she said, 'but if it's Mr Grahame you're waiting for, he's waiting for you at the other bridge.' Eileen didn't know where to look; she blushed, she laughed, and finally joined her hands and said, 'Oh, thank you, thank you,' and ran like the wind.

It was like them to meet that way, miles from home, because they were pursued by the sense of guilt. They felt more pity for their mothers than for themselves and did their best to hide their dreadful secret out of some instinctive understanding of the fear of loneliness and old age that besets women whose families have grown and whose husbands are dead. Perhaps they even understood it too well, and apprehended more of it than was really there.

Mrs Grahame, whose intelligence service was better than Mrs Clery's, was the first to speak of the matter to them.

'I hear you're great friends with a girl called Clery from the Cross,' she said one evening in a tone of modest complaint. Jim was shaving by the back door. He started and turned to her with a look of amusement, but she was absorbed in her knitting, as always when she did not wish to look him in the face.

'Go on!' he said. 'Who told you that?'

'Why wouldn't I hear it when the whole road knows it?' she replied, avoiding his question. She liked her little mysteries. 'Wouldn't you bring her up some night?'

'You wouldn't mind?'

'Why would I mind, child? Little enough company we see.'

This was another of her favourite myths; that she never saw or spoke to anyone, though Jim could do little or nothing that she didn't hear about sooner or later.

One evening he brought Eileen home for tea, and though she was nervous and giggly, he could see that his mother took to her at once. Mrs Grahame worshipped her son, but she had always wished for a daughter, someone she could talk to as she could not talk to a man. Later in the evening, Eileen, realizing that she really was welcome, began to relax, and she and his mother exchanged the sort of gossip they both loved.

'Ah, Dinny Murphy was a bad head to her,' his mother would say darkly, referring to some object of charity in the neighbourhood.

'No, no, no, Mrs Grahame,' Eileen would say hastily, in her eagerness laying her hand on Mrs Grahame's arm. 'Poor Dinny wasn't the worst.'

'Look at that now!' Mrs Grahame would cry, putting down her knitting to fix Eileen with eyes that were bleak with tragedy. 'And the things they said about him! Eileen, haven't people *bad* tongues?'

'No, he wasn't, he wasn't,' Eileen would repeat, shaking her head. 'He took a drop, of course, but which of them doesn't, would you tell me?'

And Jim, who said nothing, smiled as he noticed how the voice of Eileen, young, eager, and intelligent, blended with his mother's in a perfect harmony of gossip. Mrs Grahame did not let her go without hinting delicately at her lost and lonely condition that made it impossible for her to know the truth about anything, and made her promise to come again. She became accustomed to Eileen's visits, and was quite hurt if a week went by without one. She even said with great resignation that of course she was no company for a lively young girl like that.

Then it was Mrs Clery's turn. She might hear of Eileen's visits to the Grahames, and be upset, but, on the other hand, she might be equally upset by an unexpected visit. So Eileen had to prepare her by telling her first how Jim was situated with regard to his own mother so that she wouldn't think he came to the house with any designs on Eileen. All they had to live on was Eileen's earnings and a few shillings pension which her mother drew.

They lived in a tiny cottage in a terrace off the road, with a parlour, a kitchen that they used as a living room, and two attic bedrooms upstairs. Mrs Clery was a shrewd old lady with a battered humorous face. She suffered from a variety of ailments, and, being slightly deaf, complained of them at great length in a loud, hectoring tone. She would put a firm hand on her interlocutor's knee while she talked, to make sure he didn't escape, and then stare blankly at the fireplace in concentration.

'So then, Jim, I had this second pain I was telling you about, and I had Dr O'Mahoney to the house, and he said – what did Dr O'Mahoney say about the second pain, Eileen?'

'He said you were an old humbug,' bawled Eileen.

'Dr O'Mahoney?' her mother said in wonderment. 'He did not. Ah, you divil you!'

At home, Eileen talked nervously, at the top of her voice, interrupting, contradicting, and bantering her mother till the old woman's face wrinkled up with glee and she blinked at Jim and groaned: 'Didn't I say she was a divil, Jim? Did you ever hear a girl talk to her mother that way? I'll engage you don't talk like that to your own poor mother.'

'His mother isn't always grousing,' Eileen yelled blithely from the backyard.

'Grousing? Who's grousing?' asked Mrs Clery, her eyes half closing with pleasure, like a cat's when you stroke it. 'Oh, my,

I live in terror of her, Jim, boy, you never heard such a tongue! And the lies she tells! Me grousing!'

All the same it was pleasant for Jim and Eileen to have a place to turn to on a wet night when they didn't want to go to the pictures. Mostly, they went to Jim's. Mrs Grahame was more jealous than Eileen's mother. Even a hint of slight on the part of either of them would reduce her to mutinous tears, but if they sat with her for half an hour, she would get up and tiptoe gently out of the room as though she thought they were asleep. Her jealousy was only the measure of her generosity.

'Wisha, Jim,' she said roguishly one evening, putting down her knitting, 'wouldn't you and Eileen make a match of it?'

'A match?' Jim repeated mockingly, looking up from his book. 'I suppose you want to get rid of me?'

His mother could usually be diverted from any subject by teasing because she took everything literally even if she rarely took it far.

'Indeed, what a thing I'd do!' she said in a huff and went on with her knitting, full of childish rage at his reception of her generous proposal. But, of course, it didn't last. Ten minutes later, having forgotten her huff, she added, this time as though speaking to herself:'Why, then, you wouldn't find many like her.'

'And where would we live?' he asked with gentle irony.

'My goodness, haven't ye the house?' she said, looking at him severely over her glasses. 'You don't think I'd stop to be in your way?'

'Oh, so you'd go to the workhouse and let Mrs Clery come here?'

'Wisha, aren't things very peculiar?' she said vaguely, and he knew that she was brooding on the coincidence by which he and Eileen had been drawn together. His mother and he were both familiar with the situation in its simple form, common as it is in Ireland, and could have listed a score of families where a young man or woman 'walked out' for years before he or she was in a position to marry, too often only to find themselves too old or tired for it.

'We're not thinking in that direction at all, Mrs Grahame, thank you all the same,' he said, giving her a sweet smile. 'It's got to be a double murder or nothing at all.'

He knew that in spite of her jealousy, Mrs Grahame resented

this fate for them, but Mrs Clery jovially pretended that they should be grateful for their good fortune.

'Ye don't know how well off ye are,' she said. 'Ye're young and healthy; a lot ye have to complain of. The way they rush into marriage you'd think they were robbing a bank. Soon enough they get tired of it, and then, oh, my! nothing is bad enough for them to say about one another.'

'So you don't approve of marriage, Mammy?' Eileen would ask demurely.

'Who said I don't approve of marriage?' her mother asked suspiciously, certain that the 'divils' were trapping her again. 'What matter whether you approve of it or not? That doesn't make it any better. Let ye be young while ye can, Jim,' she counselled, laying a rocky hand on Jim's knee. 'Ye'll be married long enough.'

But, of course, Eileen and himself did not share her views. On their evening walks they usually passed through one of the new developments, glanced into half-built houses with the enthusiasm of the children who played Cowboys and Indians in them; chatted with young husbands digging in little patches of garden that were mainly builders' rubble, and let themselves be invited in for cups of tea by young couples in all the pride and joy of recent possession. They saw nothing of the ugliness of it. They saw only the newness of everything as though it were life itself renewed; the way the evening sunlight brought up the freshness of the paint, the whiteness of the curtains, the tender green of the new grass. Later in the evening Eileen would say, shaking her head: 'I didn't think the curtains were right in the big corner windows, Jim, did you?' and Jim would know she had furnished the house in her own mind.

That year Jim suggested that he and Eileen should take their holidays together. This didn't suit Mrs Clery at all. She was sure it would give Eileen a bad name. Mrs Clery was all for their being young while they could, but only as long as they were being young under her eye. Jim knew it wasn't Eileen's good name that her mother worried about at all, but the possibility that their holiday might start something she could not control. He had his way; they went to a seaside place north of Dublin, and walked and swam and sunbathed to their hearts' content for a fortnight, going into the city when it rained.

On their way home, looking out at the Galtee mountains from the window of their carriage, he said: 'Next time we go on holidays like that, we should be married. It's not the same thing.'

'No, Jim, it isn't,' she agreed. 'But what can we do?'

'What's to stop us getting married?' he asked with a smile.

'Now?' she asked in alarm. 'But what would we do with our mothers?'

'What we do with them now,' he said with a shrug.

'You mean get married and go on the way we're going?'

'Why not? Of course, it's not what we want, but it's better than nothing.'

'But suppose – well, Jim, you know yourself there might be children.'

'I should hope so,' he replied. 'We can cross that bridge when we come to it. But anyhow, there's no particular reason we should have kids yet.'

'But Jim,' she asked timidly, 'wouldn't people talk?'

'Do you think they don't talk now?'

Jim was like that, and what Jim thought his mother would think, regardless of public opinion. She, of course, had seen nothing wrong with their going on holidays together, and Eileen, who had felt rather doubtful of it herself, now knew that she was right. She felt he was probably right now too, but she wasn't sure.

The more she thought of it, the more she felt he was, though her reasons were of a different kind. Jim didn't want to wait; he didn't want to grow old and sour in expectation of the day when they could get married; he wanted something, however little it might be, of the pleasure of marriage while they were still young enough to enjoy it. Eileen thought of it in a more mystical way, as a sort of betrothal which would bind them to one another, whatever life might have in store for them. She knew it was too much to hope that she and Jim would both be set free at the same time; one would be bound to be free long before the other, and then the real temptation would begin.

But she knew that even this she would not get without a fight with her mother. Mrs Clery was conventional to the heart, and besides she knew what happened in marriage. Eileen was very sweet and gentle now, but Eileen as wife or mother would be an altogether different proposition and one an old lady might be unable to handle at all.

'What a thing you'd do!' Mrs Clery gasped with one hand on her hip. 'What sort of marriage would that be? Him living there and you living here! You'd have the whole town laughing at you.'

'I don't really see what they'd have to laugh at, Mammy,' Eileen said earnestly. 'Any more than they have now.'

'Go off with him!' her mother said brokenly. 'Go off with him! I'd sooner go to the workhouse than be disgraced by ye.'

'But, Mammy,' persisted Eileen, laughing in spite of herself, 'we won't do anything to disgrace you, and you won't have to go to the workhouse or anywhere else.'

Mrs Grahame was upset too, but it was her pride that was hurt. What the neighbours would say did not worry her at all, but it seemed to her that it was her dependence on Jim that forced him into this caricature of a marriage. If by getting out of his way she could have made it easier for him, she would cheerfully have gone into the workhouse. But when Jim explained that even if he agreed to her doing so, it would change nothing regarding Eileen and her mother, she saw that he was right. When next Eileen called, Mrs Grahame embraced her and muttered: 'Ye poor children! Ye poor, distracted children!'

'You don't think we're doing wrong, Mrs Grahame?' Eileen asked, beginning to be tearful herself.

'Sure, how could you be doing wrong, child?' Mrs Grahame exclaimed angrily. 'Why would ye care what anybody thinks? People who never sacrificed a thing in their lives!'

Then Mrs Clery threw a fit of the sulks, would not speak to Jim when he called, and finally refused to attend what she called 'the mock wedding'. Mrs Clery had little experience of that sort of thing, but she did know when she had been tricked, and she had been tricked by Jim. He had come to the house as a friend and stolen her only daughter from under her eyes. As for all this talk of putting her first, she didn't believe a word of it. A man who would do what he had done would think nothing of putting arsenic in her cup of tea.

Before she left for the church that morning, Eileen went in to her mother and asked gently: 'Mammy, won't you even wish me luck?' But all her mother said was, 'Go away, you bold thing!'

'I'll be back tomorrow night in time to get your supper, Mammy,' Eileen said meekly.

'You needn't come back at all,' said her mother.

Eileen was very upset, but Mrs Grahame only scoffed at it when they said goodbye outside the church.

'Ah, she'll get over it, child,' she said. 'Old people are all lick alike. I'm the same myself, if the truth was known. I'll see her on the way home and give her a bit of my mind.'

'And, Mrs Grahame, if you wouldn't mind making her an egg flip, she'd be easier to talk to,' Eileen said earnestly. 'She's very fond of egg flips, and she likes a lot of whiskey in them.'

'I'll give her an egg flip,' said Mrs Grahame, suddenly light-hearted because her own savage jealousy melted in the thought of comforting another old woman in her tantrums. She had a job on her hands, even with the egg flip.

'Don't talk to me, ma'am!' cried Mrs Clery. 'Young people today are all the same; all selfish, all for pleasure.'

'How can you say it, Mrs Clery?' Mrs Grahame asked indignantly. 'There isn't a better daughter in Ireland. I'd be the last to criticize Jim, but I only wish I had one like her.'

'And when the children start coming?' asked Mrs Clery, looking at her as if she were out of her mind.

'You reared one yourself.'

''Tisn't alike, ma'am,' said Mrs Clery and refused to be comforted. She was intelligent enough to realize that the presence of another baby in the house might rob her of some of the attention to which she felt entitled, and might even result in her being totally deprived of her privileges. Young people today were so selfish!

After their one-day honeymoon, Jim and Eileen obediently returned to their duties as though they had never been married at all. Yet Eileen, when you met her on the road, was exceedingly lighthearted and lightheaded, sporting her ring like any young bride. She needed all the joy her new position gave her because her mother had been shrewd enough in her summing up of what the neighbours' attitude would be. The marriage had become a matter of scandalous jokes, and remained so as long as it lasted. Even from intimate friends, Eileen got little jabs that reminded her of her anomalous wifehood. It wasn't that the neighbours were uncharitable, but their feelings about marriage, like their feelings about death, had a certain fierceness that was obvious even in their dislike of second marriages. This marriage that seemed to end at the church door was a mockery of all they believed in, so they took their revenge as people will whose dearest beliefs have been slighted.

Jim affected not to notice the scandal. He had his mother's curious imperviousness to public opinion, and he dropped in on Eileen as though nothing in particular could be said against him. Eileen dropped in rather more frequently on him and his mother, and Jim and she went off for a fortnight in the summer to Kerry or Connemara. It took Mrs Clery a full year to get used to it, and all that time she watched Eileen closely, expecting her each week to show signs of pregnancy. Perhaps it was fortunate that there were none. Heaven alone knows what she might have done.

Then Mrs Grahame fell ill, and Jim nursed her by day while Eileen took over from him at night. She was dying, and in the intervals of consciousness, she moulded Eileen's hands with her own and said: 'I always wanted a daughter, and I had my wish. I had my wish. Ye'll be happy now that ye have the house to yerselves. You'll look after Jim for me?'

'I'll look after him for you,' Eileen said, and on the night when his mother died she let him sleep on.

'I thought I'd better not wake you, Jim,' she said when she roused him next morning. 'You were so tired and Mammy went so peacefully . . . That's the way she'd have wished it, Jim,' she added gravely when she saw his look of surprise.

'I dare say you're right, Eileen,' he agreed.

But their troubles were far from being at an end. When they proposed to shift into Jim's house, Mrs Clery raised more of a hullabaloo than she had raised over the marriage.

'Is it up among strangers?' she cried aghast.

'Strangers half a mile away, Mammy?' Eileen exclaimed, still unable to conceal a laugh at her mother's extraordinary reception of every new proposal.

'Half a mile?' her mother echoed dully. ''Tis a mile.'

'And you think your old friends would desert you?' asked Eileen.

'I wouldn't ask them,' her mother replied with dignity. 'I couldn't sleep in a place where I wouldn't hear the sound of the trams. Jim's mother died in her own house. Oh, my, isn't it a queer thing he wouldn't let me die in mine!'

And once more Jim and Eileen had to resign themselves to frustration. They could offer no adequate substitute for the soothing squeak of the trams climbing Summerhill from the city, and as Eileen saw, it would be folly for them to give up Jim's excellent house, which they would need later on, and come to share her own tiny cottage with a cranky mother-in-law.

Instead, they played at being married. On a couple of evenings each week, Eileen would give her mother supper early and then come to Jim's house and have supper ready for him when he got in from the shop. When she heard his key in the lock, she ran to the front door to meet him in her white housecoat, and he would let on to be suitably astonished at seeing her. As they went in, she would point silently to the big fire she had lit in the living-room, and they would have supper together and read or talk till he saw her home coming on to midnight. Yet, even with extra work, it gave them both a deep pleasure to make the big bed that Eileen never slept in except as a visitor, to wash up together, or, best of all, to entertain some friends, just as though Eileen did not, like Cinderella, have to fly back at midnight to her old part as daughter and nurse. Some day, they felt, the house would really be theirs, and she would open the door in the morning to milkman and breadman.

But this was not how things happened. Instead, Jim fell seriously ill, and rather than consent to the conflict which he knew this would set up in Eileen's mind between her duty to him and her duty to her mother, he chose to go to hospital. Two years after his mother's death, he died there.

Something seemed to happen to Eileen at this point that made even her mother afraid. There was no argument between them as to what she should do. She shut up her own cottage, and her mother joined her in Jim's house where she received his relatives. The body had been taken to the church, and when Jim's family came, Eileen had lunch ready for them, and chatted as she served, as though the trouble had been theirs rather than hers. It was a cold lunch, and she was full of apologies. At the graveside while they wept, she showed no sign of tears. When the grave had been covered over Jim and his mother, she stood there silently, her head bowed, and Jim's aunt, an enormous woman, came up and took her two hands.

'You're a great little girl,' she whispered huskily. ''Twon't be forgotten for you.'

'But, Auntie,' Eileen replied, 'that's the way Jim would have liked it. It makes me feel close to him, and it won't be long till we're together again. Once Mammy goes, there'll be nothing to keep me.'

There was something about her words, and her dry-eyed air and her still-youthful face that the other woman found disconcerting.

'Ah, nonsense, child!' she said lightly. 'We all feel that way. You'll be happy yet, and you'll deserve it. One of these days you'll have a houseful of your own.'

'Oh, no, Auntie,' Eileen replied with a sweet smile that was curiously knowledgeable and even condescending, as though Jim's aunt were too much of a child to understand. 'You know yourself I could never find another husband like Jim. People can't be as happy as that a second time, you know. That would be too much to ask.'

And relatives and even neighbours began to realize that Eileen was only telling the truth; that in spite of everything she had been intensely happy, happy in some way they could not understand, and that what had seemed to them a mockery of marriage had indeed been one so complete and satisfying that beside it, even by their standards, a woman might think everything else in the world a mere shadow.

(1957)

Unapproved Route

Between men and women, as between neighbouring states, there are approved roads which visitors must take. Others they take at their peril, no matter how high-minded their intentions may be.

When I lived in England I became friendly with another Irishman, named Frankie Daly. Frankie was the sort of man men like. He was scrupulous, but not so as to irritate people who might have scruples of a different kind. Exacting with himself, he was tolerant of others. The good qualities he had – conscientiousness, loyalty, and generosity – were not those he demanded of his friends, and, as a result, they made great efforts to show them where he was concerned. Even Mick Flynn, who lived by borrowing, made a hullabaloo about paying back a pound he owed to Frankie.

Frankie and I were also friendly with two school-mistresses who had a little cottage in School Lane, and they frequently joined us in the pub for a drink. Rosalind and Kate could have been sisters, they had so little in common. Kate was a born spinster, lean, plain, and mournful, and with the kindest heart in the world. She was very left-wing and tended to blame most of her troubles on capitalism. Rosalind was a good-looking girl with a fat and rather sullen face who was always up and down with some man, usually – according to Kate, at any rate – of the shadiest kind. Women with a man on their hands usually vote Tory – they dislike being interrupted – and Rosalind was a Conservative. Cooking being a form of activity associated with love-making, she was also an excellent cook, while Kate, who adored food, not only couldn't cook herself, but was driven into hysterics of fastidiousness by the mere sight of cooking fat. She felt about grease as she felt about men, and I sometimes had a suspicion that she identified the two. I often wondered how she could face the liquidation of capitalists and all the blood and mess it would involve.

One day another fellow coutryman of Frankie and myself turned up on a temporary job. He was a shambling, good-natured, high-spirited man, given to funny stories and inexplicable fits of morose anger. Lodgings were scarce and hotels expensive, so the girls offered him a room in the cottage. He settled down so well with them that inside a week or so he and Rosalind were lovers. She simply could not be kept away from men.

Kate then devoted herself entirely to the task of hating Jim Hourigan, and being as rude to him as she dared with Rosalind there. Having a lover of Rosalind's in the cottage was like having endless greasy frying-pans to dodge; she couldn't move without seeing a masculine singlet or a pair of socks. Kate derived enormous pleasure from her own griefs, and she told us with gloomy humour that it had been bad enough before, lying awake and wondering what Rosalind was up to, but this had been nothing to lying awake and knowing what she was up to. She couldn't kick up a row with Rosalind, who had an unpredictable and violent temper where men were concerned. Kate rationalized this to herself by saying that Rosalind, being a girl of exceptional intelligence, knew they were all wasters, but was too proud to admit it. She told us that Rosalind never had had any taste, that all the men she knew had exploited her, that Jim Hourigan was only another of them, and that the only consolation was that she was there herself, ready to pick up the pieces when the inevitable disillusionment came. Frankie and I only laughed at Kate's groans. We didn't know what sort Jim Hourigan was, and we didn't really care much.

When his job ended, he returned to Ireland, after making many promises of bringing the girls for a long summer holiday there, and of returning himself at the first opportunity. Kate was very cheerful because she was quite convinced that he didn't mean a word of it – she had the lowest view of his character and motives – and was delighted to have Rosalind and the cottage to herself again. Rosalind, too, was cheerful because, never before having had anything to do with an Irishman, she took all his promises for Gospel, had everything ready for her holiday in the summer, and was certain that Hourigan would then ask her to marry him. She wrote him long, animated letters, cleverly recalling our little town and the characters he had met there, and quoting Kate's doleful predictions about the weather, the European situation, and the cost of living.

There was an alarming lack of response to her letters; finally they did produce a wet spark of a picture postcard, saying how much Hourigan looked forward to coming back, that might have encouraged a more persevering correspondent, but merely infuriated Rosalind. She wasn't accustomed to having her brilliant letters treated with such lack of ceremony and told him so, but this didn't produce even a spark. Kate began to put on weight, though how she did was a miracle, because Rosalind was so upset she refused to cook and Kate had not only to eat sausages – which she loathed – but even to clean the disgusting frying-pan herself.

But that wasn't the end of Kate's troubles. Imprudent as usual, Rosalind was having a baby. Now, in the natural way of things, a nice baby without any messy father to get in the way would have been Kate's idea of bliss, but bliss of that sort is not contemplated in English provincial towns. To begin with, Rosalind would lose her job; women teachers cannot have babies without marriage lines; the thing is unknown. Besides, the landlady would be bound to ask them to leave; this was also part of the drill, and even if the landlady had been a considerate woman, which she wasn't, she would still have found it difficult to overlook such conduct. They would have to try and hush things up, and put the baby out to nurse.

This was where Rosalind became completely unmanageable. She said she wanted to keep her baby, and she didn't mind who knew. Just the same she stopped coming to the public house with the rest of us, and Kate, gloomier than ever, came alone. She was depressed by her failure to make Rosalind see reason. It would only be for a couple of years, and then they could make some arrangement, like pretending to adopt the baby.

'That wouldn't be so very good, Kate,' Frankie said when she mentioned it to him.

'Well, what else can she do, Frankie? Go out as a charwoman?'

'Those are questions that answer themselves, Kate,' he said stubbornly. 'A baby put out to nurse is a question that never answers itself.'

Next evening, without saying anything to Kate or me, he called to the cottage and found Rosalind sitting alone over the fire.

'Coming down to the pub, Rosa?' he asked cheerfully.

'No, Frankie, thanks,' she said, without looking up.

'Why not? You know it's not the same without you.'

She covered her face with her hands. Frankie sat awkwardly with his legs stretched out, sucking his pipe.

'Kate tells me you don't want to part with the child.'

'It seems I'm not likely to be asked.'

'All the same, I think you're right and Kate is wrong,' he said gravely.

'That's easily said, Frankie,' she replied. 'It isn't so easy for Kate, with her job to mind.'

'If that's how you feel about it, wouldn't it be better for you to marry?'

'The man who got me would get a treasure,' she said savagely. 'Whistled after in the street!'

'That's a matter for him,' said Frankie. 'Plenty of men would be very glad to marry you. You mustn't let a thing like this make you undervalue yourself.'

'Ah, talk sense, Frankie!' she said wearily. 'Who'd marry me in the middle of all this scandal?'

'I would, to begin with – if you hadn't anyone you liked better.'

'You?' she asked incredulously.

'And consider myself very much honoured,' Frankie added steadily.

'Are you serious, Frankie?' she asked, almost angrily.

'Of course I'm serious.'

'And face all the humiliation of it?'

'There isn't any humiliation,' he said flatly. 'That's where you're mistaken. There's no humiliation where there hasn't been any offence. The offence is in deceiving others, not in being deceived ourselves.'

'Oh, I can't, Frankie, I can't,' she said desperately. 'I've made a fool of myself over this waster, and I can't let another man shoulder my burdens.'

'There's no particular burden either,' he said. 'You mustn't think I'm asking you only because you're in a fix. I'd have asked you anyway when this thing was all over and you could make up your own mind. I'm only asking now in case it might make the immediate future a bit easier.'

'Why didn't you ask me before?'

'Maybe because I felt I hadn't much to offer you,' Frankie said, with a shy smile.

'My God,' she said, rising. 'I'd have married you like a shot.'

She sat on his knee and hugged him despairingly. He was a clumsy lover. He talked in an apologetic, worried tone about his job, his home, and his family; how much he earned and where they could live. She didn't listen. She thought of what it would mean to her to start life again, free of this nightmare. Then she took him by the shoulders and looked into his eyes with the air of a sleepwalker.

'I'll do it,' she said. 'God help me, Frankie, I hate it, but I'll do it for the kid's sake. All I can say is that I'll make it up to you. You needn't be afraid of that. I'll make it up to you all right.'

Kate, whose low view of life had led her to take a low view of its Creator, almost got converted because of it. She had always liked Frankie, but her experience of people she liked had been that they only got her into fresh trouble, and that it was better, if you could manage it, to have nothing to do with anybody. She wasn't the only one who admired Frankie's behaviour. It dawned on others of us that he had done exactly what we would have done ourselves except for what people might think. Actually, as we discovered, 'people', meaning the neighbours with one or two exceptions, liked Rosalind and were pleased to see her escape the machine of social ignominy reserved for women with more feeling than calculation in them.

Frankie and Rosalind were married quietly and went to live in a little cottage some miles outside the town, a rather lonely cottage with low beams, high chimneys, and breakneck staircases, but it had a big garden which Rosalind enjoyed. She kept on her job; she knew the other teachers knew, but now it only amused her. It was wonderful to have Frankie there as a prop. Up to this, all the men she had lived with had taken advantage of her, and she had accepted it in a cynical, good-humoured way, as part of the price you had to pay for being too fond of them. She believed, as Kate did, that men were like that, but she was lacking in any desire to reform them.

Under Frankie's care she grew round as a tun, stupid, and quite remarkably beautiful, while Kate managed to look as like the anxious father of her unborn child as a girl could look. But the change in Frankie was even more remarkable. He had always kept a youthful freshness, but now he suddenly began to look like a boy of seventeen. It might have been something to do with Rosalind's cooking – Kate, who had begun to feel the lack of it, visited them every day – but he rang her up regularly at school to see that she was all right, raced for his bus to get home early in the evenings, and took her for her evening walk to the pub. He was full of banter and tricks, and Rosalind looked on with the affectionate calm of a woman watching the man she loves make a fool of himself. And it really was pleasant those summer evenings outside the public house, watching that late flowering of emotion, the bachelor crust of caution breaking up, the little shoots of sentiment beginning to peer out.

Their happiness was lyrical. It was only at odd times that Rosalind remembered her griefs, and usually it was in the early morning when she was waked by the heaving of the child within her, listened to the birds outside their window, and felt deserted even with Frankie beside her. Not to wake him, she sniffled quietly into her handkerchief, her back turned on him and her body shaken with suppressed sobs. When he woke, she still tried to keep away from him.

'What ails you now didn't ail you before?' he would ask humorously.

'What you've got in me.'

'What's that?'

'I told you – a daisy!'

'No, that was what I told you,' he said, and slapped her bottom affectionately.

Then she bawled without restraint and beat her stomach.

'Why can't it be yours?' she cried despairingly.

'One thing at a time,' said Frankie.

He believed her; that was his mistake. He really thought when he heard her lonely weeping that it was merely the ambiguity of her position that caused it, and not the humiliation of being rejected and hounded into marriage with someone else by a tramp like Hourigan. Frankie was a decent man; he didn't realize that in circumstances like those no woman can ever be happy, even with the best man in the world – even with the man she loves. Love, in fact, has nothing to do with it. To ignore that is to ignore a woman's vanity, the mainspring of her character.

Her time came in the middle of the night, and Frankie returned from the nursing home in the early morning in a stupor of misery and astonishment; misery at the mere possibility that her life might be in danger, astonishment that anyone's life could possibly mean so much to him. He lit the fire, but then found that he couldn't bear the little cottage without her; it too seemed in a stupor of misery, wondering when she would come back, put on that housecoat, boil that kettle, and wash those dishes. He wanted to make himself breakfast, but could not bring himself to touch the things that were properly hers and that stood waiting for her with the infinite patience of inanimate things. He swore at himself when he realized that he was identifying his grief with that of a common tea-kettle. He had some breakfast in a café, and then went off, walking through the countryside, merely halting for a drink while he rang up the nursing home. It was evening before everything was over and Rosalind and the child – a son – safe, and then he took a car straight there.

She was still stupefied with drugs when he was admitted, but she clung to him passionately.

'Don't look!' she said fiercely. 'Not till the next time.'

'I thought he was yours,' Frankie said with a grin and smiled down at the little morsel in the cot. 'Cripes!' he added savagely. 'Wouldn't you think they could get them out without clawing them?'

'Did you hear the children playing on the doorstep?' she asked happily.

'No,' Frankie said in surprise. 'What were they playing?'

'*Hamlet*, I think,' she said closing her eyes, and, seeing how her thoughts drifted in and out of the drug, he tiptoed out. In sheer relief he knocked back three whiskeys in quick succession, but failed to get drunk. Then he tried for some of the old gang to sit and drink with, but, by one of those coincidences that always occur at moments like that, we were all out. It was just that he didn't want to go home. When he did get out of the bus and crossed the common towards the cottage he saw a man's figure step out of the shadow of the trees beside it and knew at once who it was. His heart sank.

'Frankie!' Jim Hourigan said imploringly. 'I'd like a word with you.'

Frankie halted. He had a sudden feeling of foreboding.

'You'd better come inside,' he said in a troubled voice.

He went ahead into the sitting room and switched on the light, and the electric fire which stood in the big open hearth. Then he turned and faced Hourigan, who was standing by the door. The man looked half distracted, his eyes were wild, his hair was in disorder.

'What is it?' he asked curtly.

'Frankie,' Hourigan muttered. 'I want a word with Rosalind.'

'Rosalind is in hospital.'

'I know, I know,' Hourigan said, flapping his hands like an old man. 'She said she was going there. But I wanted to see you first, to get your permission. It's only to explain to her, Frankie – that's all.'

Frankie concealed his surprise at Hourigan's statement that Rosalind had told him anything.

'I don't think she's in a state of seeing anybody, you know,' he said in a level tone. 'The boy was born only a couple of hours ago.'

'Christ!' Hourigan said, beating the table with his fist and shaking his head as though tossing water from his eyes. 'That's all that was missing. I came late for the fair as usual. My first child is born and I'm not even there. All right, Frankie, all right,' he added in a crushed tone, 'I see 'tis no good. But tell her all the same. Tell her I never knew a thing about it till I got her letter. That God might strike me dead this minute if the idea ever crossed my mind!'

Frankie looked at him in surprise. There was no mistaking the man's abject misery.

'What letter was this?' he asked.

'The letter she sent me before she went in,' Hourigan hurried on, too distraught to notice the bewilderment in Frankie's voice. 'You don't think I'd have treated her like that if I knew? You can think what you like of me, Frankie, and it won't be anything worse than I think of myself, but not that, Frankie, not that! I wouldn't do it to a woman I picked up in the street, and I loved that girl, Frankie. I declare to God I did.' He began to wave his arms wildly again, looking around the little sitting room without seeing anything. 'It's just that I'm no damn good at writing letters. The least thing puts me off. I'd be saying to myself I'd be there before the letter. I said the same thing to her on a card, Frankie, but then, the mother died, and I was in a terrible state – oh, the usual things! I know 'tis no excuse, and I'm not making excuses, but that's the way I am. If I had any idea I'd have been over to her by the first boat. You must tell her that, Frankie. She must know it herself.'

'When did you get this letter?' asked Frankie.

'Oh, only yesterday, Frankie,' exclaimed Hourigan, entirely missing the import of Frankie's question. 'I swear to God I didn't waste an hour. I'm travelling all night. I couldn't sleep and I couldn't eat. It was all that damn letter. It nearly drove me out of my mind. Did you see it, Frankie?'

'No,' said Frankie.

'Well, you'd better. Mind, I don't blame her a bit, but it's not true, it's not true!'

He took the letter from his wallet and passed it to Frankie. Frankie sat down and put on his glasses. Hourigan bent over the back of the armchair, reading it again in a mutter.

'Dear Jim Hourigan,' Frankie read silently. 'By this time tomorrow I'll be in a hospital, having your child. This will probably be more satisfaction to you than it is to me and my husband. I am sure you will be disappointed to know that I have a husband, but in this life we can't expect everything.'

'Now, that's what I mean, Frankie,' Hourigan said desperately, jabbing at the lines with his forefinger. 'That's not fair, and she knows it's not fair. She knows I'm not as mean as that, whatever faults I have.'

'I wouldn't worry too much about that,' Frankie said heavily, realizing that Hourigan and he were not reading the same letter. It was almost as though they were not concerned with the same woman. This was a woman whom Frankie had never seen. He went on reading.

'If the child takes after you, it might be better for more than Frank and myself that it shouldn't live. My only hope is that it may learn something from my husband. If ever a good man can make up to a child for the disaster of a bad father, your child will have every chance. So far as I can, I'll see that he gets it, and will never know any more of you than he knows now.' It was signed in full: 'Rosalind Daly'.

Hourigan sighed.

'You explain to her, Frankie,' he said despairingly. 'I couldn't.'

'I think it would be better if you explained it yourself,' Frankie said, folding up the letter and giving it back.

'You think she'll see me?' Hourigan asked doubtfully.

'I think she'd better see you,' Frankie said in a dead voice.

'Only for ten minutes, Frankie; you can tell her that. Once I explain to her, I'll go away, and I give you my word that neither of you will ever see me here again.'

'I'll talk to her myself in the morning,' Frankie said. 'You'd better ring me up at the office some time after twelve.'

Hourigan shambled away across the common, blabbing poetic blessings on Frankie's head and feeling almost elated. How Frankie felt, he never said. Perhaps if Hourigan had known how he felt, he might have left that night without seeing Rosalind. He wasn't a bad chap, Jim Hourigan, though not exactly perceptive, even as regards the mother of his child.

But Rosalind had perception enough for them both. When Frankie called next morning, the effect of the drug had worn off, and she knew from the moment he entered that something serious had happened. He was as gentle as ever, but he had withdrawn into himself, the old Frankie of the days before his marriage, hurt but self-sufficient. She grabbed his hands feverishly.

'Is anything wrong at home, Frankie?'

'Nothing,' he replied in embarrassment. 'Just a visitor, that's all.'

'A visitor? Who?'

'I think you know,' he said gently.

'What brought that bastard?' she hissed.

'Apparently a letter from you.'

Suddenly, she began to weep, the core of her hysteria touched.

'I didn't tell you because I didn't want to upset you,' she sobbed. 'I just wanted him to know how I despised him.'

'He seems to have got the idea,' Frankie said drily. 'Now, he wants to see you, to explain.'

'Damn his explanations!' she cried hysterically. 'I know what you think – that I sent that letter without telling you so as to bring him here. How could I know there was enough manliness in him to make him even do that? Can't you imagine how I felt, Frankie?'

'You know,' he said paternally, 'I think you'd better have a word with him and make up your mind about exactly what you did feel.'

'Oh, Christ!' she said. 'I tell you I only meant to hurt him. I never meant to hurt you, and that's all I've succeeded in doing.'

'I'd rather you didn't let your feelings run away with you again and hurt yourself and the child,' Frankie said in a gentler tone.

'But how can I avoid hurting myself when I'm hurting you?' she asked wildly. 'Do you think this is how I intended to pay you back for what you did for me? Very well; if he's there, send him up and I'll tell him. I'll tell him in front of you. I'll tell you both exactly how I feel. Will that satisfy you?'

'He'll call this afternoon,' Frankie said firmly. 'You'd better see him alone. You'd better let him see the child alone. And remember,' he added apologetically, 'whatever you decide on, I agree to beforehand. I may have behaved selfishly before. I don't want to do it again.'

He smiled awkwardly and innocently, still bewildered by the disaster which had overtaken him, and Rosalind held her hands to her temples in a frenzy. She had never realized before how hurt he could be, and probably not even known that she might hurt him.

'I suppose you think I'm going to let you divorce me so that I can go back to Ireland with that waster? I'd sooner throw myself and the child into a pond. Oh, very well, I'll settle it, I'll settle it. Oh, God!' she said between her teeth. 'What sort of fool am I?'

And as he went down the stairs, Frankie knew that he was seeing her for the last time as his wife, and that, when they met again, she would be merely the mother of Jim Hourigan's child, and realized with a touch of bitterness that there are certain forms of magnanimity which are all very well between men, but are misplaced in dealing with women, not because they cannot admire them, but because they seem to them irrelevant to their own function in life. When he saw Hourigan again he knew that the change had already taken place. Though nothing had been decided, Jim Hourigan was almost professionally protective of Frankie's interests and feelings. That was where the iron in Frankie came out. He made it plain that his interests were not in question.

There were plenty – Kate among them – to say that he had behaved absurdly; that with a little more firmness on his part the crisis would never have arisen; that Rosalind was in no condition to make the decision he had forced on her and needed only gentle direction to go on as she had been going; that, in fact, he might have spared her a great deal of unhappiness by refusing to see Jim Hourigan in the first place.

As for unhappiness, nothing I have heard suggests that Rosalind is unhappy with Jim Hourigan. It is a grave mistake to believe that that sort of thing leads to unhappiness. Frankie's conduct certainly does, but is that not because to people like him happiness is merely an incidental, something added, which taken away, leaves them no poorer than before?

(1952)

Music When
Soft Voices Die

During the lunch hour the male clerks usually went out, leaving myself and the three girls behind. While they ate their sandwiches and drank their tea, they chattered away, thirteen to the dozen. Half their conversation I didn't understand at all, and the other half bored me to tears. I usually drifted into the hallway with a Western. As a boy, I acted out whatever I was reading – taking steady aim, drawing rein, spurring to the rescue, and clutching at my shoulder where an Indian arrow had lodged – and the girls interrupted me with their comments.

They were nice girls, though. Joan, who was nineteen, was my favourite. She was masterful and warmhearted; she would take my part when I got in trouble, and whenever she saw me with the sign of tears, she would put her arm round me and say, 'Look, Larry – *you* tell Mr Scally if he says *another* word to you, I'll tear his *eyes* out.' She talked like that, all in italics. I liked Nora, too, but not so much. Sometimes she was very sweet and sometimes she didn't see you, and you never knew which it would be. Marie I didn't really like at all in those days. She was the prettiest of the three – thin, tall, and nunlike, with a queer stiff way of holding herself and an ironic intonation in her beautiful voice. Marie usually just didn't see you. I thought she was an old snob.

The three girls had fellows, and I knew these, too, mostly from seeing them hang about the office in the evening. Joan was going with a long-haired medical student called Mick Shea, with no hat and no religion, and she was always making novenas for his conversion. Nora went with a dressy fellow in Montenotte, the classy quarter of Cork, but she had a sort of underground understanding with a good-looking postman called Paddy Lacy, who used to stop me in the street and give me gallant messages for her. She never walked out with him that I knew of, but he was certain she loved him, and it shocked me that a superior fellow like a postman would not have more sense. Marie was going strong with a chap called Jim Holbrook, a rather snobbish intellectual type, who lived up my way.

Thirty years has turned the girls and myself into old friends. Only Nora is still at the office. Joan owns a private hotel, and Marie is the harassed mother of two wild children. She is still beautiful, sedate, and caustic. Not one word of their conversation ever seemed to register in my memory, which was full of valuable information about American states and Indian nations, wigwams, Colts, Derringers, and coyotes; yet now that I cannot remember anything of what I read, it seems to me that I can hear the girls as though they were in the same room with me, like the voices of Shelley's poem, trembling on the edge of pure music.

'Do you know, I have a *great* admiration for that girl?' Joan begins in her eager italics.

'Go on!' Nora says lightly. 'What did she do?'

'I admire her pluck, Nora,' Joan says, emphasizing three syllables out of seven. 'When I *think* what she went through!'

'Ah, for God's sake, what did she go through?' Nora asks sceptically.

'That's all you know, Nora,' Joan says in a bloodcurdling voice. 'You never had an illegitimate kid to support, and Susie had.'

'Good job, too,' Nora says. 'I can't support myself.'

'What did you say she had, Joan?' Marie asks incredulously.

'A kid.'

'Well!' Marie exclaims, looking brightly from one to the other. 'The friends some people have!'

'Oh, it's true, Marie.'

'That's what makes it so peculiar, Joan,' Marie says with a shrug.

'What did she do with it?' Nora asks inquisitively.

'I suppose I really shouldn't say it, Nora, but of course it's really no secret. With the way the police watch girls like that, everything leaks out eventually. She had to farm him out in Rochestown. He must be about twelve now.'

'And does he know who his mother is?' asks Nora.

'Not at all, girl,' says Joan. 'How could she tell him? I suppose she's never even seen him. Gosh, I'm sorry for that girl!'

'I'd be sorrier for the kid,' Nora says.

'Oh, I know, Nora, I know,' Joan says earnestly. 'But what

could the poor girl do? I mean, what would *we* do if we were in her place?'

And now that the voices grow clearer in my mind, I realize that Joan is the leader of the trio. It is she who sets the tempo, and it is her violin that holds it all together. Marie, with her deep beautiful voice, is the viola; Nora, for all that her voice sounds thin and squeaky, is the cello.

'Honestly, Joan, the things you say!' Marie cries, but without indignation. Marie sometimes behaves as though Joan is not really right in the head, and manages to suggest that she herself alone, with her nunlike air and caustic tongue, represents normality.

But Joan, who believes that Marie cultivates a blind spot for anything it doesn't suit her to see, only smiles knowingly. 'Well, we're all human, girl,' she says.

'Ah, nonsense, Joan!' says Marie. 'There must be something wrong with a girl like that.'

'There's something wrong with every girl or else she'd be a man,' says Nora.

'Ah, with the best will in the world, girl, I couldn't imagine myself going on like that,' says Marie. 'I suppose I mustn't be human,' she adds with a shrug, meaning that if this is what it's like to be human, so much the worse for humanity. 'Of course,' she ends, to show she has feelings, like anyone else, 'we all like a bit of sport, but that's different.'

'Oh, but it's not different, Marie,' Joan says warmly, and again the fiddle proclaims the theme. 'That's where you make your big mistake. What you call "a bit of sport" is only a matter of degree. God knows, I'm not what you'd call a public menace, but if I didn't watch my step, I could very easily see it happening to me.'

'So could I,' Nora says, and then begins to blush. 'And I don't know what I'd do about it, either.'

'Well, what could you do?' asks Marie. 'Assuming that such a thing could happen, which is assuming quite a lot.'

'I suppose I'd have to go to England and have it there,' says Nora gloomily.

'England?' says Marie.

'That would be all right if you knew someone in England, Nora,' says Joan. 'I mean, someone you could rely on.'

'"All right"?' echoes Marie. 'I should think starting life again in a foreign country with a baby, like that, would hardly be described

223

as "all right". Or maybe I'm lacking in initiative?'

'Well, it would either be that or make him marry you,' says Nora.

'I was wondering when you'd think of marriage,' says Marie.

'That mightn't be as easy as it sounds, either, Marie,' says Joan. 'I think Nora means the fellow wouldn't want to marry you.'

'Yes, and I think it's rotten!' says Nora. 'A fellow pretending to a girl that she's the only thing in the world he cares for, till she makes a fool of herself for him, and then he cuts his hook.'

'Well,' Joan says practically, 'I suppose we're all the same when we get what we want.'

'If that's all a man wants, couldn't somebody give it to him on a spoon?' says Nora.

'I'd simply say in a case like that that the man began to see what sort the girl was,' Marie says, having completely misunderstood Nora's remark.

'And what sort would you say *he* was?' Nora asks.

'Ah, well,' Marie replies comfortably, 'that's different, Nora. Considering the sort of sheltered lives women lead, it's up to them to set a standard. You can't expect the same sort of thing from men. Of course, I think he should be made to marry her.'

'But who'd make him, Marie?' asks Joan.

'Well, I suppose his family would, if it was for nothing but to avoid a scandal.'

'Ask any mother in Cork would she sooner a scandal or a daughter-in-law,' Nora says cynically.

'Then of course the priest would have to make him,' says Marie, still unperturbed.

'That's what I find so hard to imagine, though,' Joan says, and then her tone changes, and she becomes brilliant and mocking. 'I mean, it's all very well talking about it like this in the peace and quiet of the office, but imagine if I had to go up tonight after dark to the presbytery and talk to old Canon Cremin about it. "Excuse me, Canon, but I've been keeping company with a boy called Mick Shea, and it just so happens that he made a bit too free with me, and I was wondering would you ever mind running down and telling him to marry me." Cripes, if I was the Canon, I'd take my stick to a one like that!'

'Lovely marriage 'twould be anyway,' says Nora.

'Exactly, Nora,' Joan says, in her dramatic way, laying her hand on Nora's arm. 'That's just what I mean. How on earth could you spend the rest of your life with a man after having to do that to get him to marry you?'

'How he could spend the rest of his life with me is what I'd be worrying about,' says Nora. 'After all, I'd be the one that was to blame.'

'Never mind about him at all, now, girl,' Joan says with a jolly laugh. 'It's my own troubles that I'm thinking about. Honestly, do you know, I don't think I could face it!'

'I'm full sure I couldn't,' says Nora, lighting a cigarette.

'But what else could you do?' Marie asks. She obviously thinks they are two very peculiar girls, and no wonder. They were peculiar, like all delightful girls.

'Do you know, Marie,' says Joan, 'I think I'd sooner marry the first poor devil that came the way.'

'Aren't you lucky, being able to pick them up like that?' Marie asks drily.

'Ah, well, Marie,' says Joan, 'a girl would be in a bad way entirely if there wasn't one man that would take her on.'

'Like Paddy Lacy,' says Nora, with a giggle. 'He stopped me on the road the other day while he was delivering the letters, and I declare to God I didn't know which way to look.'

'I see,' says Marie. 'So that's why you keep Paddy Lacy on. I was wondering about that.'

'You needn't,' Nora says with sudden temper. 'I'm pretty sure Paddy Lacy would be just as tough as the rest of them if I went along and told him a thing like that.'

'But why would you have to tell him, Nora?' Joan asks anxiously. 'Wouldn't you let him find out for himself?'

'And a nice situation I'd be in when he did!'

'Oh, I wouldn't be too sure,' Joan says with another laugh. 'Before a man made up his mind about a thing like that, I'd like him to have a chance of seeing the full beauty of my character. Like the boatman in Glengarriff, I'm at my best on a long stretch.'

'I think I'd as soon live with a man I forced to marry me as one I tricked into marrying me,' Nora says. 'And I'd sooner do either than what your pal did – farm out a child. I don't think I'd ever have a day's luck after.'

'Now, you're misjudging the girl there, Nora,' Joan says earnestly. 'You are, really! It's not the same thing when you never have the chance of getting attached to a child. And when there isn't a blessed thing you can do about it, I don't honestly believe that there's any moral responsibility.'

'Responsibility?' Nora says, getting up. 'Who's talking about responsibility? I'd live in dread of my own shadow for the rest of my days. I wouldn't be able to see a barefooted kid in the street without getting sick. Every knock that came to the door, I'd be in dread to open it. Every body that was picked out of the river, I'd feel it was my kid, and I was the one to blame. For God's sake, don't talk to me!'

'There's another cup of tea left, Nora,' Joan says, a little too brightly. 'Would you like it?'

'In a minute, Joan,' says Nora, and goes out to the Ladies'. When she returns a few minutes later, she looks as though she had been crying. To me it is a great mystery, because no one speaks crossly to her. I assume that, like myself, she has a father who drinks.

'Cripes, I'm sorry for poor May Jenkins,' Joan begins on another day, after Nora has poured out the tea. That is her time for a new theme, when there is no serious danger of interruption.

'Who's *she* when she's at home?' Nora asks lightly.

'May Jenkins? You'd hardly know her, Norah. She's from the south side.'

'And what ails her now didn't ail her before?' asks Nora, who is full of local quips and phrases.

'Oh, the usual thing,' says Joan with a shrug. 'Phil Macken, her husband, is knocking round with the Archer girl, on the Wellington Road – the Yellow Peril.'

'Really, Joan,' Marie says, 'I don't know where you come across all those extraordinary people.'

'I don't see what's so extraordinary about that at all,' Nora says. 'People are always doing it.'

'And people are always getting terrible diseases, only we don't go out of our way to inquire,' says Marie primly. 'Really, there must be something wrong with a woman like that.'

'Like May, Marie?' Joan asks in mock surprise.

'No, like that other creature – whatever you said her name was.'

'Oh, I wouldn't say that at all, Marie,' says Joan. 'Some very respectable people live on the Wellington Road. And a lot of men find her attractive.'

'Then there must be something wrong with the men.'

'Or the wife, why don't you say?' cries Nora.

'Or the wife,' Marie agrees, with perfect placidity. 'She should be able to mind her own husband.'

'She'd want roller skates,' says Joan, and again I hear the high note of the violin, driving the trio onward. 'No, Marie, girl,' she says, resting her chin on her hands, 'you have to face the facts. A lot of women do get unattractive after marriage. Of course, I'm not blaming them. We'd be the same ourselves, with kids to mind and jobs to do. They can't waste time dancing and dolling themselves up like Maeve Archer, and if they did, their houses would soon show it. You see, it's something we all have to be prepared for.'

'If I felt that way, Joan, I'd go into a convent,' Marie says severely.

'But after all, Marie,' says Joan, 'what could you do? Suppose you were married to Jim and a thing like that happened?'

'What could I do?' Marie echoes, smiling at the thought of anything of the sort happening with Jim. 'Well, I suppose I could walk out of the house.'

'Ah, come now, Marie,' Joan says. 'It's not as easy as all that. Where would you walk to, in the first place?'

'What's wrong with going home?'

'With a houseful of kids?' says Joan. 'Of course, I know your father is very fond of you and all the rest of it, but all the same, we have to be reasonable.'

'I could go somewhere else,' says Marie. 'After all, Jim would have to support me – and the kids, as you say.'

'Of course he would. That's if you didn't mind spending the rest of your days as a grass widow. You know, Marie, I saw one or two women who did that, and it didn't look too promising to me. No, in the way of husbands and fathers and so on, I don't think you can beat men. A dog won't do.'

'But do you mean you'd let him go on seeing a filthy creature like that?' asks Marie. 'Really, Joan, I don't think you can be serious.'

'Oh, I never said that,' Joan says hastily, 'I'm sure I'd make it pretty uncomfortable for him.'

'Which mightn't be such a bad way of making the other woman more attractive,' Nora says drily.

'Oh, we all know what Nora would do,' Joan retorts with

227

affectionate mockery. 'She'd sit down and have a good cry. Wouldn't you, love?'

'I might,' Nora replies doubtfully. 'I'd sooner that than calling in the neighbours.'

'Oh, I admit you'd have to keep your dignity, Nora,' Marie says, being particularly susceptible to any appeal to her ladyhood. 'But surely someone would have to interfere.'

'I saw too much interference, Marie,' Nora says grimly. 'It's mad enough thinking you can spend your whole life with a man and still be in love with him, but 'tis dotty entirely if you imagine you can do it with half Cork acting as referee.'

'All the same, Nora,' Joan says, in her practical way, 'before I saw a woman like that making off with a husband of mine, I'd get a fistful of her hair, and I wouldn't mind who knew it, either. I'd read and spell her, I give you my word.'

'I certainly wouldn't degrade myself by quarrelling with a creature like that,' says Marie.

'I wouldn't have the nerve,' says Nora, lighting a cigarette. 'Look, it's all very well to talk about it like that, but suppose it was the other way around? Suppose you were making a fool of yourself over another man, and your husband disgraced you all over Cork by fighting him?'

'Really, Nora,' says Marie, with her Mona Lisa smile, 'you have a remarkably vivid imagination.'

'Oh, I don't know that that's all imagination, either, Marie,' says Joan, who enjoys nothing better than imagining things. 'That could happen, too, mind you!'

'But that would make you no better than the woman you're just talking about,' says Marie.

'Who said we were any better?' asks Nora. 'I might be worse, for all anyone knows.'

'But do you know, Nora,' Joan says, 'I'm not at all sure but I'd like Mick to do it.'

'To shame you all over Cork?' Nora asks.

'Oh, no. Just to stand up for his rights. Nobody wants a doormat.'

'Give me doormats every time,' says Nora, with a sinister pull at her cigarette.

'But, Nora,' Marie asks in horror, 'you don't mean you'd just sit at home and do nothing?'

'I don't know, girl. What could you do?'

'And wait till he changed his mind and came back to you?'

'Maybe,' says Nora, with a shrug. 'I mightn't be there when he got back. I might have a fellow, too.'

'Really,' Marie says, scratching her long neck. 'I'm beginning to see a number of uses for this Paddy Lacy of yours.'

'That's where women have the worst of it,' Joan says quickly, to head off a reply from Nora about Paddy Lacy. 'It's not as easy for a married woman with a couple of kids to find someone to go off with. It's too chancy giving children a stepfather, no matter how fond you might be of him. No, what I can't imagine,' she adds earnestly, 'is what you'd do when he did change his mind. I often wonder could you ever behave in the same way to him.'

'Of course not, Joan,' Marie says. 'Naturally, if there were children, I could understand remaining in the same house with him, just for their sake, but living with him as husband and wife is a thing I could never imagine doing.'

'Ah, now, Marie, you're a girl of great character,' Joan says, 'but that sounds to me too much like giving up sweets in a sweetshop. Of course, I know people do it when they get tired of one another, but it never seems natural to me. I wouldn't do it just for fun,' she adds gravely. 'I'd want to be pretty sure that he was still fond of me.'

'I'm afraid I wouldn't have much faith in the affections of a man like that,' Marie says.

'What about you, Nora?' Joan asks.

'Me?' Nora says, blushing. 'Oh, I suppose 'twould depend.'

'You mean, depend on how he behaved to you?'

'Yes,' Nora replies with a frightened air. 'And how he behaved to the other one.'

'Well, really, Nora, this is going beyond the beyonds!' Marie exclaims, putting down her cup with a ladylike air of finality. 'Are we supposed to take *her* feelings into consideration as well?'

'I suppose she might have feelings, too?' Nora replies gloomily.

'I know what Nora would do!' Joan says triumphantly, bringing her hand down flat on the table. 'I know it just as if I was there. She'd tell her husband to go to blazes, and skelp off to the other woman's house to console her.'

'By the way she's talking, it sounds as if she'd leave her husband and live with the other one,' Marie says.

'I might even do that,' says Nora, moving towards the door.

'Ah, go on, girl!' Joan says boisterously. 'Don't you know we're only making fun of you? I know what's going to happen to you,' she adds comfortingly. 'You'll marry a fine steady slob of a man that'll stick his two heels on the mantelpiece and never look at the side of the road another woman is walking at. Look, there's a cup of tea in the pot still!'

'I don't want it, Joanie, thanks,' says Nora, and goes off to the Ladies'.

Marie gives a shrug. 'For an intelligent girl, Nora does talk the most extraordinary nonsense,' she says with finality.

'Oh, I wouldn't be too sure it was nonsense, Marie,' Joan says, in her loyal way. 'I think Nora might surprise us all.'

But Nora, worse luck, has never had the opportunity of surprising anyone; nor has Joan – two fine women who have never met with men astute enough to grab them. As for Marie, she rules her husband gently but firmly, like a reverend mother dealing with a rather dull undergardener. Of the three, she is now the one I am most intimate with. Sometimes I even think that if I were to forget myself and make advances to her, instead of slapping my face indignantly she would only laugh and say, 'Ah, Larry, will you have a bit of sense?' – which from Marie would be almost like a declaration of love. And I think the reason is that like me, she hears those voices 'vibrate in the memory' and wonders over them.

'Ah, Larry,' she says, grabbing me eagerly by the hands, 'do you remember all the old nonsense we used to talk in the office, and Joan saying what she'd do with an illegitimate baby, and me saying what I'd do if Jim went off with another woman? And look at us now – three old women!'

No doubt she realized that she can afford to say things like that to me, for while the music of those voices lingers in my mind she and they will never be old.

(1958)

Sue

God forgive me, I could never stand my sister's young men. Even if she had had taste, I should still have resented them. Our house on the outskirts of Cork was small, and there simply wasn't room in it for me and a courting couple. After a day's work in the office I would get settled with a book by the fire in the front room, and then I would hear the creak of the gate, the steps on the path, the knock, the boisterous voice in the hall – my hall! Sometimes I continued to read, and dared the fellow to come in and interrupt me, but there was never any false modesty about Sue's young men. They always had a warm corner in their hearts for themselves. Occasionally I went off to read in the kitchen, but there, apart from Mother's solicitude about whether I was warm enough and whether I could see with 'the old gas' – meaning the gaslight fixture that I was reading by – I was almost certain to be interrupted again by the arrival of one of her old cronies, come to sit and gossip with her in the kitchen. So, most often, when I heard Sue's young man, I went off, cursing, to my own bedroom, where there was no heat and 'the old gas' was worse even than in the kitchen. There, lying on my bed with a blanket over my feet, I listened to the cheerful voices of Sue and her young man sitting in comfort downstairs before the fire – my fire! Is it any wonder I grew lepping mad? Sue, of course, said I was sulky and unsociable, and Mother, who had an excuse for everybody, said the Horgans were all like that. I grew up with a considerable respect for the sensitiveness and intelligence of the Horgans.

Sue never had any taste in young men. There was a long string of them, only one of whom I ever liked, and she dropped him inside a fortnight. She said he was dull! Mind, I had no very exaggerated notion of *her* charms. I knew she wasn't steady and was always excited or depressed about something, and when she had nothing to be excited or depressed about, she came up with the most extraordinary old pisherogues and superstitions that were supposed to be lucky or unlucky, according to the mood she was in. But she was warmhearted and generous, and she had a very good intelligence whenever the fancy took her to be intelligent. At any rate she was a cut above the fellows she walked out with, though it wasn't until Harry Ridgeway came on the scene that I began to appreciate what an interesting girl she was.

I had also better be fair and admit that Ridgeway had his points, even though I didn't like him. I always thought him a bit too much of a dandy. He had a pink-and-white complexion like a girl's, and he dressed as carefully as any girl. Usually he wore a well-cut, tight-fitting suit that never had a trace of beer or tobacco ash on it, and a pale, correct-looking tie. And he had the impudence to jeer at my tweeds and my battered old tie and about how I needed a haircut. At a party he was always in charge of entertaining the dolls, while I sat with a couple of friends and a half-dozen of stout hidden behind the sofa, and hoped to God the dolls would let us alone to talk politics or religion. Ridgeway had no politics, and his religion was like his ties – pale and correct. What I really mean is that he was a lightweight, a ladies' man, though with occasional flashes of wit and intelligence, but definitely not the sort with whom you'd like to go to a bar and spend the evening discussing what was wrong with the country.

Still, I was rather puzzled by Sue's behaviour, because, though she went out quite a lot with Ridgeway, she continued to go out as well with Sidney Healy, who had now been the resident pest for close on six months. I saw no reason for having two of them about the house, disturbing me.

'Are you going steady with that masher?' I asked her one evening while she was ironing and Mother washing up.

'What masher?' she asked, growing nervous and defensive, though I hadn't even raised my voice.

'How do you expect me to remember all their names? The sickly fellow with the queer ties.'

'Harry Ridgeway?' she said in the same tone. 'Why would I go steady with him? Sure, he's mad on Judy Holmes.'

'Then why the hell doesn't he go to Judy Holmes' house instead of coming here?' I asked. 'Who is this Holmes one, anyway?'

'She's the bank manager's daughter from Montenotte.'

'Old Holmes' daughter?' I asked in surprise. 'But aren't they Protestants?'

'I suppose they are. What about it?'

'Nothing, only he's not going to find it very easy to marry her, is he?'

'I don't know. I suppose he can get a dispensation. They have money enough, anyway. I advised him to propose to her months ago.'

'Very handsome of you, I'm sure,' I said with a sniff.

'There's nothing handsome about it. She's the right sort of girl for him, and she has a bit of money. The poor devil is crazy to get out of that house of his. His old fellow drinks, and his poor mother is in and out of hospital the whole time.'

'I see,' I said. 'And because Mr Ridgeway isn't happy at home, he thinks he's entitled to come and make sure that I'm not happy here.'

That evening I didn't move when Ridgeway came in. It's bad enough getting out of a comfortable room for another man, but at least you have the feeling that one of these days things are going to even out. But to let him have it as a free gift – chair, fire, gaslight, and all – was more than anyone could expect. Ridgeway didn't seem to resent my staying, and except for that silly-looking tie of his and his mincing way of balancing a teacup on his knee, I had nothing to complain of. The man had plenty of conversation, of a kind. Later in the evening Sue asked him about Judy Holmes, and he didn't seem to resent that, either.

'Oh, Judy's playing at the School of Music concert next week,' he said excitedly.

'Go on!' said Sue. 'What's she playing?'

'The Mozart E-flat, with Humphreys doing the violin part.'

'Cripes, I'd love to hear her,' said Sue.

'We can go together, if you like. What about you, Jack?'

'No, thanks,' I said with a smile. I was fond of music, all right, but I avoided the local amateurs.

However, when Sue returned from the concert, she was full of Judy Holmes, and I knew there must have been something to her playing, for Sue in one of her intelligent phases was quite a good critic. She could have been a good pianist as well, but, being Sue, she never took the trouble to practise. She sat at the piano to illustrate what she was saying, and I filled in the violin part with three fingers while she showed how Judy did it, and when she played a wrong chord she used a dirty word. I laughed.

I was always amused at the contrast between Sue's character and the language she used.

In a funny way, hearing about the concert gave me a sort of personal interest in the Holmes girl, and next time I met her in town I raised my cap to her. She smiled back rather coolly, and I wondered if she even knew who I was. She was a tall, thin girl with a long, pale face, and a good figure concealed in a wide coat like a tent. Her hat was a plain felt one, like a schoolgirl's. She was dressed expensively, but plainly. After that, whenever I found myself daydreaming, I would think of her as the sort of girl you could take up as you took up politics or religion – a girl of natural seriousness, who could play Mozart as he should be played, and with no nonsense about her. Now when Ridgeway talked about her to Mother and Sue, I found myself listening to him. They were fascinated by everything he told them about the Holmeses, and it wasn't only the money and the bit of style that interested them, though clearly, for them as for Ridgeway, it had the appeal of a fairytale. But besides this they both had a genuine admiration for the qualities of character the Holmeses displayed: Judy's daily two hours of piano practice, her dutifulness in answering letters and remembering birthdays, her mother's social work, and the strict and narrow piety of an Irish Protestant family. How narrow that could be I was reminded one night when Ridgeway reported that one of Judy's girlfriends had used a Biblical phrase by way of a joke and Mrs Holmes had pointed out that it was blasphemy.

'Sure, when the girl didn't mean it!' protested Mother, who never really minded what people said so long as they smiled at her while they were saying it.

'Ah, they don't look at it that way at all, Mrs Horgan,' Ridgeway said with a frown. 'Of course the girl didn't mean it, but still they don't think you should say such things. And I can't help admiring them for it.'

I could see that Ridgeway had Mother and Sue admiring them for it as well.

But then an extraordinary thing happened. Ridgeway proposed, but he proposed not to Judy, but to Sue. I couldn't understand it. I knew that he wanted to make a home of his own, and it wasn't only that his father drank and his mother was so sickly that she could not keep abreast of the housekeeping. He wanted a background to go with the ties and suits, and he must have been miserably selfconscious about any friends that called to his house. You could see the sort of place he would try and make for himself – a small house in a modern terrace, with a neatly covered suite of furniture, bought on time, a few watercolours, and a vase of flowers; and there he would give little musical parties, and tea would be served in rather dainty cups. But Sue's background was just the same as his own, and imagine Sue keeping a house like that for him. She would wreck the damn place in a week.

I could see that the proposal had come as a real shock to Sue. She couldn't understand it, either, and as a result she couldn't stop talking of it.

'But you like him,' I said. 'Why shouldn't you marry him if you want to?'

'Ah, how could I?' she asked doubtfully. 'He's not in love with me. Isn't that enough?'

'How sure you are of it!' I said. I wasn't really any fonder of Ridgeway than I had been, but I realized that he would make someone an excellent husband and that Sue was the sort of girl who might very easily marry the wrong man – or no man at all. 'Isn't that for him to say?'

'Ah, it's not that,' she said, and she still sounded doubtful. 'I suppose he felt he had to ask me.'

'He needn't have felt that at all,' Mother said earnestly, 'but it showed very nice feeling. I was always very fond of Harry, and I only wish you could marry him.'

'Oh, for God's sake, hold on!' I said, getting angry with them again. 'I don't think Sue even knows what she's doing. Nobody ever proposes to a girl just out of nice feeling.'

'Harry would,' Sue said flatly. 'He's too soft for his own good. I dare say he thought people were talking about us.'

'Nonsense!' I said shortly. 'He knows more about girls than that. Probably he proposed to Judy Holmes and got the cold shoulder.'

'I wouldn't say so,' Sue said thoughtfully. 'I think he'd have told me.'

'For a man you won't marry you seem to have a remarkably high opinion of him,' I said sarcastically. 'I'd wait and see about that.'

'Ah, I don't think so,' Sue said complacently. 'Even if he did propose to her, she'd hardly talk about it.'

'She'd be the first woman in history that didn't,' said I.

'I wouldn't be too sure about that, either,' said Sue. 'Harry probably has his own reasons for not proposing to her. I dare say his family wouldn't like his marrying a Protestant.'

And suddenly she rang a bell in my head. You see, there were certain things that I seemed always to have known about myself. One was that if I fell in love there would be no walking out with other girls. Another was that if I did fall in love with someone I knew my family and friends would disapprove of – a Jew or a Protestant – I would not allow myself to be influenced by them. Whatever other faults I might have, I knew myself to be a man of seriousness and strength of character. And these, I knew, were precisely the qualities that Ridgeway hadn't got.

'Ah, so that's the reason!' I said, and I dare say triumph showed in my voice, for Sue turned on me.

'And what's wrong with it?' she asked.

'Nothing,' I said. 'Except that now you're talking sense.'

I liked that explanation because it enabled me to go on looking down on Ridgeway. But I still couldn't understand why Sue didn't want to marry him when, quite clearly, she liked him so much. I knew that she wasn't acting like the heroine of a sentimental novel and refusing him for fear of injuring his career. Apart from anything else, Sue had never read enough novels to know that a heroine might be expected to act in this peculiar way, and if you had explained it to her, she would merely have gaped and asked in her commonest tone, 'What sort of bloody idiot do you think I am?' No, the girl had got it firmly fixed in her head that Ridgeway didn't care for her, and for that reason would not marry him.

Yet they continued to go out together. After his proposal, I felt that Ridgeway was entitled to whatever facilities the house offered, and I left the parlour to them. One night, I was sitting with Mother in the kitchen. Sue and Ridgeway were supposed to be courting in the front room. All at once a most unholy row began. We couldn't hear what they said, but he was talking in a low, bitter voice and Sue was yelling her head off at him. Mother clasped her hands in prayer and made to get up, but I signalled to her to stay where she was.

'The poor child!' Mother moaned. 'God direct me!' she added, meaning that she distrusted my direction. The sitting-room door opened and I distinctly heard Ridgeway use a dirty word. Two dirty words! Fortunately, Mother either didn't hear or didn't understand. Then the front door slammed behind him, and Mother, with another glance at the ceiling, from which God could be supposed to be directing her, muttered, 'And without even saying goodnight to me!' It was a real tragedy for Mother, because she loved Harry Ridgeway's little airs of politeness, so different from the roughness of Sue and me. Then Sue came into the kitchen, bawling, and for five minutes it was impossible to get a stime of sense out of her.

'Child!' Mother cried, with what she clearly believed to be sternness. 'You must tell your brother and me what he said to you.' When she referred to me as Sue's brother, she promoted me to a position of authority.

'He asked me to marry him again,' sobbed Sue.

Mother, being one of the sympathetic souls of the world, was just on the point of saying, 'The blackguard! He should be ashamed of himself!' when she realized that it wouldn't be altogether appropriate, so she just wrung her hands and said, 'Well! Well! Well!'

'After all, that's nothing to snivel about,' I said coldly.

'Who's snivelling?' Sue asked, flaring up, as I had expected her to do. 'He said things were desperate in his house. It's not the only bloody house things are desperate in, if you ask me.'

'Oh, Sue—' Mother was beginning when I broke in.

'And what did you tell him?'

'The same thing I told him before, of course. So he said he was going straight off to ask Judy Holmes.'

'All right,' I said. 'And isn't that what you wanted?'

'Whether I wanted it or not has nothing to do with it,' she said. 'How the hell could I marry a fellow like that, that would hate the very sight of me before the honeymoon was over?'

'Oh, Sue, how can you say things like that?' Mother exclaimed indignantly.

'Because it's true, woman. I know Jack thinks he is a bit of a snob. What's wrong with that? Ye're all terrified out of your lives of trying to make yourself out a bit better than ye are. I'd be a snob, too, if only I had something to be a snob about. He hates a girl even to use a dirty word.'

'And perfectly right he is!' Mother cried. 'What right has any decent girl to use language like that, picked up at street corners?'

237

'Then what does he want with me? He heard me use it. He told me if I ever used a word like that again he'd slap my face.'

'And what did you do?' I asked, knowing perfectly well what Sue would do if I told her that.

'I said it, of course.'

'Sue, you didn't!' exclaimed Mother.

'I did,' said Sue, and then began to giggle faintly.

'And what did he do?' I asked.

'Oh, he slapped my face, all right,' said Sue, her face lighting up. Obviously the incident had made a favourable impression. 'What should he do?'

'He should talk to you seriously, Sue,' Mother said passionately. 'He should not do a thing like that. I'm surprised at him – such a nice boy! Eleven years I lived with your poor father, God rest him, and never once did he lift a hand to me.'

'A pity he didn't lift it to us a bit oftener,' said Sue.

'The dear knows, it's hard to know what to do,' Mother said, turning away and shaking her head despondently.

'Anyway,' I said, realizing what was in Sue's mind, 'you know he's not going to ask Judy.'

'That's all you know about him,' Sue replied, beginning to sob again. 'He's probably asking her now. And she's the right girl for him, whatever his family or anyone else thinks.'

Then she went up to her room to live it all through again, and bawl a bit more, while Mother sat by the fire and sighed over the contrariness of everything. Of course, she knew that Sue was doing the right thing, but she couldn't help wishing she wasn't. As for me, I was beginning to make discoveries about my extraordinary sister. I knew now that she had refused to marry Harry Ridgeway because she genuinely believed he didn't care for her. The poor fool had so often expressed his admiration for Judy and her family that he had even persuaded those two romantic women to admire them as well, and Sue could only think of love in terms of admiration. Admiration, that is, of positive virtues she recognized and respected. She was quite certain that she had none of those particular virtues herself, and yet she would keep on hoping that some day some man would discover something positive to admire in her. Perhaps, after all, she wasn't even so extraordinary; perhaps a lot of other women confuse love and admiration in the same way, and never realize that a man may love them as much for their faults as their virtues, and may think with delight of the way they begin to sparkle when everyone else is going home, or forget themselves and swear. At the same time, I knew it was something I should never be able to explain to Sue, and for some reason this made me feel unusually tender to her in the weeks that followed. I even took her to the pictures a couple of times, when she and everyone else knew I hated the pictures.

But she had been right about Harry Ridgeway. That night or next day he had gone straight to Judy Holmes and proposed to her and been accepted. He'd even induced herself and her family to sign along the dotted line in connexion with the religion of the children. I had to admit that when it came to the point, Ridgeway, ties and all, was masculine enough.

It might have been better for him if he hadn't been. I met the pair of them one night on Patrick's Bridge. She was, as usual, plainly dressed, while Ridgeway was even more the dandy than before. Between them they made me feel very awkward, with my long hair, my cap, and my rough tweeds, but Ridgeway seemed very pleased to meet me.

'You've heard of Sue's brother, Jack,' he said to Judy.

'Almost as much as I've heard of Sue,' she said with a thin smile. 'I suppose he's another charmer?'

'Oh, begod, he is not,' Ridgeway said with a loud laugh. 'Sourest blackguard you'll find about this town.'

'Ah, he probably only needs a girl to make a lot of him, as you do of Sue,' she said archly.

'Come on, Holmes!' he cried. 'You never heard the half of Sue.'

'No, you didn't get much chance of telling about her, did you, poor fellow?' she said in a mocking drawl. 'But you do get these dreadful obsessions with people.'

We said goodnight, and I went on through town. It was only when I was half-way down Patrick Street that it dawned on me that Judy hadn't been exactly pleasant to me. For some reason I always approach people on the assumption that they intend to be nice to me, and it usually takes time before I realize that they haven't been. I had gone the full length of the street before I thought, 'My God, that girl is a devil!'

As I strolled home that night, I could see as clearly as if I were living through it how dearly Ridgeway was going to pay for his harmless snobbery. I could also see why he might have been afraid of bringing a girl like that into his own family. People of our class are plain and rough, but nobody is so plain and rough that they wouldn't resent her tone, and from this time on Ridgeway would have to depend for his friendships on his wife's family and their friends.

I was so full of my own discovery that while I was telling Mother and Sue, it never once struck me that they might feel differently about it. They listened in silence, and then Sue lit a cigarette and said, 'God damn her!' and Mother didn't even protest. She was too shaken. 'The poor, deluded boy!' she said softly, clasping and unclasping her hands.

Then I saw that both had tears in their eyes, not only for Harry Ridgeway and his aspirations but for their own. It was as if life had betrayed them by being less generous than they themselves were. I kissed them before I went to bed. It was not a custom of mine, but I felt extraordinarily proud of them both.

(1958)

A Mother's Warning

One winter evening Father Fogarty's housekeeper let in a strange young woman. She was tall and thin with a slight pale face, and her good manners barely contained a natural excitability of manner. Though he was normally shy of women he was attracted by her and offered her coffee.

'When you know what I came about you probably won't ask me to have coffee,' she replied with a rueful grin.

'In that case I'd better order it first,' he said, responding to her tone.

'You'd better hear what I have to confess and *then* order it,' she suggested slyly.

'By the way, it's not Confession you want, is it?' he asked professionally.

'That comes afterwards too, like the coffee,' she replied.

'I don't know what your name is yet,' he said as she sat down.

'Sheila Moriarty.'

'You're not from this part of the world?'

'No. I'm from Limerick. I'm working here in Carr's Stores.'

'How do you like it?'

'The shop is all right. The place itself is fine. Too fine. I suppose that's what got me into the mess I'm in. Oh, I didn't realize it in time, but I was probably brought up too sheltered.'

'How many of you are there?' he asked.

'Six. Three boys, three girls. Daddy is an insurance agent; Mummy – well, I suppose Mummy is a saint.'

'A what?' he asked in surprise.

'Oh, I don't mean it that way, but she is, really. Trying to bring up six of us on Daddy's couple of quid and see that we had everything – education, music, religion. I'm damn full sure I couldn't do it. Now, here I am after less than a year away bringing disgrace on her!'

'What did you do?' he asked quietly.

'Stole stuff from the shop,' she replied sullenly. In Fogarty's experience there were two sorts of women criers, the ones who cried at once and the ones who got sullen. She was the sort who got sullen. 'Nice, aren't I?' she asked with a bitter little smile.

For a few moments he could say nothing. With her looks and temperament he would have expected her to say that she was pregnant, but you could never tell with women.

'How serious is it?' he asked gravely, and she opened her handbag and put a brooch on the little table beside her. It looked to him as silly as any other brooch – a sort of golden leaf that he couldn't imagine anyone's risking a job for.

'How much is it worth?' he asked doubtfully.

'Three quid,' she said.

'Can't you put it back?' he asked, and she shook her head slowly.

'I'm in a different department now.'

'Or put the price of it in the till?'

'Not without its being spotted.'

'All right,' he said. 'Send them a postal order anonymously. They won't ask any questions.'

'It's not as simple as that,' she said. 'Somebody knows I stole it.'

'Oh!' he exclaimed. 'Somebody in the shop?'

'Yes. An assistant manager. He encouraged me, in fact. He said the whole staff did it. Maybe they do; I don't know, but it doesn't matter anyhow. I should have known better.'

'I take it this manager fellow is a man?'

'Yes. His name is Michael Joyce. He lives in St Mary's Road.'

'Is he married by any chance?'

That did it. She began to sob drily and bitterly. Then she dabbed her nose viciously with a handkerchief and went on talking as though at random.

'Cripes, and before I left home Mummy told me never to take anything that belonged to my employers. I went into hysterics on her. It shows you the way we were brought up. I didn't know people could do things like that. And *then* she told me not to have anything to do with married men because they weren't all like Daddy! We always thought she was so blooming innocent. She wasn't as innocent as we were, though.'

'You'd better tell me the rest of this,' Fogarty said sternly. 'How far has this thing gone?'

'Too far.'

'You mean you and he have been living together?'

'Near enough to it anyway. And that's what he wants.'

'But it's not what you want?'

'Not now,' she said almost angrily. 'At first, I suppose I let myself be dazzled. I must have when I let him persuade me to pinch that, mustn't I? Now that I know what he's like I'd sooner pitch myself in the river.'

'What is he like?' Fogarty asked.

'Oh, he's not what you think,' she said ruefully. 'He's clever. I know he's smooth and he's a liar, but he could probably get round you too if it was worth his while.'

'What do you mean when you say he's a liar?' Fogarty asked, weighing it up.

'I mean he told me things about his wife, and *they* were lies.'

'How do you know?'

'Because I met her.'

'Oh, so you know his wife?'

'I do. He made me come to his house one night after work for a bit of supper. It nearly choked me. That was when I turned against him. He brought me there deliberately to show me off to her. He watched us the whole time. And everything he'd said was wrong. She was decent and she was as frightened of him as I was. There's a devil in that man.'

'Is that all?' he asked.

'Isn't it enough?' she retorted. 'I think only for that last evening he could have done what he liked with me. But he isn't normal.'

'I mean, could we have the coffee in now?' he asked with an encouraging smile. Then he went to the head of the stairs and bellowed, 'Mary! Coffee!' He shut the room door behind him and swaggered back to the mantelpiece. 'I'll have to think what's the best thing to do,' he said, sounding more confident than he felt. 'About this, to begin with,' he added, picking up the brooch. 'I gather you have no further use for it?'

'I wish to God I'd never seen it,' she said.

'You won't see it again,' he said, and put it in his coat pocket. 'I have to think about Mr Joyce as well. Meanwhile, whatever you do, don't go anywhere with him. Don't even talk to him.

If he annoys you, tell him to go to hell. I suppose he's trying to blackmail you over the brooch?'

'I suppose so, in a way,' she replied uncertainly. 'He's not as crude as that, of course.'

'They never are,' he said from the depths of his worldly wisdom. 'But remember, there's nothing he can do to you that wouldn't injure himself a great deal worse.'

'I wouldn't be too sure of that,' she said doubtfully. 'A fellow in a position like that doesn't have to say, "Miss Moriarty stole a brooch from the jewellery counter."'

'I don't think he'll say anything,' Fogarty said forcefully. 'Does he know you were coming to me?'

'No. I never told him anything.'

'If he starts anything, tell him I know everything about it,' he said. 'There's nothing these fellows dread more than a third party who's in on the game. Meanwhile forget about it. But remember, next time you meet a married man, what your mother told you. They're *not* all like your father. She was right there.'

When they had drunk their coffee he saw her to the door and held her hand for a moment.

'Give me two days to see what I can do,' he said. 'I'll be here on Friday night if you want me. Until then, forget about it.'

But this was more than he could do himself. Fogarty, partly because of his character, partly because of his circumstance, was a man who lived a great deal in his own imagination, and something about the girl had set his imagination on fire. Even the few words she had dropped had made him see the sort of home she came from, and the anxious, pious mother who tried to spread out her husband's little income into a full and comfortable life for six children who probably didn't even realize the sacrifices she was making for them, and wouldn't realize it till she was dead and buried. 'A saint,' the girl had said, and she was probably right. He had known saints like that whose lives nobody would ever know about, much less write about. He could even see how a girl brought up in a poor, pious, cheerful home like that, where no quarrel was ever allowed to occur that could not be reported later as a joke to friends, and who was then left alone in a cheerless town, would be readier than the next to grasp at whatever society offered itself. And he had no difficulty at all in imagining the sinister figure of Joyce, trying to lure the girl from one small

244

misdemeanour to another until eventually he could exercise a moral blackmail on her. He had seen a few men like that as well. What would have happened to the girl if she hadn't had the sense to consult a priest required no imagination at all. But, in spite of his burning determination to frustrate Joyce, he wasn't at all sure what he should do.

Clearly, the first thing was to get some information, and the following evening he called on the curate in Joyce's parish. He was a tall, gentle young man called Rowlands, with whom Fogarty had spent a few months in another part of the diocese.

'Information, Ed!' Fogarty said. 'Information about one of your parishioners!'

'I'm sorry, Jerry, but the seal of the confessional is strictly observed in this parish,' Rowlands said with his old-maidish humour. 'Who is it, tell me?'

'A fellow called Joyce in St Mary's Road.'

'A manager in Carr's?' Rowlands said, stroking his long jaw thoughtfully. 'I know the man you mean. He's a small, bouncy little chap. It wouldn't be woman trouble, would it?'

'Why?' Fogarty asked keenly. 'Did he have woman trouble?'

'Oh, I heard something I didn't pay much attention to. About two years ago. He used to be a traveller for Carr's before he got the big job.'

'Anything else?'

'Let me see! It's coming back to me. Mind you, I couldn't say it was anything but old talk. He was supposed to be having something to do with a married woman called Trench. She was a Protestant, of course. Anyway, herself and her husband left in a hurry. Is that the sort of thing?'

'More or less,' Fogarty said grimly. 'This time it isn't a Protestant, and I see no reason why the woman should leave town in a hurry. Don't you think I'm right?'

'Oh, I'm sure you are, but all the same I'd be careful, Jerry. That sort of thing can get you into a nasty mess.'

'Ah, aren't I always careful?' Fogarty said with a jolly laugh.

'You are,' Rowlands said cautiously, 'but in unorthodox ways. I'm very orthodox, Jerry. I like to go by the books.'

But Fogarty had heard what he came to hear and his mind was made up. Next morning he rang Joyce up at the shop and suggested that it might be more convenient for both if they met that evening at the presbytery. Joyce fell in with this enthusiastically and arrived that evening at the presbytery, looking as though he hoped to sell Fogarty a new suite of furniture. As a subtle touch Fogarty had left the stolen brooch lying on the little table where Sheila had placed it, but he was disappointed in his hope of seeing Joyce discountenanced. He smiled and picked up the brooch.

'That's a nice little article, Father,' he said. 'Fifty bob in the store.'

'Three pounds, I believe,' Fogarty said sternly.

'As much as that?' Joyce said, in what appeared to be genuine surprise. 'Probably costs four and tuppence to make. But that's how we come to be millionaires, Father.'

'It belongs to the store,' said Fogarty. 'It might help to make millionaires of you quicker if you took it back there.'

'Me, Father?' Joyce asked innocently. 'Of course, I'll take it back if you like, but it might be a bit difficult to explain, mightn't it?'

'Oh, I wouldn't say so,' said Fogarty, beginning to lose his temper. 'You could tell them it was stolen at your instigation.'

'At my instigation?' Joyce repeated quietly. He took a few steps forward and faced Fogarty from the hearth, his arms folded. 'That's a very serious charge, Father,' he went on after a moment. 'Are you sure you're in a position to prove it?'

Fogarty was taken aback. The scene wasn't going at all as he had planned it; he was in no position to prove anything, and because of it he began to bluster.

'Yes, and you know who the witness would be,' he said angrily. 'Sheila Moriarty.'

'Sheila Moriarty?' Joyce repeated phrases and names in the manner of one who thinks while he talks, to give himself time. 'And do you think seriously, Father, that the Bishop is going to accept the story of a girl you say is a thief and consider that it entitled you to go round making wild charges against me?'

'You tried to seduce that girl,' shouted Fogarty, trying to brazen it out.

'And what else, Father?' Joyce asked impudently.

'I believe there is also a lady called Trench, who may have something to say about it,' Fogarty said furiously.

'I see,' Joyce said, but he didn't, again he was only playing for time. Then he suddenly changed from defence to attack, but even then he was very much master of himself as Fogarty was not.

'Has it struck you, Father, that Sheila is very well able to look after herself?'

'It hasn't,' Fogarty said shortly.

'Yet when she wants to be protected against me – that's her story, anyway, according to you – she goes to you and not the parish priest! Doesn't that seem peculiar?'

It didn't, so far as Fogarty was concerned. Whatever happened to Irish priests in the course of their career, young people who got into trouble always took care to avoid them when they became parish priests. And Dempsey, Fogarty's parish priest, was somebody whom anybody, old or young, would avoid.

'That's her business,' he said, raising his hand.

'You're trying to make it mine, Father,' Joyce said reproachfully. 'By the way, have you told the parish priest?'

'That's none of your business either,' Fogarty said, losing his temper again.

'Oh, but I might have to see the parish priest if this persecution went any further, Father.'

'Persecution?' Fogarty growled furiously.

'Yes, Father, persecution,' Joyce said steadily. 'Hysterical young women with sex on the brain going to young priests, who accept everything they say without making proper inquiries! That is persecution, and I hope it doesn't go any further. In the meantime,' Joyce added contemptuously, 'you'd be wise to put that brooch in the dustbin and forget about the whole business.' Then his tone changed again and became insolently personal. 'Before I go, Father, did Sheila Moriarty ever tell you what her mother's advice was before she left home?'

'I'm not discussing her business with you,' said Fogarty.

'You should really ask her some time,' said Joyce, and then he turned on his heel and went jauntily down the stairs.

Fogarty was furious. He knew he had been outmanoeuvred all over the shop, and by somebody he thoroughly despised and believed to be an arrant coward. He had an aching regret that he hadn't hit the man when he had the opportunity. It was clearly a public duty on someone's part to hit him. But he had been foxed, and the result was that though he had summoned Joyce merely to warn him off, it was himself who had been warned off. And Fogarty was not a man who was accustomed to being warned off.

And yet, when he woke next morning, he was full of cheerfulness and bounce. When he analysed the scene all over again, everything about it seemed all right. An unpleasant duty had been done, no matter how inadequately. In spite of his bluff Joyce was a coward and much too afraid to pursue Sheila further. Above all, he would say nothing about the brooch. Sheila's word against his might not count, but Sheila's word and that of her priest would satisfy any reasonable person that he was at the bottom of any offence she had committed. But though Fogarty knew he had won, he realized too that for the future he must be more careful in his dealings with businessmen and would have to get advice, if not from the parish priest, at least from some priest older than himself. It was all very well to know a few thousand sins theoretically, but to know a few of them practically gave the other fellow an immense advantage.

When Sheila Moriarty came that evening she saw at once from his manner that things had gone well. This time he told Mary to bring up the coffee at once and till it arrived he talked to Sheila about her native place. When he had poured out the coffee he smiled knowingly at her.

'I had a visitor last night,' he said.

'What did you think of him?' she asked ruefully.

'To tell you the truth, I didn't like him very much. Smooth, of course. A smart salesman. Not one you could do business with, though.'

'Do you think I don't know it?' she asked wearily. 'What did he say for himself?'

'Nothing much for himself, a lot for other people. I'll be quite honest with you, he was too smart for me altogether, not to mind you. But I'm sure of one thing. He'll give you no more trouble unless you make an opportunity for him.'

'I promise you I won't do that if I can avoid it.'

'You'll have to avoid it,' Fogarty said sternly. 'Anything you have to do with that man for the future is going to injure you. He's frightened and sore, and he'll hurt you in any way he can.'

'And the brooch?'

'Never mind about that. Tell it in Confession, of course, but say you've taken steps to return it. I'll find a way myself sooner or later.'

'I'm not going to thank you,' she said. 'Only for you I don't know what would have happened me.'

'I did nothing only what I'd be bound to do for anyone,' he said. 'And even that much I mightn't have been able to do except that I knew something about him.'

'What was it?'

'Nothing much. Just an unfortunate married woman who found it advisable to leave town as a result of her association with him. That was something he didn't want brought up.'

'I suppose I should have guessed it,' she said despondently. 'It's our vanity that we can never bring ourselves to believe there could have been anyone else, isn't it? What else did he say?'

Fogarty realized with surprise that, bitter as she was, and perhaps because she was bitter, she could go on all night talking about Joyce.

'Oh, he told me to ask you what the advice was that your mother gave you,' Fogarty replied with a jolly laugh.

'He told you that?' she asked sharply, and at once he knew he had said the wrong thing. What there was wrong about it he couldn't see, unless it was that she was still so sore that every word she had uttered in confidence to a man she was in love with hurt her when it came from someone else.

'Naturally, I didn't say you'd already told me,' he added to comfort her.

'I'm glad of that anyway,' she said and got up.

'There's no need to go so soon,' he exclaimed. 'I can drive you wherever you want to go.'

'I think I'd better go just the same, Father,' she said with a smile, but he could have sworn she was fighting back tears. Something had gone wrong, dreadfully wrong, but he had no idea what it was and felt a complete fool.

'You'll keep in touch with me anyway?' he said.

'Indeed I will.'

'And if that fellow annoys you again, don't waste any more time. Come straight out of the shop and let me know. You understand that?'

'I promise, Father.'

Then she was gone and Fogarty felt let down. Let down, bewildered, frustrated, and he didn't know why. What her mother had said couldn't possibly have anything to do with it. It was advice that any mother might have given her daughter when she was leaving home for the first time, except for saying that 'all married men weren't like her daddy', which only showed the ingenuousness of the poor woman.

But why then had Sheila withered up when he referred to it, and above all, why had Joyce worn that complacent insolent smile when *he* referred to it? Then he understood and he withered up too. Sheila's mother had said something else, something about not throwing temptation in the way of priests because they were more vulnerable than other men. And quite innocently she had thrown temptation in his way and quite innocently he had been tempted, and Joyce in his coarse worldly way had seen it all. Her mother had known she was a lonely vulnerable girl and realized where it might carry her. And where it might have carried her – and him – God only knew, if he had not accidentally shown her how it all looked in an enemy's eye.

Now, Fogarty had a strong impression that he would never meet the girl again and never know what her mother had really said to her about not associating with a priest, because priests were weaker than other men, because they were more unprotected than other men. And suddenly the loneliness he was for ever trying to banish descended on him in all its black bitterness and he added aloud, 'O God, we are, we are!'

(1967)

The Corkerys

May MacMahon was a good-looking girl, the only child of Jack MacMahon, the accountant, and his wife, Margaret. They lived in Cork, on Summerhill, the steep street that led from the flat of the city to the heights of Montenotte. She had always lived the life of a girl of good family, with piano lessons, dancing class, and crushes on her schoolfriends' brothers. Only occassionally did she wonder what it was all about, and then she invariably forgot to ask her father, who would certainly know. Her father knew everything, or almost everything. He was a tall, shy, good-looking man, who seemed to have been expecting martyrdom from his earliest years and drinking Irish whiskey to endure it. May's mother was small and pretty and very opinionated, though her opinions varied, and anyway did not last long. Her father's opinions never varied, and lasted for ever.

When May became friendly with the Corkery family, it turned out that he had always had strong opinions about them as well. Mr Corkery, a mild, inarticulate solicitor, whom May remembered going for lonely walks for the good of his health, had died and left his family with very limited means, but his widow had good connexions and managed to provide an education (mostly free) for all six children. Of the boys, the eldest, Tim, was now a Dominican, and, Joe who came next in line, was also going in for the priesthood. The Church was in the family's blood, because Mrs Corkery's brother was the Dean and her sister was Mother Superior of the convent of an enclosed order outside the city. Mrs Corkery's nickname among the children was 'Reverend Mother', and they accused her of imitating her sister, but Mrs Corkery only sniffed and said if everybody became priests and nuns there would soon be no Church left. Mrs Corkery seemed to believe quite seriously that the needs of the Church were the only possible excuse for sex.

From knowing the Corkerys May began to realize at last what

251

life was about. It was no longer necessary to ask her father. Anyway he wouldn't know. He and her mother were nice but commonplace. Everything they said and did was dull and predictable, and even when they went to Mass on Sunday they did so only because everyone else did it. The Corkerys were rarely dull and never predictable. Though their whole life seemed to centre on the Church, they were not in the least pietistic. The Dean fought with Mrs Corkery; Father Tim fought with Joe; the sisters fought with their brothers, who, they said, were getting all the attention, and fought one another when their brothers were not available. Tessie, the eldest girl, known as 'The Limb of the Devil', or just 'The Limb', was keeping company with a young stockbroker who told her a lot of dirty stories, which she repeated with great gusto to her brothers, particularly to Father Tim. This, however, was for family reasons, because they all agreed that Tim was inclined to put on airs.

And then The Limb astonished everybody by entering the convent where her aunt was Mother Superior. May attended the Reception in the little convent chapel, which struck her to the heart by its combination of poverty and gentility. She felt that the ceremony might have been tolerable in a great cathedral with a choir and thundering organ, but not in that converted drawing-room, where the nuns knelt along the side walls and squeaked like mourners. The Limb was laid out on the altar and first covered with roses as though she were dead; then an old nun clipped her long black hair with a shears. It fell and lay at her head as though it too had died. May drew a quick breath and glanced at Joe, who was kneeling beside her. Though he had his hands over his face, she knew from the way his shoulders moved that he was crying. Then she cried, too.

For a full week the ceremony gave her the horrors every time she remembered it, and she felt she should have nothing more to do with such an extraordinary family. All the same, a week with her parents was enough to make her realize the attraction of the Corkerys even more than before.

'Did it scare you, May?' Rosie, the second girl, asked with a wicked grin. 'Cripes, it put the fear of God into me. I'm not having any of that *de profundis* stuff; I'm joining a decent missionary order.' This was the first May had heard of Rosie's vocation. Inside a year, she, too, was in a convent, but in Rome, and 'having a gas time', as she casually reported home.

They really were an extraordinary family, and the Dean was as queer as any of them. The Sunday following the ceremony May was at dinner there, and he put his hand firmly on her shoulder as though he were about to yank off her dress, and gave her a crooked smile that would have convinced any reasonable observer that he was a sex maniac, and yet May knew that almost every waking moment his thoughts were concentrated on outwitting the Bishop, who seemed to be the greatest enemy of the Church since Nero. The Bishop was a Dominican, and the Dean felt that a monk's place was in the cloister.

'The man is a bully!' he said, with an astonishment and grief that would have moved any audience but his own family.

'Oh, now, Mick!' said Mrs Corkery placidly. She was accustomed to hearing the Bishop denounced.

'I'm sorry, Josephine,' the Dean said with a formal regret that rang equally untrue. 'The man is a bully. An infernal bully, what's more. I'm not criticizing you or the order, Tim,' he said, looking at his nephew over his spectacles, 'but monks simply have no place in ecclesiastical affairs. Let them stick to their prayers is what I say.'

'And a queer way the world would be only for them,' Joe said. Joe was going for the secular priesthood himself, but he didn't like to see his overwhelming uncle get away with too much.

'Their influence on Church history has been disastrous!' the Dean bellowed, reaching for his cigarette case. 'Always, or almost always, disastrous. That man thinks he knows everything.'

'Maybe he does,' said Joe.

'Maybe,' said the Dean, like an old bull who cannot ignore a dart from any quarter. 'But as well as that, he interferes in everything, and always publicly, always with the greatest possible amount of scandal. "I don't like the model of that church"; "Take away that statue"; "That painting is irreverent". Begob, Joe, I don't think even you know as much as that. I declare to God, Josephine, I believe if anyone suggested it to him that man would start inspecting the cut of the schoolgirls' panties.' And when everyone roared with laughter, the Dean raised his head sternly and said, 'I mean it.'

Peter, the youngest boy, never got involved in these family arguments about the Bishop, the orders, or the future of the

Church. He was the odd man out. He was apprenticed in his father's old firm and would grow up to be owner or partner. In every Irish family there is a boy like Peter whose task it is to take on the family responsibilities. It was merely an accident that he was the youngest. What counted was that he was his mother's favourite. Even before he had a mind to make up, he knew it was not for him to become too involved, because someone would have to look after his mother in her old age. He might marry, but it would have to be a wife who suited her. He was the ugliest of the children, though with a monkey ugliness that was almost as attractive as Father Tim's film-star looks and Joe's ascetic masculine fire. He was slow, watchful, and good-humoured, with high cheekbones that grew tiny bushes of hair, and he had a lazy malice that could often be as effective as the uproarious indignation of his brothers and sisters.

May, who saw the part he had been cast for, wondered whether she couldn't woo Mrs Corkery as well as another girl.

After Rosie there was Joe, who was ordained the following year, and then Sheela did what seemed – in that family, at least – the conventional thing and went into the same convent as Tessie.

It was an extraordinary family, and May was never quite able to understand the fascination it had for her. Partly, of course – and this she felt rather than understood – it was the attraction of the large family for the only child, the sheer relief of never having to wonder what you were going to play next. But beside this there was an attraction rather like that of a large theatrical family – the feeling that everything was related to a larger imaginative world. In a sense, the Corkerys always seemed to be playing.

She knew that her own being in love with Peter was part of her love affair with the family as a whole, the longing to be connected with them, and the teasing she got about Peter from his brothers and sisters suggested that they, too, recognized it and were willing to accept her as one of themselves. But she also saw that her chance of ever marrying Peter was extremely slight, because Peter was not attracted by her. When he could have been out walking with her he was out walking with his friend Mick MacDonald, and when the pair of them came in while she was in the house, Peter behaved to her as though she were nothing more than a welcome stranger. He was always polite, always deferential – unlike Tim and Joe, who treated her as though she were an extra sister, to be slapped on the bottom or pushed out of the way as the mood struck them.

May was a serious girl; she had read books on modern psychology, and she knew that the very quality that made Peter settle for a life in the world made him unsuitable as a husband. It was strange how right the books were about that. He was dominated by his mother, and he could flirt with her as he never flirted with May. Clearly, no other woman would ever entirely replace his mother in his heart. In fact (May was too serious a girl not to give things their proper names), Peter was the very type of the homosexual – the latent homosexual, as she learned to call it.

Other boys *wanted* to go out with her, and she resented Peter's unfailing courtesy, though in more philosophic spells she realized that he probably couldn't help it, and that when he showed his almost boyish hero-worship of Mick MacDonald before her it was not his fault but Nature's. All the same, she thought it very uncalled-for on the part of Nature, because it left her no particular interest in a world in which the only eligible young man was a queer. After a year or two of this, her thoughts turned more and more to the quiet convent where the Corkery girls contentedly carried on their simple lives of meditation and prayer. Once or twice she dropped a dark hint that she was thinking of becoming a nun herself, but each time it led to a scene with her father.

'You're a fool, girl!' he said harshly, getting up to pour himself an extra drink. May knew he didn't altogether resent being provoked, because it made him feel entitled to drink more.

'Now, Jack, you must not say things like that,' her mother said anxiously.

'Of course I have to say it. Look at her! At her age! And she doesn't even have a boy!'

'But if there isn't a boy who interests her!'

'There are plenty of boys who'd interest her if only she behaved like a natural girl,' he said gloomily. 'What do you think a boy wants to do with a girl? Say the rosary? She hasn't behaved naturally ever since she got friendly with that family – what's their name?'

'Corkery,' Mrs MacMahon said, having failed to perceive that not remembering the Corkerys' name was the one way the poor man had of getting back at them.

'Whatever their name is, they've turned her into an idiot. That's no great surprise. They never had any brains to distribute, themselves.'

'But still, Jack, you will admit they've got on very well.'

'They've got on very well!' he echoed scornfully. 'In the Church! Except that young fellow, the solicitor's clerk, and I suppose he hadn't brains enough even for the Church. They should have put him in the friars.'

'But after all, their uncle is the Dean.'

'Wonderful Dean, too,' grumbled Jack MacMahon. 'He drove me out of twelve-o'clock Mass, so as not to listen to his drivel. He can hardly speak decent English, not to mind preaching a sermon. "A bunch of baloney!"' he quoted angrily. 'If we had a proper bishop, instead of the one we have, he'd make that fellow speak correctly in the pulpit at least.'

'But it's only so that his congregation will understand him, Jack.'

'Oh, his congregation understands him only too well. Himself and his tall hat and his puffed-up airs! Common, that's what he is, and that's what all the family are, on both sides. If your daughter wants to be a nun, you and the Corkerys can arrange it between you. But not one penny of my money goes into their pockets, believe me!'

May was sorry to upset him, but for herself she did not mind his loathing of the whole Corkery family. She knew that it was only because he was fond of her and dreaded being left without her in his old age. He had spoiled her so long as she was not of an age to answer him back, and she guessed he was looking forward to spoiling his grandchildren even worse because he would not live long enough to hear them answer him back. But this, she realized, was what the Corkerys' had done for her – made all that side of life seem unimportant.

She had a long talk with Mother Agatha, Mrs Corkery's sister, about her vocation, which confirmed her in her resolution. Mother Agatha was very unlike her sister, who was loud-voiced and humorous. The Mother Superior was pale, thin, cool, and with the slightest trace of an ironic wit that might have passed unnoticed by a stupider girl. But May noticed it, and realized that she was being observed very closely indeed.

She and her mother did the shopping for the trousseau, but the bills and parcels were kept carefully out of her father's sight. Drunk or sober, he refused to discuss the matter at all. 'It would only upset him just now, poor man,' her mother said philosophically. He was drinking heavily, and when he was in liquor he quarrelled a lot with her mother about little things. With May he avoided quarrels, or even arguments, and it struck her that he was training himself for a life in which he would no longer have her to quarrel with. On the day of the Reception he did not drink at all, which pleased her, and was icily polite to everybody, but when, later, she appeared behind the parlour grille, all in white, and the sun caught her, she saw his face in the darkness of the parlour, with all the life drained out of it, and suddenly he turned and left without a word. It was only then that a real feeling of guilt sprang up in her at the thought of the miserable old age that awaited him – a man like him, who loved young creatures who could not answer him back, and who would explain to them unweariedly about the sun and moon and geography and figures. She had answered him back in a way that left him with nothing to look forward to.

All the same, there was something very comforting about the life of an enclosed order. It had been organized a long, long time before, by people who knew more about the intrusions of the outside world than May did. The panics that had seized her about her ability to sustain the life diminished and finally ceased. The round of duties, services, and mortifications was exactly what she had needed, and little by little she felt the last traces of worldliness slip from her – even the very human worry about the old age of her father and mother. The convent was poor, and not altogether from choice. Everything in the house was mean and clean and cheerful, and May grew to love the old drawing room that had been turned into a chapel, where she knelt in her own place, through the black winter mornings when at home she would still be tucked up comfortably in bed. She liked the rough feeling of her clothes and the cold of the floor through her sandals, though mostly she liked the proximity of Tessie and Sheela.

There were times when, reading the lives of the saints, she wished she had lived in more heroic times, and she secretly invented minor mortifications for herself to make sure she could endure them. It was not until she had been in the convent for close on a year that she noticed that the minor mortifications were liable to be followed by major depressions. Though she was a clever woman, she did not try to analyse this. She merely lay awake at night and realized that the nuns she lived with – even Tessie and Sheela – were not the stuff of saints and martyrs, but ordinary women who behaved in religion very much as they would have behaved in marriage, and who followed the rule in the spirit in which her father went to Mass on Sundays. There was nothing whatever to be said against them, and any man who had got one of them for a wife would probably have considered himself fortunate, but all the same there was something about them that was not quite grown-up. It was very peculiar and caused her great concern. The things that had really frightened her about the order when she was in the world – the loneliness, the austerity, the ruthless discipline – now seemed to her meaningless and harmless. After that she saw with horror that the great days of the Church were over, and that they were merely a lot of perfectly commonplace women play-acting austerity and meditation.

'But my dear child,' Mother Agatha said when May wept out her story to her, 'of course we're only children. Of course we're only play-acting. How else does a child learn obedience and discipline?'

And when May talked to her about what the order had been in earlier days, that vague, ironic note crept into Mother Superior's voice, as though she had heard it all many times before. 'I know, Sister,' she said, with a nod. 'Believe me, I do know that the order was stricter in earlier times. But you must remember that it was not founded in a semi-arctic climate like ours, so there was less chance of the sisters dying of double pneumonia. I have talked to half the plumbers in town, but it seems that central heating is not understood here . . . everything is relative. I'm sure we suffer just as much in our very comfortable sandals as the early sisters suffered in their bare feet, and probably at times rather more, but at any rate we are not here for the sole purpose of suffering mortification, whatever pleasures it may hold for us.'

Every word Mother Agatha said made perfect sense to May while she was saying it, and May knew she was being ungrateful and hysterical, but when the interview was over and the sound of her sobs had died away, she was left with the impression that Mother Agatha was only another commonplace woman, with a cool manner and a sarcastic tongue, who was also acting the part of a nun. She was alone in a world of bad actors and actresses, and the Catholicism she had known and believed in was dead.

A few weeks later she was taken to a private nursing home. 'Just for a short rest, Sister,' as Mother Agatha said. 'It's a very pleasant place, and you will find a lot of other Religious there who need a rest as well.'

There followed an endless but timeless phase of weeping and confusion, when all May's ordinary life was broken up and strange men burst into her room and examined her and asked questions she did not understand and replied to questions of hers in a way that showed they had not understood them either. Nobody seemed to realize that she was the last Catholic in the world; nobody understood her tears about it. Above all, nobody seemed to be able to hear the gramophone record that played continuously in her head, and that stopped only when they gave her an injection.

Then, one spring day, she went into the garden for a walk and a young nurse saw her back to her room. Far ahead of them, at the other end of a long, white corridor, she saw an old man with his back to her, and remembered that she had seen his face many times before and had perceived, without paying attention to, his long, gloomy, ironic face. She knew she must have remembered him, because now she could see nothing but his back, and suddenly the words 'Who is that queer old man?' broke through the sound of the gramophone record, surprising her as much as they seemed to surprise the young nurse.

'Oh, him!' the nurse said, with a smile. 'Don't you know him? He's been here for years.'

'But why, Nurse?'

'Oh, he doesn't think he's a priest, and he is one really, that's the trouble.'

'But how extraordinary!'

'Isn't it?' the nurse said, biting her lower lip in a smile. 'Cripes, you'd think 'twas something you wouldn't forget. He's nice, really, though,' she added gravely, as though she felt she had been criticizing him.

When they reached Mary's room, the young nurse grinned again, in a guilty way, and May noticed that she was extravagantly pretty, with small gleaming front teeth.

'*You're* getting all right, anyway,' she said.

'Oh, really?' May said vaguely, because she knew she was not getting all right. 'Why do you think that, Nurse?'

'Oh, you get to spot things,' the nurse said with a shrug, and left May uncomforted, because she didn't know if she really did get well how she could face the convent and the other nuns again. All of them, she felt, would be laughing at her. Instead of worrying about the nuns, she went into a mournful daydream about the old priest who did not think he was a priest, and next day, when her father called, she said intensely, 'Daddy, there's a priest in here who doesn't believe he's a priest – isn't that extraordinary?' She did not hear the tone of her own voice or know how reasonable it sounded, and so she was surprised when her father looked away and started fumbling mechanically in his jacket pocket for a cigarette.

'Well, you don't have to think you're a nun either,' he said, with an unsteady voice. 'Your mother has your own room ready for you when you come home.'

'Oh, but Daddy, I have to go back to the convent.'

'Oh, no you don't. No more convents for you, young lady! That's fixed up already with Mother Superior. It was all a mistake from the beginning. You're coming straight home to your mother and me.'

Then May knew she was really going to get well, and she wanted to go home with him at once, not to go back up the stairs behind the big iron door where there was always an attendant on duty. She knew that going back home meant defeat, humiliation, and despair, but she no longer cared even about that. She just wanted to take up her life again at the point where it had gone wrong, when she had first met the Corkerys.

Her father brought her home and acted as though he had rescued her from a dragon's den. Each evening, when he came home from work, he sat with her, sipping at his drink and talking quietly and comfortably. She felt he was making great efforts to ensure that she felt protected and relaxed. Most of the time she did, but there were spells when she wanted her mother to put her back in the nursing home.

'Oh, I couldn't do that,' her mother said characteristically. 'It would upset your poor father too much.'

But she did discuss it with the doctor – a young man, thin and rather unhealthy-looking, who looked as though he, too, was living on his nerves – and he argued with May about it.

'But what am I to do, Doctor, when I feel like this?' she asked plaintively.

'Go out and get jarred,' he said briskly.

'Get what, Doctor?' she asked feebly.

'Jarred,' he repeated without embarrassment. 'Stoned. Polluted. Drunk. I don't mean alone, of course. You need a young fellow along with you.'

'Oh, not that again, Doctor!' she said, and for some reason her voice came out exactly like Mother Agatha's – which was not how she intended it to sound.

'And some sort of a job,' he went on remorselessly. 'There isn't a damn thing wrong with you except that you think you're a failure. You're not, of course, but as a result of thinking you are you've scratched the surface of your mind all over, and when you sit here like this, looking out at the rain, you keep rubbing it so that it doesn't heal. Booze, love-making, and hard work – they keep your hands away from the sore surface, and then it heals of its own accord.'

She did her best, but it didn't seem to heal as easily as all that. Her father got her a job in the office of a friend, and she listened, in fascination, to the chatter of the other secretaries. She even went out in the evening with a couple of them and listened to their common little love stories. She knew if she had to wait until she talked like that about fellows in order to be well, her case was hopeless. Instead, she got drunk and told them how she had been for years in love with a homosexual, and, as she told it, the story became so hopeless and dreadful that she sobbed over it herself. After that she went home and wept for hours, because she knew that she had been telling lies, and betrayed the only people in the world whom she had really cared for.

Her father made a point of never referring at all to the Corkerys, the convent, or the nursing home. She knew that for him this represented a real triumph of character, because he loathed the Corkerys more than ever for what he believed they had done to her. But even he could not very well ignore the latest development in the saga. It seemed that Mrs Corkery herself had decided to become a nun. She announced placidly to everyone that she had done her duty by her family, who were now all comfortably settled, and that she felt free to do what she had always wanted to do anyhow. She discussed it with the Dean, who practically excommunicated her on the spot. He said the family would never live down the scandal, and Mrs Corkery told him it wasn't the scandal that worried him at all but the loss of the one house where he could get a decent meal. If he had a spark of manliness, she said, he would get rid of his housekeeper, who couldn't cook, was a miserable sloven, and ordered him about as if he were a schoolboy. The Dean said she would have to get permission in writing from every one of her children, and Mrs Corkery replied calmly that there was no difficulty whatever about that.

May's father didn't really want to crow, but he could not resist pointing out that he had always said the Corkerys had a slate loose.

'I don't see anything very queer about it,' May said stubbornly.

'A woman with six children entering a convent at her age!' her father said, not even troubling to grow angry with her. 'Even the Dean realizes it's mad.'

'It is a little bit extreme, all right,' her mother said, with a frown, but May knew she was thinking of her.

May had the feeling that Mrs Corkery would make a very good nun, if for no other reason than to put her brother and Mother Agatha in their place. And of course, there were other reasons. As a girl she had wanted to be a nun, but for family reasons it was impossible, so she had become a good wife and mother, instead. Now, after thirty years of pinching and scraping, her family had grown away from her and she could return to her early dream. There was nothing unbalanced about that, May thought bitterly. *She* was the one who had proved unbalanced.

For a while it plunged her back into gloomy moods, and they were made worse by the scraps of gossip that people passed on to her, not knowing how they hurt. Mrs Corkery had collected her six letters of freedom and taken them herself to the Bishop, who had immediately given in. 'Spite!' the Dean pronounced gloomily. 'Nothing but spite – all because I don't support his mad dream of turning a modern city into a medieval monastery.'

On the day of Mrs Corkery's Reception, May did not leave the house at all. It rained, and she sat by the sitting-room window,

looking across the city to where the hills were almost invisible. She
was living Mrs Corkery's day through – the last day in the human
world of an old woman who had assumed the burden she herself
had been too weak to accept. She could see it all as though she
were back in that mean, bright little chapel, with the old woman
lying out on the altar, covered with roses like a corpse, and an old
nun shearing off her thin grey locks. It was all so intolerably vivid
that May kept bursting into sudden fits of tears and whimpering
like a child.

One evening a few weeks later, she came out of the office in
the rain and saw Peter Corkery at the other side of the street. She
obeyed her first instinct and bowed her head so as not to look at
him. Her heart sank as he crossed the road to accost her.

'Aren't you a great stranger, May?' he asked, with his cheerful
grin.

'We're very busy in the office these days, Peter,' she replied,
with false brightness.

'It was only the other night Joe was talking about you. You
know Joe is up in the seminary now?'

'No. What's he doing?'

'Teaching. He finds it a great relief after the mountains. And,
off course, you know about the mother.' This was it!

'I heard about it. I suppose ye're all delighted?'

'*I* wasn't very delighted,' he said, and his lips twisted in pain.
''Twas the most awful day I ever spent. When they cut off her
hair—'

'You don't have to remind me.'

'I disgraced myself, May. I had to run out of the chapel. And
here I had two nuns after me, trying to steer me to the lavatory.
Why do nuns always think a man is looking for a lavatory?'

'I wouldn't know. I wasn't a very good one.'

'There are different opinions about that,' he said gently, but he
only hurt her more.

'And I suppose you'll be next?'

'How next?'

'I was sure you had a vocation, too.'

'I don't know,' he said thoughtfully. 'I never really asked
myself. I suppose, in a way, it depends on you.'

'And what have I to say to it?' she asked in a ladylike tone,
though her heart suddenly began to pant.

'Only whether you're going to marry me or not. Now I have the house to myself and only Mrs Maher looking after me. You remember Mrs Maher?'

'And you think I'd make a cheap substitute for Mrs Maher, I suppose?' she asked, and suddenly all the pent-up anger and frustration of years seemed to explode inside her. She realized that it was entirely because of him that she had become a nun, because of him she had been locked up in a nursing home and lived the life of an emotional cripple. 'Don't you think that's an extraordinary sort of proposal – if it's intended to be a proposal.'

'Why the hell should I be any good at proposing? How many girls do you think I've proposed to?'

'Not many, since they didn't teach you better manners. And it would never occur to yourself to say you loved me. Do you?' she almost shouted. 'Do you love me?'

'Sure, of course I do,' he said, almost in astonishment. 'I wouldn't be asking you to marry me otherwise. But all the same—'

'All the same, all the same, you have reservations!' And suddenly language that would have appalled her to hear a few months before broke from her, before she burst into uncontrollable tears and went running homeward through the rain. 'God damn you to Hell, Peter Corkery! I wasted my life on you, and now in the heel of the hunt all you can say to me is "All the same". You'd better go back to your damn pansy pals, and say it to them.'

She was hysterical by the time she reached Summerhill. Her father's behaviour was completely characteristic. He was the born martyr and this was only another of the ordeals for which he had been preparing himself all his life. He got up and poured himself a drink.

'Well, there is one thing I'd better tell you now, daughter,' he said quietly but firmly. 'That man will never enter this house in my lifetime.'

'Oh, nonsense, Jack MacMahon!' his wife said in a rage, and she went and poured herself a drink, a thing she did under her husband's eye only when she was prepared to fling it at him. 'You haven't a scrap of sense. Don't you see now that the boy's mother only entered the convent because she knew he'd never feel free while she was in the world?'

'Oh, Mother!' May cried, startled out of her hysterics.

'Well, am I right?' her mother said, drawing herself up.

'Oh, you're right, you're right,' May said, beginning to sob again. 'Only I was such a fool it never occurred to me. Of course, she was doing it for me.'

'And for her son,' said her mother. 'And if he's anything like his mother, I'll be very proud to claim him for a son-in-law.'

She looked at her husband, but saw that she had made her effect and could now enjoy her drink in peace. 'Of course, in some ways it's going to be very embarrassing,' she went on peaceably. 'We can't very well say, "Mr Peter Corkery, son of Sister Rosina of the Little Flower" or whatever the dear lady's name is. In fact, it's very difficult to see how we're going to get it into the Press at all. However, as I always say, if the worst comes to the worst, there's a lot to be said for a quiet wedding . . . I do hope you were nice to him, May?' she asked.

It was only then that May remembered that she hadn't been in the least nice, and in fact, had used language that would have horrified her mother. Not that it would make much difference. She and Peter had travelled so far together, and by such extraordinary ways.

(1966)

The School for Wives

The real trouble with love is that people want contradictory things out of it. Like Jimmy Maguire and his wife. Jimmy was a tall thin fellow with an eager face, and in his younger days he used to be something of a Don Juan. There was a little group of them – the Doctor, Con Bishop, and two or three other bachelors – and they were all out for a good time. They used to go shooting and fishing, and one year, I remember, they took a house in Clare. The things that went on! Any excuse for a party, and it didn't much matter to them where the party was to be – Limerick, Galway, or Cork, what was it, after all, but a day's outing? Jimmy was the most reckless of them. They would be returning to Dublin from one outing when he would hear of a party somewhere else, and decide they ought to crash it. The Doctor, who shared a flat with Jimmy, lived in a continual state of alarm at what Jimmy would do next. Jimmy would do anything if the mood struck him, and, whatever he did, the Doctor was swept protesting into his orbit.

'But it's all right,' Jimmy would say, raising a hand. 'The man is an old friend. I've done business with him for years.'

'Business?' the Doctor would say. 'You don't even know his name.'

'Oh, what's a little thing like that between friends?'

And Jimmy would go up to the house of a perfect stranger and brazen it out. You wouldn't think from his rather formal manners that he was so audacious, but he was. And he could get away with things, for he was personable and plausible. Not only would he gain admittance to the party, he would end by becoming the centre of it. The secret of Jimmy's success was his fondness for women. He really liked women, and had a quite genuine interest in their affairs, and a woman could never be with him for long without telling him her troubles. Whatever wonderful way he had of easing their minds, women who confessed to him wanted to go on confessing, and that was where the Doctor came in, because he

266

would talk to them over the telephone in that wonderful, vague, syrupy voice of his, sympathizing with them in their inability to find Jimmy, while Jimmy in stockinged feet tip-toed around him, making hideous faces.

All this greatly scandalized the Doctor. But for all his alarm and pretended disapproval he loved it, of course. He had been devoted to his mother and, as a result, he was still unmarried and likely to remain so. Jimmy was his secret life, his wild oats. He was lonely and sweet-natured and for ever thinking and talking of love. You would go to see him, and he would fuss about with the drinks, murmuring in his gentle, worried way about Jimmy and his girls. 'And some of them married, my dear fellow,' he would whisper, giving you a dark look over his spectacles. 'I forget whether you like soda. Personally, I think it gives you indigestion. And he's so pious! Every year of his life off to Lough Derg on the pilgrimage, trailing round the holy stones on his bare feet. And even there – did I put too much water in it – he picks them up. At the same time – here's health, old man – he keeps trying to reform me. I admit my beliefs mightn't be all that orthodox, but I can't help feeling that his aren't completely sincere. Mind you, he's quite charming about it. He says I'm putting the cart before the horse, and that sins against morals are less important than sins against faith. According to him, I'm a Protestant. He says it's all in the importance you attach to the First Commandment, or something. I really can't follow that sort of argument – I mean, this difference between sins against faith and sins against morals. Can you?'

At last, after years of piety and skirt-hunting, Jimmy found the girl he wanted to marry, and he took her by storm. She was called Roisin Mooney, and I must say he showed great taste. She was a really nice girl, the sort you'd swear would be especially reserved as a reward for virtue. She was enraptured with religion, with the sacraments, with prayer, and with every form of emotional religion. Nor did marriage seem to disillusion her. At least twenty times a day that girl must have told herself that she was the luckiest girl in the world to be married to a king of men like Jimmy, and twenty times a day wondered if God would give her the grace to be worthy of him. It is the unworldly type of woman whose mind is fixed on the saints, suffering, and sublimation who really appreciates the miracle of a man in the bed when she wakes in the morning.

267

She asked him over and over to explain again from the beginning what he had felt when he first met her and how it was he had seen anything in such a plain, stupid, uneducated girl as herself. And Jimmy, who found it difficult to remember even where he had met her and whose approach to all women had been standardized down the years, tried to look portentous and understanding, and said that a legal training was a great aid in seeing through appearances. Roisin shook her head doubtfully. She had known other lawyers, and they had never seen through her. Clearly it couldn't be anything but inspiration, and she worried her own vivid recollections, trying to see portents and miracles in them, but she couldn't, because, as she recognized herself, she wasn't clever.

Jimmy had a rajah's life with her. To say that Roisin was a good housekeeper would be an absurdity. She kept house for him as a musician writes a symphony or a saint pursues a meditation – on her knees, in quest of the absolute. When he got home from the office, she knelt at his feet and took off his shoes, while Jimmy made faces to indicate the various inconsiderate ways in which she hurt his feet. When she had got him a drink and asked him for the tenth time if it was all right, she sat on a little stool and looked up adoringly at him while that scoundrel pontificated. And when he came home drunk and climbed into bed, with his bowler hat down over his eyes and his umbrella resting neatly on his left arm, she gently relieved him of both, took off his shoes and socks, opened his collar and tie, and crept into bed beside him, thanking God for the gift of a wonderful husband. She was a real pet.

Those who had known Jimmy in his bachelor days wondered how long exactly it would take him to grow tired of living with a saint and long for the open road again and the wild parties in Galway and Cork. But that was not how it happened at all. Instead, Jimmy began to drop all his old friends, the Doctor among them. He didn't do it blatantly or rudely, because, whatever faults Jimmy may have had, he was a thorough gentleman. But he dropped them just the same. Occasionally the Doctor would run into him in Dame Street, coming from his office, and Jimmy's face would light up, and the pair of them would drop into the Wicklow Bar or Davy Byrne's, while Jimmy sketched the wonderful party he was going to give for all his old friends, till that glazed look came in his eye and he had to go home in a cab.

But the Doctor noticed that no matter how glazed Jimmy's eyes got, the invitation never became more precise.

'Jimmy,' he said dryly, 'I don't want to be offensive or personal in any way, but if you'd put a tenth of the energy into giving that party that you put into talking about it, we might have some chance of attending it before we die.'

'Next week definitely, Pat,' said Jimmy, drawing himself up with a frown. 'Thursday or Friday, depending. I'll ring you.'

But the next week came and he didn't ring, and there was no party. The Doctor was hurt. He realized that Jimmy was dropping the old crowd for business acquaintances, clients, and priests. Particularly priests. A man who is trying to exorcize his past can't do better than priests. Now when he got a bit high, Jimmy talked about the Dialogue Mass instead of ankles, or the difference between ourselves and the Greek Orthodox Church. He took Roisin to the pictures, wearing the impeccable bowler hat and carrying the umbrella. Jimmy was on the way up. In no time now he would be solicitor to half a dozen government agencies.

Jimmy's old friends couldn't help being curious about the eager, dark-haired girl he had married, but what they didn't know was that Roisin was even more curious about them. Marriage was still wonderful. She was having a baby, and she lit candles to Jimmy, she was full of Jimmy, but none of the people he brought to the house really knew Jimmy. When Roisin had one drink in – one drink was always enough to loosen her tongue – she had to tell the whole amazing story of Jimmy's courtship. 'And do you know how that fellow proposed to me?' she would say. 'He made me sit on the side of the road and then took out his handkerchief and *knelt* in front of me as if I was a statue. "Jimmy Maguire!" says I. "Get up out of that or you'll ruin your new trousers."'

But when she looked at their polite, vague, smiling faces, she had the feeling that they only thought her a fool. And in the middle of the night she woke Jimmy to ask him to tell her frankly whether she hadn't ruined his life. Jimmy yawned and said no, she was doing fine.

'But I want to know the truth. I'd sooner know it now when I might be able to do something about it,' she would say, as if she were begging the specialist to hold nothing back from her. 'I do my best, but I know I haven't the brains. I was always the same. I never could do sums. No wonder if they think I'm mad.'

269

And all the time at the back of Roisin's mind was the thought that the person who would really understand her was Josephine Hanrahan. She knew that Jimmy and Josephine Hanrahan had been very thick. She did not know in which way, nor did she very much care, but she was certain that a woman who had been so fond of Jimmy would understand her feelings. This was where the first rift occurred between Jimmy and herself, for Jimmy did not like the idea at all. Not that he showed how troubled he really was. Instead, he pretended to consider the matter judicially.

'Now, Josephine is a delightful woman,' he said in a harsh tone, 'but she isn't your class. Please don't think I'm being snobbish. There's nothing I dislike more. But we have to face facts, and it wouldn't be in the woman's best interests.'

To sacrifice a pleasure in order to spare pain to Josephine appealed immensely to Roisin's idealistic mind, but all the same she couldn't help wondering if it was really necessary. And Jimmy, in his quiet Machiavellian way, fed her another curate, who kept her quiet for a few months, till she started to wonder what sort of man the Doctor was.

'Well, Paddy is a fellow you might find interesting,' Jimmy said thoughtfully, filling his pipe. 'As a study, that is. But unfortunately the way we're situated we can't very well ask him to the house. You see, Paddy is an atheist.'

'An atheist?' Roisin said, brightening up at once. She had never met an atheist. 'You never told me that.'

'Ah, well, it's not right to say things like that about your friends,' Jimmy said loyally. 'But he might just make an offensive remark in front of poor Father Joe that would upset him.'

Of course it was a slander; the Doctor was incapable of being offensive to anybody, but Roisin didn't know this and had to rest content with the excuse. Then, after racking his brains, Jimmy dug up some old businessman who had painted watercolours in his youth and had known everybody; one night when he was drunk Yeats had brought him home. But his conversation with Yeats seemed to have been of much the same kind as his conversation with Roisin. By this time, Little Liam was born, and for quite a while Roisin's attention was diverted from everything else in the world. Except that even then she was slipping out to the optician's wife next door for a cup of tea or a glass of sherry – anything to escape the curates. The optician's wife was a shrewd, interfering woman.

She didn't know what Jimmy was up to, but she knew Jimmy was trying to keep his wife to himself, and that was enough for her.

One evening the Doctor was sitting in the lounge of the Wicklow Hotel with Jimmy when Josephine Hanrahan looked in. The Doctor, who was very polite and very fond of her, jumped to his feet and signalled to her.

'Don't bother to get up, Paddy,' she said. 'I'm not staying. If I'm not good enough to drink with a man in his own house, I see no reason for doing it in public.'

'Oh, really, Josephine!' Jimmy protested.

'I didn't think you'd do it, Jimmy,' she said bitterly. 'I really didn't. I thought you were too big a man to drop your old friends.'

Jimmy looked owlishly at the Doctor, then at her, and held out his hands. 'Do I look like a man who's dropped his old friends?' he asked triumphantly.

'Oh, you're too clever for that, Jimmy,' she replied. 'You're not obvious. But you won't ask us to your house, and you won't let us meet your wife. Has Paddy been there?'

'No, dear,' the Doctor said, trying to make his voice sound smooth. 'Are you sure you won't have a drink?'

'Quite, Paddy,' she said. But she was not to be shut up. She turned on Jimmy again. 'But you'll invite people who never spoke to you a year ago and wouldn't speak to you tomorrow if you hadn't money in your pocket.'

Jimmy took his glasses off and wiped his long, pale face as though to reveal the true features below. The character he was trying to assume now was the haggard, patient, overworked family man, and to give him his due he did it well. 'My dear girl,' he said kindly, wagging his glasses at her, 'in my business I have to entertain people I don't much care for.' He stopped and picked up the bowler hat. 'This is a façade. And you know it.'

'Lies, Jimmy Maguire!' she said in a whisper. 'I know your faults. I probably know them better than you do yourself. But you're not mean, and you're not calculating and you're not avaricious.'

He drew himself up, smiled, and raised the bowler to her, 'Thank you, my dear.'

'You didn't let me finish,' she went on. 'I never said you weren't jealous.'

'Jealous?' he echoed as though he didn't know what she meant.

'Yes, jealous.'

'But of whom, Josephine?' Jimmy said, with an elaboration of astonishment that did not seem genuine.

'Of your wife.'

'That shows all you know about Roisin.'

'No, that shows all you know about her. You're afraid she'll do what other wives have done – wives well known to you.'

The Doctor didn't know where to look. Jimmy didn't like it either. 'Really, Josephine,' he said, 'that's pretty far-fetched, even from you.'

'You never made a bigger mistake in your life, Jimmy Maguire,' she said contemptuously. 'And you'll regret it.'

'Extraordinary ideas women get into their heads,' Jimmy said when she had gone. 'I hope that husband isn't giving her more trouble.'

The Doctor could see he was disturbed. That evening he did not reach the glazing stage, and they separated at the bus stop by Trinity College. The Doctor went away feeling thoughtful. For he, too, had been to the optician's house and wondered afterwards why on earth he had been invited and why the optician's wife had pressed him to come again. He began to feel that he was involved in an intrigue.

The next time he went there, he saw Con Bishop in a corner, and then he knew that he was right. Con was another of the old group. He was an architect, an excitable young man with an Oxford accent. He flirted with the optician's wife as he flirted with everybody. The Doctor was sitting with another medical man, drinking his whiskey, when the door opened and Roisin Maguire came in. Ignoring everyone else, she went straight up to the Doctor and took his hands in hers and dragged him over to the sofa.

'I'm always wanting to talk to you,' she exclaimed intensely, gazing into his eyes.

'It's mutual,' he said, never having seen a technique like this before – if it was a technique, which he couldn't be sure of. 'But I don't see as much of Jimmy as I used to.'

'Ah, who does?' she said in a husky voice. 'You can't see him for curates. I love my religion – you probably think I don't, but I do – only I can't bear too many priests round the house. Maybe I shouldn't say it to you, but I can't help it.'

'Why on earth shouldn't you say it?' asked the Doctor, overwhelmed by her manner.

'I shouldn't – not to an atheist.'

The Doctor was on the point of asking who had told her this when their hostess, who felt this was all much too sudden and public, descended on them. Still Roisin did not let go of the Doctor's hands. Instead, she looked over her shoulder at Mrs Lacey and said, 'Ah, Kitty, haven't I waited long enough for a chance to talk to this fellow? Be a sport and bring me an old drink. Anything at all will do. It all has the same effect on me . . . Aren't I awful?' she asked the Doctor. 'I can never tell the difference between one drink and another.' But her mind was not on the drink any more than it was on the party. She had a sort of rapt, entranced quality, as though she were a sleepwalker living out a dream. 'Tell me, aren't you the one that bailed Jimmy out when he was arrested in Limerick?'

'No,' the Doctor said with amusement. 'I'm afraid that was Con, the fair-haired chap over there.'

'I want to talk to him, too,' she said, squeezing the Doctor's hands. 'I'm always hearing about ye. And there was a woman in the car with him the same night, wasn't there? He won't tell me who she was. That fellow is the devil. Do you know was it Josephine Hanrahan?'

'No,' the Doctor said cautiously, 'I don't think it was.' He knew quite well who the woman was, but he felt that this was dangerous ground.

'He'll never tell me anything,' she said. 'But that's a girl I'd love to meet – Josephine, I mean.'

'I fancy she'd like to meet you, too,' the Doctor said politely.

'Ah, listen, Paddy,' she whispered, laying a hand on his knee, 'would you ever bring me round to her place some night? You couldn't tell Jimmy, of course. He has some daft notion that she's not class enough.'

'Not class enough? Mrs Hanrahan?'

'Ah, sure, what was my own father only a floorwalker in the Munster Arcade?' she said impatiently. 'I'd ask Kitty Lacey here to invite her, only Kitty is so blooming inquisitive. She'd want to know what you had for your dinner. And I can't help blabbing everything to her. I'm that sort, Paddy. I blab. Isn't it terrible? Do you notice the way I'm blabbing now?'

The suggestion that anyone might apply the word 'blabbing' to anything so enchanting as Roisin's conversation came to the Doctor as a shock as great as hearing himself described as an atheist and Josephine as a woman of no class. At the same time, he began to see what the dream was that gave Roisin the air of a sleepwalker. It was a dream of Jimmy. She loved the thought that he was a wild, romantic, reckless man, and when she was polishing his shoes, cooking the dinner, or bathing the child, she was sustained by that vision of him.

He was touched by it, and soon after that he took her to Josephine's little house in Rathgar. He felt nervous about doing it, but then, as I have said, the Doctor rather liked being in the position of having to be nervous. Besides, Roisin herself was in such a state that by force of comforting her he put himself at ease. She 'blabbed', as she called it, all the way.

'Tell me, Paddy, do you think I'm mad? Sometimes I think myself I'm not in my right mind. What will Jimmy Maguire say if he hears of it? He might kill me. Did it ever strike you that he has a distinct look of Henry VIII? I call him that sometimes. He only laughs at me.'

The Doctor laughed himself at the thought of the ascetic-looking Jimmy, who resembled an El Greco saint, being compared with Henry VIII, but now that he realized Roisin had a hankering after that side of him, it struck him that if the matter were not so delicate and if only Jimmy had remained intimate with him, it might do no harm to indicate to him that an occasional touch of the firebrand would go down well at home. But Jimmy was cautiously extinguishing every bit of the firebrand in himself – either because, as Josephine thought, he was jealous, or because he wanted to get on in the world, or possibly even for a third reason, which the Doctor could not at the moment put his finger on. He had ceased to be hurt by Jimmy's defection. He was almost beginning to feel sorry for him.

The visit to Josephine was a success. When she opened the door to them, she smiled in a way that suggested that she would presently burst into tears, but as Roisin rattled on nervously, Josephine relaxed. When Roisin went upstairs for a moment, Josephine turned to the Doctor and said, 'That old humbug! He would have all the luck, wouldn't he?'

'Are you sure it's luck, dear?' the Doctor asked doubtfully.

'Why? There's nothing wrong, is there?'

'No. But I thought you said he'd regret it.'

'Oh, that!' she said with a shrug. Like all women, she lacked the courage of her intuitions.

Roisin went home after that visit and the fat was in the fire. If she had been coming back from a date with a man, she couldn't have been more terrified. For now that it was all over she realized her own duplicity. What was worse, she had made an appointment for lunch and shopping with Josephine the following week. She knelt before a picture of the Sacred Heart in her bedroom and asked for strength to be able to tell Jimmy. She explained to the Sacred Heart, as she had to the Doctor or would have explained to anyone else, that she couldn't keep a thing to herself. She was, as the Sacred Heart knew, a blabber. And she asked the Sacred Heart not to let Jimmy be too mad with her. Then, having built up a crisis out of it, she told Jimmy in an offhand way that would have made any man mad, even one without a past like Jimmy's.

'Oh, Jimmy, do you know who I ran into today? Josephine Hanrahan.' There was no response at all. 'God, Jimmy,' Roisin rattled on despairingly, 'she's a lovely woman. Why didn't you let me meet her before? We went into her place for a minute.'

'We?'

'I met her with Paddy, and she asked us in.'

Jimmy knocked the ashes out of his pipe and slowly turned on her. He frightened her. His face looked old and sour and caved in. He said, 'Does this mean you intend to defy me?'

'Defy you, Jimmy?' she said, her hands pulling nervously at her dress. 'Sure, I never defy you. I said I'd have lunch with her. Is there anything wrong with that?'

'That remains to be seen.'

'But what could I say, Jimmy? I didn't want to hurt her feelings.'

'You could have put her off,' he said. 'As you'd put off any other unsuitable invitation.'

'But I don't see what there was unsuitable about it. I liked the girl, the little I saw of her.'

'The little you saw of her, precisely,' Jimmy said, holding up his finger in warning. 'You don't really know that woman, and I do. There are things about her I'd sooner not discuss. Things I'd prefer not to say about an old friend.'

'What things, Jimmy?' Roisin asked eagerly.

'I said I'd sooner not discuss them,' Jimmy replied severely. But his training as a lawyer probably made him feel that this was unconvincing. Evidence was what was needed. 'I don't remember too well, but there was some talk about a girl in Drumcondra that jumped out of a third-storey window.'

'Is it in Drumcondra?' exclaimed Roisin, who found it difficult to keep up another person's tone. 'Sure if I was living there I'd jump out of a window myself.'

'Well, maybe it wasn't Drumcondra,' he conceded. 'Anyway, she was killed. I'm not saying it was ever brought home to Josephine. For all I know, she may be as innocent as yourself. But you do not want to be mixed up with people like that. Particularly while she's knocking around with a fellow like Paddy Baldwin.'

'Ah, for goodness' sake, you're not going to say there's anything between the pair of them!' cried Roisin. 'I don't believe a word of it, Jimmy. I think he's lonely and she just mothers him.' Jimmy laughed harshly, and she looked up at him in surprise.

'Paddy is an old friend,' he said, 'and I have no wish to criticize him. His mother, God rest her, could have told you the truth.'

'His mother?' Roisin cried incredulously. 'But Josephine says he was crazy about her.'

'She died of a broken heart,' Jimmy said.

Then he did an extraordinary thing. He went on his knees and joined his hands. You can imagine Jimmy, six foot of him, on his knees. 'Roisin,' he said, 'won't you keep away from that crowd, for my sake? You're too good for them. They'll only corrupt you the way they've corrupted others, all for their own amusement. I know them of old, and I curse the day I had anything to do with them. That's what I wanted when I married you – to get away from it all. And there's another thing,' he added, closing his eyes and staring up in agony at her like a blind man asking for a penny. 'I didn't want to tell you, but you'd better know before it's too late. My family were all a little unstable mentally. On my father's side, of course. I couldn't bear a mental shock. My uncle was insane when he died. You wouldn't want to drive me to that.'

'Your uncle?' Roisin cried. 'Which uncle?'

'Willie,' he replied humbly. 'It was kept a great secret. We didn't want anyone to know.'

'I think,' Roisin said, speaking with real indignation, 'I might have been told before now.'

Extraordinary as it was for her to see this great man at her feet, it wasn't him she was thinking of now. It was Little Liam. Liam was a curious child. He always hated to be denied anything, and if you spoke severely to him he screamed with rage. Was it possible that Liam had inherited the family weakness, and had she in her innocence made it worse by frustrating him when she should have comforted him and given in to him? For the first time she was really angry with Jimmy, and went upstairs to look at the child, and then knelt by his bedside and promised the Sacred Heart that she would never cross him again, whatever he wanted.

She was a serious girl, and she knew that she could not imperil her marriage by doing something that Jimmy disapproved of, so she rang up Josephine and excused herself because of illness. But she was also a rotten liar. When Josephine, a woman who'd give you the shift off her back, heard that Roisin was ill, she announced that she was coming over to look after the house for her. Then Roisin's heart misgave her, and she asked Josephine over for tea. She felt terrible about it because she knew that she was no good at explaining things if the explanation involved any improbabilities, and she was certain that Josephine would see through it all. She did. Within five minutes she knew that Roisin was acting under Jimmy's orders and went white with rage. It was bad enough that he would not invite her to the house. To make it plain that he did not think her a proper acquaintance for his wife was too much. When he was ill and a bachelor, he simply packed his bag and came to her house and stayed there till he was well. So she told Roisin this, and Roisin shook her head despairingly.

'What can I do?' she asked.

'Whatever you like,' said Josephine. 'I wouldn't allow my husband to give me orders like that.'

Roisin realized unhappily that a partial explanation was not enough. 'But it isn't only that, Josephine,' she said. 'I'm afraid to contradict him. You see, it's in the family. He had an uncle that was queer.'

'It's the first I've heard of it,' Josephine said.

'Well, to tell you the truth, it's the first I heard of it, too,' said Roisin.

'But who told you?' Josephine persisted.

'He did – Jimmy, I mean. He told me it was dangerous for him to be upset.'

'And you're quite sure he's not making it up?'

'Would a man say a thing like that about his own family if it wasn't true? Sure, that would be crazy out and out. I'd sooner 'twas true. You don't think it isn't?' she added anxiously.

'I'll make it my business to find out,' Josephine said grimly.

'But if that's not true,' Roisin wailed, 'then I suppose Paddy's mother didn't die of a broken heart, either.'

'Paddy's mother?' cried Josephine. 'She worshipped the ground he walked on. And with good reason. I don't know what's come over your husband, Roisin. I never knew him to tell lies like that.'

'It isn't lying, that's the awful part of it,' Roisin said in distress. 'Josephine, I've never breathed it to a soul, and I wouldn't say it now only I know it's not true. Actually, I knew all the time it wasn't true. You will understand me, won't you? I'm only telling you to show how crazy he is. That woman in Drumcondra that was supposed to have committed suicide because of you . . .'

At that point, Josephine nearly went crazy herself, and nothing but loyalty to Roisin prevented her from going straight to Jimmy's office and demanding a signed retraction. Anyway, it made no difference. For if there is one impression a man must never leave upon his wife it is that he is emotional and unstable, because it means that the woman at once begins to feel the whole business of judgement and decision devolves upon her, and a woman who feels that no longer respects her husband. So Roisin continued to meet the gang, and take one drink, which always made her tight, and she developed a violent crush on Con Bishop, whose Oxford accent probably reminded her of Henry VIII. She and Josephine were devoted to one another, though not in the way Roisin would have wished, with Josephine as the confidante of her passion for Jimmy. Rather, she was the confidante of Roisin's doubts of Jimmy, the woman she would rush to whenever there was trouble between them. Jimmy, on the other hand, for ever alienated from all his old friends by his slanders, took to going to chapel in the evenings and praying that his wife would not do something it would have taken a convulsion of nature to make her do, and at home he was ordered about as if he were a child.

(1966)

The American Wife

Elsie Colleary, who was on a visit to her cousins in Cork, was a mystery even to them. Her father, Jack Colleary's brother, had emigrated when he was a kid and done well for himself; he had made his money in the liquor business, and left it to go into wholesale produce when Elsie was growing up, because he didn't think it was the right background for a girl. He had given her the best of educations, and all he got out of it was to have Elsie telling him that Irishmen were more manly, and that even Irish-Americans let their wives boss them too much. What she meant was that *he* let her mother boss him, and she had learned from other Irish people that this was not the custom at home. Maybe Mike Colleary, like a lot of other Americans, did give the impression of yielding too much to his wife, but that was because she thought she knew more about things than he did, and he was too softhearted to disillusion her. No doubt the Americans, experienced in nostalgia, took Elsie's glorification of Irishmen good-humouredly, but it did not go down too well in Cork, where the men stood in perpetual contemplation of the dangers of marriage, like cranes standing on one leg at the edge of the windy water.

She stood out at the Collearys' quiet little parties, with her high waist and wide skirts, taking the men out to sit on the stairs while she argued with them about religion and politics. Women having occasion to go upstairs thought this very forward, but some of the men found it a pleasant relief. Besides, like all Americans, she was probably a millionaire, and the most unwordly of men can get a kick out of flirting with a real millionaire.

The man she finally fell in love with did not sit on the stairs with her at all, though, like her, he was interested in religion and politics. This was a chap called Tom Barry. Tom was thirty-five, tall and thin and good-looking, and he lived with his mother and two good-looking sisters in a tiny house near the barrack, and he couldn't even go for a walk in the evening without the three of them lining up in the hallway to present him with his hat, his gloves, and his clean handkerchief. He had a small job in the courthouse, and was not without ambition; he had engaged in several small business enterprises with his friend Jerry Coakley, but all they had ever got out of these was some good stories. Jerry was forty, and *he* had an old mother who insisted on putting his socks on for him.

Elsie's cousins warned her against setting her cap at Tom, but this only seemed to make her worse. 'I guess I'll have to seduce him,' she replied airily, and her cousins, who had never known a well-bred Catholic girl to talk like that, were shocked. She shocked them even more before she was done. She called at his house when she knew he wasn't there and deluded his innocent mother and sisters into believing that she didn't have designs on him; she badgered Tom to death at the office, gave him presents, and even hired a car to take him for drives.

They weren't the only ones who were shocked. Tom was shocked himself when she asked him point-blank how much he earned. However, he put that down to unworldliness and told her.

'But that's not even a street-cleaner's wages at home,' she said indignantly.

'I'm sure, Elsie,' he said sadly. 'But then, of course, money isn't everything.'

'No, and Ireland isn't everything,' she replied. It was peculiar, but from their first evening together she had never ceased talking about America to him – the summer heat, and the crickets chattering, and the leaves alive with fireflies. During her discussions on the stairs, she had apparently discovered a great many things wrong with Ireland, and Tom, with a sort of mournful pleasure, kept adding to them.

'Oh, I know,' he said regretfully.

'Then if you know, why don't you do something about it?'

'Ah, well, I suppose it's habit, Elsie,' he said as though he wasn't quite sure. 'I suppose I'm too old to learn new tricks.'

But Elsie doubted if it was really habit, and it perplexed her that a man so clever and conscientious could at the same time be so lacking in initiative. She explained it finally to herself in terms of an attachment to his mother that was neither natural nor healthy. Elsie was a girl who loved explanations.

On their third outing she had proposed to him, and he was so astonished that he burst out laughing, and continued to laugh whenever he thought of it again. Elsie herself couldn't see anything to laugh at in it. Having been proposed to by men who were younger and better-looking and better-off than he was, she felt she had been conferring an honour on him. But he was a curious man, for when she repeated the proposal, he said, with a cold fury that hurt her, 'Sometimes I wish you'd think before you talk, Elsie. You know what I earn, and you know it isn't enough to keep a family on. Besides, in case you haven't noticed, I have a mother and two sisters to support.'

'You could earn enough to support them in America,' she protested.

'And I told you already that I had no intention of going to America.'

'I have some money of my own,' she said. 'It's not much, but it could mean I'd be no burden to you.'

'Listen, Elsie,' he said, 'a man who can't support a wife and children has no business marrying at all. I have no business marrying anyway. I'm not a very cheerful man, and I have a rotten temper.'

Elsie went home in tears, and told her astonished uncle that all Irishmen were pansies, and, as he had no notion what pansies were, he shook his head and admitted that it was a terrible country. Then she wrote to Tom and told him that what he needed was not a wife but a psychiatrist. The writing of this gave her great satisfaction, but next morning she realized that her mother would only say she had been silly. Her mother believed that men needed careful handling. The day after, she waited for Tom outside the courthouse, and when he came out she summoned him with two angry blasts on the horn. A rainy sunset was flooding the Western Road with yellow light that made her look old and grim.

'Well,' she said bitterly, 'I'd hoped I'd never see your miserable face again.'

But that extraordinary man only smiled gently and rested his elbows on the window of the car.

'I'm delighted you came,' he said. 'I was all last night trying to write to you, but I'm not very good at it.'

'Oh, so you got my letter?'

'I did, and I'm ashamed to have upset you so much. All I wanted to say was that if you're serious – I mean really serious – about this, I'd be honoured.'

At first she thought he was mocking her. Then she realized that he wasn't, and she was in such an evil humour that she was tempted to tell him she had changed her mind. Then common-sense told her the man would be fool enough to believe her, and after that his pride wouldn't let him propose to her again. It was the price you had to pay for dealing with men who had such a high notion of their own dignity.

'I suppose it depends on whether you love me or not,' she replied. 'It's a little matter you forgot to mention.'

He raised himself from the car window, and in the evening light she saw a look of positive pain on his lean, sad, gentle face. 'Ah, I do, but —' he was beginning when she cut him off and told him to get in the car. Whatever he was about to say, she didn't want to hear it.

They settled down in a modern bungalow outside the town, on the edge of the harbour. Elsie's mother, who flew over for the wedding, said drily that she hoped Elsie would be able to make up to Tom for the loss of his mother's services. In fact, it wasn't long before the Barrys were saying she wasn't, and making remarks about her cooking and her lack of tidiness. But if Tom noticed there was anything wrong, which is improbable, he didn't mention it. Whatever his faults as a sweetheart, he made a good husband. It may have been the affection of a sensitive man for someone he saw as frightened, fluttering, and insecure. It could have been the longing of a frustrated one for someone that seemed to him remote, romantic, and mysterious. But whatever it was, Tom, who had always been God Almighty to his mother and sisters, was extraordinarily patient and understanding with Elsie, and she needed it, because she was often homesick and scared.

Jerry Coakley was a great comfort to her in these fits, for Jerry had a warmth of manner that Tom lacked. He was an insignificant-looking man with a ravaged dyspeptic face and a tubercular complexion, a thin, bitter mouth with bad teeth, and long, lank hair; but he was so sympathetic and insinuating that at times he even gave you the impression that he was changing his shape to suit your mood. Elsie had the feeling that the sense of failure had eaten deeper into him than into Tom.

At once she started to arrange a match between him and Tom's elder sister, Annie, in spite of Tom's warnings that Jerry would never marry till his mother died. When she realized that Tom was right, she said it was probably as well, because Annie wouldn't put his socks on him. Later she admitted that this was unfair, and that it would probably be a great relief to poor Jerry to be allowed to put on his socks himself. Between Tom and him there was one of those passionate relationships that spring up in small towns where society narrows itself down to a handful of erratic and explosive friendships. There were always people who weren't talking to other people, and friends had all to be dragged into the disagreement, no matter how trifling it might be, and often it happened that the principals had already become fast friends again when *their* friends were still ignoring one another in the street. But Jerry and Tom refused to disagree. Jerry would drop in for a bottle of stout, and Tom and he would denounce the country, while Elsie wondered why they could never find anything more interesting to talk about than stupid priests and crooked politicians.

Elsie's causes were of a different kind. The charwoman, Mrs Dorgan, had six children and a husband who didn't earn enough to keep them. Elsie concealed from Tom how much she really paid Mrs Dorgan, but she couldn't conceal that Mrs Dorgan wore her clothes, or that she took the Dorgan family to the seaside in the summer. When Jerry suggested to Tom that the Dorgans might be doing too well out of Elsie, Tom replied, 'Even if they were, Jerry, I wouldn't interfere. If 'tis people's nature to be generous, you must let them be generous.'

For Tom's causes she had less patience. 'Oh, why don't you people do something about it, instead of talking?' she cried.

'What could you do, Elsie?' asked Jerry.

'At least you could show them up,' said Elsie.

'Why, Elsie?' he asked with his mournful smile. 'Were you thinking of starting a paper?'

'Then, if you can't do anything about it, shut up!' she said. 'You and Tom seem to get some queer masochistic pleasure out of these people.'

'Begor, Elsie, you might have something there,' Jerry said, nodding ruefully.

'Oh, we adore them,' Tom said mockingly.

'You do,' she said. 'I've seen you. You sit here night after night denouncing them, and then when one of them gets sick you're round to the house to see if there's anything you can do for him, and when he dies you start a collection for his wife and family. You make me sick.' Then she stamped out to the kitchen.

Jerry hunched his shoulders and exploded in splutters and giggles. He reached out a big paw for a bottle of stout, with the air of someone snaring a rabbit.

'I declare to God, Tom, she has us taped,' he said.

'She has you taped anyway,' said Tom.

'How's that?'

'She thinks you need an American wife as well.'

'Well, now, she mightn't be too far out in that, either,' said Jerry with a crooked grin. 'I often thought it would take something like that.'

'She thinks you have *problems*,' said Tom with a snort. Elsie's favourite word gave him the creeps.

'She wouldn't be referring to the mother, by any chance?'

For a whole year Elsie had fits of depression because she thought she wasn't going to have a baby, and she saw several doctors, whose advice she repeated in mixed company, to the great embarrassment of everybody except Jerry. After that, for the best part of another year, she had fits of depression because she was going to have a baby, and she informed everybody about that as well, including the occasion of its conception and the probable date of its arrival, and again they were all embarrassed except Jerry. Having reached the age of eighteen before learning that there was any real difference between the sexes, Jerry found all her talk fascinating, and also he realized that Elsie saw nothing immodest in it. It was just that she had an experimental interest in her body and mind. When she gave him Bourbon he studied its taste, but when he gave her Irish she studied its effect – it was as simple as that. Jerry, too, liked explanations, but he liked them for their own sake, and not with the intention of doing anything with them. At the same time, Elsie was scared by what she thought was a lack of curiosity on the part of the Cork doctors, and when her mother learned this she began to press Elsie to have the baby in America, where she would feel secure.

'You don't think I should go back, Tom?' she asked guiltily. 'Daddy says he'll pay my fare.'

It came as a shock to Tom, though the idea had crossed his mind that something of the kind might happen. 'If that's the way you feel about it, I suppose you'd better, Elsie,' he replied.

'But you wouldn't come with me.'

'How can I come with you? You know I can't just walk out of the office for a couple of months.'

'But you could get a job at home.'

'And I told you a dozen times I don't want a job in America,' he said angrily. Then, seeing the way it upset her, he changed his tone. 'Look, if you stay here, feeling the way you do, you'll work yourself into a real illness. Anyway, some time you'll have to go back on a visit, and this is as good an occasion as any.'

'But how can I, without you?' she asked. 'You'd only neglect yourself.'

'I would not neglect myself.'

'Would you stay at your mother's?'

'I would not stay at my mother's. This is my house, and I'm going to stop here.'

Tom worried less about the effect Elsie's leaving would have on him than about what his family would say, particularly Annie, who never lost the chance of a crack at Elsie. 'You let that girl walk on you, Tom Barry,' she said. 'One of these days she'll walk too hard.' Then, of course, Tom walked on *her*, in the way that only a devoted brother can, but that was no relief to the feeling that something had come between Elsie and him and that he could do nothing about it. When he was driving Elsie to the liner, he knew that she felt the same, for she didn't break down until they came to a long grey bridge over an inlet of water, guarded by a lonely grey stone tower. She had once pointed it out to him as the first thing she had seen that represented Ireland to her, and now he had the feeling that this was how she saw him – a battered old tower by a river mouth that was no longer of any importance to anyone but the seagulls.

She was away longer than she or anyone else had expected. First there was the wedding of an old schoolfriend; then her mother's birthday; then the baby got ill. It was clear that she was enjoying herself immensely, but she wrote long and frequent letters, sent snapshots of herself and the baby, and – most important of all – had named the baby for Jerry Coakley. Clearly Elsie hadn't forgotten them. The Dorgan kids appeared on the road in clothes that had obviously been made in America, and whenever Tom met them he stopped to speak to them and give them the pennies he thought Elsie would have given them.

Occasionally Tom went to his mother's for supper, but otherwise he looked after himself. Nothing could persuade him that he was not a natural housekeeper, or that whatever his sisters could do he could not do just as well himself. Sometimes Jerry came and the two men took off their coats and tried to prepare a meal out of one of Elsie's cookbooks. 'Steady, squad!' Tom would murmur as he wiped his hands before taking another peep at the book. 'You never know when this might come in handy.' But whether it was the result of Tom's supervision or Jerry's helplessness, the meal usually ended in a big burn-up, or a tasteless mess from which some essential ingredient seemed to be missing, and they laughed over it as they consoled themselves with bread and cheese and stout. 'Elsie is right,' Jerry would say, shaking his head regretfully. 'We have problems, boy! We have problems!'

Elsie returned at last with trunks full of new clothes, a box of up-to-date kitchen stuff, and a new gaiety and energy. Every ten minutes Tom would make an excuse to tiptoe upstairs and take another look at his son. Then the Barrys arrived, and Elsie gave immediate offence by quoting Gesell and Spock. But Mrs Barry didn't seem to mind as much as her daughters. By some extraordinary process of association, she had discovered a great similarity between Elsie and herself in the fact that she had married from the south side of the city into the north and had never got used to it. This delighted Elsie, who went about proclaiming that her mother-in-law and herself were both displaced persons.

The next year was a very happy one, and less trying on Elsie, because she had another woman to talk to, even if most of the time she didn't understand what her mother-in-law was telling her, and had the suspicion that her mother-in-law didn't understand her either. But then she got pregnant for the second time, and became restless and dissatisfied once more, though now it wasn't only with hospitals and doctors but with schools and schoolteachers as well. Tom and Jerry had impressed on her that the children were being turned into idiots, learning through the medium of a language they didn't understand – indeed, according to Tom, it was a language that nobody understood. What chance would the children have?

'Ah, I suppose the same chance as the rest of us, Elsie,' said Jerry in his sly, mournful way.

'But you and Tom don't want chances, Jerry,' she replied earnestly. 'Neither of you has any ambition.'

'Ah, you should look on the bright side of things. Maybe with God's help they won't have any ambition either.'

But this time it had gone beyond a joke. For days on end Tom was in a rage with her, and when he was angry he seemed to withdraw into himself like a snail into a shell.

Unable to get at him, Elsie grew hysterical. 'It's all your damned obstinacy,' she sobbed. 'You don't do anything in this rotten hole, but you're too conceited to get out of it. Your family treat you as if you were God, and then you behave to me as if you were. God! God! God!' she screamed, and each time she punched him viciously with her fist, till suddenly the humour of their situations struck him and he went off into laughter.

After that he could only make his peace with her and make excuses for her leaving him again, but he knew that the excuses wouldn't impress his sisters. One evening when he went to see them, Annie caught him, as she usually did, when he was going out the front door, and he stood looking sidewise down the avenue.

'Are you letting Elsie go off to America again, Tom?' she asked.

'I don't know,' Tom said, pulling his long nose with an air of affected indifference. 'I can't very well stop her, can I?'

'Damn soon she'd be stopped if she hadn't the money,' said Annie. 'And you're going to let her take young Jerry?'

'Ah, how could I look after Jerry? Talk sense, can't you!'

'And I suppose we couldn't look after him either? We're not sufficiently well read.'

'Ah, the child should be with his own mother, Annie,' Tom said impatiently.

'And where should his mother be? Ah, Tom Barry,' she added bitterly, 'I told you what that one was, and she's not done with you yet. Are you sure she's going to bring him back?'

Then Tom exploded on her in his cold, savage way. 'If you want to know, I am not,' he said, and strode down the avenue with his head slightly bowed.

Something about the cut of him as he passed under a street lamp almost broke Annie's heart. 'The curse of God on that bitch!' she said when she returned to her mother in the kitchen.

'Is it Elsie?' her mother cried angrily. 'How dare you talk of her like that!'

'He's letting her go to America again,' said Annie.

'He's a good boy, and he's right to consider her feelings,' said her mother anxiously. 'I often thought myself I'd go back to the south side and not be ending my days in this misfortunate hole.'

The months after Elsie's second departure were bitter ones for Tom. A house from which a woman is gone is bad enough, but one from which a child is gone is a dead house. Tom would wake in the middle of the night thinking he heard Jerry crying, and be half out of bed before he realized that Jerry was thousands of miles away. He did not continue his experiments with cooking and housekeeping. He ate at his mother's, spent most of his time at the Coakleys, and drank far too much. Like all inward-looking men he had a heavy hand on the bottle. Meanwhile Elsie wavered and procrastinated worse than before, setting dates, cancelling her passage, sometimes changing her mind within twenty-four hours. In his despondency Tom resigned himself to the idea that she wouldn't return at all, or at least persuaded himself that he had.

'Oh, she'll come back all right,' Jerry said with a worried air. 'The question is, will she stay back . . . You don't mind me talking about it?' he asked.

'Indeed no. Why would I?'

'You know, Tom, I'd say ye had family enough to last ye another few years.'

Tom didn't look up for a few moments, and when he did he smiled faintly. 'You think it's that?'

'I'm not saying she knows it,' Jerry added hastily. 'There's nothing calculating about her, and she's crazy about you.'

'I thought it was something that went with having the baby,' Tom said thoughtfully. 'Some sort of homing instinct.'

'I wouldn't say so,' said Jerry. 'Not altogether. I think she feels that eventually she'll get you through the kids.'

'She won't,' Tom said bitterly.

'I know, sure, I know. But Elsie can't get used to the – the irremediable.' The last word was so unlike Jerry that Tom felt he must have looked it up in a dictionary, and the absurdity of this made him feel very close to his old crony. 'Tell me, Tom,' Jerry added gently, 'wouldn't you do it? I know it wouldn't be easy, but wouldn't you try it, even for a while, for Elsie's sake? 'Twould mean a hell of a lot to her.'

'I'm too old, Jerry,' Tom said so deliberately that Jerry knew it had been in his mind as well.

'Oh, I know, I know,' Jerry repeated. 'Even ten years ago I might have done it myself. It's like jail. The time comes when you're happier in than out. And that's not the worst of it,' he added bitterly. 'The worst is when you pretend you like it.'

It was a strange evening that neither of them ever forgot, sitting in that little house to which Elsie's absence seemed a rebuke, and listening to the wind from the harbour that touched the foot of the garden. They knew they belonged to a country whose youth was always escaping from it, out beyond that harbour, and that was middle-aged in all its attitudes and institutions. Of those that remained, a little handful lived with defeat and learned fortitude and humour and sweetness, and these were the things that Elsie, with her generous idealism, loved in them. But she couldn't pay the price. She wanted them where she belonged herself, among the victors.

A few weeks later Elsie was back; the house was full of life again, and that evening seemed only a bad dream. It was almost impossible to keep Jerry Og, as they called the elder child, away from Tom. He was still only a baby, and a spoiled one at that, but when Tom took him to the village Jerry Og thrust out his chest and took strides that were too big for him, like any small boy with a father he adored. Each day, he lay in wait for the postman and then took the post away to sort it for himself. He sorted it by the pictures on the stamps, and Elsie noted gleefully that he reserved all the pretty pictures for his father.

Nobody had remembered Jerry's good advice, even Jerry himself, and eighteen months later Elsie was pregnant again. Again their lives took the same pattern of unrest. But this time Elsie was even more distressed than Tom.

'I'm a curse to you,' she said. 'There's something wrong with me. I can't be natural.'

'Oh, you're natural enough,' Tom replied bitterly. 'You married the wrong man, that's all.'

289

'I didn't, I didn't!' she protested despairingly. 'You can say anything else but that. If I believed that, I'd have nothing left, because I never cared for anyone but you. And in spite of what you think, I'm coming back,' she went on, in tears. 'I'm coming back if it kills me. God, I hate this country; I hate every goddamn thing about it; I hate what it's done to you and Jerry. But I'm not going to let you go.'

'You have no choice,' Tom said patiently. 'Jerry Og will have to go to school, and you can't be bringing him hither and over, even if you could afford it.'

'Then, if that's what you feel, why don't you keep him?' she cried. 'You know perfectly well you could stop me taking him with me if you wanted to. You wouldn't even have to bring me into court. I'll give him to you now. Isn't that proof enough that I'm coming back?'

'No, Elsie, it is not,' Tom replied, measuring every word. 'And I'm not going to bring you into court, either. I'm not going to take hostages to make sure my wife comes back to me.'

And though Elsie continued to delude herself with the belief that she would return, she knew Tom was right. It would all appear different when she got home. The first return to Ireland had been hard, the second had seemed impossible. Yet, even in the black hours when she really considered the situation, she felt she could never resign herself to something that had been determined before she was born, and she deceived herself with the hope that Tom would change his mind and follow her. He must follow her. Even if he was prepared to abandon her he would never abandon Jerry Og.

And this, as Big Jerry could have told her, was where she made her biggest mistake, because if Tom had done it at all it would have been for her. But Big Jerry had decided that the whole thing had gone beyond his power to help. He recognized the irremediable, all right, sometimes perhaps even before it became irremediable. But that, as he would have said himself, is where the ferryboat had left him.

Thanks to Elsie, the eldest of the Dorgans now has a job in Boston and in the course of years the rest of them will probably go there as well. Tom continues to live in his little bungalow beside the harbour. Annie is keeping house for him, which suits her fine, because Big Jerry's old mother continued to put his socks on for him a few years too long, and now Annie has only her brother to worship. To all appearances they are happy enough, as happiness goes in Cork. Jerry still calls, and the two men discuss the terrible state of the country. But in Tom's bedroom there are pictures of Elsie and the children, the third of whom he knows only through photographs, and, apart from that, nothing has changed since Elsie left it five years ago. It is a strange room, for one glance is enough to show that the man who sleeps there is still in love, and that everything that matters to him in the world is reflected there. And one day, if he comes by the dollars, he will probably go out and visit them all, but it is here he will return and here, no doubt, he will die.

(1961)

The Cheat

1

The only thing that distinguished Dick Gordon from the other
young men of my time in Cork was his attitude to religion. As
an engineer he seemed to feel that he could not afford to believe
in anything but the second law of thermo-dynamics: according to
him, this contained everything a man required to know.

For years he courted a girl called Joan Twomey, and everyone
expected he would marry her and settle down, as most men of his
kind do. Usually they are of a serious disposition and settle down
more easily than the rest of humanity. You often see them in their
later years, carrying round the collection bag at twelve-o'clock
Mass, and wonder what has happened to all their wild dreams of
free thought and social justice. Marriage is the great leveller.

But Joan's mother died, and she had to do the housekeeping
for a father and two younger sisters, so she became serious too,
and there was no more reckless behaviour in the little seaside
house they rented in summer. She was afraid of marrying a
man who did not believe in anything and would probably bring
up his children the same way. She was wrong in this, because
Dick was much too tolerant a man to deprive his worst enemy
of the pleasure of believing in eternal damnation, much less his
wife, but Joan's seriousness had developed to the dimensions of
spiritual pride and she gave him up as she might have given up
some pleasure for Lent.

Dick was mystified and hurt: it was the first shock to his feeling
of the basic reasonableness of life; but he did not allow it to change
him. After all, his brother, Tom, was an ex-cleric, and he had been
worked on by experts. Some time later he met a girl called Barbara
Hough, who was a teacher in a Protestant school, and started to
walk out with her. On the surface Barbara was much more his
style. She was good-looking and urbane, vaguely atheistic and left-
wing in her views, and she thought that all Irish people, Catholic

and Protestant, were quite insane on the subject of religion. All the same, for a young fellow of good Catholic family to take up with a Protestant at all was a challenge, and Barbara, who was a high-spirited girl, enjoyed it and made the most of it. His friends were amused and his family alarmed. Of course, Dick could get a dispensation if Barbara signed the paper guaranteeing that their children would be brought up as Catholics, but would Barbara, who was a rector's daughter, agree to it? Characteristically, when Tom asked him this, Dick only smiled and said, 'Funny, isn't it? I never asked her.' He would probably have been quite safe in doing so, for though Barbara herself did not recognize it, she had all the loneliness of one brought up in a minority religion, always feeling that she was missing something, and much of Dick's appeal for her was that he was a Prince Charming who had broken the magic circle in which she felt she would be trapped until the day she died. But Dick did not ask her. Instead he proposed a quiet registry-office marriage in London, and she was so moved by his consideration for her that she did not even anticipate what the consequences might be.

You see, it was part of Dick's simplicity of mind that he could not realize that there were certain perfectly simple things you couldn't do without involving yourself in more trouble than they were worth, or, if he did see it, he underrated its importance. A few of his old friends stood by him, but even they had to admit that there was an impossible streak in him. When Barbara was having a baby the family deputed his brother, Tom, to warn him of what he was doing. Tom was tall, good-looking, dreamy and morbidly sensitive. He did not want to approach Dick at all, but seeing that he was the nearest thing to a priest in the family, he felt that it might be his duty.

'You know what people are going to think, Dick,' he said with a stammer.

'The same as they think now, I suppose,' Dick replied with his gentle smile.

'This is different, Dick.'

'How, Tom?'

'This concerns a third party, you see,' said Tom, too embarrassed even to mention such things as babies to his brother.

'And a fourth and a fifth, I hope,' Dick said cheerfully. 'It's a natural result of marriage, you know. And children do take after their parents, for the first few years anyway.'

'Not in this country, they don't,' Tom said ruefully. 'I suppose there are historical reasons for it,' he added, being a great student of history.

'There are historical reasons for everything in this country, Tom,' said Dick with a jolly laugh. 'But because some old fool believes in the fairies for good historical reasons is no excuse for bringing up my kids the same way.'

'Ah, well, it's not as foolish as all that, Dick,' said Tom, looking more miserable than ever. 'It's poetic, or fanciful or whatever you like, but it's what we were brought up to believe, and our fathers and grandfathers before us.'

'And the monks told us that Ireland was such a holy country that we'd have the end of the world eight years before anywhere else . . . I'm not sure what the advantage was supposed to be . . . I don't suppose you still believe that?'

'Why would I?' asked Tom. 'It's not an article of faith.'

'It was an article of faith to you and me, and I wouldn't have liked to be the fellow that disbelieved it,' said Dick with a sniff. 'Anyway, it's no worse than the rest of the nonsense we listen to. That sort of thing is looked on as childishness everywhere else today, and it'll be looked on as childishness here, too, in your lifetime and mine. In fifteen years' time people will only laugh at it.'

That was Dick all out, entirely reasonable and tolerant, and yet as big a misfit as if he had two heads. How could any responsible superior recommend a man as pig-headed as that for promotion? The sensible thing for Dick would have been to emigrate and start all over again in England or America, where apparitions were not so highly regarded, but there was a dogged, cynical streak in him that derived a sort of morose pleasure from seeing some devotee of apparitions promoted over his head and making a mess of some perfectly simple job.

He had a number of friends who sympathized with his views and who met at his little house in the College Road on Sundays to discuss the latest piece of jobbery in the university. They grew mad about it, but Dick's attitude of amused tolerance rarely varied. At most he sighed: it was as though he saw things that they could not see. One old schoolteacher called Murphy used to grow furious with him over this. He was a gloomy-looking, handsome man who was at the same time very pious and very anti-clerical. Passion made him break out in angles, as when he called his old friends 'Mister'.

'Mister Gordon,' he shouted one night, 'you're out of your mind. A hundred years from now the descendants of those hobblers will still be seeing apparitions behind every bush.'

'They won't, Ned,' Dick said with a smile. He was particularly fond of Murphy and enjoyed seeing him in a rage.

'What'll stop them, Mister Gordon?'

'Facts, Ned!'

'Facts!'

'Facts impose their own logic, Ned. They're imposing it now, at this very minute, here and elsewhere, even though we may not see it. It's only an elaboration of skills. Skills here are still too rudimentary. But women are beginning to do men's work, and they'll have to think men's thoughts. You can't control that, you know. The world you're talking about is finished. In ten or fifteen years' time it'll be a joke. Simple facts will destroy it.'

2

That was all very well. Dick might have a good eye for what was going on in the outside world, but he had no eye at all for what was going on in his very own house. One evening, after they had been married for ten years, Dick was at home and Barbara out with their son, Tom, when there was a knock at the door. Outside was a young priest; a tall, thin, good-looking man with a devil-may-care eye.

'Can I come in?' he asked, as though he had no doubt whatever of his welcome.

'Oh, come in, come in!' said Dick with a thin smile. He hated those embarrassing occasions when people with more self-confidence than manners inquired how his soul was doing. He was a friendly man and did not like to have to appear rude or ungrateful.

'Mrs G out?' the priest asked cheerfully.

'Yes, gone into town for some messages,' Dick said resignedly. 'She won't be long.'

'Ah, it gives us the chance of a little chat,' said the priest, pulling at the legs of his trousers.

'Look, Father, I don't want a little chat, as you call it,' Dick said appealingly. 'This town is full of people who want little chats with me, and they can't understand that I don't appreciate them. I gave up religion when I was eighteen, and I have no intention in the world of going back to it.'

'Did I ask you to go back to it?' the priest asked with an air of consternation. 'I wasn't expecting to see you at all, man! I came here to talk to your wife. You are Mrs Gordon's husband, aren't you?'

'Yes,' Dick replied, somewhat surprised by the priest's tone.

'Well, she's been receiving instruction. Didn't you know that?'

'Instruction? No, I didn't.'

'Crumbs, I'm after saying the wrong thing again!' the priest said angrily. 'I shouldn't be let out without a male nurse. Look, I'm terribly sorry. I'll come back another time.'

'Oh, as you're here, you may as well stay,' Dick said amiably. It was partly pride, partly pity. He could see that the priest was genuinely distressed.

'Another time! Another time!'

'Who will I say called?' Dick asked as he saw him to the door.

'The name is Hogan. Mr Gordon, I wouldn't have wished it for a hundred pounds.'

'It was hardly your fault,' Dick said, with a friendly smile.

But as he closed the door the smile faded and he found himself cold and shaking. He poured himself a drink, but it only made him feel sick. Nothing that could have happened to him would have been quite so bad as this. He had been betrayed shamelessly and treacherously, and he could already see himself as the laughing-stock of the city. A man's loneliness is his strength and only a wife can really destroy him because only she can understand his loneliness.

He heard her key in the lock and wished he had left before her return. He liked to be master of himself, and now he feared he had no control over what he did or said.

'Dick!' she called in her clear ringing voice and opened the living-room door. 'Is something wrong?' she asked as he did not turn round. 'One moment, Tom!' she said to the child in the hall. 'Run upstairs and take your things off. I'll call you when tea is ready. Don't argue now, sweetheart. Mummy is busy.' She closed the door behind her and approached him. 'I suppose Father

Hogan called,' she added in her weary, well-bred voice. 'Was that it? You should know I intended to tell you. I wanted to make up my own mind first.' Still he did not reply and she burst out into a wail, 'Oh, Dick, I've tried to tell you so often and I didn't have the courage.'

She knew the moment he looked at her that she had fooled herself; persuaded herself that he was dull and tolerant and gentle and that nothing she did to him would affect their relationship. It is the weak spot in the cheat, man or woman.

'You hadn't the courage,' he repeated dully. 'But you had the courage to make a fool of me before your clerical friends.'

'I didn't, Dick,' she said hotly. 'But you know yourself it's something I can't discuss with you. It's a subject you can't be reasonable about.'

The word 'reasonable' stung him.

'Is that what you call being reasonable?' he asked bitterly. 'I should have been reasonable and made you conform before I married you. I should have been reasonable and brought Tom up as my family wanted him brought up. Every day of my life I had to accept humiliation on your account when I could have been reasonable about it all. And then you don't even have the courage to discuss with me what you're going to do or what the consequences will be for Tom. You prefer to bring him up believing that his father is damned! There's reasonableness for you!'

'But I'd discuss it with you now, Dick, if only you'd listen to me patiently.' She began to wring her hands. 'It's not my fault if I can't live without believing in something.'

'In Heaven,' he said cynically.

'In Heaven, if you like. Anyway, in something for you and me and Tom. I was brought up to believe in it, and I threw it away because I didn't value it, and now I need it – maybe because I haven't anything else. If only you wouldn't tell me it's all just nonsense!'

'Why should I tell you anything?' he asked. 'You have better advisers now.'

In fact, he never did discuss it with her. He even allowed Tom to go to Mass with her and attend the local monks' school without protest. The older Tom was Barbara's biggest surprise. She knew that in arguments with Dick he had taken her side, but when they discussed it together he seemed to judge her far more severely than Dick. It was curious, because the diffidence, the slight stammer, the charming smile did not change.

'Of course, Barbara, as a Catholic I am naturally pleased, for your sake and the kid's, but as Dick's brother I can't help feeling that it's unfortunate.'

'But don't you think it may help Dick to see things a bit differently in the course of time?'

'No, Barbara, I don't,' he said with a gentle, almost pitying smile.

'But, Tom, I don't see that it should make any more difference than it does between you and Dick.'

'Marriage is different, Barbara,' he said, and she didn't even see anything peculiar about being told of marriage by a man who had almost been given up by his own family as unmarriageable. 'People don't know it, but they marry for protection as much as anything else, and sometimes they have to be protected at the cost of other people's principles.'

'And you think Dick needs protection?' she asked wonderingly.

'I think Dick needs a great deal of protection, Barbara,' he said with an accusing look.

There was a good deal of talk in the city, much of it ill-natured, though on the whole it did Dick less harm than good. He had ceased to be an active force for evil and become a mere figure of fun, as vulnerable to ridicule as any university intriguer. It had even become safe to promote him.

But it was old Ned Murphy who said the thing that stuck. He and two of Dick's other friends were drinking in a public house one night, and the others – Cashman, and Enright who was a bit of a smart alec -- were making good-humoured fun of Dick. Murphy alone did not laugh at all. He scowled and rubbed his forehead with his fist till it grew inflamed.

'It's like your wife having an affair with another man,' he said sourly, and because he was unmarried Cashman and Enright laughed louder. Still there was something uncomfortably apt about the analogy; both were married men and there had been a small scandal about Enright's wife, who had had an affair with a commercial traveller. They knew there was always another man, a shadowy figure, not real as they were, and they dreaded his presence in the background.

'Still, you'd think he'd have given her some cause,' said Cashman.

'He gave her plenty of cause,' said Murphy.

'But they always got on well together.'

'They got on all right,' Murphy admitted. 'But she must have had a terrible life with him. She's a religious girl.'

'Lots of religious girls marry men like that, though,' said Enright, as though he were following the conversation, which he wasn't.

'Not men like Dick Gordon,' Murphy said broodingly. 'He's an optimist, and optimism is the plague of a religious mind. Dick has no notion how intolerable life can be. A man like that doesn't even believe in Evil.'

3

Dick's optimism was tested severely enough a few years later. He was ill, and word was going round that he would never be well again.

This put half Cork in a flutter, because everyone who had ever had a conversation with him seemed to feel a personal responsibility for seeing that he was converted, and those who might see him were warmly advised of what they should do and say. His boss put a car at the disposal of his friends so that they could rush a priest to his bedside at any hour of the day or night. 'Vultures are a breed of bird that has always fascinated me, though I thought they were supposed to be extinct,' said Ned Murphy. Barbara was exasperated by all the hysteria, more particularly because it put her in such a false position, and her replies became shorter. 'I'm afraid it is a matter I never discuss with my husband,' she said. 'There are certain things that are too personal even for a wife.' Even that did not put people off the subject. They said that converts were never really like their own people.

One rainy evening Dick was alone in the house, trying to read, when a strange priest called. He was tall and fat and very grave.

'Mr Gordon?' he said.

'Yes,' said Dick.

'Can I come in for a moment?'

'Oh, certainly. Sit down.'

'You don't know who I am, Mr Gordon,' the priest said jovially as he took a chair. 'I know quite a lot about you, though. I'm the parish priest, Father Ryan.'

Dick nodded.

'Mr Gordon, I want to talk to you about your soul,' he said with a change of tone.

Dick smiled and lit a cigarette. He had been through it all so often.

'Surely, among your congregation you could find plenty of others,' he suggested mildly.

'Not many in such danger, shall we say,' the priest replied with a smile. Something about the smile shook Dick. It seemed to radiate a sort of cold malice which was new to him.

'Considering that we've only just met, you seem to know a lot about the state of my soul,' Dick said with the same weary sarcasm.

'Mr Gordon,' the priest said, raising his hand, 'I wasn't speaking only of your spiritual danger. Mr Gordon, you're a very sick man.'

Dick rose and opened the door for him.

'Father Ryan, you're concerning yourself with things that have nothing to do with you,' he said icily. 'Now, do you mind getting out of my house?'

'Your arrogance won't last long, Mr Gordon,' the priest said. 'You're dying of cancer.'

'You heard me?' Dick said menacingly.

'You have less than three months to live.'

'All the more reason I shouldn't be persecuted by busybodies like you,' Dick said with sudden anger. 'Now get out before I throw you out.'

He scarcely raised his voice, but anger was so rare with him that it had a sinister quality that overawed the priest.

'You'll regret this,' he said.

'Probably,' Dick said between his teeth. 'I'll regret that I didn't treat you as you deserve.'

Afterwards he went back to his book, but he was even more incapable of reading or of understanding what he read. Something about the priest's tone had upset him. He was himself almost devoid of malice and had shrugged off the opposition to himself as mere foolishness, but this was something more and worse than foolishness. This was foolishness going bad, foolishness turning into named evil. And Dick, as Ned Murphy had said, did not really believe in Evil.

When Barbara came in he was still sitting in darkness before the fire, brooding.

'Hullo, dear,' she said with false brightness. 'All alone?'

'Except for a clerical gentleman who just called,' he said with an air of amusement.

'Oh, dear!' she said in distress. 'Who was it?'

'His name is Ryan. A rather unusual character.'

'What did he want?'

'Oh, just to tell me I had cancer and had less than three months to live,' Dick said bitterly.

'Oh, God, no, Dick! He didn't say that?' she cried, and began to weep.

He looked at her in surprise and concern and then got up.

'Oh, don't worry about that, Babsy!' he said with a shrug. 'It's only their stock-in-trade, you know. You should have heard the pleasure with which he said it! Where would they be without their skeleton to brandish?'

It was only the sort of thing he had said to her in the early days of their marriage and had not said since her conversion. She did not know whether he really meant it or said it just to comfort her. After their years of married life he was still gentle and considerate. His brother, Tom, was little help to her.

'I'll only have to try and be at the house more,' he said gloomily. 'This thing could happen again.'

'But can't we complain to the Bishop about it?' she said angrily.

'I'm afraid that wouldn't do much good, Barbara. The Bishop would be more likely to take Father Ryan's side. By the way, have you confidence in that doctor of yours?'

'Dr Cullen? Oh, I suppose he did what he could.'

'I don't mean that,' Tom said patiently. 'Are you sure he didn't go to Father Ryan himself?'

'Oh, God, Tom!' she said. 'What sort of people are they?'

'Much like people everywhere else, I suppose,' he said despondently.

After this, she dreaded leaving Dick alone. She knew now the hysteria that surrounded them and knew that those who indulged in it were ruthless in a way that Dick would never understand.

One day she was upstairs, chatting with him when the door-bell rang. She answered it and saw Father Hogan outside. He was now parish priest in a village ten miles outside the town, and they saw less of him. He was one of the few friends she had whom Dick seemed to like.

'Come in here, please, Father,' she said, and led him into the little front room. She closed the door and spoke in a low voice. 'Father, I can't have Dick persecuted now.'

'Persecuted?' he asked in surprise. 'Who's persecuting him?'

'You know what he believes,' she said. 'I dare say he's wrong, and if you catch him in a moment of weakness he may say he's wrong, but it will be his weakness, not him.'

'What the hell are you talking about?' he asked angrily. 'Are you out of your mind? I rang him up when I heard he was sick and he asked me to call for a drink. I'm not going to do anything to him – except maybe give him conditional absolution when it's all over, and that won't be on his account. There are people in this town who'd try to refuse him Christian burial. You don't know it, but you wouldn't like it. No more would his family.'

'You had nothing to do with the man who told him he was dying?'

'Why?' he asked quietly. 'Did someone do that?'

'The parish priest did it.'

'And am I to be held responsible for every fool and lout who happens to wear a soutane?' he asked bitterly. 'He asked me in for a drink, Barbara, and I'm going to have it with him, whatever you may think . . .' Then with one of his quick changes of mood he asked, 'Did it upset him?'

'Fortunately, he didn't believe it.'

'Didn't believe it, or pretended not to believe it?' he asked shrewdly and then threw the question away. 'Ah, how would you know? I won't disturb him, Barbara,' he added gently. 'I wish I was as sure of my own salvation as I am of his.'

'So do I – now,' she said, and he knew as though he were inside her that she was regretting the weakness of years before and wishing that she could go into the dark with her husband as they had both imagined it when they were in love. It was the only way that would have meant anything to Dick now. But he was a good priest, and he could not afford to brood on what it all meant. He still had a duty to the living as well as to the friend who was about to die.

(1965)

Requiem

Father Fogarty, the curate in Crislough, was sitting by the fire one evening when the housekeeper showed in a frail little woman of sixty or sixty-five. She had a long face, with big eyes that looked as though they had wept a great deal, and her smile lit up only the lower half of her face. Father Fogarty was a young man with a warm welcome for the suffering and the old. A man with emotions cut too big for the scale of his existence, he was for ever floundering in enthusiasms and disillusionments, wranglings and reconciliations; but he had a heart like a house, and almost before the door closed behind her, he was squeezing the old woman's hand in his own two fat ones.

'You're in trouble,' he said in a low voice.

'Wisha, aren't we all, Father?' she replied.

'I'm sorry, I'm sorry,' he said. 'Is it something I can do for you?'

'Only to say Mass for Timmy, Father.'

'I'll do that, to be sure,' he said comfortingly. 'You're cold. Sit down a minute and warm yourself.' Then he laid a big paw on her shoulder and added in a conspiratorial whisper, 'Do you take anything? A drop of sherry, maybe?'

'Ah, don't be putting yourself out, Father.'

'I'm not putting myself out at all. Or maybe you'd sooner a sup of whiskey. I have some damn good whiskey.'

'Wisha, no, Father, I wouldn't, thanks. The whiskey goes to my head.'

'It goes to my own,' he replied cheerfully. 'But the sherry is good, too.' He didn't really know whether it was or not, because he rarely drank, but, being a hospitable man, he liked to give his visitors the best. He poured a glass of sherry for her and a small one for himself, and lit one of his favourite cheroots.

The old woman spread her transparent hands to the blaze and sipped at her wine. 'Oh, isn't the heat lovely?' she exclaimed with girlish delight, showing her old gums. 'And the sherry is lovely, too, Father. Now, I know you're surprised to see me, but I know all about you. They told me to come to you if I was in trouble. And there aren't many priests like that, Father. I was never one to criticize, but I have to say it.'

'Ah,' he said jovially, throwing himself back in his big leather chair and pulling on his cheroot, 'we're like everybody else, ma'am. A mixed lot.'

'I dare say you're right,' she said, 'but they told me I could talk to you.'

'Everyone talks to me,' he said without boastfulness. It was true. There was something about him that invited more confidences than a normal man could respect, and Father Fogarty knew he was often indiscreet. 'It's not your husband?' he added doubtfully.

'Ah, no, Father,' she replied with a wistful smile. 'Poor Jim is dead on me these fifteen years. Not, indeed, that I don't miss him just the same,' she added thoughtfully. 'Sometimes I find myself thinking of him, and he could be in the room with me. No, it's Timmy.'

'The son?'

'No, Father. Though he was like a son to me. I never had any of my own. He was Jim's. One of the last things Jim did was to ask me to look after him, and, indeed, I did my best. I did my best.'

'I'm sure you did, ma'am,' said Father Fogarty, scowling behind his cheroot. He was a man who took death hard, for himself, and for others. A stepchild was not the same thing, of course, but he supposed you could get just as attached to one of those. That was the trouble; you could get attached to anything if only you permitted yourself to do so, and he himself was one who had never known how to keep back. 'I know how hard it is,' he went on, chewing at his cheroot till his left eyebrow descended and seemed to join in the process, and he resembled nothing so much as a film gangster plotting the murder of an innocent victim. 'And there's little anyone can say that will console you. All I know from my own experience is that the more loss we feel the more grateful we should be for whatever it was we had to lose. It means we had something worth grieving for. The ones I'm sorry for are the ones that go through life not even knowing what grief is. And you'd be surprised the number of them you'd meet.'

'I dare say in one way they're lucky,' she said broodingly, looking into the fire.

'They are not lucky, ma'am, and don't you believe it,' he said gruffly. 'They miss all the things that make life worthwhile, without even knowing it. I had a woman in here the other night,' he added, pointing his cheroot at the chair she sat in, 'sitting where you're sitting now, and she told me when her husband gave the last breath she went on her knees by the bed and thanked God for taking him.'

'God help us,' the old woman said, clasping her hands. 'I hope no one does the same thing over herself some day.'

'Thanked God for taking him,' Fogarty repeated with his troubled boyish frown. 'What sort of mind can a woman like that have?'

'Oh, she's hard, she's hard,' agreed the old woman, still looking into the fire.

'Hard as that hearthstone,' he said dramatically. 'My God, a man she'd lived with the best part of her life, whatever his faults might have been! Wouldn't you think at least she'd have some remorse for the things she'd done to him in all those years?'

'Oh, indeed, 'tis true,' she said. 'I often blamed myself over poor Jim. Sometimes I think if only I might have been a bit easier on him, he might be here yet.'

'Most of us have to go through that sooner or later,' he said, feeling that perhaps he had gone too far and reopened old wounds. His own old wounds were never far from breaking open, because often a light or careless word would bring back the memory of his mother and of his diabolical adolescent temperament. 'We have to be careful of that, too,' he added. 'Because it's not the guilty ones who go on brooding, but the others – the people who're only partly guilty, or maybe not guilty at all. That can happen, too. I had a man here last week talking about his wife's death, and nothing I could say would persuade him but that he'd wronged her. And I knew for a fact that he was a husband in a million – a saint. It's something we can't afford to indulge. It turns into a sort of cowardice before life. We have to learn to accept our own limitations as human beings – our selfishness and vanity and bad temper.'

He spoke with passion, the passion of a man teaching a lesson he has never been able to learn himself. Something in his tone made the old woman look at him, and her face softened into a sweet, toothless old smile.

'Haven't you great wisdom for such a young man!' she exclaimed admiringly.

'Great,' he agreed with a jolly laugh. 'I'm the biggest idiot of them all.'

But she shrugged this off. 'Ah, what else were the saints?'

'Look here, ma'am,' he said, rising and standing over her with mock gravity. 'Don't you be going round talking about me as a saint or you'll be having me sent to a punishment parish. The poor Bishop has trouble enough on his hands without having to deal with saints. I'll say eight-o'clock Mass on Sunday for your boy. Will that do you?'

'My boy?' she said in surprise. 'But Timmy wasn't my son, Father. Sure, I said I had no children.'

'No. I took it he was your stepson.'

'Is it Jim's?' she exclaimed with a laugh of genuine amusement at his mistake. 'Ah, sure, Jim wasn't married before, Father. Don't you see, that's why I had to come to you?'

'I see,' he said, though he didn't, and anyhow he felt it was none of his business. The woman, after all, hadn't come to make her confession. 'What was his surname so?'

'Ah, Father,' she said, still laughing but in a bewildered way, 'I'm so distracted that I can't explain myself properly. You have it all mixed up. Sure, I thought I explained it.'

'You didn't explain it, ma'am,' he said, repressing curiosity. 'And anyway it's nothing to me who Timmy was. That's a matter between you and your confessor.'

'My what?' she cried indignantly. 'Ah, Father, you have me distracted completely now. This has nothing to do with confession. Oh, my, what's that Timmy was? If I could only think!'

'Take your time, ma'am,' he said, but he wondered what was coming next.

'A poodle' she exclaimed. 'Now I have it.'

'A what?'

'A poodle – a French poodle is what they called him,' she said, delighted to remember the proper term. And then her big eyes began to fill with tears. 'Oh, Father, I don't know how I'm going to get on without him. He was everything to me. The house isn't the same without him.'

'You don't mean you're asking me to say Mass for your *dog*?'

'Oh, I'm not asking you to do it for nothing,' she added with dignity, opening her handbag.

'Are you a Catholic at all, ma'am?' he asked sternly, fixing her with a glowering look that only seemed to amuse her. She tossed her head with a sudden saucy, girlish air.

'Wisha, what else would I be?' she asked gently, and he felt that there was nothing much he could say in reply.

'And do you know what the sacrifice of the Mass is?' he went on.

'Well, as I go every morning of my life, Father, I should have some idea,' she replied, and again he had the feeling that she was laughing at him.

'And don't you know that you're asking me to commit sacrilege? Do you even know what sacrilege is?'

'Ah, what sacrilege?' she exclaimed lightly, shrugging it off. She took three five-pound notes from her old handbag. He knew she intended the money as an offering; he knew it was probably all she had in the world, and he found himself torn between blind rage and admiration.

'Here,' he said. 'Let me get you another drink. And put that blooming money back in your bag or you'll be losing it.'

But the very sound of his voice told him that he was losing conviction. The terrible little old woman with her one idea exercised a sort of fascination over him that almost frightened him. He was afraid that if he wasn't careful he would soon find himself agreeing to do what she wanted. He poured her a drink, threw himself back again in his armchair, and at once gave way to his indignation.

'I cannot stand this damn sentimentality!' he shouted, hitting the arm of his chair with his clenched fist. 'Every day of my life I have to see good Christians go without food and fire, clothes and medicine, while the rich people taunt them with the sight of their pampered pets. I tell you I can't stand it!'

'Why, then, I'm sure you're right, Father. But I'm not rich, and no poor person was ever sent away from my door with nothing, as long as I had it.'

'I'm sure of that, ma'am,' he said humbly, ashamed of his outburst. 'I'm sure you're a better Christian than I am, but there are different needs and different duties, and we must not confuse them. There are animal needs and human needs, and human needs and spiritual needs. Your dog has no need of the Mass.'

'He was very fond of Mass. Every morning he came with me and lay down outside the chapel door.'

'And *why* did you leave him outside the chapel door?' asked Fogarty.

'Why?'

'Yes, why? Wasn't it that you made a distinction between an animal and a spiritual need?'

'It was nothing of the kind,' she said hotly. 'It was the parish priest that asked me, because some old fools complained. Hah, but I often sneaked him in when they weren't looking, and let me tell you, Father, none of those old craw-thumpers behaved as devotionally as my Timmy. Up with the Gospel and down at the Elevation, without my saying a word to him. And don't tell me that Our Blessed Lord wasn't as pleased with Timmy as with them.'

'I'm not telling you anything of the sort,' he said, touched and amused. 'All I am telling you is that now that your dog is dead, prayers can make no difference to him. Your dog couldn't incur guilt. Your prayers may make a difference to your husband because, like the rest of us, he did incur guilt in this life and may have to atone for it in the next.'

'Ah, it's easy seen you didn't know Jim, Father. Poor Jim was innocent as a child. He never did anything wrong only taking the little sup of whiskey when I wouldn't be looking. I know he got a bit cranky when he had a drop in and I wouldn't give him any more, but sure that's a thing you wouldn't give a second thought to . . . No, Father,' she added thoughtfully, looking into the fire again, 'I don't mind admitting that the first day or two after he died I wasn't easy in my mind at all. I didn't know what little thing he might have said or done on the side, unknown to me, or what little taste of punishment they might give him. I couldn't rest, thinking of him burning down there in Purgatory, with people he didn't know at all. A shy man, like that, and a man – I won't belie him – that would scream the house down if he as much as got a splinter in his nail. But then I realized that nobody in his right mind could be doing anything to him. Oh, no, Father, that's not why I get Masses said for Jim.'

'Then why do you get them said for him?' Fogarty asked, though he knew the answer. His own big heart answered for him when his reason didn't.

'Sure, what other way have I of letting him know I'm thinking about him?' she asked with a childlike smile. 'He's always in my mind, morning, noon, and night. And now Timmy is the same.'

'And when I tell you that it makes no difference to Timmy – that Timmy can't know he's in your mind?'

'Ah, well, Father, these things are great mysteries,' she replied comfortably, 'and we don't know all about them yet. Oh, I know there's a difference, and I'm not asking for anything impossible. Only one small Mass, so that he'll know. But when I talk to people about it, you'd think I was mad from the way they go on. They tell me he has no soul, because he never committed sin. How does anybody know he didn't commit sin? A little child doesn't commit sin and he has a soul. No, Father,' she went on with iron determination, 'I know I'm old and I have no one to advise me, and my head isn't as good as it was, but thank God I still have my wits about me. Believe me, Father, a dog is no different from a child. When I was feeling low coming on to Jim's anniversary, Timmy would know it. He'd know it as if he could read what I was thinking, and he'd come and put his head on my lap to show how sorry he was. And when he was sick himself, he'd get into my bed and curl up beside me, begging me with his eyes to make him better. Yes, indeed, and when he was dying I felt the same way about him as I felt about poor Jim – just the way you described it, thinking of all the times I was hard on him when he didn't deserve it at all. That is the hardest part of it, Father, when you have to try and forgive yourself.'

'I'm sure you have very little to forgive yourself for, ma'am,' Fogarty said with a smile. 'And God knows, if it was anything I could do for you I'd do it, but this is something that, as a priest, I can't do.'

'And there's no one else I could go to? You don't think if I went to the Bishop myself he'd let you do it?'

'I'm quite certain he wouldn't, ma'am.'

'Ah,' she said bitterly as she raised herself heavily from her chair, 'if I was younger and smarter with my pen I'd write to the Pope about it myself.' She turned to the door, and Fogarty sprang to open it for her, but the courtesy was lost on her. She looked at him with deep mournful eyes that seemed to contain all the loneliness in the world. 'And it's wrong, Father, wrong,' she said in a firm voice. 'I'm as good a Catholic as the next, but I'd say it to the Pope himself this minute if he walked into this room. They *have* souls, and people are only deluding themselves about it. Anything that can love has a soul. Show me that bad woman that thanked God her husband was dead and I'll show you someone that maybe hasn't a soul, but don't tell me that my Timmy hadn't one. And I know as I'm standing here that somewhere or other I'll see him again.'

'I hope you do, ma'am,' he said, his big voice suddenly growing gentle and timorous. 'And whenever you say a prayer for him, don't forget to add one for me.'

'I will not indeed, Father,' she said quietly. 'I know you're a good man, and I'll remember you with the others that were good to me, and one of these days, with God's help, we'll all be together again.'

(1957)

Variations
on a Theme

1

Kate Mahoney was sixty when her husband died. After that, she had, like many another widow, to face the loss of her little house. It was a good house in a good lane. There was a sandstone quarry behind, so that no one could overlook them except from a great distance, and though there was a terrace of really superior houses between them and the road, and it had no view and little or no sunlight, it was quiet and free of traffic any hour of the day or night – a lovely place for children, as she often said.

Her two daughters, Nora and Molly, were married, one in Shandon Street and the other on the Douglas Road, but even if either of them had been in a position to offer her a home she would have had doubts about accepting it. What she said was that the people in Shandon Street were uncivilized and the people on the Douglas Road had no nature, but what she really thought was that her daughters shouted too much. The truth was that Kate shouted enough for a regimental sergeant-major, and the girls – both gentle and timid – had learned early in life that the only way of making themselves heard was to shout back. Kate did not shout all the time: she had another tone, reserved for intimate occasions, which was low-pitched and monotonous and in which she tended to break off sentences as though she had forgotten what she was saying. But, low-pitched or loud, her talk was monumental, like headstones. Her hands and legs were twisted with rheumatics, and she had a face like a butcher's block in which the only really attractive feature was the eyes, which looked astonishingly young and merry.

She loved the lane and the neighbours – so different from the nasty strange people you met in Shandon Street and the Douglas Road – but mostly she longed to die in the bed her husband had died in. With the rheumatics she could not go out and do a day's work as other widows did to stretch out their couple of halfpence.

It was this that turned her mind to the desperate expedient of taking in a foster-child – this and the realization that the lane was a lovely place for children. She could hardly help feeling that it would be a good influence on a child.

It was a terrible thing to descend to, more particularly for a woman who had brought up two children of her own, but there didn't seem to be any alternative. Motherhood was the only trade she knew. She went with her problem to Miss Hegarty, the nurse, who owned one of the bigger houses between her and the road. Miss Hegarty was a fine-looking woman of good family, but so worn out by the endless goings-on of the male and female that she admitted to Kate that most of the time she could not be bothered to distinguish between honest and dishonest transactions. 'Aha, Mrs Mahoney!' she said triumphantly. 'They all start out in a laugh and all end up in a cry.' Even to women in labour she would call out joyously, 'Last year's laugh is this year's cry, Mrs Hartnett.' The funny thing about Miss Hegarty was that though nobody had ever mentioned a man's name in connexion with her, she seemed to know of every girl within fifty miles who was in trouble.

Kate, however, found her a good counsellor. She advised her against taking foster-children from the local council because they paid so badly that you would have to take three or four to make a living out of them. The thing to do was to take a child of good family whose mother would be able to support it. Even then you couldn't rely on vagabonds like that because they were all unstable and might skip off to foreign parts without warning, but you would still have the grandparents to fall back on. 'Oh, Mrs Mahoney, if they have it they'll pay to keep their precious daughter's name out of the papers. Fitter for them to keep her off the streets!'

Miss Hegarty knew of a girl of that kind from Limerick who was going to England to have her baby and would probably be glad of a good home for it in Ireland, but not too close to her family. When Mrs Mahoney told Nora and Molly, Molly didn't seem to mind, but Nora got very dramatic and said that personally she'd choose the poor-house – a remark Kate did not like at all, though it was only what you'd expect from a giddy creature like Nora.

From Nora she borrowed back the old family perambulator, and one spring morning it appeared outside the door in the lane with a baby boy asleep inside, while Kate herself sat on the window-sill to explain her strange position. 'My first!' she shouted gaily, and then went on in the monotonous voice she used for solemn occasions to explain that this was no ordinary child such as you would get from the workhouse, but the son of a beautiful educated girl from one of the wealthiest, best-bred families in Limerick, who herself was manageress of a big shop there. Of course, the neighbours smiled and nodded and groaned, and agreed it was a sad case, but that times were changing; and did not believe a word that Kate told them because they knew a girl like that must have the bad drop, and the bad drop was bound to be passed on. All the same they were sorry for Kate, an old neighbour and a respectable one, who had no choice but to put the best face she could on it. The young married women who, as they said themselves, had paid for their titles, were not so charitable and said that you could not allow decent children to grow up in an atmosphere like that, and that the priest or the landlord should stop it because it was lowering the value of morality and property in the lane. They did not say it too loud, because, however humiliated she might be, Kate was a very obstinate old woman, and a vulgar one as well if she was roused.

So Jimmy Mahoney was permitted to grow up in the lane along with the honest transactions and turned into a good-looking, moody kid, cheerful and quarrelsome, who seemed to see nothing wrong in his mother's being so old. On the contrary, he seemed to depend on her more than the other children did on their real mothers, and sometimes when she left him alone and went off to see Nora or Molly he refused to play and sat and sulked on the doorstep till she got home. Even that ended one day when he simply went after her, without as much as the price of the tram, and walked to the other side of the city to Molly's on the Douglas Road.

'Oh, you divil you!' Kate shouted when she looked round and saw him staring accusingly at her from the front door. 'I thought you were a ghost. A nice position I'd be in if you went and got yourself killed on me!' Then she grinned and said, 'I suppose you couldn't get on without me.' Molly, a beautiful, haggard woman, gave him a smile of mortification and said quietly, 'Come in, Jimmy.' It was a thing she would not have wished for a pound because she knew it would have to be explained to the neighbours as well as her own children. But afterwards, whatever she or Nora might think, Kate brought him with her wherever she went. They might imagine that he had no such claim on their mother, but Jimmy thought otherwise.

But by the time he was five or six things were again going hard with Kate. Money wasn't what it had been and her little margin of profit was contracting. She paid another visit to Miss Hegarty, and this time the nurse had an even more staggering story. It seemed there was this well-to-do girl in Bantry who was engaged to a rich Englishman and then went and had an affair with a married man she had known from the time she was twelve.

'A married man!' exclaimed Kate. 'Oh, my, the things that go on!'

'Don't talk to me, Mrs Mahoney!' Miss Hegarty cried dramatically. 'Don't talk to me. If you knew the half of what was going on, 'twould make you lose your religion.'

Kate felt it her duty to warn Jimmy that he was getting a little brother. Miss Hegarty herself advised that, but whatever Miss Hegarty knew about flighty girls she seemed to know very little about small boys. When Mrs Mahoney told him, he began to roar and kick the furniture till she was sure the whole lane was listening. He said that he didn't want any little brother. He said if she brought one into the house that he'd walk out. He said she was too old to be having babies and that she'd have everyone talking about them. As she sighed afterwards, a husband wouldn't have given her such dogs' abuse. And what Jimmy said was nothing to what her daughters said.

'Ah, Mammy, you're making a holy show of us!' Nora cried when she came to call.

'I'm making a show of ye?' Kate cried wonderingly, pointing at her bosom with the mock-innocent air that maddened her daughters. 'I do my business and I don't cost ye a penny – is that what ye call making a show of ye?'

'Ah, you'd think we were something out of a circus instead of an old respectable family,' stormed Nora. 'That I can hardly face the neighbours when I come up the lane! Ahadie, 'tis well my poor daddy doesn't know what you're making of his little house.' Then she put her hands on her hips like a common market-woman and went on. 'How long do you think you'll be able to keep this up, would you mind us asking? You think you're going to live for ever, I suppose?'

'God is good,' Kate muttered stiffly. 'I might have a few years in me yet.'

'You might,' Nora said mockingly. 'And I suppose you imagine that if anything happens to you, Molly and myself will keep up the good work, out of Christian charity?'

'Aha, God help the innocent child that would be depending on Christian charity from the likes of you!' Kate retorted with sudden anger. 'And their people have plenty, lashings of it – more than you'll ever be able to say with your husband in a steady job in the Brewery! How sure you are of yourself! My goodness, that we'd never do anything at all if we were to be always thinking of what was round the next corner. And what about my rent? Are you going to pay it?'

'Ah, 'tisn't the rent with you at all, and it never was,' Nora said with growing fury. 'You only do it because you like it.'

'I like it?' her mother asked feebly, as though she were beginning to doubt Nora's sanity. 'An old woman like me that's crippled with the rheumatics? Oh, my!' she added in a roar of anguish, 'that 'tis in a home I ought to be if I had my rights. In a home!'

'You and your home!' Nora said contemptuously. 'That's enough of your lies now, Mammy! You love it! Love it! And you care more for that little bastard than you ever did about Molly or me.'

'How dare you?' Kate cried, rising with as much dignity as the rheumatics permitted. 'What way is that to speak to your mother? And to talk about a poor defenceless child like that in my house, you dirty, jealous thing! Yes, jealous,' she added in a wondering whisper, as though the truth had only dawned on her in that moment. 'Oh, my! Ye that had everything!'

All the same, Kate was a bit shaken, not because of the row, because the Mahoneys had always quarrelled like that, as though they all suffered from congenital deafness, and they got the same pleasure out of the mere volume of sound they could produce that certain conductors get out of Wagner. What really mortified her was that she had given herself away in front of Nora, whose intelligence she despised. Now if it had been Molly she wouldn't have minded so much, for though Molly was apparently serving her time to be a saint, she had the intelligence to see through Kate's little dodges. It was true that Kate had taken Jimmy in for perfectly good mercenary reasons, and that without him she would have no home at all; and it was very wrong under the circumstances for Nora to impute sentimental motives to her; but all the same she wasn't so far wrong. Motherhood was the only trade Kate knew, and she liked to practise it as her poor husband had liked to make little chairs and tables in the last year of his life, when no one cared whether he made them or not; and though her rheumatics were bad and her sight wasn't all it used to be, she felt she practised it better the older she got. It was also true enough to say that she enjoyed Jimmy more than she had enjoyed her own children, and if you had pressed her about it she would have said that in those days she had been young and worried about everything. But if you had pressed her hard enough, you would also have discovered that there wasn't a boy in the whole road that she thought was a patch on Jimmy. And what was wrong with that? she might have added. You might say what you like but there was a lot in good blood.

She would not have understood at all if you had accused her of being an old dreamer who was attracted to Jimmy by the romance and mystery of his birth – the sort of thing she had missed in her own sober and industrious youth, but, just the same, Jimmy gave her the chance of sitting over the fire in the evening with some old crony and discussing like a schoolgirl things she would scarcely have known existed.

'Oh, when I seen Jimmy's mother that day in the solicitor's office she was like something you'd see in a shop window, Mrs Summers,' she would chant. 'She was beautiful, beautiful! And I could see by that set face of hers that she had a month of crying all bottled up inside her. Oh, Mrs Sumners, if you seen her the way I did you'd know that nothing she could do would be bad.'

And later, when she had tucked Jimmy in for the night and lay awake in the other room, saying her rosary, she would often forget her prayers and imagine how she would feel if one stormy night (for some reason she made it stormy) there came a knock to the door and Kate saw Jimmy's father standing in the lane, tall and handsome with a small black moustache and the tears in his eyes. 'Mr Mulvany,' she would say to the teacher (she was always making up names and occupations for Jimmy's unknown father), 'your son wants nothing from you,' or (if she was in a generous mood), 'Senator MacDunphy, come in. Jimmy was beginning to think you'd never find him.'

But dreamers are for ever running into degrading practicalities that they have failed to anticipate, and there was one thing about her extraordinary family that really worried Kate. Before she had even laid eyes on him, the second boy had also been christened James, and because she was terrified of everything to do with the law she did not dare to change his name. But so that Jimmy should not be too upset, she left his name as it was, plain James – an unnatural name for any child as she well knew.

James was a very different sort of child from Jimmy. He was a baby with a big head, a gaping mouth, and a cheerless countenance that rarely lit up in a smile. Even from the first day it was as though he knew he was there only on sufferance and resigned himself to the fact.

Fortunately, Jimmy took to him at once. He liked being left in charge, and was perfectly happy to change and entertain him. He explored the neighbourhood to study all the other babies and told Kate that James was cleverer than the whole lot of them. He even got Kate's permission to wheel the old perambulator up and down the main road so that people could see for themselves what James was like and came back with great satisfaction to report any approving remarks he happened to elicit. As he had a violent temper and would fight anyone up to twice his weight, the other kids did not make any public remarks about this sissified conduct.

2

A couple of times a year Jimmy's mother, whom he knew only as Aunt Nance, came to stay with friends in Cork, and Jimmy visited her there and played with the two children, who were called Rory and Mary. He did not like Rory and Mary because they ganged up on him at once, and he only went on his aunt's account. She was tall and good-looking with a dark complexion and dark, dark hair; she talked in a crisp nervous way, and was always forgetting herself and saying dirty words like 'Cripes!' and 'Damn!' which delighted Jimmy because these were words that were supposed to be known only to fellows.

When he got home, Kate asked him all sorts of questions about his visit, like how many rooms there were in the house, what he ate there, what sort of furniture there was and what size was the garden – things that never interested Jimmy in the least.

When James began to grow up, he too asked questions. He wanted to know what school Rory and Mary went to, what they learned there, and whether or not Mary played the piano. These were questions that did not interest Jimmy, but it dawned on him that James was lonely when he was left behind like that and wanted to see the Martins' place for himself. It seemed an excellent idea to Jimmy, because James was a steady, quiet kid who would get on much better with Rory and Mary than he did, but when he suggested it Kate only said James was too young and Aunt Nance said she'd see.

It ended by his suspecting that there was something fishy about James. There had always been something fishy about him, as though he didn't really belong to the family. Jimmy wasn't clear how you came to belong to the family, but he knew it had to happen in a hospital or in the house, and he couldn't remember anything of the sort happening to James. One evening, when Kate was complaining of her rheumatics, he asked her casually if she hadn't gone to hospital with it.

'Ah, how would the likes of me go to hospital?' she asked sourly. 'I was never in a hospital in my life and I hope I never am.'

James was in the room, and Jimmy said no more for the time being. Later that night he returned to the subject.

'You're not James's mother, are you, Mammy?'

'What's that you say?' she cried in astonishment.

'I said you're not James's mother, that's all.'

'Oye, what queer things you think of!' she said crossly.

'But you're not,' he said with a shrug. 'You only took him in because his own mother didn't want him, isn't it?'

'You inquisitive puppy!' she hissed. 'Don't let the child hear you saying things like that.'

'But it's true, isn't it?' She's the one you get the money from.'

Kate threatened him into silence, but she was terrified. 'Oh, my, the cunning of him!' she said next day to Mrs Sumners. 'The way he cross-hackled me – that poor Jack Mahoney never did the like all the long years we were married! And what am I to say to him? Who will I get to advise me?' The neighbours could not advise her, and even if they tried it would be useless, because they had no more experience than herself. Miss Hegarty might have been able to advise her, but Kate felt that asking her advice would be a sort of admission that she had failed in the job.

And all the time Jimmy's behaviour grew worse. At the best of times it wasn't very good. Though occasionally he got into high spirits and entertained herself and James by the hour, telling funny stories, the high spirits rarely lasted long, and he sulked on his bed with a comic. After this he would go out with other, rougher kids, and return late with a guilty air she could spot from the end of the lane, and which meant he had broken a window or stolen something from a shop. She watched him from the back door when she saw him in the quarry, because she was sure he had a hidey hole there where he kept the things he stole, but when she poked round there by herself she could never find anything. At times like these she was never free of anxiety, because she knew it imperilled the sufferance the neighbours extended to him, and if ever a policeman – which God forbid! – came to her door, they would be the first to say it was all you could expect of a boy like that. But this was the worst bout yet.

Finally, she decided to tell him the truth about James, or as much of it as she thought he could understand, and one night when James was asleep she sat with him in the darkness over the kitchen fire and told him in her monotonous voice about this beautiful, beautiful girl in Bantry and how as a girl she was in love with this nice young man, and his cruel parents made him marry a girl he did not love at all, and then the girl's parents persuaded her to marry this rich Englishman with motor-cars and yachts and big houses in all parts of the world, but at the last moment the poor girl's heart misgave her and she tried to be reunited to the one she truly loved. She told it so movingly that by the end she was in tears herself, but Jimmy's first words startled her out of her daydream.

'All the same, Mammy, James should be with his own mother,' he said.

She was astonished and dismayed at the maturity of his tone. This was no longer any of the Jimmys she had known, but one who spoke with the sort of authority poor Jack had exercised on the odd occasions when he called his family to order. She even found herself apologizing to poor Jack.

'Ah, wisha, how could she without that husband of hers knowing?'

'Then she ought to tell him,' Jimmy said, and again it was like her dead husband's voice speaking to her.

319

'Tell him? Tell him what?'

'Everything.'

'Is it to be upsetting the child?' she asked complainingly.

'If she doesn't upset him, somebody else will,' he said with his brooding, old-mannish air.

'They will, they will, God help us!' she sighed. 'People are bad enough for anything. But the poor child may as well be happy while he can.'

But it was Jimmy, not James, she was concerned about. James might get by, a colourless, studious, obedient boy like him, without giving much offence to anyone, but one day Jimmy would beat another boy or steal something from a shop and the whole truth would come out. For a few moments she was tempted to tell him, but she was afraid of what his mother would say when she knew.

Meanwhile, she saw to her surprise that she seemed to have given Jimmy a purpose in life, though it was something she might have expected. Jimmy was always like that, up or down, full of initiative and independence or shiftless and dependent. Now he took over James personally. He announced that it was bad for the kid to be so much alone and took him with him when he went down the Glen or up the river with bigger boys. It was not James' notion; he didn't like bigger boys and didn't in the least mind being left alone with the bits of clean paper he managed to pick up for his writings and drawings, but Jimmy said it was for his good and anything anyone said was good for James he would give a fair trial to. When he came home he repeated his adventures to Kate in the literal gloomy manner of a policeman making a report.

'Jimmy took me down the Glen with Bobby Stephens and Ted Murtagh. I don't like Ted Murtagh. He says dirty words. Jimmy and me fished for thorneybacks. Then he showed me a blackbird's nest. You can't touch a bird's nest because the bird would know and leave the young ones to die. Ted Murtagh robs birds' nests. I think that's wrong, don't you, Mammy?'

James collected bits of information, right and wrong, apparently under the impression that they would come in handy one day, and to each of them he managed to attach a useful moral lesson. No wonder he sometimes made Jimmy smile.

But Jimmy still continued to brood on James's future. He waited until Aunt Nance came to Cork again, and when he got her to himself he poured it all out on her. He had managed to convince himself that Kate had not understood, but that Aunt Nance who was cleverer would only have to hear the facts to do something about it. Before he had even finished the story she gave him a queer hurt look and cut him off.

'You'll know what it's all about one of these days,' she said.

'But don't you think he should be with his mother?' he asked.

'I don't know,' she said with her boldest air, and then took out a cigarette. 'And even if I did, I wouldn't criticize,' she added.

'Well, I think it's wrong,' he said sullenly. 'The poor kid has no one to play with. Couldn't I bring him over here tomorrow?'

'Begod, you couldn't, Jimmy,' she said. 'Too many blooming kids they have on this place already, if you ask me.'

He left her in one of his mutinous, incoherent fits of rage. He did not take the bus home, even though he had the money, but walked and stood on the river's edge, flinging stones. It was late when he got home, but he told Kate the whole story. 'Ah, what business have you to be interfering?' she asked miserably. He went to bed, and she heard him tossing and muttering to himself. Finally she lit the candle and went into the little attic room that he shared with James. He sat up in bed and looked at her with mad eyes.

'Go away!' he whispered fiercely. 'You're not my mother at all.'

'Oye!' she whimpered, sleepy and scared. 'You and your mother!'

'You're not, you're not, you're not!' he muttered. 'I know it all now. I'm like James, only you wouldn't tell me. You haven't the decency. You tell me nothing only lies.'

'Whisht, whisht, whisht, and don't wake the child!' she whispered impatiently. 'Come into the other room.'

He stumbled out ahead of her in his nightshirt, and she sat on the edge of her bed and put her arm round him. He was shivering as if he had a fever, and she no longer felt capable of controlling the situation. She felt old and tired and betrayed.

'What made you think of it, child?' she asked wearily.

'Aunt Nance,' he said with a sob.

'Was it she told you?' She knew she didn't even sound surprised.

'No. She wouldn't tell me anything, only I saw she was afraid.'

'Who was she afraid of?'

'I asked her to get James's mother to bring him home with her and she got frightened.'

'Oh, oh, oh, you poor desolate child, and you only did it for the best!' she wailed.

'I want to know who my mother is,' he cried despairingly. 'Is it Aunt Kitty?' (Kitty was the mother of Rory and Mary.)

'Why then, indeed, it is not.'

'Is it Aunt Nance so?'

'Wisha, child, lie down here and you can sleep with Mammy.'

'I don't want to sleep,' he said frantically. 'How can I sleep? I want to know who my mother is, and you won't tell me.' Then, turning suddenly into a baby again, he put his head on her lap and wept. She patted his fat bottom under his nightshirt and sighed. 'You're perished,' she said. 'What am I going to do with you?' Then she lifted him into her bed and pulled up the clothes.

'Will I get you a cup of tea?' she asked with feigned brightness, and, as he shook his head, she added, 'I will, I will.' A cup of tea in the middle of the night was the greatest luxury she could think of. She put on an old coat and went downstairs to the kitchen where the oil lamp was turned low. There was still a spark of fire left and she blew on it and boiled the big iron kettle. When she climbed awkwardly back up the stairs with the two mugs of tea she heard him still sobbing and stopped. 'God direct me!' she said aloud. Then she sat on the edge of the bed and shook him. 'Drink this, my old *putog*!' she said humorously. It had always made him laugh to be called a sausage.

'I don't want it,' he said. 'I want to know who my mother is.'

'Drink it, you dirty little caffler!' she said angrily. 'Drink it or I won't tell you at all.'

He raised himself in the bed and she held the mug to his mouth, but he could not stop shivering and the tea spilled over his nightshirt and the bedclothes. 'My good sheet!' she muttered. Then she took her own cup and looked away into a corner of the room as though to avoid his eyes. 'She is your mother, your Aunt Nance,' she said in a harsh, expressionless voice, 'and a good mother she is, and a good woman as well, and it will be a bad day for you when you talk against her or let anyone else do it. She had the misfortune to meet a man that was beneath her. She was innocent. He took advantage of her. She wasn't the first and she won't be the last.'

'Who was it?' he asked.

'I don't know, and I don't want to know.'

'Who was it? Because I'm going to find out and when I do I'm going to kill him.'

'Why then, indeed, you're going to do nothing of the sort,' she said sharply. 'He's your father, and he's there inside you, and the thing you will slight in yourself will be the rock you'll perish on.'

The dawn came in the window, and she still rambled on, half dead with sleep. Later, when she reported it to her cronies, she said with a sour laugh that it was nothing but lies from beginning to end, and what other way could it be when she hadn't a notion how a girl like that would feel, but at the time it did not seem to be lies. It seemed rather as though she were reporting a complete truth that was known only to herself and God. And in a queer way it steadied Jimmy. The little man came out in him again. Once she had persuaded him of the truth of his mother's being a victim, he had no further thought for his own trouble.

'Mammy, why didn't she bring me to live with her?' he asked earnestly. 'I could look after her.'

'Oye, you will, child, you will one of these days,' she said sourly. Though later it seemed funny to think of Jimmy looking after his mother, at the time it only hurt her because she would never have a son who would feel that way about her. Daughters were a poor thing for a mother to be relying on.

'Mammy, does this mean that there's something wrong with James and me?' he asked at last, and she knew that this was the question that preoccupied him above all others.

'Indeed, it means nothing of the sort,' she cried, and for the first time it seemed to herself that she was answering in her own person. 'It is nothing. Only bad, jealous people would say the likes of that. Oh, you'll meet them, never fear,' she said, joining her hands, 'the scum of the earth with their marriage lines and their baptismal lines, looking down on their betters! But mark what I say, child, don't let any of them try and persuade you that you're not as good as them. And better! A thousand times better!'

Strange notions from a respectable old woman who had never even believed in love!

*

3

When Jimmy was fourteen and James between eight and nine, Jimmy's mother decided it was time for him to come and live with her. At first things seemed to have turned out well for her. After Jimmy's birth she had met a very nice young man who fell in love with her. She had told him the whole story, and unlike the general run of fellows in her neighbourhood, who sheered away from her the moment they caught a whiff of scandal, he accepted it as a normal event that might have happened to any decent girl. This seemed to her much too good to be true, and she had held off marrying him for years. The irony of it was that when she knew he was really in love with her and she with him, it was too late. After long years of marriage they had no children of their own. Even before this became obvious he had wanted to adopt Jimmy and bring him up as their own child, but she had put it off and off. First, she said, she wanted them to have the pleasure of a normal child in normal surroundings; Jimmy would come later. But now there was little chance of that, and she had begun to blame herself, to feel, even, that it was a sort of judgement on her for having given Jimmy up originally. Finally, her husband had laid down the law. They were having Jimmy to live with them and the neighbours could say what they pleased.

It was a terrible shock to Kate, though why it should have been she didn't know, since for years it was she who had argued with her neighbours that the time had come for Jimmy to have a proper education and mix with the right class of people. Now she realized that she was just as jealous and possessive as anyone else. She had never criticized Jimmy's mother or allowed anyone else to do so, but now she hadn't a good word to say for her. 'She neglected him when it suited her, and now when it suits her she wants him back,' she complained to Mrs Sumners. 'Ah, now you have to be fair, ma'am,' Mrs Sumners, replied philosophically. 'Fair? Why have I to be fair?' Kate retorted angrily. 'Let them that have it be fair. Them that are without it are entitled to their say.'

Besides, Jimmy provoked her. He was always up or down, and now he was up all the time, thinking only of the marvellous new world that was opening before him and without a thought for herself and James. He told her blithely that he would always come back for the holidays and comforted James by saying that his turn would come next and he'd be going to London. 'He will, he will,' she said and began to weep. 'And neither of ye will care what happens to me.' At this he grew frantic and shouted, 'All right, I won't go if you don't want me to.' Then she turned the full force of her malice on him and shouted, 'Who said I didn't want you to go? How could I keep you here, and me with nothing? Go to the ones with the cars and the fur coats! Go to the ones that can look after you!'

And yet when his stepfather came and took him away she had a feeling of immense relief. She realized that she was not the one to look after him. He was too wild; too big and noisy and exacting; he needed a man to keep him in order, and besides, now that she had become old and stiff and half blind, the housekeeping was more of a strain. She would decide to give herself and James a treat and go to town for the good stewing beef, and suddenly realize when she got back to the house that she had forgotten how to make stew. 'God direct me!' she would say aloud, closing her eyes. 'How was it I used to make it when I was younger? 'Delicious' poor Jack used to say it was.'

James was an easier proposition altogether, a boy who wouldn't notice whether you gave him stew or a can of soup or a mug of tea so long as he got the occasional penny for his exercise books. It was music with him now, and he spent hours carefully ruling over the exercise books and making marks that he said were operas and singing them over to her in a tuneless sort of voice. Signs on it, he had almost ruined his eyes and she had to get black glasses for him. He was having trouble in school as well, for the headmaster, who lived up the road, knew who he was and disliked having such a boy in his good clean Catholic school.

One day James came home and said in his unemotional way, 'Mammy, Mr Clancy said to me today, "James Mahoney, or whatever your name is." I don't think it was very nice of him to say that, Mammy, do you?' Kate went a little mad. Her first notion was to complain Mr Clancy to the Dean, but she had a suspicion that the Dean and Clancy were hand-in-glove and that any justice she got she would have to take for herself. So she donned her old hat and coat, took her umbrella by way of a walking-stick and went up the road to the headmaster's big house. When he appeared at the door, she asked him what he meant by insulting her child, and he called her 'an impudent old woman' and slammed the door in

325

her face. Then she banged on the knocker, beat the door with the handle of her umbrella, and read and spelt him for two generations back. She saw by the way that the curtains along the road were being twitched that she had an audience, and she recounted how his mother, known to the Coal Quay as 'Norry Dance Naked', had owned slum property and refused to supply doors for the conveniences. It must be admitted that she was a very vulgar old woman, and after that James had to go to the monks. The monks did not mind who his mother was, because they soon satisfied themselves that James was a born examination-passer who was worth good money to them.

But the loss of Jimmy showed her how precarious was her hold on James, and in the evenings when they were alone she encouraged him to talk about what he would do when he was grown up. James, it seemed to her, had only one ambition, and that was to become a statue. He knew all the statues in town, and for a while had been rather depressed because it had seemed to him that the only way to become a statue was to be a martyr for Ireland, a temperance reformer, or the founder of a religious order, none of which attracted him. But then he discovered from a library book that you could also be a statue for writing books or composing music, which was why he worked so hard making up operas. Looking at his big solemn face in the firelight, Kate thought that there was something of the statue about it already.

Jimmy had been a great boy to raise a laugh, particularly against himself, and James, who knew the way she felt about him, tried to be funny too; but if she was to be killed for it, she could not raise a laugh at James's jokes. And yet she knew that James was gentler, steadier, and more considerate. 'Jimmy have the fire, but James have the character' was how she summed them up.

Then early one morning she heard a hammering on the front door and started up in panic, feeling sure something had happened to Jimmy. He had been on her mind for a week, and she had been scolding James to stop blinding himself over his old books and write to his brother to see was he all right. It was a queer way for a woman to behave who had been congratulating herself on having got rid of him, but Kate's mental processes were never very logical. Without even waiting to ask who was there she opened the door and saw Jimmy outside. Instantly she was lightheaded with relief and joy.

'Oh, child, child!' she sobbed, throwing her arms round his neck. 'Sure, I thought you'd never come home. How did you get here at all?'

'I walked most of it,' he said with a characteristic dash of boastfulness.

'You did, you did, you divil you, you did!' she muttered impatiently and then her voice rose to a squeal of anguish. 'Are them your good trousers?'

'Who is it, Mammy?' James shouted petulantly from upstairs.

'Come down and see, can't you?' she retorted, and went to tinker with the fire while James came downstairs in his nightshirt.

'Sorry I'm back, James?' Jimmy said with a grin, holding out his hand.

'No, Jimmy, I'm very glad you're back,' James said in a small voice.

'Put on your topcoat, you little devil!' cried Kate. 'How often have I to be telling you not to go round in your shirt? Out to the yard, and everything . . . That fellow!' she sighed to Jimmy. 'He have the heart scalded in me. I'd want ten eyes and hands, picking things up after him.'

They had breakfast together just as the sun was beginning to pick out the red quarry behind the house, and it tinged Jimmy's face with fresh colour as he told them of his all-night trip. It was a marvel to Kate how she had managed to listen to James all that time, remembering how Jimmy could tell a story. Whatever James told you always seemed to begin or end with something like 'Mammy, wasn't I clever?', but Jimmy began by revealing himself a fool and ended by suggesting something worse, but it never crossed your mind that he was a fool at all.

'And what did you do with the money for the fare?' Kate asked suspiciously. 'Spent it, I suppose?'

'What fare?' he asked, blushing.

'I suppose she gave you the money for the train at any rate?'

'Oh, I didn't tell her.'

'You didn't what?' Kate asked slowly. 'Oh, my! I suppose you had a fight with her and then walked out of the house without a word to her or anybody? I declare to God you're never right.'

'She doesn't mind what I do,' Jimmy said with a defiant shrug.

'She doesn't, I hear!' Kate said ironically. 'I suppose she didn't pay you enough attention? And now she'll be blaming it all on me.

327

She'll be saying I have you ruined. And she'll be right. I have you ruined, you little caffler!' She opened the back door and looked up at the great sandstone face of the quarry reflecting the morning light. 'Oh, my! There's a beautiful morning, glory be to God!'

A half an hour later she heard the unfamiliar sound of a car turning into the lane and cocked her head in alarm. It stopped immediately in front of the cottage. She spun round on Jimmy, who was now as white as she felt herself. 'Is that the police?' she asked in an angry whisper. She knew it was the wrong thing to say, but Jimmy did not appear to hear her. All the glow seemed to have gone out of him. 'If that's Uncle Tim I'm not going back with him,' he said dully. Kate went to the front door and saw Nance's husband, a good-looking young man with the sort of pink-and-white complexion she called 'delicate'.

'Here we are again, Mrs Mahoney,' he said without rancour.

'Oh, come in, sir, come in,' she said obsequiously, wiping her hands in her sack apron, and now she was no longer the proud, possessive mother, but the old hireling caught in possession of property that was not rightly hers. The young man strode into the kitchen as if it was his own and stopped dead when he saw Jimmy sitting by the window.

'Now, what made me come here first?' he asked good-naturedly. 'Mrs Mahoney, I have the makings of a first-class detective in me. Tim the Tracer, that's my name. Criminals shudder when they hear it.' When Jimmy said nothing he cocked his head reproachfully. 'Well, Jimmy?' he asked. Kate could see that Jimmy both liked and dreaded him.

'I'm not going back with you, Uncle Tim,' he said with an indignation that was half an appeal.

'Begor, you are, Jimmy,' his stepfather said, but still with no trace of resentment. 'It wouldn't be much use me going back to Limerick without you. And if you think I'm going to spend the rest of my days chasing you round Ireland, you're wrong. This last jaunt was enough for me.' He sat down, and Kate saw he was exhausted.

'Wisha, you'll have a cup of tea,' she said.

'I will, and a whole teapot-full, Mrs Mahoney,' he replied. 'I didn't even have time to get my breakfast with this fellow.'

'I don't want to go back, Uncle Tim,' Jimmy said furiously. 'I want to stop here.'

'Listen to that, ma'am,' Tim said, cocking his head at Kate. 'Insulting Limerick, and in Cork of all places!'

'I'm not saying anything about Limerick,' Jimmy cried despairingly, and again he was a child and defenceless against the dialectic of adults. 'I want to stop here.'

Screwing up her eyes as she filled the teapot again and put it on the table, Kate tried to intervene on his behalf.

'Wisha, 'tis only a little holiday he wants, sir,' she said humbly, but this only made Jimmy madder than ever.

'It isn't a holiday I want,' he shouted. 'I want to stop here for good. This is my home, and I told my mother so.'

'And don't you think that was a pretty hard thing to say to your mother, Jimmy?' his stepfather asked drily.

'It's true,' Jimmy said angrily.

'Come on and have your cup of tea, sir,' Kate said, trying to smooth things down. 'Will you have another, Jimmy?'

'I will not,' Jimmy said, beginning to cry. 'And it isn't that I'm not fond of her, but she left it too late. She shouldn't have left it so late, Uncle Tim.'

'You might be right there, son,' his stepfather said wearily, pulling his chair up to the table. 'You can let things like that go too far, and maybe you are too old to get used to your mother. But you're not going the right way about it either.'

'All right then,' Jimmy cried, at the end of his tether. 'What should I do?'

'Don't run out of a situation whenever it gets too hard,' his stepfather said, going on with his skimpy breakfast of bread and tea. 'People's feelings are hurt when you do things like that. Talk to her and tell her how you feel. Maybe the best thing would be for you to come back and go to a proper school here, but leave it to her to make the arrangements. You see, you don't seem to understand what it cost your mother to bring you home at all. It may have been the wrong thing to do; it may have been a failure, but you don't want to leave her feeling that her life is nothing but failures.'

'He's right, Jimmy, boy, he's right,' Kate said, recognizing the deep feeling in his tone. 'If you don't go back now you could never go back with all the old talk there would be. But if you go back now, you can always go home for the holidays.'

'Oh, all right,' Jimmy said with despair.

329

And it was real despair as she well knew, not play-acting. Of course, he indulged in a bit of that as well. He would not kiss her when he was leaving, and when James said cheerfully, 'You'll be back with us in a couple of weeks,' Jimmy took a deep breath and said, 'I may or I may not,' leaving it to be understood that he did not rule out the possibility of suicide. But she knew that he did not want to go, that he looked on her house as the only home he knew, and she had great boasting about it among the neighbours. 'A boy of fourteen, ma'am, that was never away from home all the days of his life, travelling back like that through the night, without food or sleep – oh, my, where would you find the likes of him?'

And at the end of his stay with his mother they resumed their existence together more or less where it had been broken off. There was only one major change in their relationship. A couple of days after his return Jimmy said, 'I'm not going to call you "Mammy" any more.' 'Oye, and what are you going to call me?' she asked with sour humour. 'I'm going to call you "Granny",' he said. 'The other sounds too silly.' After a few weeks, James, who had continued to call her by the old name, said 'Granny' too, as though by mistake, and she suddenly lost her temper and flew at him. 'Glad enough you were of someone to call "Mammy"!' she shouted. Though she knew it was only fair, she did not like it. Like the young married women who had objected to Jimmy and himself in the first place, she felt she had paid for her title.

4

A year later, what with the rheumatics and the bronchitis, Kate had to go to hospital, and Nora and Molly each agreed to take one of the boys, but when it was put up to them neither of them would agree. They stayed on in the little house by themselves, and each week one of the girls came up a couple of times to clear up after them. They reported that the mess was frightful, though you could always tell which of the boys was responsible, because Jimmy was a conscientious messer, who piled everything into one enormous heap, apparently in the hope that Santa Claus would find it, while James left things wherever he happened to be whenever an idea struck him. As a result Kate left hospital too soon, but even then she was too late to prevent mischief, for while she was away Jimmy had quietly left school and got himself a job in a packers'.

'Oh, you blackguard!' she sighed fondly. 'I knew you'd be up to something the minute my back was turned. Oh, my, that I'd want a hundred eyes! But back to school you go tomorrow, my fine gentleman, if I have to drag you there myself. And 'twouldn't be the first time.'

'How can I go back to school?' Jimmy asked indignantly. 'They could have the law on me unless I gave a month's notice.' Jimmy knew that she was terrified of policemen, lawyers, and inspectors, and even at her advanced age was always in dread of being marched off to jail for some crime she never committed.

'I'll talk to the manager myself,' she said. 'Who is he?'

'You can't talk to the manager,' said Jimmy. 'He's away on holidays.'

'Oh, you liar!' she muttered happily. 'There's no end to the lies you tell. Who is it, you scamp?'

'Anyway, I have to have a job,' Jimmy said in a grown-up voice. 'If anything happens to you, who's going to look after James?'

'Oh, you divil out of hell!' she said, because it was something that had worried her a lot, and she knew now that Jimmy realized it. But at the same time she knew that Jimmy was the sort of bossy kid who would take on a responsibility like that because he could show off about it, but he would have his own good reasons, which you wouldn't see until later.

'A lot he have to hope for if 'tis you he's relying on!' she shouted. 'Did you tell your mother?'

'That's right,' he said bitterly, confounded by her injustice. 'What time have I to write to my mother?'

'Plenty of time you have to write to her when 'tis money you want,' Kate said with a knowing air. 'Sit down there and write to her now, you vagabond! I suppose you want me to take the blame for your blackguarding.'

Jimmy with his usual martyred air sat at the table and agonized over a note to his mother.

'How do you spell "employment", James?' he asked.

'Aha!' she exclaimed malevolently. 'He wants to give up school and he don't know how to spell a simple word.'

'All right, spell it you, so!' he retorted.

'In my time, for poor people, the education was not going,' she replied with great dignity. 'People hadn't the chances they have now, and what chances they had, they respected, not like the ones that are going today. Go on with your letter, you thing!'

And again his stepfather came and argued with him. He explained patiently that without a secondary education of some sort Jimmy would never get into a college and would probably never rise above being a common labourer. Jimmy knew his stepfather liked him and began to cry, but he was in one of his obstinate moods and would not give in. He said again and again that he wanted to be independent. When his stepfather left, he accompanied him to the car, and they had a long conversation that made Kate suspicious.

'What were ye talking about?' she asked.

'Oh, nothing,' Jimmy said lightly. 'I only asked him who my father was. He says he doesn't know.'

'And if he says it, he means it,' snapped Kate. 'How inquisitive you're getting.'

'He said I was entitled to know,' Jimmy replied angrily. 'He told me I should ask Nance.' (Sometimes he called his mother 'Mother' and sometimes 'Nance', and whichever he said sounded awkward.)

'You should,' Kate said ironically. 'I'm sure she's dying to tell you.'

But when next he came back from a visit to his mother he had a triumphant air, and late in the evening he said boastfully, 'Well, I found out who my father was anyway.'

'It didn't take you long,' said Kate. 'How did you do it?'

'It was Uncle Tim, really,' he admitted. 'I was arguing with Nance when he walked in. He was mad! He just said, "Get out, Jimmy!" and I did. Half an hour later he came into me and said, "Now go and talk to your mother!" She was crying.'

'Small wonder!' Kate said with a shrug. 'Who was it?'

'Nobody in particular, actually,' Jimmy admitted with a defeated air. 'The name was Creedon. He had some sort of grocery shop in North Cork, but he's left that for years. She thinks he's in Birmingham, but I'm going to find out.'

'For what?' she asked. 'What good will it do you to find out?'

'I can go to see him, can't I?' he asked defiantly.

'You can what?'

'Go and see him,' he grumbled with some doubt in his voice. 'Why wouldn't I?'

'Why wouldn't you, indeed, and all the attention he paid you!' she retorted. 'You're never right.'

And, indeed, there were times when she thought he wasn't. For months on end he seemed not to think at all of his parentage, and then he began to daydream till he worked himself into a fever of emotion. In a fit like that she never knew what he might do. He was capable of anything, and even though it might never come to violence, she did not know from day to day what deep and irreparable hurt some casual remark might inflict on him.

One day he went off. A sailor on the Fishguard boat had arranged for him to travel free. While he was away she fretted, and, of course, being Jimmy, he did not even send a card to say where he was. She nursed the vague hope that Jimmy would not be able to locate his father; that he would have moved; but, knowing Jimmy's obstinacy in pursuit of an obsession, she had little confidence in this. She tried to imagine what their meeting would be like and hoped only that his father would not say anything to provoke him.

'Oh, my!' she sighed to James. 'If Jimmy took it into his head, he'd kill him.'

'Oh, no, Granny!' James said in his bored way. 'Jimmy isn't going to England just to kill him. He has more sense than you think.'

'Oye, and what is he going for?' she asked. 'Since you know so much about him?'

'It's only curiosity,' James said. 'Jimmy is always looking for something that was never there.'

Then, one autumn morning, after James had left for school at the other side of the city, Jimmy walked in, looking dirty and dishevelled. He had had no breakfast, and she fumbled blindly about the kitchen, trying to get it for him in a hurry, and cursing old age that made it such a labour. But her heart was light. She had only been deceiving herself, thinking that Jimmy and his father might quarrel, when all that could have happened that would have made a difference to her was that they might have got on too well.

'Oh, you blackguard!' she said fondly, leaning on the kitchen table and grinning into his face, to see him better. 'Where were you?'

'Everywhere.'

'And did you find him?'

'Of course I found him. I had to follow him to London.'

'And what do you think of him now you have him?' she asked, too jovially to be true.

'Ah, he's all right,' Jimmy said casually, and his tone didn't sound true either. 'I don't think he has long to live though. He's drinking himself to death.'

Instantly she was ashamed of her own jealousy and pettiness – she could afford to be, now that she had him back.

'Ah, child, child, why do you be upsetting yourself about them?' she cried miserably. 'They're not worth it. Nobody is worth it.'

She sat in the kitchen with for two hours. It was just as when he had run away from his mother's house, as though he had been saving it all up for her – the tramp across Wales and England, the people who had given him lifts, and the lorry-driver who had given him dinner and five bob when Jimmy had told his story. She felt she could see it all, even the scene when he knocked at the door in the shabby London lodging-house and an unshaven man with sad red eyes peered out suspiciously at him, as though no one ever called except to harass him further.

'And what did you say?' Kate asked.

'Only "Don't you know me?"' Jimmy recited, as though every word of it was fixed in his memory. 'And he said, "You have the advantage of me." So I said, "I'm your son."'

'Oh, my!' Kate exclaimed, profoundly impressed and a little sorry for Jimmy's father, though she had resolved to hate everything she learned about him. 'And what did he say then?'

'He just started to cry.'

'Fitter for him do it fifteen years ago!' Kate shouted in a sudden access of rage.

'I said, "Well, it's all over and done with now," and he said, "'Tisn't, nor 'twill never be. Your mother missed nothing when she missed me. I was a curse to others, and now I'm only a curse to myself."'

'How sorry he is for himself!' said Kate.

'He has reason,' said Jimmy, and went on to describe the squalid room where he had stayed for a week with his father, sleeping in the same unmade bed, going out with him to the pub to put a few shillings on a horse, yet Kate felt a little touch of pride in the way

Jimmy described the sudden outbursts of extravagant humour that lit up his father's maudlin self-pity. And then, being Jimmy, he could not help laughing outright at the good advice which was all his father had to give him – warnings against drink and betting, but mostly against being untrue to himself.

'The cheek of him!' cried Kate, who could see nothing in the least humorous in it. 'Oh, that 'tis me he should have had! I'd soon give him his answer, the night-walking vagabond!'

'I don't care,' Jimmy said with a defiant shrug of his shoulders. 'I like him.'

Kate could scarcely reply to this, it was so unjust. She was furious at the thought that after all her years with Jimmy she might have lost him in a single day to the man who had never raised a finger to help him, nor asked whether he was living or dead. But she knew, too, that it was fear that made her angry, because she had gone closer to losing Jimmy than she had ever done before.

5

At first, when Jimmy got a girl of his own, Kate paid no attention. She thought it was only foolishness, but when it went on for more than six months, and Jimmy took the girl out every Friday night, she began to grow nervous. She told Mrs Sumners that she was afraid Jimmy might marry 'beneath him'. When this got back to the girl's people, they were outraged, because they were afraid that Mary was going to do the same thing. 'A boy that nobody knows who he is or where he comes from!' they went around saying. 'Or is she in her right mind at all?'

Kate dreaded Friday evenings on that account. Jimmy would come in from work, and shave and strip and wash under the tap in the backyard. Then he would change into his best blue suit and put brilliantine on his hair, and she watched every move he made with gloom and resentment.

'You're not going to be late again?' she would ask.

'Why wouldn't I be late?' Jimmy would ask.

'You know I can't sleep while you do be out.' (This was true; any other night of the week she had no trouble in sleeping.)

Finally James ticked her off. One Friday evening he closed his book, raised his glasses on his forehead, and said, 'Granny, you worry too much about Jimmy and that girl. Jimmy is steadier than you give him credit for.'

'He is, I hear,' she retorted rudely. 'He have as much sense as you have, and that's not much, God knows. Wouldn't you go out and have a game of handball like a natural boy?'

'That has nothing to do with it,' James said equably. 'I know Jimmy better than you do. There's nothing wrong with Jimmy only that he has very little confidence in himself, and he's too easily influenced. That's why he prefers to go with stupid people instead of clever ones. They make him feel superior. But he has a very good intelligence if he ever tries to make use of it.'

At the same time Kate wondered often if Jimmy would ever outgrow his attitude to his family. So far as his immediate neighbours were concerned, the whole thing was forgotten except to his credit. He was as much one of themselves as any of the honest transactions brought up in the locality. But it was as if Jimmy himself could never really forget that he was an outsider; again and again the old fever broke out in him, and each time the form it took came as a surprise to Kate. Once he took off on his bicycle to a little town eighty miles away where his uncle ran a grocery store. His uncle had kept his father supplied with small money-orders that promptly went on horses. Jimmy didn't get much of a welcome because his uncle quite unjustly suspected that Jimmy wanted money-orders as well, and, besides, he did not want the job of explaining his nephew to the townspeople. In spite of his tepid welcome, Jimmy came home in high spirits and gave Kate and James a really funny description of his uncle; a frightened, cadaverous, clever little man, who lectured Jimmy on the way the country was going to the dogs, with people neglecting religion, working less and expecting more. Jimmy felt he had the laugh on his uncle, but at Christmas it was his uncle who had the laugh on Jimmy, because he sent him a small money-order as well. Jimmy was deeply touched by it; once or twice they saw him take it out of his pocket and study it with a smile as though it were a long and intimate letter.

Worse still, there was the summer when he took his bicycle and, with the help of his sailor friend, stowed away again on the Fishguard boat. This time he cycled through southern England to the little Dorset town where his mother had lodged while she was having him, all alone, without husband, lover, or friend to encourage her. Kate thought this whole expedition very queer and grumbled again that he was 'never right', but somewhere inside herself she realized that it was part of his way of getting to belong. And she knew, whatever anyone said, he would go on like that to the end of his days, pursued by the dream of a normal life that he might have lived and a normal family he might have grown up with.

James observed it too, with considerable interest, but with a fundamental disapproval. He had never shown much curiosity about his own blood-relations, though he knew he had brothers and sisters who went to expensive English schools, and he let it be seen that he thought Jimmy cheapened himself by the way he sought out his own.

'Ah, that's only because I always had to live too close to them,' Jimmy said. 'Boy, if I was like you, I'd never have anything to do with any of them again.'

'Oh, I don't know,' James grumbled. 'I don't see why I should avoid them. I'd like to meet my mother and my brothers and sisters. It's only natural, but I don't want to meet them yet.'

'You're right, boy,' Jimmy said with sudden depression. 'Because all they'd do is look down on you. Oh, they'll be polite and all the rest of it, but they'll look down on you just the same.'

'Oh, you always take things to the fair,' James said petulantly. 'You think people look down on you because you haven't enough confidence in yourself. You always think there's something wrong with you, and it's not that at all. It's something wrong with them. They're people who pay far too much attention to what other people think. If I meet them when I'm a civil servant or a teacher in the university they'll be delighted to know me. People like that never neglect anyone who may be of use to them.'

Kate, amused by James's juvenile lecturing, knew that there was a sad wisdom in what he said. While Jimmy, who had something of his father's weakness and charm, might prove a liability, James would work and save, and it would be his curiosity about his family that would be satisfied, not theirs about him. And James would make perfectly certain that no member of it patronized him. She was very old, and her grip on life had slackened, but she did very much long to see how James would deal with his family.

All the same, she knew she wouldn't see it. She fell ill again and Molly came to the house to nurse her, while Nora and usually one or both of their husbands came to relieve her in the evenings.

Her presence made an immediate change in the house. She was swift and efficient; she fed the boys and made conversation with callers, leaning against the doorpost with folded arms, and then would slip away into the front room or out the yard and weep savagely to herself for a few minutes, as another woman might do for a quick drink. The priest came, and Molly chatted with him about the affairs of the parish as though she had no other thought in mind, and then dashed up to her mother's room again. Kate asked to see Jimmy and James. The two boys went quietly up the stairs and stood at either side of the big bed. Each of them took one of her hands.

'Don't upset yeerselves too much, boys,' she said. 'I know ye'll miss me, but ye need have no regrets. Ye were the two best sons a mother ever reared.' She thought hard for a moment and added something that shocked them all. 'I'm proud of ye, and yeer father is proud of ye.'

'Mammy!' Molly whispered urgently. 'You forget. 'Tis Jimmy and James.'

Kate opened her eyes for a few moments and looked straight at her.

'I know well who it is,' she said. Then her eyes closed again and she breathed noisily for some minutes, as though she were trying to recollect herself. 'Don't do anything he'd be ashamed of. He was a good man and a clean-living man, and he never robbed anyone of a ha'penny. Jimmy, look after your little brother for me.'

'I will, Mammy,' Jimmy said through his tears.

Something about that sudden reversion to the language of childhood made Molly break down. She took refuge in the front room to weep. Nora scolded her as all the Mahoneys had always scolded one another.

'Ah, have a bit of sense, girl!' she said lightly. 'You know yourself poor Mammy's mind is wandering.'

'It is not wandering, Nora,' Molly said hysterically. 'I saw her and you didn't. She knew what she was saying, and Jimmy knew it too. They were her real children all the time, and we were only the outsiders.'

That night, when Kate was quiet at last in her brown shroud, clutching the rosary beads on her breast, the neighbours came in and sat round her in the candlelight. They were asking the same question that Molly had already asked herself: how it was that a woman so old could take the things the world had thrown away and from them fashion a new family, dearer to her than the old and better than any she had known. But Kate had taken her secret with her.

· (1960)

Julian Barnes
Before She Met Me   £3.99

'An intelligent and addictive entertainment . . . Barnes has
succeeded in writing one of those books that keep us up until
2 a.m. reading just one chapter more . . . few will be able to resist
its easy humour and almost insidious readability' NEW YORK
TIMES BOOK REVIEW

'Frighteningly plausible . . . stunningly well done' GUARDIAN

'Graham Hendrick, an historian, has left his disagreeable wife
Barbara for the more agreeable Ann, and is well pleased with
the exchange.He can hardly believe his luck, and spends his time
dwelling on her and listing what she is wearing in a notebook.
This blissful state continues until the day he catches her
committing adultery on celluloid. Ann was, sometime before they
married, a mediocre film actress. Soon he is pouncing on small
clues, examining her books for inscriptions of byegone lovers nd
continually re-seeing the few bad movies she appeared in. It's not
that he blames Ann for having a past before they met, but history
matters to him . . . Funny, sad and faintly ominous . . . making
jealousy tangible and dangerous' HARRIET WAUGH, SPECTATOR

'I find it coming back like a personal memory. Barnes's hilarious
wit is individual, but jealousy (its theme) is unfashionably
universal' PHILIP LARKIN, OBSERVER BOOKS OF THE YEAR

'A remarkably original and subtle novel'
FRANK KERMODE, NEW YORK REVIEW OF BOOKS

'Disciplined and rich. If this were a play there would be a mad
scramble for all the parts'
ADAM MARS-JONES, FINANCIAL TIMES

'It is rare to come across a novel that's so funny and odd, and at
the same time, so resonant and disturbing' NEW YORK TIMES

'There is an irresistible bland of wit and intelligence in his work'
NEW STATESMAN

Graham Swift
Learning to Swim and Other Stories   £3.99

'Swift acquires strength from the interleavings and interweavings
of his collection. Almost all the stories are versions of the 'family
romance', protective inventions attempting to cope with the
tensions and rifts within families, whether children and parents or,
by extension, husbands and wives. Children, teenagers, doctors
and patients, a refugee Hungarian boy, a Greek restaurant owner
– all are clearly yet subtly presented, in their obsessions and
deceptions' THE OBSERVER

'An admirable collection. Each story has its subtle nuances of
narrative and language which establish a quite distinct character.
A most impressive work of fiction' THE TIMES

'. . . among the most promising young writers in Britain . . .
Graham Swift should be read by everyone with an interest in the
art of the short story' PAUL BAILEY, THE STANDARD

Graham Swift
Waterland   £4.99

'At once a history of England, a Fenland documentary, and a
fictional autobiography . . . a beautiful, serious and intelligent
novel' OBSERVER

'Swift spins a tale of empire-building, land reclamation, brewers
and sluice minders, bewhiskered Victorian patriarchs, insane and
visionary relics . . . a startling cast of characters going about their
business as though it were utterly normal and preparing the way,
down the centuries, for a trio of deaths' BOOKS AND BOOKMEN

'Positively Faulknerian in its concentration of murder, incest, guilt
and insanity' TIME OUT

'One of the most important talents to emerge in English fiction'
GLASGOW HERALD

All Pan books are available at your local bookshop or newsagent, or can be ordered direct from the publisher. Indicate the number of copies required and fill in the form below.

Send to: **CS Department, Pan Books Ltd., P.O. Box 40, Basingstoke, Hants. RG21 2YT.**

or phone: 0256 469551 (Ansaphone), quoting title, author and Credit Card number.

Please enclose a remittance* to the value of the cover price plus: 60p for the first book plus 30p per copy for each additional book ordered to a maximum charge of £2.40 to cover postage and packing.

*Payment may be made in sterling by UK personal cheque, postal order, sterling draft or international money order, made payable to Pan Books Ltd.

Alternatively by Barclaycard/Access:

Card No. | | | | | | | | | | | | | | | | | | |

Signature:

Applicable only in the UK and Republic of Ireland.

While every effort is made to keep prices low, it is sometimes necessary to increase prices at short notice. Pan Books reserve the right to show on covers and charge new retail prices which may differ from those advertised in the text or elsewhere.

NAME AND ADDRESS IN BLOCK LETTERS PLEASE:

....

Name————————————————————————————

Address————————————————————————————

—————————————————————————————————

—————————————————————————————————

—————————————————————————————————

3/87